D1612170

Withdrawn

For She Is
Wrath

For She Is Wrath

Emily Varga

WEDNESDAY BOOKS
NEW YORK

This is a work of fiction. All of the characters, organizations, and events portrayed in this novel are either products of the author's imagination or are used fictitiously.

First published in the United States by Wednesday Books, an imprint of St. Martin's Publishing Group

FOR SHE IS WRATH. Copyright © 2024 by Emily Varga. All rights reserved. Printed in the United States of America. For information, address St. Martin's Publishing Group, 120 Broadway, New York, NY 10271.

www.wednesdaybooks.com

Designed by Jen Edwards

The Library of Congress Cataloging-in-Publication Data is available upon request.

ISBN 978-1-250-87738-3 (hardcover)
ISBN 978-1-250-87739-0 (ebook)

Our books may be purchased in bulk for promotional, educational, or business use. Please contact your local bookseller or the Macmillan Corporate and Premium Sales Department at 1–800–221–7945, extension 5442, or by email at MacmillanSpecialMarkets@macmillan.com.

First Edition: 2024

10 9 8 7 6 5 4 3 2 1

For my dad, who loved fantasy books.
I just wish you got to read this one.

And for my mom, who made me believe it was
possible for me to pursue my dreams. Thank
you for always being there for me.

For She Is Wrath

One

The light was good for escape today.

It filtered through the iron bars like golden paint splashed across a dirty canvas, and if I stretched high enough, I could feel its warmth on my fingers. I could close my eyes and imagine that I was outside, face in the sun, free.

But I wasn't.

Instead, I was encased in crumbling gray granite and cold stone floors.

If it was up to the prison warden, I'd never feel the sun on my face again.

If.

I picked up my rock that I had spent weeks sharpening to a point and etched a single line in the stone above my head. *Three hundred and sixty-four.*

I'd been here almost one year.

One year since I'd heard voices different from the guards who took my waste bucket every evening, the other prisoners' sobs as they dwelled on their unfortunate fate, or the warden's endless painful interrogations. One year since I'd tasted my grandmother's earthy mutton karahi and felt the heat of those spices on my tongue. One year since I'd embraced my father and told him that everything would be okay, that I would be coming home.

And when I thought of the boy who had stolen all that, I wanted to tear down every stone that surrounded me and bury him beneath them. Let him feel the crushing weight. Let him feel the shame that shouldn't have been mine to bear. Three hundred and sixty-four days of rage brewing inside my veins.

Three hundred and sixty-four days of plotting my escape.

I gauged the position of the sun through the iron bars, calculating the hour—noon. It was almost time. I pressed the tip of my finger into the sharp point of the rock, a huff of relief spilling out when it broke the skin and a thin bead of blood trickled down. It was ready.

I was ready.

Weeks of planning, of listening to the whispers of the guards, of knowing the warden would be away—now was my chance.

My empty food pan waited below the open slot in the metal door to be refilled. I crouched low beside it, the rock poised in my hand.

Today, I would be free. I would reunite with Baba.

And then I would wreak hell upon the ones who put me here.

Steps thudded down the hall, bouncing off the walls of the prison. The rusty squeak of a door flap opening. The bang of the ladle against a corroded metal dish. The greedy slurps of other prisoners receiving their rations.

Thump, thump.

I could measure how close the guard was to my door by the sound of his footsteps. I closed my eyes, imagining I was on the training field, sword in my hand, my opponent drawing closer.

Thump, thump.

With each pause as he doled out the prison rations, I exhaled.

I bit my lip hard to distract myself from the dread coursing through my body. If I focused on being afraid, I would never leave this place, and all my plans and plotting would come to nothing.

He stopped. The crack in his knees echoed like thunder as he crouched down. Then his arm shot through the opening and the battered metal ladle upended the foul slop into my bowl with a slap.

I nearly cried out with surprise and pressed my hand to my mouth. He was quick, but I was quicker. At the last second I grabbed his rough sleeve, yanked it back through the gap, and smashed his face into the door.

His head hit the metal with a satisfying smack, and he wrenched against my grasp. I struggled to hold him, pressing my feet against the door for leverage and fumbling with the sharpened rock. I managed to push his sleeve up and stabbed the point into the fleshy part of his forearm, dragging downward to his hand. The guard let out a choked scream and thrashed, desperately trying to jerk free. I wrapped my fingers tight and pulled his arm with all I had, slamming his face back into the door.

Again.

And again.

His sounds grew more garbled, a suffocated whimper. My arms shook as I continued, sweat dripping down my neck from the exertion. I focused only on the singular violence of what I was doing, of what I needed to do to get out of here. Blood dribbled from the small square opening like crimson rain.

Soon, he grew silent, and stopped completely. My fingers trembled as I released him. His body flopped down, lifeless, hitting the floor with a wet thud. The metallic tang of fresh blood nearly overwhelmed me, and for a minute I pressed my face to the cool stone floor, letting the stale air of my cell flow through my lungs.

But soon the other guards would notice his absence.

I sat up and pushed my arms through the opening of the door, running my hands along his torso, feeling his blood-soaked uniform until I found the metal loop of keys attached at his waist. I unhooked them, ready to combust from elation. Finally, *finally,* one of my plans was succeeding.

I was going to get out of here. I was going to see my father again.

The rusty keyhole took a few tries before it unlocked, the door snapping open with a click. I deliberately looked away from the bloody body as I grabbed his legs and dragged him back into my cell.

Looking at him meant I might feel regret.

The number of times the guards had hauled me out of my cell to be tortured meant I had no room left in my heart for regret. Not for them.

Not for anyone.

This time, I was walking out of my cell on my own terms, with my own two feet, stained with the blood of the guard I had just killed.

I glanced down the hall, making sure it was empty before stepping out and heading toward the door at the end. It was eerily silent. As if all the prisoners on my wing had collectively held their breath at my audacity in killing a guard.

I glanced up to find a pair of dark eyes staring at me from the barred window on one of the doors.

It would only be a matter of time before the alarm was raised.

I had to move.

I ran blindly, my bare feet slapping against the cold floors, sharp spikes of pain running up my thighs from the impact.

I could nearly taste the fresh breeze on my tongue, smell the salty scent of the ocean on the wind. Possibility buoyed my steps—that I would actually make it out of here alive, that I would see my family again.

That I would make *him* pay for what he did to me.

Cells flanked my sides and prisoners pressed their faces against the iron bars at the top of their door. They shouted and banged with empty ration pans. Soon it was as if a hundred of them were yelling at once, and I couldn't tell if they were jeering or celebrating that one of their own had made it out.

If the warden were here, I might be more concerned, but with warden Thohfsa gone, security would be more relaxed, the guards lazier.

This time, I was going to get out.

I unlocked the door to the outside, scrambling with the keys in my hand, the metal clanging like a terrible wind chime.

Nothing could have stopped me as I stepped into the open air of the prison yard, and into my freedom.

Nothing, except the row of guards waiting outside with the prison warden, their blades pointed straight at me.

———

"How fortunate that I returned early," came Thohfsa's nasal drawl as she walked toward me.

She wore her usual plum sherwani, the long coat billowing behind her, her thick hair braided in a crown on top of her head. Her mouth was a menacing slash across her face, and the deep lines on her cheeks stood out in the midday sun.

The bottom dropped out of my stomach.

I couldn't turn around—all that awaited me in that direction was my cell. But I couldn't fight my way out, not when I had a meager pebble asa weapon, and they six sharp scimitar blades.

I wished I had one of my old throwing daggers, so I could at least put up a decent resistance, but they'd taken those from me when I was arrested. I stared at the scimitars pointed in my direction and my heart pounded against my chest. Normally, I welcomed the thrill of battle and swordplay.

But Thohfsa's smile was worse than any sword.

The acidic sting of bile hit my throat. At another prison, I might have been executed for this attempt. Here, I would pray for death.

Because Thohfsa wanted her prisoners to live. She wanted to make them suffer.

I knew that after three hundred and sixty-four days.

"Looks like I will be executing the first-floor guard for letting your poor attempt at escape proceed."

"Too late," I retorted, calling across the yard. "I already did it for you."

Thohfsa huffed out a surprised snort and a few of the guards gasped at my audacity, but I didn't spare them a glance. I focused all my anger on Thohfsa, rolling the sharp stone in my hand and running over my slim options.

Thohfsa turned to the men around her. "Give the prisoners on the first floor an extra ration. They deserve it after alerting us to Dania's escape. And prepare the interrogation room for her."

"No need for interrogation, I'd hate to spend more time with you than necessary." My voice was so hoarse from disuse, it sounded like a sad wheeze, but it didn't stop my retort. "I'd rather keep company with the fleas in my cell."

Thohfsa laughed, a cruel bark she often gave before enacting a punishment.

I could trace the marks she had made on my skin—as if the scars on my body created a map of my own disobedience. Just the thought of them flooded me with renewed rage. I wasn't going to just stand here and let her arrest me again without putting up a fight. I gripped the sharpened stone so hard my fingers felt numb. Thohfsa tilted her chin up, looking at me like I was a slug underneath the heel of her boot.

Fuck it. If I was going down, I would take the bitch with me.

I rushed at her, stone in hand, scream ripping from my throat.

She didn't move, except to flutter her hand at the guards flanking her.

A sharp pain exploded in the back of my skull, and blackness consumed me.

———

My skin burned from the fresh welts coating it. Every attempt to move brought renewed waves of agony so strong I threw up the non-existent contents of my stomach. After retching, I tried to push my body up from my cell floor.

I could barely drag myself, not when the worst of Thohfsa's torture centered around my limbs. The smell was sharp and acrid—there was nothing like the scent of your own charred flesh to remind you of your position in life.

They had dumped me here after Thohfsa was done beating me, and I lay facedown on the cold stone, wishing I could turn to stone myself. Then I wouldn't have the constant companion of this pain. I wouldn't have the familiar ache of not knowing what became of my family after I left.

Of not knowing what happened to my father, my grandmother, even my cat.

I had been accused of murder. Treason. That would have tainted them all. I rolled my tongue across my teeth, tasting the bitter anger that had lived with me every day since I had been charged.

Since I had been framed for a crime that had never been mine.

Now, because of that, I had a family with no honor. My father likely couldn't operate his smith anymore, and my grandmother's friends would have turned away from her in disgust. I wanted to tear out my hair at the thought of them going through all that without me, and there was nothing I could do to help.

Why hadn't the emperor just executed me? I exhaled slowly, stopping myself from spiraling. I needed to focus on surviving. Just being alive, one more day, despite the pain, despite the darkness.

Escaping. Seeing my family again.

Revenge.

A soft scratching jolted me from my thoughts.

I turned my head, pain splintering through my brain at the movement. I looked around my cell for the source of the sound, the moonlight pouring through the bars in the window above, creating shadows on the floor.

But nothing was there. My cell was empty except for a few loose bits of straw and my waste bucket.

Could it have been a rat?

My belly had a loud reaction to that, and I eyed my empty food bowl. A rat for dinner would be something different, at least, though I wasn't sure I could catch one in the state I was in.

I heard it again and stiffened. It was undeniable, a scraping against the stone.

It bounced off the granite walls and surrounded me as if it were echoing inside my head. I pressed my hands to my ears, wondering if I'd finally gone mad from all this.

But the sound was still there, insistent.

Louder.

I forced myself to sit up, even as blackness crept into the edges of my vision. A wave of nausea hit me and I struggled to stand, my legs giving way beneath me. Bracing myself against the floor instead, I held my breath trying to listen.

Scratch, scratch, scratch.

It was coming from underneath me, a relentless tapping. I pressed my cheek to the cool granite and a slight vibration rippled across my face. I jerked back.

Scratch, scratch.

It seemed to be coming from the opposite corner of the room, near the window—a sliver of space in the stone that was no more a window than a cat was a lion. I crept slowly toward that corner, the vibration intensifying with every inch I moved.

The noise went from a soft tap to an all-out thud, a cracking against rock. I yelped and scrambled back, every cut and burn along my thighs screaming in torment.

The ground burst open, fragments of the floor flinging every which way, the sound like splintering earth.

I cried out and wrapped my arms around my head as debris flew in my direction and small shards of stone peppered my skin. A large piece of rock bounced off my shoulder and I picked it up, arming myself.

This was clearly no rat.

Like the squeezing of mango flesh out of its skin, a human head erupted from the ground. I suffocated a surprised scream and hurled my rock, every thought emptying from my brain as I stared at the face of another person staring back at me from the floor of my cell.

"Ah, shit," the girl said as she lifted her eyes to look around the room.

Two

"What are you?" I whispered as a girl about my age lifted herself from the dark hole where the floor had once been. "Are you a ghoul? Finally come to devour me?"

"I'm not a very cunning ghoul if I had to get imprisoned myself to steal your soul." Her eyes roved over me, a frown deepening her face. "And you look awful. You'd think I'd find healthier humans to feast on."

She was shorter than me, with curly dark hair that hung wildly about her shoulders, dirty and matted like an animal. I pet my own and wondered what I looked like after so many months. In the early days of my imprisonment I'd braided it down my back to keep it manageable, but now I'd given up trying to look presentable. Caring about my appearance meant I had someone to look presentable for, instead of four vacant gray walls.

The girl's cheeks hung from her, like the flesh had been sucked from her bones. But if the rest of her looked dead and ghoulish, her eyes were like a crackling fire.

"I really thought I was close this time." She raked her filthy hands over her face.

I glanced at her fingernails, thick with dirt. "You're digging out of prison," I said slowly.

The girl stopped pacing and turned to look at me. "Quick one, aren't you?"

My face twisted into a scowl. "Forgive me if the sight of another prisoner breaking through the floor was startling." I was surprised I still had the capacity for sarcasm. "It's been a year since I've talked to someone other than Thohfsa or the guards."

I wondered if I'd finally lost my mind and was sitting here talking to myself, imagining another person.

She looked at me, assessing. "Try three."

Three years. I exhaled through my teeth. Three years was a long time to be alone, surrounded by stone walls and the smell of human filth.

But soon enough, that would be me.

I glanced up at her through my tangled hair. This girl had managed to get beyond her prison door, something I had only done once and it ended in utter failure.

"How did you manage it? Escape?" I gestured to the mess she'd made of the floor.

"Well, I didn't quite do it, did I? I ended up here instead of outside. A year of digging and I'm in an even worse cell than the one I started in." She sniffed the air. "With a worse smell too."

I laughed, the sound cackling out of me and going so unnaturally long I was sure I appeared unhinged. I cleared my throat and gestured to my wounds. "I wasn't expecting visitors. Otherwise, I would have cleaned up."

The girl grimaced. "Thohfsa do that to you?"

"I didn't do it to myself, did I?"

She narrowed her eyes. "You're the one that tried to escape, aren't you? You nearly got me caught! The guards searched all other prisoners for weapons after they recaptured you." She tilted her head. "Did you really think you could just run out of this place in the middle of broad daylight?"

"Just like you thought you could dig your way out, but instead you ended up here?" I shot back.

"Fair enough." She stretched her arms up and looked around again. "Your cell is much smaller than mine. What did you do? Kill someone you shouldn't have?"

I grimaced. "Something like that."

More like he was already dead at my feet.

Footsteps echoed down the hall—a guard on his usual patrol. I sat up, ignoring the ache in my shoulders as I did so.

"Be quiet, or they'll find you," I snapped at her, my voice low.

We sat in silence as the echo of his booted feet sounded between us. When he had moved past, the girl raised her brows.

"Another prisoner would give me away instantly," she whispered back. "Why don't you call out to them? Collect the extra rations they provide to turn in escapees?"

I returned her astute gaze. She was right that I could get rewarded for turning her in—that's exactly what happened with me. But I would be damned if I subjected another person to Thohfsa's punishments, no matter how much my stomach growled.

But more than that, an idea was percolating in my head, one that grew stronger with every passing moment she was sitting here.

"I'm not interested in betraying another prisoner," I said honestly. "Not after my last escape. You want to try to get out of here? Be my guest." I gestured to my fresh injuries. "They'll do the same to you."

She smiled, but it was more of a suggestion on her face, as if she didn't really know how to smile anymore and was trying it on. I understood that—I'd forgotten how to smile too.

"What is your name?"

I straightened. No one had asked for my name in the past year.

Names had meaning. Names were power. I knew that if my name had been different, if my family had been different, I might not be in this prison at all. But *here,* we were all the same.

We were all nothing.

And my name had no meaning behind these stone walls.

"Dania," I answered. "My friends call me Dani."

Not that I had any anymore.

"I'm Noor." She sat cross-legged on the ground. I glanced at the small opening in my door. There wasn't another guard patrol for a few hours, but I didn't know if Thohfsa was keeping a closer eye on me after my escape attempt.

"And they won't catch me," she continued. "I *will* dig my way out of here. I am going to escape."

Her words were so sure, so *bold* in the middle of my dark chamber, that a startled laugh escaped me.

The idea that had begun to take over screamed louder as I looked at the gaping hole she had made in the floor.

"It would be faster to dig with two people." I said the words slowly, as if they were just coming to me, as if I didn't plan them.

This girl had dug here, and if she had dug here, she could dig out as well.

We could dig out.

Her eyes narrowed on me, so shrewd I felt as if my very bones were being examined.

"Yes, it would be." She cocked her head. "I've been digging for a year. By my estimation, your cell is on the other side of the prison. I must have gotten turned around when they brought me in. I've been digging the wrong way."

"Ah." I leaned toward her, keeping my face a mask of calm, as if I casually welcomed visitors to my dingy cell all the time.

"Don't they notice you digging?"

She shook her head. "I'm always back to put my waste and food bucket out. I'm never gone more than a day—I don't really have enough candle left for the light." She waved her hand over the bag of supplies she had dumped on the floor. A small stub of wax and a dented tin cup spilled out from the opening.

My eyes widened at the two foreign objects. I'd never been given so much as a spoon to eat my lentils.

"How did you get those?" I never thought I'd have wonder in my voice as I looked at a rusted tin cup, but it was funny the things I missed when they were taken away.

The girl grinned, but no humor lit in her eyes. "You really want all my secrets, don't you? The guards are very interested in why I'm here and what I have to offer them. Sometimes they give me things in exchange for information, or with the expectation that one day I will return the favor."

"Well, they certainly don't offer me any kind of favor."

"Didn't you just kill one of them?"

I scowled. "What did you do that was so special?"

Noor leaned back on her hands. "I was an assistant to a chieftain who cultivated Emperor Vahid's crops of zoraat."

I sucked in the air against my teeth, surprised she'd said the words so simply.

As if she hadn't just admitted that she helped grow the entire source of the emperor's power—the coveted seeds he'd bargained for with a djinn to take over the empire. Djinn were powerful magical beings who did not part with their gifts lightly and with whom you did not want to bargain if you could help it. They didn't even exist in our world, but in the world of the unseen.

"My chieftain stole a large amount of zoraat and hid it, along with a small fortune," she continued.

I whistled low. Ever since Vahid struck a bargain with a djinn for those first magical seeds, they had been guarded intensely—after all, they were how he had forcibly annexed the five kingdoms and the northern tribes under his new rule. Zoraat had given him healing magic, an endless food supply, and an indestructible army. But Emperor Vahid solely controlled that power, and he wasn't willing to share.

"I can't imagine the emperor took kindly to *that*."

"No." She looked away, her eyes shadowed. It was a moment before she spoke again. "The emperor killed my chieftain for his betrayal." She swallowed, a harsh smile twisting her lips. "And Emperor Vahid didn't believe I knew nothing about where he had hidden the seeds, so he had me tortured and thrown in here."

I grew still. "And did you? Know where he had hidden them?"

Another shadow of a smile passed her lips. Instead of answering me, she swept her gaze around the room again, lighting her eyes on the tally of days I had etched into the wall, a macabre countdown to my death.

"Comfortable lodgings, don't you think? This is the ends of the earth, a barren island where they throw those they don't want others to find."

I sat up straighter at my unanswered question. Access to the emperor's stash of djinn magic was considerable power.

If Noor possessed it, she could control anything.

The kingdom. The emperor. The world.

As if Noor could read my machinations, she focused those sharp eyes on me once more. "Why are you here, Dania? What did *you* do?"

I swallowed. The truth felt hard to say out loud, even though it repeated through my mind on a daily basis. Saying it out loud meant it was real, and that I hadn't just imagined it. The lump in my throat grew thick.

"I was tricked. Accused of murdering a chief from the northern tribes." I kept my eyes down, studying my hands, trying not to think of the burned husk of a body that had sat at my feet the day they arrested me, devoured from the inside out.

"Murder and treason."

Noor whistled. "And did you do it?"

An echo of my own question. Two could play this game. "As soon as you start telling me the truth, I'll start telling you."

She crossed her arms over her chest. "If you're going to join me, I need to know whether you're likely to stab me in the back."

"After a year in here, I would do anything to escape. But to answer your question, no, I didn't kill him."

I clenched my fists. I wasn't the one who'd killed him. I knew exactly who had, and why.

I repeated their names nightly.

Especially the one person I never saw coming.

"I was . . . betrayed. Framed. I thought I could trust someone, but it turns out he wasn't on my side."

Those words stung the most.

More than admitting I'd been outwitted.

It was the sheer fact that I'd been betrayed by my best friend, my first love, and that was the reason I was rotting alone in a dark cell, on a forgotten island.

Mazin had been the one to put me here.

Even just thinking his name had anger thrumming through my blood like the gathering of water behind a dam threatening to break loose. Soon, it would. But today, a slow exhale calmed the rage simmering beneath my skin.

"I can't do much about it, not when I'm in here, and they out there."

Noor toyed with the edge of her filthy kurta, the dirt coloring the garment so that it was crusted and gray. "And what if you weren't in here anymore?"

I closed my eyes at her words, at how they latched on to my heart with sharp hooks and refused to let go. "If I wasn't imprisoned anymore, I . . ."

I thought of my family, of my father who must be worrying about me. Then I thought of those who'd framed me.

Mazin to whom I'd entrusted my whole heart, for him to skewer it beneath his scimitar. Darbaran, the head of the palace guard who'd arrested me. Emperor Vahid who'd used me to get rid of a powerful political opponent without a thought about my life or my family. I curled my bruised and bloodied hands into tight fists.

If I were free, I would make them all pay the price for what they had done.

They would feel every bruise, every moment of humiliation and betrayal.

But somehow, I couldn't say it. Not yet. Not when I'd only repeated these words to myself for the past year.

"I'm not sure."

Noor gave me a look as though she didn't believe me, as if she could see every thought I'd had for the past three hundred and sixty-five days and was aware I knew exactly what I would do as soon as I broke out of here.

She chewed the inside of her cheek.

"I want freedom," she said finally. "I want it so badly I can taste it. But I also want retribution. Emperor Vahid stole my entire life from me. And I want it back."

Her words were vehement, and suddenly we weren't just two girls sitting in a prison cell together with no hope of a future. For a moment it felt like we might have the power to actually do something.

"And you're right," she said finally. "Digging on my own takes an awful long time."

I stilled, afraid to move.

"It would be much faster with a partner." She glanced over at me. "Though you'd need to recover first." She reached forward, as if to touch me, and I shriveled back in surprise. I hadn't been touched by another human in kindness since before my arrest.

But instead, she extended her hand. I glanced at it warily, before reaching out in return. Her fingers curled in mine and we shook hands, sealing our bargain.

"Together, it won't take us another year to get out of here," I said, my voice as hopeful as the rising pressure of possibility in my chest.

She nodded, and that spark of hope spread through me.

"But you didn't answer my question. If you were free, Dania, what would you do?"

Mazin's face filtered through my mind, the one who had thrown me in this hell and left me here to suffer. Who had abandoned me to the royal guard, and served the emperor above all else.

But there was someone more important than revenge.

Holding my baba's newest blade in my hand.

Sparring with him in the practice yard.

Hearing his low chuckle when I bested all the other students.

Sharing a meal with him in the low light of his smith.

All the things I had longed to do came rushing forward, as if the dam inside me had broken loose and it wasn't anger that released, but pure longing.

"If I were free, I would find my father."

Three

Before

The light was good for battle today.

I held my sword up to it, making the blade glow as if it had been heated by the forge once more.

"I'm sorry, have I come to the right place? I'm looking for the swordsmith."

A boy a little older than me stood at the gate, gazing with uncertainty at my father's shop, his hands around the reins of a fine black stallion alongside him. He was tall and lanky, with a mop of black hair, a large chin, and plump cheeks he hadn't quite grown into yet. His too-big dark sherwani with gold embroidery and jeweled buttons betrayed his status.

I narrowed my eyes—he lived at the palace, and he worked for Emperor Vahid.

The emperor who had overthrown our kingdom and slaughtered half my mother's people in the north.

And I knew exactly why he had come.

"If you can't tell you are standing at the swordsmith by the various blades hanging outside of the building, I think you've got other problems besides being lost."

His uncertainty turned to a scowl.

Good. I wouldn't help him. Working for the emperor and flashing his colors around our village would mean he would get nothing from us but disdain. My father had supplied the old king with weapons that were as beautiful as they were deadly. But apparently, Emperor Vahid wanted his swords forged at the same smith.

"I prefer to be certain before making an assumption and proving myself an ass," he said with his nose in the air. "Something it seems you have no problem doing."

I inhaled sharply. Did this gaudy fool just call me an ass?

He puffed out his chest like an overgrown bird and stared down at me. "You clearly have no idea who I *am*."

A snort escaped me. This boy barely had hairs on his chin, and he was trying to lord above me? "I know exactly who you are, unfortunately. If you've come for the new emperor's sword, *my father* would be the one making it."

His mouth dropped open and I gave him a satisfied smirk.

"I've been sent by the emperor himself, and you still speak to me like this?"

"Look around you." I gestured to my small village at the edge of the mountains, the clay-packed houses embedded into the mountainside like flecks of snow, on the edge of the territory where all the northern tribes were forced to submit to the emperor. We might be a day's ride from the city where the emperor established his new court, but we were far from compliant here.

No one in this village would be impressed by Emperor Vahid's power.

These people cared about raiders coming for their family, about freedom from the imposed laws of the capital, and their ability to trade and make money from bartering their goods in the city. Not a single villager would turn their head at this boy's fine stallion—unless it was to steal it as retribution against the emperor. We were more worried about mountain marauders and the bitter winter decimating the next harvest of apricots in the valley.

I took a sidelong look at the boy's horse, decked out in Emperor

Vahid's golden emblem—the outline of a zoraat flower crested on its saddle.

"These people supported the king. He protected them. You won't find much simpering for you here, if that's what you are after."

"And yet, if your father is the smith, then he has already agreed to make the emperor's sword." He raised his chin.

Rage expanded my chest, leaving me momentarily breathless. I pursed my lips together. "He values his head."

"You obviously don't."

I picked at my nails, attempting to appear calm. "I do, I just know who has the power to remove it. It isn't you."

His hand darted to the scabbard at his waist as if to prove me wrong and pull free the curved scimitar hanging there. I knew from the plain handle that it was definitely *not* made by my father.

Ours were solid, sure, and intricately carved. My father prided himself on his silver koftgari-decorated grips and the pommels of camel bone that he usually shaped himself.

But I'd been handling knives since I was a babe, and generally the person already holding one had the upper hand. Mine flashed in the sunlight before this boy could even draw his, and he held up his hands as I pointed my double-edged talwar at him, the sharpest side in the vicinity of his throat.

"I wouldn't if I were you," I said calmly, not bothering to hide the smile in my voice.

"This is treason!" he sputtered, and I didn't miss that flash of fire in his dark gold eyes. It seemed the pretty boy had some spirit in him after all.

"Dania!" a voice shouted from across the yard.

I groaned inwardly as my father came up the path.

He bowed to the boy who was at least twenty years his junior, and I wanted to scream. I wanted to wrench his head up with the end of my sword and tell him not to bow to the emperor's lackeys ever again.

"Forgive my daughter. She is sometimes too passionate." Baba gave me a warning look, his ochre eyes narrowing on me.

I laughed instead, though I couldn't hide the bitter edge to it. "I was just playing with the boy. Honestly, does the palace not teach the guards how to fight?"

Baba frowned at me, not buying my act for a second. "He is not a guard, Dani, as you well know."

I winced. "Nanu wouldn't like us conversing with him," I muttered, only to him.

"Nanu doesn't pay our expenses," he shot back.

I folded my arms across my chest and settled for glaring at the boy instead. He gave me a dismissive glance and returned his attention to my father. I pressed my teeth together to stop myself from drawing my sword again.

"My name is Mazin, and I'm the ward of the new emperor. I've come at his behest to give the specifications for his new sword and provide payment." He paused, his face bland, but I didn't miss his eyes sliding to mine. "If your skills should prove satisfactory," he said finally.

I lunged, anger beating again at my chest. That he would dare to even suggest that my father's skills wouldn't be good enough for the emperor made my blood heat. "You know nothing about my father if you think his blades would be anything other than satisfactory. He is the most sought-after bladesmith in all the kingdoms."

My father placed a hand on my shoulder, stilling me. "It's all right, Dani. Emperor Vahid has every right to inspect my work to determine if it is up to his standards."

"So why send this silly boy, then? Especially after he took away the village protections? Why not come himself?"

"Because perhaps he trusts *this silly boy*," sneered Mazin, pulling himself to his full height, which I begrudgingly admitted was considerable.

I cocked my head, not letting him intimidate me. "I guess we always knew Vahid was a fool."

Mazin sucked in a harsh breath, surprise and something like wonder crossing his face. I guess no one had dared to insult Emperor Vahid in his presence before.

Good, he deserved a little grounding. But at my father's stricken expression, I knew I had gone too far.

"Dania!" My father yanked me back behind him. "Stay out here while we talk." He gave me a look that dared me to defy him.

Heat flooded my face as I looked at my father, incredulous. "What? You *always* have me in the shop when discussing—"

"Not this time. Perhaps when you can guard your tongue better so we *don't* get reported for treason." He said the words low so that only I could hear them, his voice sharp with frustration.

I clamped my mouth shut. Baba *never* spoke to me this way. My eyes narrowed at the boy standing beside us.

Baba and I were a team. Ever since my mother died, we were together against everything.

Mazin followed my father into his smith, and a flush of shame heated my cheeks. The boy threw the curl of a grin at me over his shoulder as he went.

I clenched my fists tight against my legs.

That boy had made an enemy today.

Four

I dug till my hands bled. After a few days I'd healed enough from my injuries that every hour was focused on tunneling underneath the floor of my cell. We moved forward in inches, and though it was the tiniest of increments, I felt like I was moving with purpose.

Freedom.

Family.

I pushed back against that tiny voice that wanted a different goal, a darker, more wrathful purpose.

Revenge.

But I couldn't afford to think about vengeance now. My only priority needed to be getting back to my father and making sure he was okay.

The first few days of digging, Noor and I worked quietly together, shifting away the black earth millimeter by millimeter. But after a year of being confined alone, I wasn't about to continue the silence. Working alongside her made me realize I wasn't impervious to the need for human companionship, as much as I wanted to pretend otherwise.

We sat in the dark tunnel, illuminated by the sun filtering through the small slice of window, as I chipped away at the earth and passed cups of dirt back to her.

"You worked for Emperor Vahid? Dealing with djinn magic?" I asked cautiously. I had been itching to talk to her about it for days, turning over her earlier words in my mind. If she had access to zoraat—the most powerful substance in our world—there was no telling what she could do once she broke out of here.

She paused, holding the tin cup in her hand. She lifted her eyes to the small window in my cell, staring at the disappearing light.

"Technically one of his chieftains," she responded finally. "His name was Souma and he was responsible for managing Vahid's zoraat farms, as well as mixing the right doses for his soldiers and healers. I worked as an herbalist in Vahid's royal apothecary, under Souma's supervision."

"All that djinn power." My words were hushed. "How were you allowed to work with it? I thought you had to be incredibly special to even touch zoraat."

"Are you saying I'm not special?" She arched a brow, but her smile faded. "Actually, I'm really not. Just an orphan who managed to be in the right place at the right time. I needed somewhere to go and Souma needed an assistant. Working with zoraat was quite dangerous and he kept . . . losing them." She winced.

"So, you weren't chosen because you were special, it was because everyone else died."

I handed her another cup of dirt. Noor emptied it in the waste bucket and came back to the tunnel.

"I suppose you could say that. But I also had a knack for zoraat blends. You must consume the djinn seeds in exactly the right proportions or the results can be catastrophic. Emperor Vahid mixes his own blends, of course—they say the djinn he bargained with for the power taught him how to use it. But for the soldiers and healers and anyone else who uses zoraat, Souma and his staff mix the blends."

"Did you try them?" I couldn't hide the awe in my voice. I had never known anyone who had eaten zoraat. I had seen Emperor Vahid a few times in passing when I'd been at the palace with Maz but hadn't ever spoken to him directly.

To be able to use raw djinn magic, to have the power to reconfigure your body, to wield a smokeless flame or shake the very earth we walked on—those kinds of abilities could come in handy. I flexed my fingers, not thinking about the djinn magic so much as my own skills—the swords I longed to hold, the daggers I dreamt to throw again.

It wasn't magic I craved, but the weight of steel in my grip.

"No, I never got to use them myself. That was only for the generals or the emperor's personal healers, and he controls their consumption very strictly. He never wants to give anyone more than they need. But Souma said I was one of the finest blenders of djinn magic he'd ever seen. It was one of the reasons he . . ."

Noor trailed away, her face shadowed in the darkness of the tunnel, the faint light catching the shimmer in her eyes. After a moment she cleared her throat. "It was one of the reasons he trusted me so much." Her voice cracked.

Souma sounded like someone important to her. Perhaps even a father of sorts. I swallowed, my throat tight. I knew what it was to miss a father.

An unfamiliar kinship tugged at my heart, recognizing the shared emotion. We were more than just two escapees, we were two daughters, two people who had been wronged, two people trying to get back what we once had, though we probably never would. This place had stolen years of our lives, and we wouldn't get the chance to live those again. I curled my fingers into the dirt, savoring the feel of it pushing under my fingernails. Someone was responsible for taking that life away from me, and I wanted to be the one to make him pay.

Noor's sniff brought me back. She scraped more of the dirt into the tin cup.

"I'm sorry," I said quietly.

She looked up at me, pushing the tangled hair from her eyes with a dirty hand. "Yeah, me too."

But there was more to this story. Souma had betrayed Vahid, and

I knew as well as anyone what happened when you were accused of betraying the emperor.

"You said Souma hid zoraat from the emperor? That he stole from him?" I ran through the implications of that. I had been thrown into a cell to rot, but I hadn't stolen djinn power from the emperor. "I'm surprised Vahid didn't destroy Souma's entire family."

Noor was silent for a moment, and I didn't expect her to respond. "Oh, he did. Vahid was furious. All Souma's sons were executed, and anyone connected with Souma was sent here and tortured for information on where the zoraat was hidden. As you can imagine, Thohfsa loved that."

Her voice was bitter and I thought about what that must have been like for her. At least I knew that my father was still alive and waiting for me. Everyone Noor had known was gone.

I chipped away at the hard packed earth and was thankful that I was the one rotting in prison and not my father.

But if Souma had hidden zoraat, did Noor know about it? And if she did, would she go back to claim it?

Access to magic like that was worth more than just breaking out of here. It was complete freedom. It was the power to go anywhere, be anything you wanted. I could escape with my father, away from the emperor, away from Maz.

But something dark and rotten answered inside me.

Did I really want to run away from Mazin?

Did I want to run?

Or make him burn?

I gave Noor a sidelong glance. She hadn't said if Vahid had recovered his missing djinn magic. Which meant she might just know where it was.

"Everyone you know is gone," I said, breaking a particularly large stone free from the earth and handing it back to her. "And Vahid killed Souma. So, what will *you* do when you break out of here?"

She'd asked me this question, but hadn't shared her own answer.

It was enough to simply want free of this place, I supposed, but she dug the stones away with fire in her veins, just as I did. This wasn't only about freedom, like my motivation wasn't just getting to my father. We both had something we hadn't wanted to confess, because confessing it meant acknowledging it.

Noor held the rock, the shadows staining her expression, making her appear more ominous than usual. She was a small girl, with a pointed chin and a mop of dark curls, but now she appeared more like a vengeful ghoul than when she'd first burst into my chamber.

"I suppose you could say I'm a loyal person," she said quietly. "And I believe that Souma deserves justice."

"And are you the person to mete that justice out?" I asked, wondering if that same need flooded through my veins.

But justice seemed more noble than what I wanted. Admirable. What I wanted from the people who betrayed me wasn't admirable.

Not when I pictured the dagger that would tear through Mazin's heart.

But even I had a greater reason to want justice than she did. Noor was an orphan, beholden to no one. It wasn't she who was accused of treason, it wasn't her own name she had to clear. It seemed odd she would focus so much on the injustice done to the man who had simply taken her in.

"I am." Her voice was gravel hard. "If not me, there isn't anyone else left."

"How?" I asked, the word curling between us like an incantation. "How would you get justice?" We both knew I was asking something much larger than the mechanics of a strategy.

How can one take down an empire?

Vahid had done it with the power of the djinn by his side. Could it could be done again?

She hesitated, her response catching in her throat. "I have a plan."

There was no doubt in my mind that plan involved djinn magic and a stolen treasure Thohfsa had been trying to torture out of people for three years. And if Noor had access to that treasure, perhaps I could as well.

Coupled with the possibility of escape, I felt hope bubbling in my chest.

But having that small kernel of hope was a dangerous thing, because if I lost it, then the despair might finally overtake me.

That much I knew from the past year.

———

"I think I have dirt so far up my fingernails it's part of my skin now."

I lay in Noor's cell, examining my hands. She was right, mine *was* worse than hers. Her chamber looked like a palace compared to where I'd been housed—it was at least three times the size, and she even had a rickety bed with a worm-eaten straw mattress that felt as good as if it had been filled with peacock feathers.

When I first saw it, I cried.

Then I lay down, my bones sighing, my back unbending from the year of sleeping on a cold stone floor.

"You said you were tricked when you were arrested." Noor's voice cut through my joy in lying on a bed again. She sat with her back against the wall, cross-legged, watching me. "Tell me what happened to put you in here."

I sat up, rolling my shoulders and ignoring my growling belly. My muscles ached from digging and I was feeling the lack of food more keenly now.

When I didn't answer right away Noor barked out a rough laugh. "You get such a look on your face when you are thinking about home that I can't help but ask about it. And sometimes when you talk about escaping, I can only describe your expression as how I would feel if Thohfsa were being dismembered in front of me."

My lips lifted involuntarily. "I know exactly what my face would look like if that were transpiring."

"So, tell me, then. What happened?"

What happened?

I had thought of nothing else. I had worked it all out, every misstep where I went wrong, every clue that signaled what they had done.

What *he* had done.

How could I have been so foolish to not realize who he was? To not think that he would choose the emperor over me, when it all came down to it?

I flexed my hands in the scratchy bedcover. "I was betrayed by someone I thought I loved. Someone I thought had my back. But he didn't."

"Bastard," Noor seethed, and I appreciated the anger on my behalf. "What was his name?"

I exhaled, filling the space between us with my rage. "Mazin. We'd known each other since we were kids. I thought I knew everything about him."

"What did he do?"

"He asked me to meet him in the palace. Instead, I found the body of a northern warlord at my feet, poisoned by djinn magic. Darbaran, the head of the palace guards, arrested me. I thought Maz would help me escape, but he just stood and watched. He didn't even defend me." The words stung so badly I trembled. "He made me believe I was loved, trusted. Then, he and the others at the palace framed me for murder. Emperor Vahid tossed me in here, condemning my family to the sin of my crime too." I swallowed thickly, not just anger rising in my chest but sorrow. Maz hadn't just taken my freedom, or my father's reputation. He'd taken away one of the few relationships I believed was safe, true.

And he lit it on fire and smiled as I burned with it.

"Who framed you?"

I felt the involuntary curl of my lips but knew my smile wasn't a smile by the expression on Noor's face—a mixture of alarm and wariness.

That same simmering fury lurked in my bones, waiting to be released, waiting to be given a sword so that it could create a bloody, vengeful path. Then, I recited the list I said every night before I went to sleep. The list of people responsible for where I was.

"Darbaran, the head of the guards who accused me, arrested me, and made sure I had no escape. Emperor Vahid, who clearly wanted to dispose of one of his political rivals without triggering a civil war and I was the one to pin it on. And Maz." I broke off, not trusting myself to speak anymore.

"Who was Maz to you?" Noor's voice was gentle.

I closed my eyes, thinking about how to answer that question. My childhood best friend? My lover, whom I'd given my heart to? The person I'd shared my darkest secrets with, held in the early rays of morning and fought alongside against anyone who stood in our way?

I looked away from Noor to the wall behind her. Noor's own scratches and marks decorated the stone, tabulating the days, triple the size of mine, a grim reminder of what my days would resemble if I stayed here. Days Mazin had condemned me to without a second thought.

"Mazin was someone I trusted when I should have known better. Someone who was always going to betray me, in the end."

Noor made a sound against her teeth. "A lover, then."

Something squeezed in my heart, and it made me inexplicably furious.

Yes. I wanted to answer.

Yes, he was a lover.

But I wasn't ready to say that yet. I hadn't quite grappled with the depths of that betrayal, and with the fact that in my dark moments my treacherous mind still thought back to those memories when I needed comfort.

As if I still had capacity to yearn for someone who was never there to begin with.

But there was no point in not being truthful now; it wouldn't erase what had happened.

At my silence, Noor cleared her throat. "How do you know they were responsible? Those names you recited."

"How do you know your chieftain trusted you?" I asked her in response. "How do you know he cared about you?"

Noor answered immediately, without hesitation. "I felt it in my bones."

"Yes," I said, the word a whispered hush. "Yes, exactly. When I was arrested, I went over it all, every step, every conversation, every strange look or absurd coincidence. Maz asking to meet me in that room, at that particular time. Darbaran coming upon me instead, catching me right as I discovered the body. Neither of them would have done this at all if Emperor Vahid had not ordered it. The body at my feet was a rival to Vahid—a northern warlord who was rumored to be starting a rebellion. If the emperor had executed him, it would have caused a civil war." My voice was steeped in bitterness. "Maz is loyal to Emperor Vahid above all, no matter what his sins are."

And Vahid had many, given the slaughter during his rise to power.

Noor's eyes darkened at the mention of Vahid's name. "Why didn't they execute *you* to silence you?"

She asked the question I'd asked myself. Why was I still alive? Why was I here?

"That part I can't figure out. I can only imagine they wanted to inflict the greatest suffering possible."

That stung the most. The knowledge that not only had Maz betrayed me, but that he wanted my torture. My pain. He wanted me to hurt.

What was most pathetic was that I cared. I cared he had made this so personal, he had put me here to rot and taken the side of the emperor.

What had I done to him to deserve that?

Or perhaps I needn't have done anything. Perhaps he always had the capacity to do this to me, and I was too in love with him to see it.

There was a heavy silence.

Noor scratched the back of her neck.

"If Maz put you in a place like this, he can't have been a very good lover," she said, laughter clinging to her words and dispelling the tension in the room.

I huffed out a rueful laugh in response, appreciating her attempt to drive the darkness from my heart.

"No," I said finally, the smile fading from my lips, my eyes tracing the cracks on the ceiling. "That was never our problem."

"Ugh, isn't that always the way? Good at one thing and terrible at everything else." She leaned back against the wall.

I thought back to the first time I had kissed Mazin.

The first time he'd wrapped his arm around my waist, pressed his lips to my neck. Even though the memories were twisted and bitter with his betrayal, I could still remember what it felt like to have my pulse beat wildly as his thumb traced my lower lip, the rush of anticipation in my stomach when he smiled against my skin. I swallowed, trying to will the memories away.

"We knew each other for a long time. I thought I knew him as well as he knew me, but obviously not."

"The ones closest to you will betray you the most," Noor said so softly I almost didn't catch her words. I wondered at them, because she sounded like she understood from personal experience.

I cleared my throat, glad to change the subject. "Is that what happened to you and Souma? Emperor Vahid found out he was stealing from him through someone close?"

Noor nodded. "His own son betrayed him. He wanted to save his family's honor but ended up massacring them all. Even the servants were arrested and imprisoned."

"Like you."

Noor looked uncomfortable by the suggestion that she was a servant but eventually nodded. "Yes, like me. But I'm not going to stay here and rot like everyone else, that's not my fate."

"Nor mine," I said, wiping the dirt from my face and looking at the dark tunnel we'd crawled out of.

Staying in this prison wouldn't be my fate. Not anymore.

Five

Our days were consumed by digging, talking, rushing back to our cells before we were discovered, and sleeping.

I slept like I'd never slept before, with all my energy focused on escape. I had a renewed motivation, a hope that I didn't expect alive in my chest. With every new inch of earth dug I moved closer to the possibility.

The light of the candle was low, the earth caking our skin like we were rodents, scrabbling in the dirt.

Thoughts of freedom drove my hands.

Hopes of seeing my father helped me ignore the hunger ripping through my belly. I thought of what I would do to Maz if I had a blade in my hand, and that kept my body moving. I was the rat, burrowing out of the trap, coming to rip out my captors' throats.

"I think we've hit a rock or something here. I can't seem to get past it." Noor's voice was strained, muffled from the tunnel. She smacked at the hard dirt with her tin cup, trying to break it up.

My heart sank. A rock, depending on how large, could take weeks to dig out.

"Is it a boulder or clay?" I tried to see around her. "Try scraping around it to see how big it is."

"It's moving!" she called back, and I released a breath. That meant we could dig it out.

"Maybe if I bang on it a little it will shake things loose." She pounded the tin against the rock with a thwap. "It's dislodging!"

"Well, that's a relief."

I began scooping up dirt again, hollowing out the excess dirt from the tunnel and emptying it into our waste buckets. I got back to Noor's cell and dumped handfuls of dirt on the floor.

A strangled scream came from the tunnel. A cloud of fresh dust erupted into Noor's cell. My stomach dropped as I rushed back to the hole.

"Noor?" I called, forgetting to lower my voice, forgetting in my panic that the guards might hear. I dove back through the hole, crawling as fast as I could through the pitch black, my eyes struggling to see her in the dark.

The candle had gone out, and no matter how many times I called, Noor didn't respond. I'd made it to the end, feeling the wall of dirt, with no Noor at all. I laid on my stomach in the dark, processing what must have happened.

Cave in.

I lurched forward, clawing at the earth. My fingernail tore against a large stone and I cried out. My throat was thick and tight, and my hands trembled as I dug.

No.

No, no, no, no.

It couldn't end like this. Not with her buried in a tunnel and me trapped in her cell and no way out.

Not when we were so close to escaping.

My fingers brushed warm, rough skin and my heart leapt to my throat. Noor's bare foot poked out of the dirt. I yanked it, not bothering to be gentle or careful, only caring about how many seconds had gone by with her face buried in the soil. I shook the earth loose from her prone body and dragged her backward through the tunnel.

Once I'd made it to the opening, I lifted her body to the floor of her cell.

"Noor, don't die now, we've still got another year of digging to do."

My hands shook as I brushed stones and debris from her mouth. Her eyes were shut, and her limbs floppy and lifeless. I pulled the hair away from her face and tried to clear the dirt from her airway.

"And if I have to do it myself that will be two years." I huffed out a deep breath, my pulse beating against my skin like a panicked bird. "And we all know I'm terrible at digging so it will take me more like four years." I pressed my ear to her chest. There was a shallow rise and fall, a small intake of breath. She was still alive. For now. I gave a delirious laugh that was more like a sob.

But then the relieved pounding of my heart stopped completely. A dark trickle of liquid pooled on the floor, pouring from the back of Noor's head from some unknown wound.

I leapt to my feet and didn't think twice about what I was going to do.

It was possible they would do nothing, that they wouldn't care whether Noor lived or died. But if the guards were even remotely invested in the fact that she may have access to unimaginable djinn power, they might actually do something to save her.

I pounded on the cell door, screaming my head off, shouting for help. They could take her to the infirmary, they could staunch the bleeding, they could prevent her from dying.

And I couldn't be here when they did.

Footsteps sounded in the hall, and distant shouts bounced off the walls. I leapt away from the door and crawled back down the tunnel, grabbing the loose piece of floor that we used to hide the escape route and closing it over my head.

Then I waited.

My chest felt tight and a cold sweat poured over me. They had to come. They had to save her.

Eventually the door opened, and the sounds of slamming and shouting filtered down to me. I pressed my hand hard to my mouth, trying not to make a single sound as guards filled Noor's cell and lifted her up off the floor.

"Shit. We have to take her to Thohfsa."

"Thohfsa will kill *us* if she's dead. Take her to the infirmary first." There was some grunting as they lifted her, and one of them swore.

Then it went quiet.

I huffed out a shallow breath, my heart beating so wildly I could barely focus. But there were no more sounds.

No footsteps, no talking.

I waited a long time before I lifted the slab up again and peeked into the room.

The cell was empty. Noor was gone.

But there was something else I hadn't expected.

The guards had left the door open.

Six

Of course they'd left the door open. To them, there was no one left to escape.

I tried to dampen the rising adrenaline flooding through me. I could leave without anyone noticing. I could slip into the night on my own.

My breath was tight in my chest as I stepped through the door. This time when I moved through the dark halls, I was soundless, and the other prisoners were sleeping. Noor's cell was on the opposite wing, adjacent to the ocean. I could almost smell the salt spray in the air, nearly touch the cool water with my fingertips.

If I hid from the guards, made it out of the main prison, and climbed the perimeter wall, I could make it to the beach without the alarm being raised.

I was close, so close to getting out of here. My stomach was in my throat, my body fairly vibrating as I slunk along the hall.

This time I was under cover of darkness, this time I didn't leave a trace.

The stone was cold against my feet. I crept along the wall, trying to remember the layout of my prison wing. This one seemed to be organized the same way, and if I kept to the outer hallway, I should make it to the exit.

I turned the corner to find two guards standing at the main door, their murmured voices carrying on the cool breeze. My back was to the granite wall as I watched the two figures illuminated in the moonlight. At last they started their next guard rotation, moving away from the doorway and heading toward the opposite end of the prison.

I took my chance and noiselessly crept to the door. The sea air slapped against me with spirited force, as if it welcomed me outside.

I slipped out and slid along the side of the building, my back pressed to the brick. The rough scuff of a footfall sounded, and I held my breath as a guard stepped around the corner of the building before turning the other way and retracing his steps in a loop. I trod carefully, gaining ground, with only one focus.

Escape, escape, escape.

I made it to the perimeter wall. There was no one else here.

I could climb over and be out in minutes.

But as I looked over my shoulder a light flickering in the distance pulled my attention. A long brick building stood separate from the main prison and the warden's tower, like a lone rider on the horizon. I recognized it from the one time I had been there, after some fairly brutal punishments from Thohfsa.

The infirmary.

Noor.

My foot paused against the mud-brick outer wall, my breath stilling in my chest.

Could I do this? Could I escape and leave her behind, the person who had allowed me to get this far in the first place? Something dark took root in my stomach, a sick feeling I couldn't shake.

If I went back for her, we'd be recaptured. Escaping when they hadn't a clue I was gone was one thing, but rescuing Noor and fighting the guards by ourselves was entirely different. I didn't even know if she was conscious. Or alive.

But Noor's sardonic grin filled my mind, her driven hands black with earth, her face full of reverence as she spoke about Souma. Noor had understood how much I missed my father. She had felt the same.

I couldn't hop that wall.

I couldn't escape. Not if it meant leaving Noor behind.

"Dania, you are such a fool," I muttered as I began retracing my steps and veering off to the right, toward the infirmary. Something churned in my gut remembering her limp body when I dragged her out of the tunnel, seeing that pool of blood spread out across the dirty floor.

She's still alive.

She has to be.

My footsteps were a whisper on the sparse grass, the flickering candle in the infirmary window like a beacon. I pressed against the wall of the prison, huddling into the shadows to avoid a guard rotation moving past me. The prison yard was dotted with low bushes and not much else, but I was thankful there were no torches lining the perimeter wall at this side.

The sharp scent of cardamom wafting in the air caught my attention and I turned my head. I hadn't drunk chai in a long time, but I'd know that smell anywhere. Two guards stood by the infirmary drinking from large cups, the steaming liquid casting vapors in the cool night. I could have easily killed them both just for a taste of it.

They stood at the only entrance, so if I was going to get caught I might as well do so with the taste of chai on my lips.

I crouched down by a thick bush, running my hands along the ground for anything I could use as a weapon.

My fingers shook with the need to hold any kind of knife.

A scimitar.

A katar over my knuckles.

I'd even take an ornamental blade.

My hand pressed against my chest as I remembered the pendant

Maz had given me, a real miniature dagger that I could have used at a time like this.

Instead, the pad of my other thumb brushed against the rough bark of a tree branch that must have blown over the wall. I grabbed it with relief and knelt low, nearly crawling toward the guards.

If I attacked them both now, they'd sound the alarm, and any advantage I had would be gone. The last time I tried to barrel through the prison without a weapon it didn't work so well, and this time I was armed no better. I tested the weight of the thick branch in my hands.

I bit the edge of my lip. Noor would never do something so risky as to fight the guards out in the open. And I needed to think a little more like Noor to get us both out alive.

I inched closer to the building, my stomach dragging over the soft grass, thankful for the blanket of darkness making me nearly indistinguishable from the shrubbery. I'd been crawling on my belly in the dirt for weeks, it didn't bother me to do it now. I stopped a few feet away from the guards and listened to their hushed voices as they drank. My breath froze in my lungs at the mention of Thohfsa's name.

"Hashim said Thohfsa is coming personally to see the prisoner. She gave orders to be informed if anything happened to her."

"You think the girl knows where Souma's stolen treasure is?"

The other guard huffed. "A weak girl like that couldn't survive Thohfsa's torture without revealing what she knew. But the warden still thinks she has information, or else why would she give her all those privileges? Or summon a healer of the unseen to heal her?"

"Well, Thohfsa won't learn anything if the prisoner's dead."

My heart stuttered at his words.

Please don't be dead, Noor.

"Hopefully the healer did her job."

I bit down on my bottom lip so hard I tasted iron. If Thohfsa herself was coming to see Noor, that meant I had limited time to get her out. And if a healer of the unseen had been summoned, that meant the emperor himself had sanctioned the use of zoraat to heal her. Emperor Vahid approving the use of one of his prized djinn magic healers meant he did suspect Noor knew something about Souma's treasure. But right now, I was more relieved than anything—if Noor was healed, she was alive. And if she was healed, I wouldn't have to carry her, and we might actually have a chance of escape.

I closed my eyes and inhaled the billowy scent of chai one final time before making my move. Then, I grabbed a large rock nearby and threw it into the bushes on the other side of the infirmary. I didn't have time to be stealthy anymore, not if Thohfsa was on her way.

My fingers clamped around my stick, the makeshift sword cutting into the meat of my palm.

"Eh, did you hear that?" One of the guards turned toward the sound. "There aren't any guards on patrol over there."

The other guard snorted. "You're in your head again. No one will attempt escape after what Thohfsa did to the last girl. And it's unlikely *she'll* try again." He gave a low laugh, and I nearly laughed right along with him.

Let them think I gave up. They would know soon enough how wrong they were.

I curled my hands tighter around the branch, ready to take them both on. But just as I was about to rise from the shadows, the first guard shook his head and walked to the other side of the building to investigate the noise.

Leaving me alone with his friend.

I rolled from the bushes, stepped into the torchlight, and raised my stick high.

The guard's eyes went wide, his mouth open in a surprised scream, but thankfully he didn't have a chance to make a sound. I clubbed him with the thick end, and he dropped to the ground.

"I did try again," I muttered as I kicked his motionless body. But I couldn't leave him here, not if the other guard was on his way back. A ring of keys hung from his waist and I grabbed them as noiselessly as I could, unlocking the front door and dragging his heavy body through the entrance, along with the tree branch I'd hit him with.

I closed the door behind us and we were encased in silence, except for my harsh breath.

The same stone floors as were in the rest of the prison graced the infirmary but with considerably less grime. In fact, the whole building was cleaner, as if it had barely been used, and with only the slight smell of turmeric from the salve they applied to our wounds after Thohfsa's interrogations. It wasn't large—only one long hall with different rooms where patients were housed. The entrance was dark except for the faint glimmer of the moon through a window above and a low light from an open door at the far end of the hall. Various unlit torches dotted the walls and a slight draft blew its way down the corridor. I shivered and wrapped my arms around myself, wishing I had some of that chai now to warm me.

I lifted the guard's arms once more and grunted with the effort of pulling him to the nearest room—an empty chamber housed with medical supplies. Once I dumped his body, I flexed my hands, working the blood back to my fingers, wishing I still had some of the physical endurance I'd come to prison with.

All the muscles I'd honed from sparring with Mazin in the training yard had melted away when met with the steady starvation rations of the prison.

I nudged the guard's leg with my toe and he didn't react. My hands raked his body, feeling for any kind of weapon, but he didn't have anything on him I could use. Pity. There wasn't anything to tie him with, so I propped one of the gray metal chairs under the door handle. Then I went in search of Noor.

Seven

My feet slapped lightly against the cool stone as I walked down the hall, keeping to the shadows along the edge. Every room I passed was an empty husk and I didn't see a sign of any other guards.

I walked toward the faint light emanating from the end. That was the only indication anyone was in the building other than me, which meant it must be where Noor was kept.

A small voice in my head repeated that I was a fool for going back for her and not escaping when I could.

But the other part of me, the part that kept my feet moving and my heart racing, knew that if I didn't go back for Noor, if I didn't try to rescue her too, I'd feel as if I never left the prison. That sick feeling was gnawing at my gut, spreading its black roots, and I knew exactly what it was.

Guilt.

I wouldn't be free of it if I just left her here to die. And what was freedom worth if I still felt imprisoned?

I crept closer, listening for any sign of life other than the dim flickering light. It wasn't until I got to the door that I heard a soft whisper and hope rose in my chest.

Noor.

Noor was alive. Noor was *talking*.

But I held back, because she certainly wasn't talking to herself.

"I told you, I don't know anything about it."

"You're lying." Another voice, just as soft, but utterly deadly, and my stomach dropped at hearing it.

Thohfsa.

"I didn't send for that djinn healer just so you could keep lying to me. You're finally going to tell me where Souma's treasure is, and you're going to do it tonight."

All the elation I felt was gone. If Thohfsa was there, guards would be as well. I leaned forward, daring a glance inside.

Noor lay in a narrow bed, wearing a pale cotton kurta with a sheet thrown over her. Her skin was leached of color, but her light eyes were alert.

Thohfsa stood at the foot of her bed, her arms crossed and a familiar scowl on her face.

"Do you hear me? I won't give you another chance, girl. You've had too long as it is. I've given you privileges, I've given you time. And now I'm going to give you more pain than you ever thought possible unless you start telling me where it is."

My nails bit into the flesh of my palm at Thohfsa's threats. I had heard them many times before, but none quite so vehement.

The room was no bigger than Noor's cell, but with more windows, and Thohfsa and Noor were completely alone. I crept closer, still cloaked in the darkness of the doorway. If there were no guards, then Thohfsa had made a fatal mistake, one that I wouldn't hesitate to take advantage of.

But why would she come here without protection? Even if Noor were incapacitated, Thohfsa never went anywhere without her guards.

You're finally going to tell me where Souma's treasure is.

I sucked in a soft breath. Of course. Thohfsa didn't want anyone around if she was going to get answers. She wanted to be the one to find it. And she didn't want to share.

But if she was alone, even without weapons, then I could fight her.

My fingers tightened around the branch in my hands, ready to display how well they could best her.

"Where is it?" Thohfsa growled, moving closer to Noor. She gripped the short sword at her waist, and I knew from the way she handled the hilt that she hadn't grown up with a sword in her hand as I did. She had training, yes, but the memory of a blade was imprinted on my fingers. My sword was an extension of who I was.

And my hands itched to get one back.

I pushed forward, all secrecy and subterfuge gone. A faint roar sounded in my ears.

"She already told you," I said, my voice carrying across the room. "She doesn't know where it is. So why don't you leave her alone and contend with someone who isn't lying prone on a bed."

Noor let out a surprised gasp and sat up. Thohfsa's eyes bulged, and a satisfying look of shock crossed her features. After months of her abuse, my skin buzzed with the anticipation of returning the favor. Sweat coated my palms as I held my tree branch tighter. I took another step into the room.

I had seconds to get this right before she raised the alarm.

I rushed at her, pulling my arms back and slamming the branch into her gut. Thohfsa jerked from the impact and let out a stuttered wheeze.

Draw your sword, draw your sword.

As if she could hear my thoughts, she pulled her short sword free of the leather scabbard at her waist. Cool calm washed over me as I set my shoulders and prepared to fight.

Thohfsa gave a cruel smile, stretching the thin skin across her face, looking like a macabre skeleton in the flickering torchlight. "I've tortured you more times than you can count and you keep coming back for more. I'm starting to think you like punishment."

I kept my concentration as I moved closer to Noor's bed. "You okay, Noor?" I asked, glancing over at her, trying to keep my voice level.

"Been better," she drawled as Thohfsa lunged at me again.

"That's debatable," I said, half out of breath as I pivoted away from the attack, "when you are lying in a warm bed, and I'm fighting off Thohfsa with a stick."

Thohfsa looked from me to Noor and back again, her round eyes narrowing. "How do you two know each other?"

I arched a brow. "I thought you knew everything that happened within your prison walls, warden?"

Thohfsa growled at the back of her throat, then raced forward, her blade high in the air. I raised my tree branch to meet it, praying the wood was fat enough, or Thohfsa's blade was dull enough, that it wouldn't cut it in half. As Thohfsa brought the blade down, Noor shouted my name, but I couldn't afford to break concentration. Thohfsa's sword struck my weapon, landed squarely in the middle.

And got stuck.

I wanted to scream in triumph. Instead, I slid my hand down the blade, grasped the hilt of her sword, and slammed it backward into her cheek.

Thohfsa stumbled back into Noor's bed, losing her balance, and I wrenched the sword from her, spinning it around with the tip of the blade aimed directly at her.

Thohfsa let out a frustrated cry as she stared down the sharp end of her own weapon. A glimmer of panic fluttered behind the harsh grooves of her face, and I tasted success on my tongue.

"You didn't do your research, Thohfsa," I said as I gave her the same slow smile she always bestowed on me. "You decided to engage in a sword fight with the daughter of the emperor's sword maker. I can best you even without a blade."

"You don't want to kill me," she stuttered back. "I can set you free. Let me go and I'll ensure your release."

"Are you trying to bargain with me? After everything you've done?" I looked her up and down, my expression grim. "I'm not in a negotiating mood." I advanced on her, the memory of every beating she'd given me fresh on my skin, the sound of every snap of the whip as it cracked against the back of my thighs echoing in my head.

"Dania." Noor's quiet voice cut through my fog of rage. Noor had shuffled to the edge of the bed and tentatively placed a toe on the floor. She braced herself against the mattress as she stood on her feet, and I released a slow breath as she walked toward me.

"Knock her out, you don't need to kill her."

"Are you joking?" I scowled, nearly baring my teeth. "I don't need to kill her? She's tortured us both for *years*."

"Listen to her!" Thohfsa's eager voice cut between us like a rough axe. "You'll have a better chance at freedom if I'm alive, I'll help you!"

I gave her a flat smile. "Noor doesn't know you like I do, warden. We won't live while you live."

Thohfsa licked the front of her teeth, that calculating gleam returning to her face. I angled my head, but before I could react, she opened her mouth and let out a loud scream.

I didn't second-guess it, not even when Noor grabbed my arm, nor when she called my name again.

I charged forward and plunged my sword into Thohfsa's stomach with a sick lurch.

A gasp escaped me—I had forgotten what it was to pierce a body with a blade, to feel the resistance of skin against steel and the rush of nausea in my throat when it finally gave way.

My sword cut her off mid-scream and we both stood staring at each other for a moment, slack-jawed.

Thick streams of crimson gushed down my blade. I closed my eyes briefly and all that rage and hatred was silent.

For a moment, it was peaceful.

Thohfsa had met her end, and it had been everything I had promised every time she'd laid a hand on me. I wrenched my sword free, the blood pooling as Thohfsa's body slumped to the ground.

I glanced over my shoulder at Noor. "You don't get to decide my retribution."

She nodded tightly, her eyes wide.

Wiping the blade clean on Noor's bedsheet, I tried to steady my erratic breathing.

It had been a long while since I'd killed someone with a blade, but dwelling on it now could cost us our lives. A mask of focused composure dropped over me, and I instinctively rolled the short sword in my hand, testing its weight, introducing myself to the new weapon. I exhaled a steadying breath.

"We have to move now. Thohsfa made enough noise to have the guards running over here. If we don't get out now, we never will."

Noor's unreadable gaze slid to Thohfsa's still-twitching body. She chewed on her bottom lip, looking as if she wanted to scold me but thought better of it. Instead she said, "Do you have a plan?"

I smiled at her, an echo of Thohfsa's earlier one. "No, but I have a sword."

Eight

Up until now I'd been missing the one thing I needed to get out of here. From memory I adjusted my gait to accommodate my sword, the heavy weight different from what I was used to with my talwar, but it would do the job.

Distant shouting and footsteps sounded at the other end of the infirmary, signaling that Thohfsa's scream had been effective.

Noor ran to the door and looked down the hall, eyes wide with fear. "How in the name of the djinn are we getting out of this one?"

I exhaled, my heart beating as loud as a tabla. I counted slowly in my head, stilling my nerves, as I rocked back and forth on my feet. With a blade, I felt sure. Powerful. I raised it in front of me. "We'll do things my way this time."

Steps pounded against the stone, the same insistent boots I'd heard for the past year. Noor jumped back as two guards entered the room, weapons drawn. I recognized one as the guard who went after the rock I'd thrown, his hair cropped short and beard closely trimmed. The other had his uniform buttoned unevenly and an unbrushed nest of curls. Their eyes went from Thohfsa on the ground to me holding her bloodied sword.

I huffed a laugh at their shocked expressions and remembered how Thohfsa used to berate them. "Don't tell me you haven't wanted to do the same?"

Noor stepped forward, her hands extended in a placating way. "The warden is dead. You can either let us escape under cover of darkness and have the chance to live, or fight us and die." She gestured to the weapon in my hand.

"I didn't know we were giving them an option." My fingers curled tighter around the hilt, and I took a step forward.

"I know you said you were good with one of those, but I'd rather get out of here with as little bloodshed as possible," Noor said through gritted teeth.

"I can't promise anything," I called back to her, my eyes narrowing.

I very much doubted we would be walking out of here without any more blood spilled.

The guards agreed, because they advanced on us, their own blades gleaming in the torchlight.

The roar inside my head quieted.

I shifted back and forth on my feet and savored the familiar rush of fight brewing in my veins. My muscles woke, remembering each drill with Baba in the training field, each bout as I honed my skill.

The first guard with the neat beard lunged and I pivoted backward and struck his scimitar down with Thohfsa's short sword. He wasn't expecting my sure strike and his sword dangled in his grasp. He gaped at me, and I didn't waste time driving the blade into his belly too. Noor gasped behind me and my arms screamed with the force of another killing blow. The guard cried out, the weak mewl of a drowning cat.

The slovenly guard came at me with a roar, but I couldn't wrench Thohfsa's sword out fast enough. I abandoned it and rolled away as he sliced the air with his double-bladed scimitar, missing me by inches.

I came to my feet, empty hands itching to steal his blades. The guard followed me, charging forward as my feet danced around him.

I reached for the pommel of Thohfsa's sword and managed to heave it out this time.

When the guard arched his scimitar high, I dove under and slammed my hilt into his jaw, letting the heavy metal handle of Thohfsa's sword swing forward with all its weight.

He fell like a boulder onto the floor.

Noor ran over to him, placing her fingers against his neck. "Well, at least this one's not dead."

"More will be," I said, my mouth curling into a grim line. "If not them, us."

I picked up the incapacitated guard's double-bladed sword by the center pommel and sliced it through the air.

"I can only use as many swords as I can hold. I'll settle for two right now." I looked down at the other scimitar, a single curved blade lying in a pool of blood on the floor. "You take that one."

Noor looked like she had just swallowed a cupful of thorns. "No thanks, I'm sure I would be more of a danger to myself than others."

"You need a weapon, take it." I walked to the doorway and looked down the hall. No other footsteps. No other guards.

Noor gingerly picked up the hilt with two fingers. It dangled limply from her grip, and her hands shook.

I gave her an incredulous look. She might be right, she didn't look like she could use the weapon at all. No wonder she concentrated her efforts on digging out of here instead of fighting her way out.

"You okay?" I asked, examining her blanched face.

Noor exhaled slowly. "The zoraat blend the healer used wasn't perfect, I could have mixed one better. I'm still feeling the effects of recovery. But at least she healed my wound and made me conscious so Thohfsa could interrogate me." She rolled her shoulders and winced, massaging the back of her neck. "My head is pounding."

"Where is the healer now?" I eyed Thohfsa's body. She wasn't moving, but there was still a slight rise and fall to her chest as she bled out.

But I was not inclined to give her a swift death given what she had put me through.

"She was ordered to leave as soon as she was done. I have to admit, I didn't expect Thohfsa to have the kind of resources to get a healer from the emperor that fast."

I chewed on the inside of my cheek. "You said the emperor wanted his zoraat back, right? It makes sense he'd be interested in you."

"I don't like the idea of that."

"I wouldn't either."

I knew what it was to have the attention of Emperor Vahid, and he was merciless.

We stepped over the bodies and crept down the hall of the infirmary, easing open the door. Outside was dark and eerily silent, but more importantly, there were no guards in sight.

We skirted around the building toward the opposite perimeter wall, the one not along the cliffside. My breath was trapped in my chest, the pressure nearly unbearable.

The other guards may not have been alerted yet, but soon they would notice Thohfsa and the others missing.

We had to be as quick as possible.

We crawled along the grass, avoiding the roving torchlight from the guard towers. Thohfsa's watchtower was next to the main entrance, and we headed there to climb up and over the perimeter wall. My breath was a white puff in the cool air.

A few more minutes and we would be free. A few more steps and we'd leave this prison behind.

But as we crouched in the grass, I froze at a yell in the distance.

Noor bumped into my back. "What?"

"I heard a shout."

After a moment, the noise was impossible to ignore. Multiple guards called out, their voices coming from the direction of the infirmary. The stamp of feet pounded the grass.

They were close.

Then, the worst sound—the sharp ringing of bells echoed through the prison.

My blood froze. Now they were looking for us.

I clutched my swords tight, like they were an anchor.

The last time I'd faced the guards head-on, it hadn't gone well.

But this time, it was different. This time, I had weapons.

With swords in my hands, I was invincible.

Noor's own sword nearly flew out of her grip when the bell sounded and she whirled on me.

"Every time you turn, I think you are going to stab my eye out," I muttered as I shifted away from her swinging sword tip.

"I told you I didn't want to hold one!" she snapped.

"You don't *hold* a sword, you wield it. And it's helpful to have in case we—"

The unmistakable hiss of a blade leaving its sheath cut underneath the chaos around us.

I could identify that sound in the middle of a storm.

I stopped short at the edge of the infirmary and dared a glance around the corner.

Half a dozen guards stood, their scimitars raised, looking for us.

"You're going to need that sword after all."

Nine

"There's no way we are getting out of this." Noor's shaking voice carved through the roar of battle in my ears.

"I've had worse odds," I whispered back.

Noor gave me an incredulous look. *"Have you?"*

I hadn't, but I didn't want to tell her that. But now at least I had a blade pointing back at them.

Correction, I had *three* blades.

"We just have to break their formation up," I said, chewing on the bottom of my lip. We couldn't go back the way we came, because we'd just encounter the guards from another angle. And we couldn't climb over the wall behind the infirmary, because there was nothing on the other side but jagged rocks and rough sea.

We'd have to take them head-on.

"I can handle a couple of them at a time, as long as they aren't coming at me at once."

Memories in the training yard flashed through my mind, causing my hands to tighten around my hilt.

But these weren't memories of training with Baba, but with Mazin.

We'd spent hours sparring, either with Baba's other students or just each other. Though Mazin's swordsmanship had needed work, in the end he was the only one who could match me.

Until he'd bested me in our final battle, the one we'd had without swords.

The one where I'd ended up in prison and he had walked free.

"Dania," Noor croaked, fear palpable through her words, "do you think I can take on six guards when I barely know how to hold this thing?"

I turned to her, the memories giving rise to what felt like ancient anger, fueling my movements and solidifying my resolve.

"Not to fight," I admitted, thinking through our strategy, "but as a distraction."

"Oh great. So, I'm the bait?"

"They don't know there's two of us. Just that you escaped from the infirmary, and Thohfsa is dead. Let's use that to our advantage."

"Okay." She nodded, her mouth white. "Just don't leave me to be skewered while you run off alone." She stood, her sword in her hand, looking like she was walking to her execution.

"If I wanted to do that, I wouldn't have come back for you."

She gave me a small smile, but it didn't meet her fearful eyes.

I wanted to reassure her, but I didn't know what was about to happen. I knew what my skills were, I knew what I had been trained to do, but I'd never really gone into a fight when I had to worry about someone else—especially someone who didn't have any fighting skills. The best thing I could do was make sure the odds were a little more even.

"I need them broken up. Lure them back here, that will give me a chance to thin them out." If they didn't know I was here, I wanted to use that.

She nodded and clutched the sword in front of her like it was a talisman instead of a weapon.

I took a deep breath, placed the flat of my hand on Noor's rigid back, and pushed her into the awaiting guards.

Shouting ensued, and the scuffle of feet grew closer.

"We have her!" A voice was dangerously close, split off from the rest. Just what I wanted.

"Did you think you could escape?" a guard said, his voice a low growl. "Alone?"

Noor ran back behind the wall, her sword held oddly. A guard came running after her but I was ready. I flicked one end of the double-sided scimitar, slicing his throat in a clean motion.

"She's not alone," I said to his twitching body on the ground.

For one brief moment, I mourned him. Another death on my hands, one that didn't need to happen. But I couldn't afford to dwell.

I was tired. I'd been digging daily on little food and even less sleep. I channeled everything I knew about fighting—everything I learned from Baba and training with Maz.

But in the end, the last voice I heard dictating my steps was my grandmother's.

Never show them your fear. The weak feed from fear.

Another guard leapt from around the corner, and I cut him down without glancing at him. The next followed and met my blade. I unsheathed the talwar and met three guards at once, never on the defense. Each hit was a killing blow, every move an attack. A guard with long dark hair and an eye patch rushed at me, meeting the slam of both my swords.

But he guarded his face with his own blade and pushed me back. He was big—much bigger than I was. I wouldn't last fighting him like this; I needed to outmaneuver him. I sidestepped him but he followed, and two other guards joined. I dove for the soldier on his right, slicing his heel with my scimitar and rolling away as he fell to the floor with a tight gasp. He clutched his foot and moaned like a baying dog. My crossed swords met the curved steel of the taller guard, and I managed to parry his heavy attacks before spinning out of reach. A short guard with a long beard and shoulders corded like thick ropes swung his scimitar with a speed that took me off guard, giving me a shallow cut across the forearm.

I smothered my yelp with a low hiss as he gave a smug smile. The pain sizzled through my veins like cold fire. My face pressed into a fierce mask. To them, I would be impenetrable. To them, I wouldn't show fear.

The weak feed from fear.

The large guard leapt toward me, slamming me to the ground and landing on top of me. My lungs compressed as all my air was snatched up by his meaty body against mine.

A thin smile stretched across his face and he was so close I could see every blackened pore on his cheeks, could smell the strong waft of sweat crawling up my nose. I couldn't move, couldn't fight, and couldn't get him off me.

Panic beat at my chest.

I had no way out.

"Is your plan to kill me with your stench?" I said, hoping he'd lose his temper enough for me to take advantage of. My legs kicked at him, but couldn't find purchase. His broad hand pinned my arms above my head, my swords pressed into the grass, useless.

He raised his sword, the tip pointing directly at my chest as if he were going to stake me to the ground.

My breath caught and I couldn't exhale. It felt as though time froze as he brought down his blade. But as he did, his arms faltered. His beady eyes rolled back into his head and he collapsed on me with a heavy thud.

I lay there, momentarily stunned. My palms pressed hard on his shoulders and I heaved his stinking body off me. Noor was poised above him, the hilt of the scimitar in front of her, as if she were about to stab herself. I blinked, my words catching in my throat.

"I thought you said you didn't know how to use a sword?" I said finally, with a thick swallow.

She tilted her head and huffed out a breath. "I'm pretty sure I used the wrong end."

Footsteps sounded behind us, and Noor whirled as another guard came upon us. I jumped to my feet, swinging my scimitar over her head and planting it in the neck of the guard. I tore it out, blood splattering us both.

A moment of weighted silence surrounded us. We walked around the corner of the infirmary and surveyed the damage.

All the guards in the yard were dead.

Noor whistled. "You did it, Dania."

I didn't celebrate. I stifled the urge to grieve the dead and swallowed the bile in the back of my throat. I yanked Noor's arm in my own and dragged her toward the perimeter wall.

"We'll have every guard coming for us in the prison in minutes if we don't get out of here now."

"Didn't you just kill them all?"

I shook my head, counting the number of bodies and running through how many night patrol guards I had counted before my previous escape attempts.

"It looks like we've only been dealing with the night patrol guards, but they've raised the alarm, so soon we'll have every prison guard descending on us. They believe one prisoner escaped. As soon as they see the massacre, they'll be coming."

Noor nodded, and then pulled her hand from mine. "But why are you dragging us to the wall?"

I gaped at her. "So we can climb over it."

Noor laughed, then held up a large gold key ring that glinted in the moonlight. "Who needs to hop the wall when I already swiped the keys to the front gate from Thohfsa?"

Ten

Shouts sounded in the distance as the rest of the prison guards ran toward the infirmary. Noor's hands shook as she unlocked the entrance and we both slipped through the main door under cover of darkness while the front patrols were distracted.

My heart pounded louder than our eager footsteps, but when my feet first hit the loose sand by the water, I felt like flying.

We'd made it to the beach.

Escape was in our sights.

We found a rickety boat and dragged it down to the water as silently as we could. My bloodied hands finally let go of my swords and picked up an oar instead.

We rowed into the night, adrenaline fueling our arms. I should have been too exhausted to move, but my skin felt alive, as if freedom had flooded me with new fire. We had no clear direction of where we were going, just that we were leaving the prison behind us.

"I can't believe we just did that. I can't believe *you* just did that." Noor's voice trembled and I wasn't sure if she was going to laugh or cry.

I felt my own giddy laughter bubbling up in my chest.

"Those guards barely had basic sword training," I said, unable to keep the grin from my face. "It wouldn't have been possible with proper soldiers."

Noor scoffed. "It shouldn't have been possible at all. Have you been consuming djinn magic? How did you do that?"

I paused in my rowing and rubbed the back of my neck. It wasn't magic that had my sword moving through the air like lightning, my reflexes quick as a cat.

It was training.

Every attack, parry, and defense was muscle memory.

Dark eyes and steady hands flashed through my mind as I thought of who I'd done all those hours of training with.

If I closed my eyes, I could even hear the whisper of his careful footsteps beside me. Until I wasn't just recalling the sparring, but the other things too. The parts of him I desperately wanted to forget—the small smile in the corner of his mouth when he watched me, the catch in his voice when he said my name. I curled my fingers into my palms, nails biting skin, trying to escape the onslaught of him, each memory as if it was ingrained on my skin.

But I buried them, those moments of softness that I didn't want to think about—because they were lies.

The only truth between us had been on the battlefield.

And I didn't want to speak his name, not now.

"I grew up with every kind of sword my entire life. My father made them, but he also made sure I knew how to use them," I said finally, suffocating the other words that threatened to leap out.

"That he did." Noor looked out at the dark ocean and for a moment we let our boat bob on the water, both consumed by bigger thoughts.

"Dani, I didn't tell you everything." Noor's low voice cut underneath the steady rush of the ocean.

I looked up, something in her voice stilling the oar in my hands.

Noor's vibrant eyes met mine across the moonlit sea. "I know exactly where Souma's treasure is."

I inhaled, the sea air winding its way around my lungs, the possibilities of her admission running through my mind better than any prison escape strategy. It replaced warm thoughts of Maz and gave me something else.

Something that felt like vengeance.

I had suspected she knew where it was. But now it was certain, the potential was limitless. All that power. All that magic.

What would I do if I had the power to make anything happen?

This time the memories that assaulted me weren't comforting, they were steeped in bitterness. Mazin's immovable face as he watched me being dragged away by the palace guards. Captain Darbaran's grubby fingers as they bit into the flesh of my arm and fastened thick chains around my wrist.

I could make them pay. But what would that get me now?

As much as I wanted to give in to hatred, it was my baba's low voice that urged me home. Vengeance wouldn't help my father—it would only make things worse. I could have all the power in the world, but right now I only wanted one thing.

"Come with me, find Souma's treasure with me." Noor's voice was so soft it was nearly snatched up by the wind, but I heard it clear enough. "Share it with me. We could go anywhere we wanted with what Souma buried." She swallowed, her eyes like fire in the moonlight. "We could get justice for what was done to us."

A low breath swept through me. "Justice?" I arched a brow. "Is that what you want? Because that isn't what I need."

She looked away, across the unfathomable dark sea.

"Revenge," she responded after a minute. "That's what I should have said."

A word I knew well.

"I want revenge on Emperor Vahid." She licked her lips nervously, as if admitting it out loud made her afraid.

But something niggled at the back of my mind. This was more than punishment for a chieftain she'd become close to. This was something else.

"Why?" I asked, tilting my head, assessing her. We'd shared so much with each other, but perhaps not enough.

"I want to destroy the man who ordered so many dead. The man who killed my . . ."

Noor trailed away, as if she were struggling for the word. I was unsure which one she would land on. Friend? Chief?

Souma hadn't been just her chieftain, hadn't been just a man who'd taught her how to use zoraat, that much was clear.

"Your . . . ?" I prompted.

She looked up, her dark eyes glistening. "Souma was my father. My real father. He had an affair with my mother, but hid my identity from his family when my mother died and he took me in. That's why I can't just hide while Emperor Vahid sits in his palace without a care in the world." Her hands curled at her side.

I smiled, but it was without humor.

"You and I both lost because of Vahid. But if he killed your father, you are owed retribution for that, Noor. I would want it if the same happened to me."

Noor looked down, as if meeting my eyes would be too much.

Revenge.

My fingers were itching to take hold of it. But vengeance wouldn't bring me to my father. It wouldn't erase what had happened.

Noor was giving me the keys to unlimited power, the ability to have djinn magic in my grasp.

Strangely, I didn't feel triumphant.

Did I want retribution for what had been done? Undoubtedly. But mostly I just wanted to hold my father's hand, feel the raised scars on his palm from so many years at the forge, and remember what it was to be loved. Her father was killed by Vahid, but mine still had breath in his lungs, and this conversation made me realize how fortunate that was.

"I can't." I weighed my words. "I can't go after Souma's treasure with you."

Her mouth twisted in disappointment.

"I need to go back for my father."

Noor nodded, though she gripped her oar so tightly her knuckles turned white. I wondered for the first time if she even had anywhere to go.

The only family she'd had was dead.

I swallowed past the lump in my throat, knowing that my father would welcome her with open arms after how she'd helped me.

I reached out to her on impulse, my hand resting lightly on her arm. "Come home with me. You have a place to stay." My voice was low and true. We hadn't known each other long, but our relationship had been forged in the dirt of a prison that had meant to kill us, and instead we'd left with bloodied hands. "We'll figure out what we want to do next when we are safe at my father's house."

Noor bit the edge of her lip and looked back at the prison, now a dark dot on the brightening horizon.

"Dania, you've already done enough for me. You went back for me and you didn't have to." Her smile was sad. "It's okay. If I had family, I'd want to be with them too."

My heart splintered, knowing that she had no one left, that she was alone now, and I still had people who loved me.

I clasped her hands in the boat, and it rocked with the force of my movement. "You're my family now too."

Eleven

My village sat at the foot of the mountains, nestled into the rock like it was part of the formations themselves. Dozens of baked brick houses protected its inhabitants from the onslaught of the glacial wind, and an outcropping in the cliff shielded us from the worst of the valley storms.

My father's smith stood at the edge of these houses, proud against the mountainside, its white walls and stone gate calling to me. Normally a smith would be in the city, close to the emperor, outfitting his armies and assassins with deadly weaponry. But my father was no ordinary smith. He refused to move from the place he'd married my mother and his village community to seek greater prosperity in the city. And still it found him.

He had a knack for forging blades that were both beautiful and deadly, that seemed to fly from your hand with surprising accuracy and balance. Emperor Vahid even asked if my father had gotten a hold of djinn magic somehow, or if his forge was heated by the smokeless fire of the djinn realms.

Of course he hadn't. My father was an ordinary man, and I loved him for it.

Noor and I managed to steal a pack mule when we arrived at the first town near the sea.

We rode through the night. If anyone was coming after us, we needed to have a head start.

"Your village better have a very deep well, I feel as though I could drink forever." Noor draped dramatically over the front of the mule while I dismounted and grabbed its reins, leading it through the dawn-lit streets of my village.

"It has a well, otherwise people wouldn't live here."

"Take me to it immediately."

I let out a snort of laughter, even as thirst pounded through my own head. Our waterskins had run out hours ago and we'd managed to survive scooping snow from the sand dunes as we crossed the cold desert. My stomach growled, the last of the wild cherries and stolen dates running out that morning. "First we go to my father's house, and we can have all the food and drink we want there, I promise you."

"Good, because I cannot subsist on dates alone. The food was better in prison."

"You can't be serious about *that*." I shuddered at the memory of the lentil slop sliding down my throat.

Noor lifted her head. "You're right. At least dates have a taste."

I hadn't minded the steady diet of apricots and almond-dusted flatbreads we'd swiped from the towns we'd passed through. Noor and I had raided what we could from the tiny settlements along the way and we had managed to pilfer two plain kurtas to replace our bloodied prison ones, as well as basic but serviceable woven shoes. If I felt a pang of remorse at the people I had stolen from, I reminded myself that I was seeing my father soon and could pay them back when I got home.

All that mattered was finding him again.

Then we could go anywhere we wanted.

"Just think, we could be eating mutton stew and rice. Spicy pickles.

Pillowy bread covered in garlic and black onion seeds." Noor licked her lips.

"We'll have a feast at my father's." I couldn't disguise the urgency in my voice. My skin was buzzing with anticipation. We were so close I could feel the burn of tears behind my eyes.

"Come on."

I led Noor through the uneven cobblestones of my village, checking that the muted dupatta wound around my face hid my features. I didn't want anyone alerting Emperor Vahid—or Mazin—that I had returned. I didn't know if he had spies in my village, but I wasn't going to take that chance.

We got closer to my father's house, the mud brick painted a bright white, jutting out of the rock of the mountain. On the side of the building was his smith, the sign with crossed daggers etched into it still hanging above the door.

But the smith was dark, with no warm glow from the smelt peeking through the cracks in the windows.

I frowned, my hand curling around the reins so tight the leather pinched. Baba always worked at the smith early in the morning.

Dread sat in my stomach, growing like a sinkhole.

"The door is ajar." Noor pulled her cloak tighter.

I glanced at the house to confirm her whispered words. I had been too busy looking at the smith to notice the door was wide open.

My steps barely left a mark on the dusty walkway as I rushed inside. The house was cast in shadows, with no candle glow to signal life inside.

Where is he?

"Baba?" I called out, my heart in my throat, my eyes roving wildly about the empty room. The mango wood bench in the front room was overturned, and the desert scrub mat shredded. A bead of sweat ran down my temple even though the house was cold.

It was the kind of cold that felt uninhabited, stale. I rushed to the back of the house, until I made it to my father's bedroom.

Everything was destroyed.

His bed was torn apart, the pillows ripped open, and the date palm mattress split in half. All the daggers my father normally had displayed on the walls of his room were removed, with only the darkened outline of their presence imprinted on the walls to signify they were ever there. I walked over and placed my palm on the outline of the dagger that had a gold handle in the shape of a jackal's head, as if to convince myself that my memories were real, that my father *had* lived here.

That this house had been warm and alive the last time I had seen it.

I shouted again and again, calling his name, shouting for my cat, Jalebi, letting the words echo through the house, looking for any sign of life.

"Where are you?" I whispered into the broken room.

"Maybe he fled?" Noor's quiet voice came from behind me, tentative, as if she didn't want to startle a wild animal. It broke through the vacancy of the room and despite her careful words, anger rose inside me.

"Not like this," I snapped, combing the empty, ravaged space for any clue as to where he would have gone.

There was nothing, not even any sign of my cat. It was as if no one had lived here in a long time.

I turned to face Noor. "He would have tried to leave me a message."

He wouldn't have left like this, not with his house destroyed and no word about where he had gone.

"Perhaps he didn't have time to leave you one." I heard the doubt in her voice. It was the same doubt that had dread pulling me down to the floor with its weight.

"Do you think Emperor Vahid took him too?"

Her mouth flattened. "That's possible. Though it doesn't explain why his belongings are missing and everything is wrecked. Perhaps the house was raided?"

Raided.

At Noor's words, I bolted to the opposite end of the house, to my room.

The same white baked brick walls I had grown up with greeted me, the same sturdy bed frame and wide window allowing shafts of sunlight to illuminate the dust in the air. Except my room was in the same state of disarray as my father's—there were a few plain kurtas strewn about the floor, but all my other clothes were gone. The room was upended, as if multiple hands had hunted through everything and took whatever they wanted.

I felt an awful, sick feeling—like I had been arrested all over again, taken from everything I loved and given a vacant cell in return. And that ever-present fear weighing on me since arriving, nearly taking me to my knees.

I pulled the bed away from the wall and worked a loose brick by the bedpost. It was stuck, and I felt a flicker of relief. I tugged and twisted until it broke free, crumbling in my hands and revealing a small compartment, a secret space only I knew about.

There. A small dark bag sat undisturbed in the corner of the hole.

Air whooshed out of me, my shoulders sagging as I pulled it out.

I loosened the indigo sack hiding my few items—a pouch of money, a braided piece of my amma's dark hair, along with her looping gold earrings, a pocket-sized folding knife made by my father, and the final piece—a necklace with a miniature dagger pendant, given to me by Mazin. I held it up in the light, watching the glow of the blade in the dawn sun. It was a real dagger, albeit small, but the blade as sharp as any of my father's. Its hilt was the head of a halmasti, the large, wolf-like creature in folklore tales of the north. It was a re-creation of a bigger dagger my father made, my favorite knife. I curled my fingers around it, the prick of the blade stinging my palm, the memory of when Mazin gave it to me fresh in my mind.

You'll wear it, won't you?

I'll never take it off.

But I had forgotten it that day, which kept it safe when they arrested me. Only for Maz to stab me in the back with a different knife.

"Whatever you've come for, there's nothing left. They've taken everything already. Don't you have any shame?"

That ragged, piercing voice tore through me and pulled me out of my memories.

I would have known it anywhere.

I whirled around. "Nanu?"

My grandmother stood in the doorway, a dusty dupatta pulled about her shoulders. She looked smaller than before, shrunken, as if the scarf she clung to had begun to swallow her up. Shock rippled through me at the change in her. Where she had once looked so much like my mother—glossy black hair, skin a vibrant warm brown as if the sun always shone on it—she had now aged significantly. More significantly than anyone should have in a year. I would have barely recognized her if it wasn't for that voice, like the rusty snap of a flame from the smith. Now her hair was a faded and streaky gray, her skin carved with deep grooves that looked like scars.

She blinked at me, her pale eyes glimmering in the dawn-drenched room. "Dania?"

It was a faint whisper, but I heard the disbelief there.

I raced to her, my eyes burning, and threw my arms around her, careful not to crush her now frail body. "Nanu, it's me, Dania. I'm back."

Holding her felt foreign, and I couldn't recall the last time we'd ever embraced. My grandmother and I had never been close, and my father had blamed that on my mother's death. Since my mother was killed, something in my grandmother had changed, like the grief of losing her only child had twisted inside her, and she couldn't stomach the rest of the world.

Especially me.

She kept her distance, and we only really saw each other at holidays and village celebrations. But that distance melted away now that she was here in front of me, and my father was not.

Her shoulders were stiff, and she didn't embrace me in return. "I thought you had died, girl." She shook her head, her eyes wide. "I thought . . ."

Her voice was still uncertain, as if she didn't believe I was real.

"Nanu." I took her by the arms and shook her. "Where is Baba?" My voice was urgent and low. "What happened?"

Her mouth dropped open, and a sound whistled out, though not discernible words. Her already blanched skin looked whiter still. Unease settled over me like a fog I couldn't quite see through.

But she didn't answer my question. Instead she looked behind me and stiffened. "Who are you?"

I looked back at Noor, who stood awkwardly in the doorway of my room, uncertainty flickering across her face.

"Nanu, relax, she's with me. She's my friend."

Nanu blinked and look back at me, chewing on the edge of her lip. "I can't believe you are here, Dania. Standing in front of me."

I exhaled, clasping her hands in mine. "I'm real, Nanu."

"They released you?" She frowned, those heavy lines on her face deepening.

I shook my head, a firm no.

Realization dawned on her face and her voice dropped to a low whisper, almost not daring her next words. "You escaped?"

Escaped.

I thought of all the guards I had killed to get out of there, of the torture I had suffered under Thohfsa. Of Noor unconscious, lying in a pool of her own blood on the floor of her dirty cell.

Escape was such a small word for what we had done. We carved a path to freedom despite what had been stolen from us.

"Yes, I escaped. And I've come to get Baba—and you, if you want to join us. I want to leave our village and run to a place where Vahid won't have power over us anymore. Where we can live in peace. Maybe we'll go north to your people there."

I wasn't sure if Nanu would join us, but I extended the offer anyway. Memories of her flitted through my mind, the way she held herself so carefully apart from me. The shadow of herself she became after my mother died.

Nanu's mouth twisted, like a poisoned snake. "Dania, I have to tell you about your father."

That dark pit in my stomach returned, but something inside me refused to acknowledge it.

"Where is he?" I looked around as if I could conjure him, my voice seeping with desperation. "We need to leave as soon as possible, Vahid might be looking for us." My words were rushed, and I refused to look at my grandmother's hollow eyes. There was something there I didn't want to see.

"Dania." Noor's cool voice cut through my frantic words and she laid a hand on my shoulder. I stilled, my blood pounding in my ears. "I think your grandmother is trying to tell you something."

An ache formed in my chest, a black gaping wound that felt as if it were going to swallow me whole. I knew the words before she said them, before she even turned her pale eyes to mine, before Noor caught me as I fell. I knew what my grandmother had been trying to tell me, and I didn't want to hear it.

Because if it was true, then I had nothing left.

"Dania, your baba is dead."

Twelve

"Tell me what happened."

Nanu took us to her little house a few minutes away and we sat in her front room, cradling cups of chai she'd poured from a pot hanging over the fire.

"The house was raided after your father was killed."

After my father was killed.

I knew it was true in my bones, the way you feel a mountain storm about to descend. My father wasn't here anymore.

And I needed to know why. But my grandmother had thus far avoided my questions and instead made up a bed for us in the main room.

"Tell me what happened," I repeated, my voice low, coming over to her as she stoked the flames. She poured more chai, and a green cardamom pod floated to the top of the milky tea. I gripped the warm cup but couldn't bring it to my lips, my tongue feeling thick.

"Drink your tea," she said firmly.

I swallowed thickly, trying to bury my frustration. She met my glare with a stoney stare of her own, so I lifted it to my lips and downed the hot liquid, not tasting a single drop, barely noticing the scalding tea as it flooded my throat.

"There." I slammed my cup on the table in front of us. "Now, *tell me what happened!*"

Noor laid a soft hand on my shoulder, and I shot her a grateful look. I closed my eyes and let a long breath flow through me, trying to calm the riot of emotions bursting to get out. I knew this wasn't my grandmother's fault, but I needed information from her.

Nanu took a deep breath. "When they took you, your father was consumed with rage. He gathered his best weapons, intending to free you. No one could talk sense into him. His friend Casildo said he would help him, so together they went at nightfall to find you."

Casildo.

My father visited him when we'd made trips to Basral and Casildo would often purchase swords from him. He had been a good friend to my father, and I considered stopping at his house when we rode here. But the fact that Casildo helped my father try to rescue me made something rise in my chest.

I didn't even know that my father *had* mounted a rescue.

My hand reached out of its own accord to grasp Nanu's cool fingers. She paused and looked down at our joined hands, a frown curling her mouth. We didn't touch often, and now I had both embraced her and held her hand in the space of a few hours. When my mother had died, it wasn't my grandmother I could turn to in my grief. But now she was the only left who knew my father as I did and who knew what he meant to me.

"I didn't know of Baba's attempt to break me out," I said, remembering those early days of imprisonment in the palace dungeon, before they had transported me to the island and left me to rot.

I had expected to be executed, but they'd sent me to a place much worse than death. And all the while my father had died trying to free me. That dark, sick feeling grew bigger and more encompassing.

"Baba is dead because of me?" I turned my face away from hers, not wanting to see the confirmation in her eyes.

"No," she said, her voice cutting through the roar in my ears.

"He was betrayed by his friend Casildo, who said he could get them into the palace prison. Instead, he led your father straight to the city guards. But your father would not go quietly. He fought them until he was overwhelmed by the soldiers. Foolish."

Nanu's words were quiet, but I heard them so loud in my head I couldn't see straight. I pictured everything—the way he would have drawn his favored filigreed talwar upon seeing the guards, the twist of his mouth when he whirled on his friend and realized his treachery. It would have been a lot like the way I had looked at Mazin before the guards took me.

He would have felt that same drop in his stomach that I did, the same rush of disbelief at the realization your closest ally had betrayed you.

The understanding that you were alone.

"Where is he now?" I asked with deadly calm.

Noor met my gaze, her feet tucked under her as she sat on the date palm mat.

She nodded at my expression.

Yes.

She knew what I wanted. Because she wanted the same thing, for the same crime. The answer to what my next steps would be was as clear as day.

Nanu watched our exchange with a tilt of her head, as if seeing our bond for the first time.

But she hadn't yet answered my question.

"Casildo?" I repeated. "Where is he?" My words were barely a growl, but the air changed with the force of them. Anger and anticipation sat heavy in the room, and I curled my fingers around my father's little pocket dagger.

Nanu narrowed her eyes. "Casildo is back in the city, still a respected merchant. If anything his betrayal advanced his position with the emperor. But before he went back, he raided your father's smith. Took all his swords. Helped himself to everything he could get."

Why didn't you stop him? I wanted to scream at her.

But I knew the answer to that. My grandmother was no warrior, and with me arrested and my father dead, there would have been no one left to defend.

"Is that why Casildo betrayed my father? For his swords?" My voice rose, the words too loud in the silence between us.

My grandmother smiled faintly. "Casildo claimed he was afraid of the emperor and that is why he turned your father in. But I know he's been showing off your father's knives in his armory ever since."

"My father's death for a collection of swords." I shook my head.

"Dania, I had no idea your father was heading to his death." My grandmother's eyes were shadowed.

"I don't blame you, Nanu." I gentled my voice, even though the old familiar rage was flooding my veins, the dam breaking wide open. "I blame the people who put me in prison."

Mazin's cold face flitted through my mind. The memory of Darbaran's smirk nearly had me spitting. Emperor Vahid had orchestrated it all to take out an opponent without inciting a civil war.

But now I could add Casildo to that list.

Casildo, who I thought was our ally and became just another betrayer.

"And I blame the man who deceived my father while pretending to be his friend."

"Don't do anything foolish, Dania," cautioned my grandmother, but without any heat. Maybe she was tired of fighting with my father for all those years, and didn't want to waste the energy on me. She knew it would be no use.

My lips lifted, a humorless smile. "Whatever I do, it will not be foolish."

Vengeance was what I wanted, and Noor had the access to make it happen.

I could tell by Noor's pursed lips that she expected my next words. She wanted to right the wrongs done against hers just as I did mine.

"We will stay here a few days to rest, and then Noor and I will continue our journey."

I didn't explain to my grandmother where we were headed or what we were seeking. If I mentioned the zoraat to her, it could be tortured out of her. It was better that she be kept in the dark.

"But you cannot leave now." Nanu took a step toward me, her eyes darker. I blinked, wondering if it was concern I heard in her voice, or something else. Nanu had never been the type to show her emotions. "I thought you were dead," she continued, her voice pleading.

Something tugged at my heart, but I had already made my mind up. My blood had turned to steel now, as if I were one of Baba's weapons, and with his death my purpose had been forged.

It wasn't about me or Nanu anymore. It wasn't about justice.

This was about revenge.

"We'll stay for a short while, but I can't risk anything else. Not with news of my escape likely reaching Vahid."

She nodded, and I could feel her disappointment. She wanted me to stay, but I couldn't. Not now. I would never be able to live with myself if I didn't do something about my father's death. I couldn't let that go unanswered, couldn't let his betrayer roam free, nor those who had played a part in betraying me. I was unleashed, and all the dark parts of me were clamoring to get out.

Casildo. Darbaran.

Mazin.

I glanced up at Noor. One name in my puzzle intersected with hers.

Vahid.

I said their names over and over again in my mind, until a plan formed, until I could visualize every step I needed to take to get there.

And the very first one was getting our hands on that djinn treasure.

━━━┿━━━

That night we feasted on stewed goat my nanu slaughtered for the occasion. I scooped the last of the gravy from my bowl with a piece of chewy flatbread and savored the black cardamom and chilis on my tongue, wondering how I ever made it through the year without eating this. I sat at the low table in Nanu's main room, picking at the remaining spicy pickles on my plate, the sour sharpness keeping me present.

Nanu had invited some of the women of the village over to assist with the food, and I kept my gaze low as they shot curious glances at Noor and me. Nanu assured me they wouldn't report us to Vahid, but I still felt uneasy about so many being aware of our escape. I didn't want anything to stand in the way of what I was about to do.

My father's death had solidified my resolve.

But I didn't cry. I didn't grieve.

All my sorrow had channeled itself into anger. The fierce need for retaliation wrapped itself around my throat, claws piercing my skin. I gripped the edges of my bowl so hard I was surprised the stone didn't crack in half.

"Are we really going where I think we're going?" Noor sidled up next to me, plopping herself down on a cushion, her plate as empty as mine. "Are you finally agreeing to go after Souma's treasure with me?"

I leaned back, releasing a heavy breath. Noor and I were both on a familiar path of revenge. And with her access to Souma's treasure, we could do much more than dream about it.

"Yes."

Noor spooned more rice onto her plate from the serving bowls in front of us and lowered her voice. "I thought you didn't care about it."

"That was before I knew my father had been murdered. Now, I understand what you wanted to do. And I agree. We both deserve a path to retribution." Those choking fingers of rage tightened on my throat, and I almost couldn't breathe.

Noor set down her bowl and rubbed the back of her neck. "Dani, I know you are angry—"

"I'm much more than angry." My voice was a low snarl.

"Right. But don't make big decisions on the heel of finding out what happened to your father. Think this through."

"And is that what you told yourself when Vahid killed Souma? When he killed your father?"

She sucked in a breath through her teeth, but I continued.

"I am thinking this through. More than anyone ever has. I am thinking of every cut, every bruise, and every blow I'm going to give in repayment for what they did to my father. For what they did to me." My mouth pressed into a grim line, and I stared at the aunties of the village laughing together. A few had come in from feeding the chickens, and another woman was rubbing warmed mustard oil into my nanu's hair. Afra, the village elder, was burning a chili in the doorway of the house, warding off the evil eye that might have followed me from prison. It was an atmosphere of festivity—the swordsmith's daughter, returning to the family of aunties who'd been there all her life.

Except that daughter was different now.

And though this was the place I'd grown up, I didn't become who I was here. Not really. It wasn't until I had lain on that stone floor in prison that the molten iron had truly entered my veins.

"I want you to be sure. Once we go down this path, we can't turn back."

I crossed my arms over my chest. "Are *you* sure? Can you go on, knowing that Souma's killer is still out there?"

Noor looked away from me, the pain flashing across her eyes before staring at her bowl.

I nodded. "I didn't think so. That isn't possible for me anymore either. Not while they live."

Mazin's face floated to the top of my mind, like the first cloud in a gathering storm.

It would always come back to him.

There were others that deserved my ire just as much, but it was Maz's betrayal that was a festering raw wound of hurt spreading to everything else.

He was the person who had betrayed me the most.

If it wasn't for him, Baba would still be alive. I swallowed and closed my eyes briefly before focusing them back on Noor. "Not while *Mazin* lives. He's the catalyst for everything. And I'm going to do whatever it takes to make sure he feels my rage."

Noor watched me, her expression inscrutable, the torchlight flickering off her bright eyes. "If this is what you truly want, then I'm ready. And I want to take him down."

I knew her *him* was different, but we were fighting two sides of the same coin.

Noor raised her chin. "I want Souma to have justice too."

"Vahid will be taken care of, trust me. Are *you* sure you want to share all that power with me?"

She nodded, and before I lost the nerve, I had to ask her the question. "Why?"

Noor sucked in a breath and watched the flames dancing in the fire. "Because when I could have been trapped in that prison with Thohfsa, you came back. And because I don't think either of us should do this on our own. Because we make a great team. And because . . ." She hesitated. "Because we both know what it's like to lose a father and be powerless. And I want us to have some of that power back."

I exhaled, some of the anger draining away. She was right, we did work well together—our escape proved that, as had the journey here. And we had a common enemy. As much as I wanted to ride into the city with my swords high, I knew I needed to be smarter about this, more subtle.

This wasn't just about punishment, this was about making them pay, with all the might I could gather.

"This won't be an easy path," I said, watching the village women, realizing that I would likely never come back here again. Not with what came next.

"Trust me, as soon as I met you I knew you wouldn't be an easy path." A slow smile spread across Noor's face.

I reached out and squeezed her hand, unused to feeling grateful. "Thank you, friend."

Noor didn't have to share her power. But I wasn't about to refuse it either.

"Thank me when you are holding the magic of the djinn in your hands. When you have the power to do nearly anything."

I nodded, but my fingers curled against the weathered wood table knowing the only thing I wanted was to have my father back.

But no djinn power could give me that.

Nothing could.

Baba was gone, and my peace would now have to come from destroying my enemies. They would pay the price for what they had done.

"I don't think we should stay here very long," Noor said, her voice low while she smiled and nodded to a woman walking by Nanu's fire. "The villagers are watching us."

I started at her words. "You think they would tell the emperor?"

Our village was loyal to our own, and I would be surprised if someone turned us in.

But then, I never thought Mazin would have done that to me either.

"A village like this? You'd kill for some extra coins in your pocket to see you through winter."

I watched some of the women singing by the fire. "We should leave at first light then."

"I'll start filling my pack with your grandmother's rotis. It's a long journey where we're going, and I've had my fill of dates."

I flashed her a smile, the first time I'd truly felt like smiling since I heard of Baba's death. "Pack the pakoras too. I saw an extra plate by the fire."

"Ohhhh, good thinking."

Noor wandered over to the food and I popped a few fennel seeds into my mouth and chewed on them as I stared into the fire.

It felt as if Baba's death had unleashed something in me, something I had kept tethered when I still had hope of him.

But now, there was no hope.

I wasn't going to rein myself in any longer.

I closed my fists tight, thinking of Casildo, the man who had double-crossed my father. They had been friends since childhood, and the man had been like an uncle to me. That he could so easily turn my father in made my skin cold. But in that coldness I found power, as if I could lock out all emotion and it would distill my goals to the only ones that mattered. Maybe that was the answer to everything. Maybe if I turned my body to ice I could become the weapon I needed to avenge my father.

To avenge myself.

Thirteen

"Noor, wake up."

Noor rubbed her eyes groggily and blinked at me. "It's still dark. The sun hasn't even started to rise." She sat up from her little pallet on my grandmother's floor. The few clothes we had were strewn around us on the floor, the room a mess from the night before, when nearly half the village had been here. "Dania, are you okay?"

"I heard something, maybe a shout?" I bit the inside of my lip. "I think we have to leave now."

Noor clambered to her feet. "I'll saddle the mule."

"Do it quickly. I'll gather our bags."

Something about the tension in the air didn't feel right, and my voice came out in urgent puffs. Noor glanced through the window. "I don't see anything, but there could be an ambush. Someone might have gotten word to the emperor's soldiers."

I folded my clothes tightly into my pack. "It would take the emperor's soldiers half a day to ride here. We need to be long gone before that happens." I paused. "Unless someone got word to the city last night."

"What about your grandmother? Don't you want to say goodbye?"

The chipped paint on Nanu's door stood out in the dim light of her compact mud-brick house. I looked at it for a long moment and thought of what I had told myself last night.

The only way to continue this was to contain any emotion, to lock everything up.

I didn't have room for my grandmother, I didn't have room for kindness.

I turned my blood to stone and continued packing. "We don't have time to wake her. Goodbyes aren't necessary."

Noor frowned. "But don't you want to—"

"No. When all this is over, maybe." I wasn't sure if there would be anything left of me when what I had planned was over, and I didn't want to contemplate that future. But I would see Nanu then. Maybe I'd come back to this village and live some hollowed-out existence.

Noor looked as if she wanted to say more but shook her head instead. "Let's go, then."

We left before the sun filtered its first rays of morning. I looked down at Basral, the emperor's city, as we climbed up through the mountains. A cloud of dust rose in the air from the valley, growing ever closer.

"Horses."

Noor looked over her shoulder. A group of black dots on the horizon signified the emperor's riders.

"Someone *did* alert them."

My heart slammed against my chest, adrenaline and anticipation cutting through my anger.

If I met with Vahid's soldiers now, I'd turn the ground red with their blood.

I fluttered my eyes closed, breathing through my nose. Fighting a few low-level soldiers wouldn't serve me, and it wouldn't give me my revenge. We had to concentrate on making a quick escape, before they could confirm we were ever here.

"They'll be tracking us."

"I wouldn't be too worried about that." Noor nodded toward the other direction, across the desert to where the sky dripped down to the earth in a gray haze.

"A storm," I breathed.

"That will cover our tracks in the interim. But we need to make haste before they catch up to us."

We traveled for days, portioning out the rations we'd taken from Nanu, and harvesting from the forest in the mountains for the rest we needed. Noor proved remarkable at knowing which plants to eat and which were djinn-made, which would *burn us from the inside out* as she put it. We ate wild red plums, roots boiled in goat's milk to remove the bitterness, and mountain scorpions that had found their way into Noor's bag roasted over the fire. And every day as we moved through the terrain and followed Souma's route, I repeated the same names like a mantra.

Casildo.

Darbaran.

Vahid.

Mazin.

It kept my feet moving, stopped me from falling to my knees and sobbing into the earth every time I thought about my father's death.

Because if I stopped moving, if I stopped plotting, I'd have to face the reality of life without him.

Noor and I traveled mostly in silence, and I could sense she was giving me space. At night she adjusted our course by mapping the stars, muttering to herself and taking us on a zigzag path through the mountains.

I spent the evenings sharpening my knife.

Mazin's pendant hung cold against my chest, and each time it slid under my kurta I took a slow breath.

A reminder.

We camped under the stars for small snatches of time, just in case the soldiers were still tracking us. Because of that, we never rode a direct route and switched back on ourselves multiple times to confuse our trail.

At last, we came to the other side of the mountains, where enormous boulders littered the ground, making it nearly impossible to travel through.

"We're here," Noor said, looking at the rocks as if she could tell each one apart from one another.

"How do you know?"

"Souma gave me the exact location and described this place well. He called it the *graveyard of stone*."

I looked around at the vast space, the formations indeed piled high like tombs. "How are you meant to find anything here?"

"There are clues. Souma gave me a map."

I shot her a look. "How did you smuggle a map into Thohfsa's prison?"

"I didn't." She tapped her temple. "It's all in here. Souma made me memorize it."

Now that we'd reached our destination, her face glowed in the morning light and her eyes shone even brighter.

"You're happy we're here," I said slowly, recognizing the lightness of her steps as she moved through the boulders.

"I finally get to see Souma's life savings." She shot me a smile. "The treasure he hid from the world."

"And confirm that he trusted you with it, over everyone?"

Noor met my eyes, her smile fading. "Yes, that's part of it too."

The treasure could be anywhere, and navigating this type of geography would be impossible. We could be overturning rocks looking for this mystical djinn treasure for the rest of our lives.

I chewed on my bottom lip, shielding my eyes from the sun. "What else did Souma say?"

"That there was a spot where four stone tombs stood in a row. Near that was a cave invisible to the eye."

I tied the mule to a dilapidated date tree and made my way to Noor. My feet stuttered to a stop when a black snake slithered across my path and into the sparse bushes. I let out a garbled scream, lost my balance, and fell in the dirt.

"Why did he pick such an unusual place to hide it?" I said, wincing and dusting the pebbles off my knees. My fresh kurta I'd taken from my grandmother's was torn and I examined the light fabric as I sat back against a large boulder.

"For the same reason you are frustrated now—it is hidden well. No one will accidentally come upon this place, in fact you would probably go around to avoid it. Look around you—there isn't much life here. There isn't anything at all."

She was right. The collection of rocks stretched across the horizon like an eerie stone army. You'd have to know exactly what you were looking for to find anything here.

I got up and kept walking, combing through the rocks, my eyes focusing on anything that resembled a tomb. Noor followed behind me, kicking at the stones with her feet. Something in the distance caught the corner of my eye and I stopped so quickly Noor ran smack into the back of me.

"What the—"

At the outcropping of the hillside were four towering rock tombs, so seamlessly placed that you wouldn't notice until you stood in the exact right place. I took a step toward them, my breath caught in my chest. Noor followed behind, just as silent. The closer we got the more obvious it became that they were intentional—larger boulders on the bottom, with the smaller rocks piled higher until one blackened stone rested on top.

"It must be near here," she breathed.

I scanned the outcropping of rocks. There was no way a cave was hidden along here. We were surrounded by boulders of all shapes and sizes that opened onto a large, desolate expanse.

"Are you sure he said 'cave'?"

"Yes," snapped Noor, seeming to come to the same realization I had. Souma's directions didn't make sense.

Noor let out an exasperated breath. "Sorry, I just don't believe he would lie to me. There has to be more to this."

I moved closer to the four rock piles, examining them. A thought occurred to me.

"Noor, he said 'tombs'?"

"Yes, why?"

Something lightened in my chest. I looked at her. "The cave is underground. Think about it—*a tomb.*"

She waited a beat before scrambling over to me, a giddy laugh erupting from her. "There must be an underground cave near here."

I got on my hands and knees, sweeping my hands over the ground around the rock piles, the rush of anticipation making my fingers shake. My fingertips hooked on something—a seam in the rock below.

Rocks don't have seams.

I exhaled a whoosh of breath.

"Here," I called out to her.

Noor rushed over to me. "What is it?"

I studied the crack in the rock, too neat and symmetrical to be anything but intentional. "An entrance of some kind, I think."

We worked together, sweeping the dirt and pebbles aside, our hands caking with dust.

Finally, we cleared a space about the size of a large man. A smooth stone surface was revealed under all the dust and rocks, with a circular armhole.

"It's a door."

Noor thrust her hand into the armhole and heaved, but the stone didn't move.

"Let's try both of us."

We both gripped the latch of the stone door and coordinated our efforts. The entrance wrenched free, releasing a cloud of dust into the air, enveloping us both.

I coughed, crawling away from the opening, trying to catch my breath.

"Dania, are you okay?"

"Fine, I just need a minute." I inhaled a breath of fresh air before rubbing the dirt from my eyes and turning back to the cavity in the earth.

Like a sinkhole about to swallow us up, the ground opened into a dark cave beneath the dirt.

"Please don't tell me you want us to go in there." I looked over the edge into the waiting dark.

"Don't be silly," she breathed. "I am not nearly as athletically inclined as you are. I want *you* to go in there."

I shot her a glare, pushed through the sick feeling of fear in my stomach, and approached the opening. If the djinn magic was in there, I would have to be the one to retrieve it.

"Souma wouldn't have laid any traps," Noor whispered from behind me. "If he had, he would have told me."

"So why aren't you going in there?" I shot back.

"Because if there is anything to fight, you are the best one for the job."

"What would there be to fight?" I said, my brows rising to my hairline.

"Something unseen."

For the first time, I realized what we were doing and what the repercussions were. We were going after a djinn treasure, a power so rare the emperor himself made a deal with a creature from another world just to use it.

And we were about to take it for ourselves.

I touched the hilt of Baba's folding dagger under my kurta.

"When this is over, I'm teaching you how to handle yourself in a fight," I called over to Noor.

"Why do that when I've got you?"

I snorted a laugh, dispelling some of the panic pressing against my chest. I swung my legs over the edge of the entrance, trying to see the bottom. I couldn't jump down when I didn't know how far it went.

"Do we have a rope?"

"No. But your grandmother gave me one of her dupattas—I could tie that around your waist and lower you down?"

"That might work."

Noor pulled out a dark red dupatta from her bag, the shawl embroidered with a soft yellow thread in a northern floral design my grandmother often wore. I tied it carefully around my waist, and Noor held the other end.

"Don't drop it."

"I can't promise anything." She flashed a quick smile at me as I bared my teeth.

Then I clambered down into the dark.

Fourteen

Light filtered through the opening above and gave me just enough visibility to see in the darkness of the tomb. The air was cool and dry, the cave protected from the elements above by the stones covering it. It wasn't that deep of a drop. I likely could have jumped down myself, but the dupatta around my waist gave me a bit of security, despite not knowing what waited for me.

My feet pressed into soft sand, and I ran my eyes along the walls of the cave.

It wasn't a big space, and it was empty save for three large bags in the corner. I exhaled at the sight of them, and gold glinted in the scant sunlight from above.

Souma's treasure.

"Are you okay down there?"

"There's some bags down here—I think it's coins."

I moved over to inspect the bags—two of them filled with hefty piles of gold, glittering emeralds, and diamonds as big as my eyes.

The third with a substance I never thought I'd see in my life.

Zoraat.

Djinn magic.

The multicolored seeds glistened like pearlescent oil in the trickle of light from above, and I wanted to dig my hands into the bag and feel their power.

But I had no idea how zoraat worked—Noor was the expert in that. Did touching them imbue some of their power? Or did one have to eat them to use djinn magic?

I laid a hand on top of the seeds, their texture like the bottom of a tide pool filled with pebbles.

With these, I could do anything.

My father's face flashed in my mind, his smile a little crooked, the circles around his eyes dark, like he'd just stayed up all night at the forge.

With these I could avenge his death.

I dipped my hand into the bag, marveling at the fish egg texture. All this power. All this possibility.

A feeling of stillness rushed through me, and a slight breeze tickled my cheek.

I frowned, looking back up. There shouldn't be a breeze in here.

Revenge.

A deep whisper shot through the cavern and I jumped, snatching my hand back. Something moved out of the corner of my eye and I whirled around, drawing my dagger, my heart in my throat.

But there was no one else here.

I frowned at the empty chamber and walked the perimeter, the sandy bottom sinking beneath my feet. That voice had felt real— rough, ageless, and filled with venom. And I could have sworn I saw the edge of a cloak in the shadowed corner of the cave. But when I walked every inch, there was nothing waiting in the dark.

I went back to the three bags of treasure, retracing my steps, until I stopped short and snapped my gaze back to the ground where I had just been. There, illuminated by the light above, were two perfect footprints, much bigger than my own, pressed into the sand.

I exhaled and wrapped my arms around myself, the air feeling much colder than before. But I couldn't just stand around chasing imaginary ghosts. I shook my head and grabbed the edge of the dupatta, tying it around the first burlap sack. My skin still prickled from that voice, from those footprints, and I didn't want to remain in the cave a moment longer.

"Noor, I'm tying the bags to the dupatta—can you lift them up?" I called up to her, my eyes focused on the djinn seeds in front of me.

"Yes, I'll attach it to the mule." Her face peered over the cave opening and I felt a rush of relief at seeing her pointed little chin.

Noor hauled up the first bag of gold that I had looped the end of the dupatta around. Then we repeated the process with the other two bags until Noor helped heft me through the opening and into the waiting sunlight.

"It looks like Souma really did trust you."

"Yeah," she replied softly, her voice heavy. "I guess he did." She looked out at the mountains, lost in thought, her lips pressed so tightly together they'd turned white.

I walked over to the bag of zoraat, seeing the vibrancy of the different colors for the first time in the full light.

"So, how do they work?"

"You have to consume them in the right doses. When Emperor Vahid made his bargain with the djinn who gave him the first seeds, it was so he could have the power of the djinn at his fingertips. I spent years perfecting the right doses based on his usage. It can be . . . disastrous if you use the wrong amount."

Her eyes shuttered, and I didn't want to ask about what horrific djinn torture she witnessed as a result of an incorrect amount of zoraat consumption.

Especially because I knew I was about to consume them.

"Have you ever tried them yourself?"

Her head snapped up. "No. Absolutely not. It wasn't allowed."

"Then how do you know the right amounts?"

She swallowed thickly. "As an apprentice we trained in all types of blends for healers of the unseen. Because my blends were so effective, Souma graduated me to . . . more intense use of the magic."

"Such as?"

"Torture. Possession. Transfiguration. The same powers the djinn themselves might harbor."

I moved closer to the seeds, daring to let my fingers dip again toward their cool glossy exterior. As soon as my skin touched the smooth surface of the seeds, I felt a growing frisson of pressure. Those same soft whispers sounded from the boulders surrounding us, and I started.

"Do you hear that?"

The whispers grew louder, like the stones themselves were speaking to me, like the earth had been cleaved in two and begun talking.

And that one word rose again, above the rest, an incantation and warning all at once.

Revenge.

"Yes," I whispered back.

A face appeared before me, eyes black, face gaunt. I reared back, a cry wrenching from my throat. I knew that face, and had thought about seeing it again every day for a year.

But it was not as I remembered. Instead of his warm crooked smile, he was a festering body, a decomposing ghoul, come to snatch me away.

My father.

The warm grip of Noor's hands yanked me back to the present as she heaved me away from the seeds.

"Dani!"

I blinked twice, and then looked at her, my chest feeling as if it were going to explode. I couldn't wipe away the image of my father's ragged face staring back at me, an apparition come to haunt me. "What was that?"

Noor stared at me. "We aren't letting you touch these again. Not without the right dose from me."

"You said you had to consume them for it to work." I shook my head to clear it. "All I did was touch them." I thought about what had happened in the cave, but that felt too unbelievable to explain.

"What did you see?" Noor asked, cocking her head. "You looked . . . vacant for a moment. I've never seen it do that before, influence someone just by touching it."

"I saw . . ." I licked my dry lips, trying to make sense of exactly what had happened.

But I couldn't form the words to tell her about my father's rotting corpse.

A shudder rippled through me. "It doesn't really matter. Do you think it will happen again?"

"I have no idea, usually the healers of the unseen consume the blended zoraat before knitting together bones and the like. They transfigure the human body with the power they ingest." She watched me a moment more. "Are you sure you want to do this?"

I wasn't sure exactly which part she was asking me about—the revenge? Consuming zoraat and possessing myself with djinn magic? But I pushed that gaunt, wretched image of my father from my mind, and thought instead of my baba's rough hands working his smelt, his deep laugh as I told him a joke I'd heard from the palace guards, or the way he always hiccupped after taking a deep sip of chai. The heat of rage filled my chest once more, replacing the fear of his ghoulish face, replacing that unsettling voice whispering from all directions.

My father would still be here if it wasn't for the ones who had taken him from me.

"Yes. I'm sure. I want to do this."

Noor nodded. "Let's get to work, then."

Fifteen

We journeyed to the emperor's city, taking a winding route that meant we didn't go back through my village. We had ample gold, which meant that at the first mountain village we traded our mule for a horse and our sleeping mats in the dirt for a room at a caravanserai.

The caravanserai was a large white mud-brick building in the shape of a square, with painted blue doors and a relatively large stable for an obscure little village. It wasn't particularly populated, which was good because we didn't have to worry that someone was about to rob us. Nonetheless, I rented the biggest room for what we were about to do.

"You've done this before, right? Transfigured someone into another person entirely?"

The clay-packed walls of the caravanserai were painted white on the inside too, and our room even had a large mirror. I looked at my reflection, memorizing my face, tracing the lines of my stubborn mouth and wide dark eyes.

Soon, different eyes would be looking back at me.

"A few times," Noor said, picking out some zoraat seeds from the sack. "But it's really just about tweaking the blend and knowing what you want. You had an odd reaction to touching the seeds, so let's start small for now."

She had separated the colors of the zoraat into a few small piles—deep turquoise, bloodred, turmeric yellow. Then she placed the separate colors into small stone bowls she'd pilfered from the kitchen, with a heavy pestle to grind them. Noor began grinding each pile into a fine powder. She took a pinch from each of the different colored piles and prepared a brownish substance on a tin plate. She looked up at me with trepidation above the little pile of the zoraat powder.

I stared back at her.

"What am I supposed to do, exactly?"

She exhaled and lifted a small spoon to the powdered blend she made. "You don't need to do anything. Not yet."

I bit my bottom lip. "If you've never ingested this, how do you know what the right combination is to make it effective?"

She hesitated a second before lifting the spoon to my mouth. My nails bit the inside of my palms as I took in the reddish-brown powder.

Even though Noor had saved my life, trusting *anyone* was difficult after one of the closest people in my life had condemned me to die.

I chewed the inside of my cheek, tamping down the urge to throw the zoraat in her face and run out of the caravanserai.

But if I didn't trust her, if we didn't trust each other, we'd never get justice for what was done to them.

For what was done to us.

I inhaled and let the air flow through me, calming all the voices in my head telling me to stop.

It was too late for that.

"At the apothecary, Souma would have me try different blends, experimenting on the healers and spies the emperor had deemed privileged enough to consume the zoraat. The other assistants at the apothecary would cause unimaginable suffering. Their subjects would be in agony—their insides going black, their eyes melting, their skin peeling off."

"You are being so inspirational right now," I said as I gestured to the powder on her spoon. "I'm really excited to see what color my insides will turn."

She shook her head. "What I am trying to say is that I dreaded inflicting that kind of pain on anyone—and many of the subjects died from those experiments. But when I blended, it was as if there was something guiding me to choose the right amounts. I felt connected to the zoraat in a way the others didn't."

"Something?" I thought again of the voice in the cave, that whispered growl that seemed to come from the earth itself.

"A . . . feeling. A hand? I'm not sure."

"And you didn't kill anyone with your mixtures?"

"Better than that—whatever Vahid wanted them to do, I could make happen. It took apothecarists years to master the techniques and amounts properly, whereas I seemed to have an affinity for it." She shrugged. "Needless to say, I've done this before, and if your skin peels off, I'm really very sorry."

I arched a brow and looked down at the spoon again.

Words met my lips and I felt the gravity of them before I even spoke. "I trust you."

We hadn't come this far for me to lose faith in her now.

The zoraat powder coated my tongue and thickened like oil in my mouth.

"What—" My teeth were sticky, and talking was difficult. I tried to swallow and immediately retched.

"It takes some getting used to."

"You think?" I gasped out and doubled over, my knees cracking against the floor. I curled my toes under and braced myself. "You didn't tell me this would feel like hell."

"Only for a moment. Try not to panic." Noor's calm voice floated over me, and surprisingly quieted my thumping heart.

My limbs felt light and heavy at the same time. My legs became loose, and I didn't have enough strength to stand. There was still a trickling sensation as the oil-like liquid spread to the rest of my body.

"What am I supposed to do now?" I said to the floorboards, my hands flat to the ground as I tried not to cry out at the twisting sensation slithering through me. I didn't want to attract attention and screaming the place down wasn't exactly subtle.

"Try and visualize what you want," Noor said, her voice louder this time, and I realized she was down on the floor with me, her knees close to my head. "Remember, I blend the seeds, but the power is in your hands once you consume it. I give you the specific dose that you need and after that the world is yours."

The world is yours.

Revenge is mine.

I curled my fingers into the floor and pushed myself up, looking into the mirror before me. My bloodshot eyes looked wild and my skin dirty from the dust of the road. But as soon as I concentrated on the power flooding inside my body, I felt it answer.

"I want to change the way I look," I said to Noor, who nodded.

"Transfiguration. One of the more difficult powers of the zoraat, but possible with the right blending. Think through how you want to change the way you look. Focus on a feature. The magic will manipulate your body as if a djinn fire could melt the skin like water softening clay."

I closed my eyes and listened to Noor, thinking about my nose, elongating it and making it slightly wider. Then I opened my eyes.

My breath died in my chest.

Noor smiled. "You look different already." Then her face took on a serious cast.

"Change as much as you like, but there is a limit if you want to keep who you are. There needs to be one thing you keep wholly the same, one physical aspect of yourself that you can't alter."

"My hands," I said without a second thought. My hands knew the balance of a blade, knew how to maneuver the hilt of a dagger to send it flying through the air before I even thought about hitting a target. If there was anything I would keep, it would be them.

"Then focus on a different feature of yourself and work on that.

Don't do too much—tweaking just a small part of yourself works to make you different enough."

I worked on my eyes, drawing them out, making them narrower, sharper. I kept my skin the same shade but made the undertones warmer, giving my cheeks a rosy flush. Then I stretched my cheek-bones, the bones crunching as they moved, pain splintering through my body as my face took on the life of someone else.

Until finally I was done.

The girl who stared back at me wasn't the one who had just fought off prison guards or found out her father was murdered.

This girl was soft, pretty, pampered. Someone who hadn't known hardship.

Noor whistled. "Mazin won't know who you are at all."

"Good," I whispered, thinking of all I would do to him with this face. "That's what I want."

"Who will you be instead of Dania?"

I reached my fingers up and traced my lips, the edges of my eyes.

"Sanaya," I said finally. "Sanaya Khara. Daughter of a wealthy northern chief." I knew the northern tribes well from my mother and grandmother. It was a lie rooted in the truth and something I could convincingly embody. But I couldn't stop staring at the new face looking back at me through different eyes. "This is remarkable."

"Yes, but it doesn't last, so we must be careful."

I faced her, my new eyes wide. "What do you mean?"

"This is temporary. Once the zoraat leaves your system, you'll start turning back to yourself. You must keep consuming zoraat in order to maintain the facade. And you shouldn't consume too much of this blend for long, even if we had an unlimited supply of seeds. I've seen some assassins turn . . . dark from having too much."

"How long?" I still stared at myself, barely hearing her words. "How long can I wear this face for?"

Noor shook her head. "I'm not certain. Three weeks, maybe. A month?"

"A month is fine." I would use whatever time I had to my advantage. But I needed more than just a new face.

I needed the power to take down an emperor.

An army.

A lover.

"We can use the seeds for other things?"

"Yes, I can give you different zoraat combinations for other djinn powers."

"Good." I turned from the mirror and faced her. "Are you going to disguise yourself?"

Noor shook her head. "Souma made me vow never to take it. Not after what he'd seen happen. But that's not a risk here. And no one knows what I look like because no one ever met me outside of Souma's storeroom. I won't need to use the zoraat and then we will have more for you. As long as we still plan on taking down Vahid, I don't need anything else."

She watched me, her eyes absorbing my face as if *she* didn't really know who I was anymore, even though she was aware it was all a mask.

"Are you sure you want to do this?" She asked the question again, but this time it had a different emphasis. She wasn't asking anymore if I was sure I wanted to consume the seeds, but rather if I wanted to do any of this at all. If I even wanted to go down this path.

Because if we started, there was no going back.

A cool calm washed over me. Baba was murdered by the emperor's soldiers. His smith stripped of his precious blades by his best friend. I had lost everything this past year and gained only pain. But Mazin still had everything, despite all he had taken. I thought of his face, that smooth impenetrable veneer right before the guards had taken me.

"Yes," I said, my voice a deep growl. "That's the only thing I want."

Sixteen

We made it to the city swiftly after buying another horse and traveling back on the direct route through the mountains. I didn't bother to cover my face given I was wearing an entirely new one. Noor's dupatta covered hers but no one would have recognized her anyway. We were strangers to this city, and that was how we wanted it.

The city rose up from the dunes like it was an extension of the earth, a natural fixture moored in the ground instead of a man-made walled city the color of sun-drenched sand stretching to the horizon.

Basral.

The city of djinn power and blood. The place where I would find my retribution.

I repeated the names that were my constant companion now.

Casildo. Darbaran. Vahid. Mazin.

They had betrayed me for gain, and they would receive much more than they ever wanted. Zoraat coursed through my veins and the same whispered word I'd heard on the wind met my ears again.

Revenge.

I tasted it on my tongue, remembering the dark figure I thought I'd seen in the cave and the two footsteps beside mine in the sand.

Remembering my father's ghoulish face. It was unsettling that just touching the zoraat could have caused those illusions, because it reminded me that I truly didn't know how much power it was capable of.

Perhaps we had enough zoraat to level this entire city.

Perhaps I could scorch the earth under Mazin's feet and make him beg me to spare his life.

A dark feeling took hold, deeper than my rage had ever been, the djinn magic in my system feeling like it had come alive. For a moment my vision shadowed, and my palms burned as if they were coated in fire.

"What should we do first?" Noor's voice cut through the blaze that had swept over me.

The first step in the plan.

I could kill them all right now if I wanted, but that wasn't why we'd come back. We wanted something more than death, something darker than retribution.

Casildo had betrayed my father for his swords, using the love for his child against him. Would he do the same for what he values? Would he fight for what he loves, as my father did? Darbaran was the head of the palace guard, and when I'd known him I'd wanted to break his fingers off for his wandering hands and lecherous stares. Money and exploiting those weaker than him were his vices—and Noor and I planned to exploit that ourselves.

Emperor Vahid only ever chased after one thing—power. If we could chip away at that, burrow ourselves into the cracks of his empire, we could disintegrate the ground he stood on. Noor wanted that most of all.

And Mazin.

He betrayed me by using our relationship, by taking advantage of my love and trust and using that to make me a scapegoat.

Now I would do the same.

I would map out every step of my vengeance.

"First, we build our image," I answered her, thinking through my list of names.

We had to be seen by the right people in order to get close enough to the emperor and noticed by Mazin.

"We have enough gold to attract some attention. So, let's use it. Then we need an introduction. We need to be able to get close to Vahid and gain access to the palace."

The palace was where Mazin would be.

Noor flashed her teeth. "I've always wanted to go shopping to my heart's content."

———

We purchased a home at the edge of the city walls, one of the more lavish houses in the entire city. Noor picked it out, looking around with a pleased huff when she spied the garden, given her affinity for herbs and plants. I walked around the halls, checking for places intruders could break in, testing the doors for security. Being ostentatious was necessary to attract the notice of Casildo, Darbaran, and Vahid. But once Mazin was aware of us, I wasn't taking any precautions on what he would do. We had to be prepared against any threat.

After our house purchase, we went straight to the bazaar, buying enough silks, suits, and jewelry to look like queens. We chose every color of shalwar kameez, lehengas, and tunics with intricate beading, mirrors, and textile patterns. I made sure to pick a few key pieces of fabric and textiles from the north—large plump flowers embroidered in pink, geometric lines, block ink patterns on the edge of sleeves— everything I had seen my mother and grandmother wear while growing up. If I was playing the part of a northern woman, I wanted to do it justice. Every piece of adornment was chosen with a purpose, as if we were donning armor.

I pictured Baba forging his blades, carving his elaborate beasts on the hilts, adding each gem with precision, and realized that I was doing the same.

Arming myself with beauty, to distract from the true weapon that

I was. And while they were busy admiring me, I'd slice their fingers off with my blade.

"Do you have a plan for getting invited to the emperor's court? Other than spending so much money they can't ignore us?" Noor lay on a pile of cushions eating slices of fresh mango as I perused the latest collection of daggers one of the city swordsmiths had brought me. Nothing compared to my father's blades, but I needed to be better armed than I was.

And if our plan with Casildo went accordingly, soon I would take back my father's swords anyway.

"That will come later." I had plans involving Vahid, but I needed to lay the groundwork. "For now, we need the attention of Casildo."

Noor nodded.

I spun the tip of a dagger on my pointer finger, the only physical part of me I still recognized.

First, I wanted my father's blades back.

"He betrayed my father, got him killed by the emperor's soldiers, and raided his smith. It's time we test this disguise out in the real world."

———

The air was thick in the bazaar as the heat sank down from the blazing sun and sat on the skin like a heavy net. I went in my finest shalwar kameez, the top a deep indigo and threaded with a bold textile pattern from the north, with trousers a matching shade of blue silk. My thick hair—now a wild mane of curls instead of my usual pin-straight locks—was twisted into an ornate braid piled on my head and laced with golden beads. My new eyes were darkly lined with kajal, and I stared through them with all the confidence I would have felt in my own skin. We wove through the market, searching for Casildo's merchant's stall.

It sat on the edge of the market, stocked with blades Casildo imported from all across the empire.

I approached the stall with a nonchalance I didn't feel. My skin flushed with rage, even though the small man selling the collection of daggers on the table was not Casildo. His muddy eyes narrowed on me, eyeing my finery and the servants at my side—one of them being Noor, posing as my personal maid.

"Good day to you, sahiba. Can I help you find something for your husband, perhaps?" Greed glinted in his eyes as he began pushing his most jeweled blades forward. My gaze swept over them—none of the knives were made by my father. I could that tell in an instant.

"I have no husband," I said as I picked up a particularly gaudy dagger, without the deadly edge to match its finery. "I am looking for a sword. I'm somewhat of a collector."

"Then you have come to the right place, sahiba. There are no finer swords than Casildo's."

I swept my gaze over the man's stall, dismissive. I picked up a katar, the handle set in silver, and slid my knuckles through the opening so that the blade rested above my fingers. Noor had wanted me to appear dainty and uncertain around the blades, but there was no way I could do that. Let him see that I knew exactly how to handle them.

"I am looking for something particular I saw once." I thought of the uniqueness of my father's knives, of every animal he had carved into the hilt, of the engravings he'd made on the blade. I tapped my lips with the point of the katar and made a humming sound under my breath.

"A halmasti head, carved with camel bone, set with emeralds and gold filigree."

The man stroked his chin, his eyes darting to the side. "Sahiba, I have seen something similar. But not here. My master, Casildo, has a larger collection of blades at his home that he sometimes shows private collectors. The largest you ever saw. But I warn you, the blades will be costly."

"Does it look to you that I cannot afford it?"

A faint smile touched his lips, his eyes lowering in deference. "No, sahiba, but I don't like to catch my customers unaware. I will speak to my master about what you seek. Where can I reach you?"

"I'm in the south of the city, a dwelling called Jasmine Koti, do you know it?"

"Ah, yes, sahiba, I know it. A fine home indeed. Beautiful gardens."

If possible, his eyes lit even brighter with hunger. He was counting on a big commission from Casildo out of this, and I would not disappoint. "I will send word to your servant in the morning about meeting to discuss Casildo's other swords. Expect to hear soon."

"I will."

That afternoon a nervous servant arrived on our doorstep to tell us that Casildo was interested in meeting with us.

"That was fast." Noor took the note from the sweaty young man and flung it on the table in the middle of the room. I sat on the large indigo divan, sunlight filtering through the sheer curtains on the surrounding windows. To anyone looking in, I would have resembled a pampered rich girl, eating handfuls of pistachios and sipping rose water chai.

Except for the daggers I was throwing across the room and embedding into the wooden wall opposite me.

"It says he wants to meet tomorrow to discuss the sword you were looking for."

"His merchant probably shouted to him about how rich we were. Especially with all the jewels in my hair." I gave a little laugh and paused in the act of throwing my next dagger.

I pressed the tip of the blade to my palm and let the edge prick my skin. I was so close to seeing Casildo. So close to meeting the eyes of the person who'd orchestrated my father's death. Anger blossomed in my chest as I looked over the note from him.

"Not to mention the diamonds gracing your fingers." Noor nodded to my hands. "We looked like a walking treasure trove. Good thing you hired all those guards around the house, or we'd be getting robbed right now."

"Greed and cowardice is Casildo's language. He was always enamored with my father's status, with his expertise and blade collection. But he waited until he was on his knees before taking advantage of him. He needs to know exactly what we have to flaunt, and that he can get some of it."

Noor picked up a dried apricot from the plate in front of me and popped it in her mouth. "By cheating you?"

"Perhaps. If given the opportunity, certainly. But he might even do worse." I threw the knife at the wall, letting the blade fly. My anger released with it.

I needed a cool head for what would come next.

Noor smirked. "You think he's going to try and rob you with that army of guards you've got waiting outside? Casildo betrayed your father because it was easy, and he had power on his side. He's a coward. He's not going to do anything that could risk his life."

"That's why he's going to think it's simple. Until it's not. That's when we strike."

"You're so bloodthirsty."

"Have you met me?" I quirked a smile, then my gaze turned serious. "Wouldn't you be?" I stood up and wrenched my dagger out of the wall.

Noor looked out the window facing the palace. "He took your father from you. I would want revenge for the exact same reason. But just be careful you don't become what you most despise. That we both don't become what we most despise."

"And what is that?"

"Greedy. Power hungry."

I considered her words. The power flooding through me was intoxicating; I couldn't deny that. But there was no danger of me succumbing to it, not when I had bigger ambitions. "I won't forget what we are here for."

Her laugh echoed through the halls of the cavernous house. "Forget is something I *know* you don't do easily."

Seventeen

We arrived at Casildo's home in all the finery we had, displaying Souma's extravagant wealth to our utmost advantage. Torches were lit all along the house, the trellis patrolled by guards. We were met at the door by his merchant from the bazaar, a broad smile on his face.

"His man must have really told tales about our means," Noor whispered as we walked.

"Then we shall have to live up to them." I pulled my dupatta close, the glittering beadwork chiming together, as if my outfit agreed.

"Welcome to my home." Casildo stood at the entrance, and it took everything in me not to rip the pin securing my dupatta from my hair and slit his throat with it. "Tarfaan has told me of your search, and that you are recently new to the city. It is my pleasure to have you here."

He looked exactly as I remembered, except his dark hair was now graying at the sides, and what once had been a warm smile now felt calculating and oily. I pressed my own mouth into a smile, my hand involuntarily floating toward the dagger strapped to my thigh. I exhaled a slow breath, steadying myself.

Killing him outright was too good for him.

Despite the boiling anger in my veins, a tremor of fear ran down my spine as he took in my face.

Had I changed my appearance enough?

Could Casildo discern who I was despite the djinn magic coursing through me?

He was the first person who had known me before I'd been arrested and I was now testing the experiment firsthand.

But his expression didn't change.

He still had that same smile, as if he were tallying the worth of my kameez. Good thing I'd worn the most expensive one I owned.

Noor was wearing a dark green kurta with fine gold embroidery at the hem. She was still posing as my maid, because she could get places I couldn't and gather information I wouldn't have access to. We would need that if we wanted to get close enough to Casildo.

If I wanted him to suffer, I was going to have to know exactly what he would hate to lose. I toyed with the neckline of my kameez and gave him a pretty smile through gritted teeth as I tried my best to soften the rage sitting in the back of my throat.

"Thank you so much for your welcome, sahib. I am happy to view your collection. Your man was most helpful in recommending your blades to me."

"Those knives were nothing compared to my private stores." Casildo beckoned us inside and we were led through to an open-air courtyard in the center of his home, filled with greenery, giant lotus flowers, and star white dahlias infusing the room with a sickly perfume.

It was a common feature for wealthier homes in the city to have this type of indoor garden, to alleviate some of the heat from the outside. A large fountain in the center took up the majority of the garden. As we moved closer, I realized it was a stone depiction of the mythical battle between the warrior Naveed slaughtering a deadly azi. The dragon's great wings were crushed under Naveed's boots, and its neck pierced by the blade of his scimitar. It was gruesome to behold, but it set the tone of the house.

Here, might and weaponry were prized.

I watched the pained eyes of the azi, who was said to be attacking a local village until Naveed fed it a poisoned goat and slaughtered its drugged body.

Another lesson—treachery wins the day.

My eyes flickered to the rest of the garden. Servants surrounded us, holding various platters with crystal goblets, golden plates, and every type of refreshment.

"Expecting others?" I turned to Casildo.

"A few friends to welcome you into the city. Your arrival has caused quite a stir, especially when you bought out half the bazaar. There are rumors about you all over Basral. I'm thankful you stopped by my bazaar stall."

"I am thankful too, sahib. If only to meet another sword collector."

"Please, call me Casildo."

I inclined my head with a smile and his eyes gleamed. "Your hospitality is most generous."

We were led to platters of roasted lamb, spicy pickles, and fresh roti my teeth were begging to sink into. I had learned since being in prison there wasn't any kind of food I would pass up if given the opportunity. I reached for a roti but Noor made a noise in her throat as I did so. Our eyes met, hers with censure. Noor stepped forward instead and began filling a plate for me.

"Please, eat your fill." Casildo gestured to the food. "Once we share a meal, we can visit the swords you are so interested in."

"I would like that very much." I bit into a piece of tender roast meat in my mouth and chewed it slowly, savoring the taste. "Tell me, where did you acquire your swords? Do you have a supplier?"

My stomach clenched as I prepared for his answer. Perhaps he would give away the entire tale, the history of how he betrayed my father. I was eager to hear him talk about it, eager to stoke the fires of my rage when he bragged about how he owned all his knives.

Will you dare speak about my father, you disgusting coward?

"I used to. But now I mostly collect from my travels. You requested a very specific sword—a pommel carved into a halmasti head?" He made a kissing sound against his teeth. "There are few who have even seen one."

"My nanu would tell me tales of them when I was a girl. I remember seeing the blade and regretting not buying it."

"Did your father not purchase it for you?"

"He had more important things to do with his time besides buying young girls ceremonial blades." I laughed, the sound falling flat to my ears, the lie like ash on my tongue. Of course, my father had gifted me beautiful daggers he'd made since I could walk. But I had to wear the skin of Sanaya Khara now.

"Your family name is an important one in the north, is it not? Quite a powerful warlord's tribe." He leaned back in his chair and studied me. "What are you doing this far from home, in the emperor's city?"

"My father wanted to make treaties and connections without leaving his people. He sent me to Basral in his stead." I scooped up a mouthful of stewed goat, the sharpness of the ginger and green cardamom alighting on my tongue. I took small, dainty bites, instead of shoveling it in my mouth like I wanted to do. "Your food is delicious. Tell me, who is your cook?"

Casildo laughed. "I'll not have you steal her away from me. At least not before you see my blades. Come." He signaled to a servant to pour steaming cups of chai. "Let us take our tea in the gallery."

"The gallery?" I asked, more harshly than I intended. "I didn't come to see paintings and sculpture."

Noor arched her brow from behind Casildo and I nearly gave her a rude gesture. I clasped my hands together, painted a demure smile on my face, and softened my voice. "I would much prefer to see your sword collection."

He gave me a patronizing smile as he patted my shoulder.

I wanted to break each finger.

"I think you shall like this gallery."

Casildo led the way and we followed, walking through the ornate halls of his grand house. When I had known him, he was a simple merchant, with a three-roomed city town house and modest means. There was only one thing that could have changed his wealth and status, and that was the profit he made from betraying my father. I raised my chin, the guilt seeping through my pores threatening to overwhelm me. I hadn't been there to help my father. He'd been alone when his closest friend had betrayed him.

I trailed my hand along a tapestry hanging at the end of the hall, depicting the battle between the former king and Emperor Vahid. On it, Emperor Vahid stood tall and proud, a pile of gleaming djinn seeds in his hand, the old king laid atop a mountain of human bodies.

I thought of the bags of zoraat hidden in our house, the vibrant colors that Noor knew exactly how to blend. If everything went as planned, Vahid's chokehold on the empire would fall, and it would be because of the zoraat he so vigilantly controlled.

"Ah, the battle of Chidkruh. A favorite of mine." Casildo came up beside me, so close I almost snapped my head backward and sent his teeth to the back of his throat. I smiled to myself, imagining it.

"The emperor gifted that to me himself." He returned my smile, as if we were in on the same joke, though he wouldn't have liked my punch line.

"You are an impressive man to be given such a gift by Emperor Vahid." I put on a tone of reverence.

He laughed. "Be careful sahiba, or I'll take your flattery to heart."

My lip curled with disgust involuntarily. Was he flirting with me?

Noor cleared her throat. I met her gaze and she shot me a look that said I wasn't keeping my true emotions out of my expression.

But really, the man was old enough to be my grandfather.

I schooled my features into something resembling a coy glance. Let him think his flirting could get him somewhere. If that helped gain his trust, then I would bat my eyelashes enough to cause a windstorm.

Casildo smiled back, clearly delighted. Revulsion rose in my chest. Ugh, this was harder than I thought.

"The emperor simply rewarded a good turn I did him."

My ears perked up at that. "A good turn?" I tried to keep my voice curious.

"I told him of a plot against his life and helped him execute a traitor. But things aren't that adventurous these days."

I snorted an amused sound, hoping that it conveyed I was pleased with his joke and not that I didn't trust myself to speak. My hands drifted down again to the dagger strapped to my thigh, snug in its sheath, waiting to be released. The dark need to slit his thick neck and have his blood splash all over the marble floor nearly took over.

I felt the djinn magic answer my rage, simmer in my veins like a low fire.

Blackness darkened the edges of my vision, and a hot tingle ran through my hands. I looked down at my twitching fingers to find a single black vein curling from the tip of my index finger to the knuckle. It looked like a dark vine winding its way under my skin, responding to the unseen magic thrumming through me. I stared at it, more in confusion than anything, then a spike of panic lodged in my throat. Was this a byproduct of the zoraat? I pressed my hand to my side, hiding the black mark.

I widened my stance, planting my feet on the ground—a fighting stance.

Noor nudged me with her shoulder, her mouth pressed into a firm line as she shook her head. Clearly Noor was aware I was about to throw all our plans out the window and commit murder right here in the middle of Casildo's hall. I shot her a venomous look but moved my hand away from my dagger.

She was right. I didn't want to lose my head now, not when we'd come all this way. I curled my fingers in on themselves, making a mental note to ask her about the strange black vein spiraling down my hand. But it wouldn't detract from what we had come here for.

"Revenge."

That same whispered voice shot through me. But I couldn't tell anymore if it was my own.

My father deserved more retribution than Casildo's slit throat. I exhaled a long breath and felt the anger draining out of me, replaced by resolve.

We came to a large room, lit by various torches affixed to the stone wall. Glass cases surrounded us, filigreed gold lining each one, the contents gleaming in the flickering light. The cases were filled not with art, but weapons.

Swords. Daggers. Knives of all kinds.

It was a swordfighter's haven.

I looked from one case to the next, nearly forgetting what I was doing here at the sight of such a magnificent collection of blades.

I stood in front of a large case filled with straight-edged saifs, the intricately notched handles gleaming in the torchlight. Then my eyes flickered to a display of sabers, their lightly curved steel blades beckoning my fingers to pick them up. All around me were jeweled daggers, carved khopeshes, wickedly curved talwars, kirpans sheathed in golden lace—enough knives and swords and daggers that I could take down hundreds of my enemies if I wanted.

I exhaled at the breadth of them.

Then that breath caught in my throat as I turned my head toward the wall at the end of the room. Swords I was familiar with stared back at me, swords that I knew better than my own hands. From floor to ceiling, blades of every type and design filled the space, but all with one thing in common—they had been made by the same swordsmith.

Casildo had an entire wall filled with the weapons he had stolen from my father.

I took a step forward involuntarily, as if I was stepping toward Baba and he was still alive, breathing, smiling, right in front of me. This was his life's work. And it was sitting in the house of the man who had murdered him.

My heart pounded furiously and I pressed my hand hard to my chest as if I could rip it out, as if I could stop the rage and sorrow from threatening to take over.

"I see I have surprised you, sahiba. I thought you might enjoy the collection I have here, being someone with an avid interest in weaponry such as yourself."

"I am speechless," I managed to grit out. I lifted my lips in an attempt at a smile, but I was sure it was a twisted grimace.

Casildo gestured to refill our chai, and more steaming liquid was poured into the tall glass in my hand. Dried rose petals floated to the top, and not even the familiar scent of hot cardamon and crushed pistachio comforted me. My fingers clenched the glass tightly, and I could have shattered it into a thousand pieces if I loosed the rage crackling through me. That black vine on my hand grew thicker and curled down to my wrist. I lifted the glass to my lips, relieved that the liquid remained steady, and I managed to swallow the scalding tea.

The door to the gallery creaked open behind us, but I didn't bother to turn my head. I still stared at the row of immaculately polished blades glistening in the torchlight, wishing that instead of them, I had my father again.

In every knife hilt I saw his weathered hands focused on the detail of his artistry, in the glow of each blade I pictured him bent over his forge, forming the metal with precision. This was him, and it was not. It was everything he valued and worked for, but he wasn't here anymore for it to matter. The only person left that could still stand up for him was me, and I needed to right the wrong that was done to him.

"Ah, you've finally joined us." Casildo greeted someone, and footsteps approached. Still, I didn't turn. If I tried to speak I would not be able to mask the fury blazing inside me.

"Meet Sanaya Khara, daughter of the Khara Chieftain, and new to Basral. Sahiba Khara, please let me introduce you to the *Hawk*."

Someone gave a short laugh, and it had the effect of a bucket of ice water being thrown over me.

I knew that laugh.

I remembered that laugh.

I used to take delight in being the one to make it happen.

"Please, I am trying very hard to bury that nickname," a deep voice responded, like the rumble of a boulder falling from a mountain.

It was a distinct voice, the voice of an orator, or politician, smooth and confident, but something about it drew you in, made you feel as though you were trusted, special.

I closed my eyes.

Not him.

I hadn't prepared myself for the sound of his voice yet. Not this soon. I thought I would have time to shore myself up, to steel myself like one of my father's talwars—impenetrable, unbreakable. But every word brought it all back, until I wasn't certain my legs could still hold me up. I could feel it, everything—his touch on my skin. His smile when I called his name.

His expression when he betrayed me.

That one hurt most of all, and instead of me being the impenetrable blade, he was—slicing through my defenses, through my trust, piercing my heart. That calm mask he wore when the guards took me away was the face that haunted me all my days in prison.

"I think it suits you," Casildo continued, oblivious to the storm of emotions raging inside me. "But have it your way. Let me introduce you to Mazin Sial, the emperor's second-in-command. Youngest second there has ever been, in fact."

I felt rather than heard Noor's intake of breath at his name being announced.

But I snuffed every riot of emotion clambering to get out.

I couldn't fall apart. Not now.

Not until it was over.

And I would be damned if *he* made me fall apart, not after everything he had done. This time, I would be the one in control, I would be the one to watch as his entire life crumbled. I took a moment to center myself before walking off the edge of the cliff, letting a slow breath run through me. Then, I made my expression a pleasant mask.

This was who I would become in front of him. A sweet, beautiful confection.

And when he bit into the honeyed sugar, it would be poison filling his mouth.

Eighteen

He looked exactly the same. The dark hair, just a little too long. The small mole sitting underneath his eye on one side, like a bold star. Broad shoulders encased in his same palace uniform—dark sherwani with gold detailing and high leather boots to his knees. Even the quirk of his eyebrow was something I'd memorized a thousand times.

And yet, bruised circles shadowed his eyes. His face was gaunt, sharper, more pronounced, as if he needed a few good meals in him. His posture was rigid, like his shoulders directed the rest of his body and they were made from the same steel as the long scimitar that hung at his side—a product of my father as well. His eyes, always dark, always filled with longing, were replaced with a different emotion. If I didn't know better, I would say it was sadness.

Good. He should be fucking sad.

He should regret every moment of every day since he betrayed me. But I knew he couldn't, not if it was in service to his precious emperor. If his life was sad now, it wasn't because of what he had done to me. But there was one thing I was sure of—Mazin wasn't happy. He was still a blazing force of authority and contradictions, but I knew him too well underneath to not see the restlessness there.

And this time the smile on my face was not forced.

You have no idea what I'm about to rain down on you.

"I am pleased to meet you, sahiba Khara."

My smile widened, and I tilted my head toward him. Noor and I had practiced this at least. I wasn't a born seducer, but I'd never had the motivation as I did now. I was going to throw the same tenacity into making Mazin fall in love with me as I did into learning the sword. Because when I revealed the truth, it would hurt far more than the sharp tip of steel.

My eyes flickered to the girl at his side, a girl I also knew very well. Her dark hair was woven into a braid and slung over her shoulder with a deep blue dupatta affixed to it and delicate earrings that made a soft tinkling sound when she moved her head.

She was also the same—innocent, trusting, lovely. And I felt not a single ounce of guilt that I was about to manipulate that trust to my heart's content.

"And who is this?"

"This is my sister, Anam."

Anam was impossible to hate, but I tried anyway. Permanent contagious smile touching her lips, predisposition to believe anyone and anything—she was a walking opportunity for every con man and imposter in the city.

Noor moved to the periphery of the room.

She was meant to leave Casildo and me to talk while she tried to gather information from his house. But I could tell from her expression she didn't want to go, not with Mazin now here.

But despite the unexpectedness, I tried to focus on the positives—Casildo had sped up the plans tenfold by introducing me to them.

"What brings you to our city, sahiba Khara?" Maz asked, and a little tremor went through me at the sound of his voice again. I didn't stop to analyze what that was.

"Please, call me Sanaya. And I am just visiting. My father wants to come to the city eventually and asked me to ready a place for his arrival." My own voice came out a little higher than I would have liked and I chewed on the edge of my lip.

"She purchased the vacant Jasmine Koti property," Casildo said, almost conspiratorially.

Mazin's eyebrows shot to his hairline.

I turned to the girl at his side. "You'll have to show me around the city, Anam. I've been to the bazaar but I have no idea who to buy from, who will cheat me, and who is lying to me."

Mazin chuckled as if I'd told a joke, and I wanted to smash his face into one of the glass cases. Instead I sidled closer to him. He'd only see what I wanted him to—Sanaya Khara, a beautiful chieftain's daughter who was unproblematic and sweet. I turned to him, a question in my gaze.

Our eyes met, and I felt unexpectedly breathless with the contact.

"Anam won't be able to help you with any of those things," he explained. "I wager my sister gets cheated regularly spending the emperor's money."

Anam looked shamefaced at Mazin's words but smiled at me. "I would love to show you the city, Sanaya, and the bazaar, despite what my brother says."

"Of course. And I don't believe his words for a minute. In fact, you are likely the one doing the bargaining, with eyes like yours."

Her gaze lit up, and she shot a look to her brother.

I turned back to Mazin, forcing myself to remember that in this body, with this face, I didn't hate him. In this skin, I wanted his adoration, as much as it made me want to retch. I wanted him to want me, just as much as he had pretended to want me before. Then I would rip his heart out while it was still beating.

"And what brings you to Casildo's home this evening, Sanaya?" He rolled my fake name on his tongue like a caress, and I felt my pulse speed up.

I remembered this about him—he was charming. Other girls

would giggle to me about him constantly, hoping that I'd introduce them to him.

"I have an interest in swords and daggers of all kinds. I saw some of Casildo's collection in the bazaar and heard he might be interested in selling some of his private collection to me."

Mazin inclined his head. "And did he agree?"

Casildo's voice entered the conversation from the back of the room. "She's looking for a particular blade, one she said she saw at a market once, though I've no idea where. A dagger with a bone hilt carved into the head of a halmasti."

Mazin stood to his full height, his mouth pressing into a thin line. I was unable to tear my eyes away from him. He was behaving differently than I imagined. He wasn't boastful or arrogant. A small muscle ticked in his jaw that I recognized from every training bout we'd had together.

He was trying to keep his emotions in check.

Why?

"Mazin is being tight-lipped." Casildo sounded amused as he came to stand beside us. He took a long drink of his chai and then extended his hand for his cup to be refilled. A servant came rushing over to him. My lip curled. Casildo used to say he was a man of the people, would drink with my father over a fire outside of his smith with the villagers in camaraderie. Now he drank tea with crushed rose petals from gold-rimmed glasses and couldn't even fill his own cup.

"He knows the exact knife you seek. Unfortunately, it is not in my collection. But I do have something similar." Casildo gestured to the back wall, the glass case containing my father's blades.

I forced myself to look away from Maz and back to the swords on display. Noor stood next to them, and I met her gaze for the briefest of moments before looking back to the glass case.

I was grateful she was still here. She was a silent presence at the edge of the room, observing us all without being noticed—but just knowing there was someone here who had my back made me a bit more confident.

Even if she was terrible with a sword.

"The dagger you seek is very unique." Mazin's voice was a low rumble beside me. He had moved closer, so close that I could smell him and nearly closed my eyes at the memories that assaulted me.

The problem when someone you loved betrayed you was that you had a lifetime of good memories with them that you had to examine in a different light. What was once a safe place to be—beside him, engulfed in his arms, inhaling the smell of rainstorms and pine—was actually the most dangerous place of all.

I exhaled slowly to calm my pounding heart.

"I know of only one smith who created a blade with a halmasti head, though I doubt you saw it at a market. The man who made it only sold his wares directly."

"Really?" I turned to Maz, our faces inches apart. I shifted slightly and the cold steel of the dagger at my thigh reminded me that I had a knife on me. But I didn't want a swift resolution. I wanted him to suffer as I had. I wanted them all to realize what they had done, and regret who they had destroyed to their very last moment.

I smiled at him, taking satisfaction instead from the way his eyes lighted on my lips and not from envisioning his spilled blood.

"Really? You must introduce me to the swordsmith. I would very much like to meet him and buy directly."

That doused the smile on his face. His eyes darted to Casildo, a look of raw emotion crossing his features, his mouth twisting into a grimace before it all settled back into a smooth mask.

"He's no longer with us, unfortunately." Maz looked away from Casildo. "He died."

I coiled my hands to my side. "What a shame. How did he pass?"

"He was a traitor." Casildo's voice rang out through the room before Mazin could respond.

"He and his family tried to betray the emperor. They were arrested and executed."

I gritted my teeth. *Not all of them.*

"Indeed? That makes his knives worth even more, then." I forced my lips to lift.

Casildo gave me a greasy smile in return. "Exactly my thoughts." He turned to the case once more. "I think you might find a blade similar to what you saw here."

"Show me, please."

I had already pinpointed the knife he wanted to show me as soon as I saw my father's collection. This one had a pommel carved into the head of a northern mountain wolf, not as large as the halmasti, but to hear my father tell it, equally as fierce. But I would have all these swords back in my possession very soon. This moment was spinning the tale for Casildo.

The tale that I was wealthy, influential, and I could afford expensive trinkets with no more than a second thought. Because that would also gain entrance into the emperor's court.

The fact that Mazin was also here was wonderfully convenient for me.

I glanced at the dagger in question and inhaled excitedly as if I hadn't known exactly where it was all along. "Why, it's so similar to the one I saw! I must have it."

"I'm afraid it will be costly, coming from my private collection."

Mazin moved behind me, and I darted a look over my shoulder. He was remarkably still, watching Casildo with a veiled gaze. But then his eyes flickered to mine.

For a second I forgot I was pretending to be someone different. I forgot that I was looking at him through unfamiliar eyes. And when he met my stare it must have showed, because his own eyes widened, and he tilted his face as if he were examining a puzzle he couldn't quite figure out.

I caught myself—I wanted him intrigued, not suspicious. I wanted him to long to meet me again, not set his soldiers on me.

I turned back to Casildo and waved my arm distractedly, as if any amount would be inconsequential to me. Which was true, I would pay anything to get my hands back on my father's legacy. But this was to create the character we needed to take Basral. "My servant will provide the sum."

I nodded at Noor. Casildo held back a smile so wide it could barely contain his glee. A rush of warmth spread through me, the satisfaction of a plan clicking together like an intricate design on a sword.

Casildo needed to know how much *possibility* I had. So when he decided to try and take it, I would destroy all of his.

We departed soon after, Casildo counting his fresh coins and one of my father's daggers resting gently in an ornate box on my lap.

The satisfaction I felt faded, leaving a hollow bitterness that was compounded by Mazin's final expression. He didn't meet my gaze to say goodbye, nor did he attempt to take my hand to kiss it so I could begin laying the foundation of my seduction. Instead, the entire time we were walking out of Casildo's grand home, Mazin never took his gaze off that box.

Nineteen

Before

THE HAWK

Baba made me start training with Mazin, despite his talent being so much less than mine. Maz trained with the other soldiers too, but the emperor decided he needed more.

"The boy is incompetent," I had grumbled to my father as he walked us to the training field at the back of the smith. Field was not perhaps the right word—the ground was so worn it was more like a yard of dirt with some sparse shrubbery.

But it was my favorite place in the world.

"Winning a battle isn't about skill, Dani. It's about heart. And Mazin has plenty of that."

I stepped onto the dirt with my talwar in my hand, watching Maz hold a too big scimitar in his as my father left us alone to spar.

"This is like charity, trying to improve your fighting prowess." I lunged forward and removed his weapon before he could blink.

And yet, he never stopped trying. I did it three more times before planting my talwar in the yard and leaning over it with a yawn. That last time was harder than I thought it would be, but I didn't want him to see my surprise.

He had improved.

Not that I would tell him.

He picked up his sword from the dirt, his jaw clenched, a muscle ticking in one corner. I thought he would lunge again, pull the same thoughtless move. Instead, he lowered his blade and looked at me.

"I'm hungry, let's stop for a moment."

I snorted. "The real reason you want to stop is that you don't want to be beaten anymore."

He puffed out an exasperated breath and planted his own blade in the ground, mimicking my stance. "Has anyone ever told you you are impossible to befriend?"

A startled laugh bubbled up. "Is *that* what you are doing? Befriending me? I have plenty of those, I don't need more."

He gave me a skeptical look and leaned toward me. Something flipped in my stomach at his intense focus. I noticed for the first time that he was not unappealing to look at—though he hadn't yet grown into his limbs and his hair was an unruly mop. He rubbed the back of his neck and my eyes traced his flexed arm before darting back to his face.

What was *wrong* with me?

"Dania, you don't have any friends. Not that I've seen. You have sparring partners. What you need is to have fun."

I stared back at him. "What I *need* is to train. Or I'll be in danger of being as terrible with a sword as you are," I retorted, crossing my arms over my chest and hoping my face wasn't as red as it felt.

He smiled, and I felt the fight go out of me.

I could stop for a few minutes. One break for luncheon didn't mean we were friends.

"Fine, one meal." I leaned against my talwar. "But then we go back to training. My father asked me to help you, so if you don't want to I'll train alone."

I grabbed the fresh parathas made by a village aunty that had been delivered that day. We sat along the wooden fence of the training yard, eating in companionable silence. The parathas were rolled and filled with spicy pickles and firm cheese. I must have forgotten how hungry I was because I practically wolfed them down.

"This may be the best thing I've ever eaten," Mazin said between mouthfuls, and leaned back against the post.

I chewed without looking at him, willing myself not to engage in conversation. But the afternoon sun cast a glow behind him, making the day seem softer, dreamier somehow. He tipped his head back and looked at the mountains framing our village, something in his eyes filled with resolve, and a little like longing. I couldn't help but follow his gaze, to want to see what he was looking at with such focus.

For a wild moment, I wished he were looking at me that way. I swallowed thickly and turned my head, my skin uncomfortably hot.

"They don't feed you at the palace?" My voice came out croaky, and I stuffed more paratha into my mouth to mask my embarrassment. I might as well fall on my talwar now and die to spare myself more humiliation.

"Not like this. Everything is a rich curry, or an overly sweet dessert. The emperor wants the best, most extravagant. But this is simple and hearty and made for short breaks in the sun. It reminds me of when I was a boy."

"You are still a boy," I reminded him, licking some of the sour pickle off my fingers.

"I mean, before I joined the emperor." He still had that hint of longing in his gaze that made me want to know more.

It bothered me that I wanted to know about his past at all, considering he worked for Vahid.

But I did. He wasn't royalty, not that I was aware of, and he spoke as if he had once lived in a village like ours. I bit the inside of my cheek until I felt the gnaw of pain, but it still didn't stop my question.

"What do you mean, *before*?"

He looked up from his paratha, pausing before taking a bite. The sun made his eyes appear golden. I scowled at the direction of my thoughts, and his lips lifted at my expression.

"I can tell you really want to know about my childhood." He took another bite of the bread.

"No, but you won't shut up about it, so I might as well know what you're talking about."

"You might as well." He tilted his head. "My sister and I come from a village in the south, where Emperor Vahid began waging his war against the king with zoraat." His tone was light, but when I glanced at his knuckles they were white.

He was like that often, I realized. *Contained*—like a clay matka pot, until the heat from the fire became unbearable and he exploded. He fought like that too, whereas I was the opposite, lashing out, always on the attack. He played the defense far too much, until the last possible moment.

"I didn't know you had a sister," I said quietly.

He met my eyes at that. "Yes. Anam was a baby when the emperor came. My mother hung her crib on the branch of a banyan tree and told me to watch Anam while she went to fetch my father. My parents both died in the fighting, killed by the king's soldiers." His throat bobbed, and he took another bite. My own throat felt dry, and the paratha in my hand seemed inedible now with his words.

"A hawk flew down and attempted to carry off my sister from the tree. I fought it off, throwing rocks and desert scrub at it while it dove at us. But the bird was huge, nearly as large as me, and its talons sharp. The bird would have carried off Anam and I wouldn't have been able to save her. But Emperor Vahid himself came upon us as I was trying to protect her. He notched an arrow and struck the hawk through the heart." Maz laid a finger near the collar of his shirt to where a necklace hung. A single black talon hung from it.

"You took a piece of it." I nodded at the talon.

"The emperor did. Cut it off and gave it to me. He said I fought bravely, and he could use someone like that by his side, someone who would defend against those who would prey on him. That's when he decided to take us in. He saved us."

He sounded almost reverent.

I snorted and his gaze shot to me. "Emperor Vahid started that war," I said with vehemence. "The one that killed your parents." I folded my arms over my chest. "He isn't your savior."

"He stopped my sister and me from getting massacred. The king was intent on slaughtering the villages in the south to teach Vahid a lesson. Vahid rescued us."

I pursed my lips and looked toward the low hills that dotted the horizon, away from the mountains. The arid landscape was dotted with trees and shrubs. A golden jackal ran across the clearing, a pup in its mouth, and made its way to a nearby walnut tree that hung crooked, as if hanging on by its last root. A bird circled above, watching for an opportunity to snatch the pup, the same threat that had sought to take Mazin's sister.

But Baba always said that hawks were cunning and patient. They would wait until the perfect time before striking.

Mazin and I were both silent until he spoke again. "It's hard to understand, I know. When my parents were mowed down by the soldiers, hate could have festered in my heart. But Emperor Vahid saved us, took us in, and made sure we didn't suffer. What else could I do but be thankful? My parents were gone, but we still had each other. I owe the emperor my life and my loyalty."

I watched him, trying to understand the perspective of a small boy who was just desperate to stay alive, and to stay together with his baby sister. Desperate enough that they would be grateful for anything, even a man who created the very war that killed his family.

Mazin met my eyes, the paratha forgotten in his hands too. But I didn't know how to respond to the silent plea for understanding, the need for approval that the love he sought from the emperor wasn't a poison.

"What are you thinking?" he said after a long moment.

I couldn't say what he wanted me to, but that wasn't who we were anyway. On the battlefield, being kind wouldn't lead to victory.

Only slaughter elsewhere.

"I think," I said, straightening from my perch and dusting myself off, "that you didn't really save your sister from a hawk that day."

Twenty

"Well, that was surprising."

Noor collapsed on my bed as I began removing my jewelry.

"Yes." I held myself as still as I could, like if I moved I would utterly fall apart.

Then I closed my eyes and allowed everything I had kept at bay wash over me.

The shock at seeing Maz.

The conflict I felt when my eyes met his.

The anger at my father's swords on display like a trophy in Casildo's house.

"I didn't expect Mazin there. It was sloppy of me. I should have imagined that possibility."

"*We* should have," she agreed. "But it doesn't change the course of things."

"No, we can just move forward with the next phase of the plan quicker."

Noor nodded. "I'll bring coins to the bazaar tomorrow and coordinate the next steps." She moved to leave the room but then paused, seeming to hesitate.

"What is it?" All the exhaustion of wearing a face and personality of someone else was catching up to me, and my voice sounded weary. The effects of the zoraat running through my veins set me on edge, like something dark gnawing at my stomach.

I remembered with a start the black mark that had appeared on my finger, like a spider crawling down my hand. But when I examined it now, it wasn't there. Sanaya's burnished brown skin was all I saw. No marks, not even a bruise.

"Are you okay?"

I exhaled, looking back up at Noor. She studied me with a frown. I spread my fingers out again, but there was nothing. Had I imagined it?

"I've been better."

"I know. When Casildo said Mazin's name . . ." She trailed away with a shudder. "You seem to be handling it well, though."

I shrugged, a gesture of nonchalance I didn't feel. "I knew I would see Maz eventually. I didn't expect it so soon, but I can adjust."

"And you're sure you want to continue with everything? His sister seems sweet."

I scowled at her. "Yes, I'm sure. I don't have a conscience where he is concerned."

She bit her lip. "Even if the sister gets hurt too?"

"He is the reason my father is dead, so yes. Even if his sister gets hurt too."

Noor nodded and her hands curled into fists. "As long as the plan is still to go after Vahid. I need to know he won't get away with everything he's done. That at the end of all this, he will be left with only ashes."

"Just as we were," I said quietly, the room seeming to darken as I did so. I cast a glance at the window, the moon casting a shadow of Vahid's palace.

She walked toward it, placing her hands on the frame and turning back to me. The moon lit her as well, and I saw the sorrow in her brown eyes. "Yes. Just like we were."

I knew she was thinking of Souma, just as I was thinking of my father.

I continued removing my jewelry, the weight lifting from me with every piece I took off. Gilt bangles on my wrists, a thick golden choker with dangling rubies around my neck, a filigreed ruby tikka pinned in my hair, a gold nath from my nose, all landed with a thud in the bowl on the table.

When I was done, I rubbed my wrists and felt as though I could breathe again.

"By the way, there's definitely something you didn't tell me," Noor said, leaning back against the window.

I stretched my arms overhead, linking my knuckles together and pushing my hands up. It had been a while since I'd trained, and I needed to build up some of the muscle I'd lost in prison. "What?"

She smirked, mirth entering her eyes. "You never mentioned how attractive Mazin was."

I stared. Then wordlessly I bent down, took off my curled-toe shoe, and lobbed it at her head.

She ducked, undeterred. "Those cheekbones? The dark eyes? No wonder you are cut up over him."

"Shut up," I muttered, spinning on my heel.

"You never told me his shoulders were that broad!"

I ordered tea as the room filled with Noor's laughter.

"Can you be serious for once?"

"Why, when you are serious enough for the both of us?"

I knew she was only doing it to lighten the mood, but there was a grain of truth in it. I hadn't handled Mazin's appearance well. He had still managed to draw me to him, and the lure of him was even stronger than before.

But I couldn't let myself fall into my own trap. I scrubbed my hands over my face and tried to let that sink in.

The door opened and a servant entered with tea. She placed it on the table, gave a bow, and then left.

I took a long sip, the hot chai warming my throat and bringing me back to myself.

"I want the world to see what a coward Casildo is," I said as Noor turned toward me. "I want his friends and family to turn their back on him. I want him to lose everything he's ever had." My hand gripped the edge of the table. "I don't have long with this face. If we don't get what we came here for, it would be the same as if we never left that prison."

Noor watched me, her unfathomable golden eyes taking me in with the same assessment she had when she first entered my cell. "Like I said, you are serious enough for the both of us."

I huffed out a breath and sat back on the divan. A gust of wind rushed through the room, rustling the curtains.

If I listened hard enough, it almost sounded like the same whispers I'd heard in Souma's cave as I touched the zoraat.

Revenge.

"I have a task for you," I said suddenly, pulling myself from those thoughts, from that memory of my father's decaying corpse.

Noor walked over, picked up the chai from my hands, and took a great gulp out of my cup.

"We have more gold than you've ever seen in your life and you can't order your own cup of chai?"

"Stealing yours tastes better."

I rolled my eyes. "I want you to follow Casildo. I want to know every move he makes, and I want to know everything that's important to him. If there's a crack in his foundation, I want to know about it."

"So you can flood it with water?"

I smiled. "So I can erode the very earth he walks on."

"Make a list of things that will destroy Casildo. Got it. What will you be doing?"

I swiped my cup of chai from her and leaned back on the divan. "I'll be going shopping."

Twenty-one

The bazaar was full today, with shouting market vendors clamoring for my attention and shoppers jostling me from every direction. I hadn't quite gotten used to my new appearance yet, and every pass by a dusty mirror took me by surprise.

It was no wonder the fabric merchants wanted my business when they saw the yards of vibrant textiles I was wearing, colors so rich the dye alone might have been a year's worth of custom. I even caught the hand of a cheeky pickpocket trying to unclasp my jeweled bracelet.

Today I was dressed in a kameez with floral embroidery and small blue beads adorning the sleeves like a thousand grains of indigo sand. My hair—which was now a lighter shade of mahogany brown—was twisted up into a knot and decorated with a golden headband with strings of pearls and golden beads covering my forehead. But the softer curve of my cheeks, round eyes, and gentle, approachable face took me aback just as much as my clothes.

Sanaya looked soft and petite, while Dania was rough and fierce.

Well, we were both fierce, my disguise just hid it better behind an intricately woven shalwar kameez, and a dupatta slung over my arms, so fine it could have been spun by the djinn.

Was this the kind of woman Mazin wanted? One who would be a gentle presence to his ferocious ambitions?

I caught myself before I went down that road.

It didn't matter what kind of love Mazin wanted. It was my job to make sure the person he chose was Sanaya. And once I destroyed him, perhaps I would finally be free of him. Free of his constant presence haunting me like a bhuta everywhere I went—his persistent ghost hounding my every thought.

I shot past the spice stalls, heaping with saffron threads, black salt, sharp dried mint, and heady mango powder. I ignored the jewelry stands that Noor would have insisted we stop at—the mirrored earrings and elaborate tikkas were some of her favorite things to buy. I didn't even spare a glance for the large piles at the fabric merchants, piled heavily with patterned textiles, cotton, silks, and organza. I was here for something else altogether.

Something caught my eye, darting through the thick crowd of people so deftly I almost didn't catch it. But when I looked closer, triumph lifted my steps.

At last, I spied what I was looking for.

Or *who*.

The boy was dirty, with wet mud crusted around his mouth as if he'd been eating it. Dirt was daubed across his face and arms like paint—and I realized it probably was. He gave the appearance of a starving orphan who hadn't been bathed in weeks. But when I cast my eyes over his frame and spied his healthy limbs poking out of his worn kurta, I knew he was getting enough to eat. This too was an act, one designed to dismiss him as a wretched beggar boy, so no one noticed that he was very practiced at his trade. When I'd last been at the bazaar with Noor, I'd let him go with a laugh when he'd tried to steal my purse.

But today I had business.

He hadn't noticed me yet. Instead, he weaved through the crowd with practiced ease. The bazaar was busy, with the workday finished and many stopping here to shop or grab a bite at the various kebab and paratha stands lining the edge of the market. Not a single customer noticed the filthy pickpocket as he made himself rich by lifting all their expensive belongings and bulging money purses.

He was quite a sight to watch. Bejeweled bangles, shining pocket watches, and thick sacks of coins—he pocketed them all in a streamlined fashion, tucking them into a small weathered bag that hung at his waist. By the time he made it to the other side of the street, I saw who I had hoped he would lead me to—an older boy waiting at the edge of the alley.

This was who he reported to.

I needed to be quick if I was going to catch them.

They slipped into the alley, a narrow space between yellowed mud-brick buildings that looked so uninviting no one else stood near it. I trailed behind, weaving through the heavy crowds and darting around a run-down jalebi stall.

I rounded the corner and stole into the alley behind them, the darkness swallowing me up.

My dagger was hidden under the folds of my kameez, and I reached for it. What I didn't expect was the cool press of steel under my chin before I could even draw my own weapon.

"You didn't think we saw you following Yashem? Sahiba, you stick out like the emperor's stallion in a herd of pack camels." The boy sounded amused, and far older than he had looked in the bazaar.

My lips lifted involuntarily, despite the surprise jolting through me that the urchin had managed to get the upper hand. I thought I'd been more prepared to deal with him. But I was more pleased than afraid, even though he was the one pressing the knife against my neck. If he could handle himself against me, he might do very well if Mazin was his opponent. I pushed my neck forward lightly to test the blade. The edge of it didn't even prick my skin with the telltale slice of a stone-sharpened knife.

Blunt. I could work with blunt.

"It's not many that have taken me by surprise with a dagger. You should consider yourself skilled."

He flicked the point up to my chin, so I had to tilt my head up. "I do."

Before he could make another move, I shot my hand to his, twisting the dagger from his fingers and turning it on him instead. I widened my stance, advancing on him with the dagger held firmly in my hands. It was heavier than I had thought it would be, a fairly decent blade. He must have stolen it from someone wealthy.

The boy held his hands up at me, fear replacing the mock bravado that I'd seen moments before. But his brown eyes grew even wider when I turned the hilt over to him.

"Go on, take it. I'm not here to fight you, I have something else in mind."

His expression shadowed with suspicion as he snatched the knife from my hand. "What?"

"A business proposition."

The boy scowled at me. "We don't kill for money, sahiba. Now leave before we rob you of all your fine silks."

I put my hands up. "I don't want you to kill anyone. With any luck, no one will get hurt. And if you do a good job and are interested in easy money, I will have plenty more work for you."

"What's the job?" His voice was harsh, dismissive even, but I could hear the greedy interest behind them, especially when I lifted a purse full of coins to show him how serious I was.

I tossed him the bag and he caught it easily with one hand.

"Anam Sial, ward of the emperor, will be shopping later in the bazaar." I swallowed thickly, pushing down the strange sensation of guilt bubbling up in my chest. But Maz had made his choice and with it, sealed her fate. Guilt was not an emotion I could afford.

"I want you to kidnap her."

The urchin barked out a laugh before tossing the bag of coins back at me. "Now I know you aren't in your right mind, sahiba. You think

I don't know who her brother is? Mazin Sial rules this city. Taking his sister would be a death sentence. He'd burn all of Basral down."

The corner of my mouth lifted at the fear I heard behind the thief's words. Mazin had built a reputation in the time I had been gone. One that I would happily tear apart.

The boy opened his mouth, but I pulled another purse of coins from my belt and any words died on his tongue. "You won't have her for long. And Mazin won't know who did this. It will be between you and me only. I can promise you that."

"How can you promise to keep the most powerful man in the city away from us, sahiba? It cannot be done." His words were firm, but his eyes stayed on the bags of coins in my hand.

"Because I'm about to burn Basral down before he even gets a chance." I held up the purse. "Do you want this money or not?"

I eyed the smaller boy, whom he called Yashem. He was looking between me and the older street thief. Maybe it was time to switch tactics.

"Yashem, is it? You clearly work together, are there more of you?"

"Yes, sahiba." His voice came out as a squeak, but then he shored up his shoulders and lifted his chin. "We are many."

He looked to the coins in my hand, and then at the older boy. Finally, the older boy rolled his eyes and nodded.

Yashem stepped forward, holding out his hands for the bags.

"And we would like to hear more about your business proposition, sahiba."

I crossed my arms over my chest and smiled.

———

A few hours later I was back at the bazaar, having been alerted by Noor that Anam and her guards were finally heading there.

I sat at one of the tables along the path by the market food stalls, taking in the smells of hot pakora, sizzling curries, the heat of chilis in the air. After a year of sameness in prison, it was as if my senses weren't yet attuned to being back in the world, and now they were bombarded. I had taken for granted all this vibrancy before. But sitting here I closed my eyes and savored the smell of hot sugar and ghee as each fresh jalebi was made.

I convinced myself that the gnawing in my stomach was from the smell of roasted meat, and not the pang of my conscience trying to stop me.

I looked down at my hands—still my own after changing my face with zoraat.

I had known immediately my hands were the only thing I couldn't have changed. They had led me to freedom, were the reason I could use a sword so well. But above all, I knew I wouldn't have been able to look down and see someone else's fingers, someone else's scars. These hands would never be locked behind bars again, would never be stopped from holding the weight of a sword hilt. These were the hands that would see me through this.

Movement at the end of the bazaar caught my eye, and I lifted my head as Anam made her way through the winding streets.

She wore a simple shalwar kameez, a soft blue, edged in delicate floral embroidery. The black nondescript cloak I was wearing over my clothes made blending in with the crowd much easier for my next task, but underneath I wasn't wearing anything so subtle as Anam. My silver beaded suit would shine garishly in the afternoon sun—I was projecting wealth, not taste. The diamond-studded bangles lining my arms would draw the eyes of every market shopper for miles. I moved closer to the banyan tree in the center of the square and farther from view.

Anam was flanked by two guards, and I recognized both.

Durab and Tishk. I'd trained with them at the palace whenever I'd come to visit Maz. They were smart enough, but I'd put my money on the pickpockets as smarter. I wiped the sweat from my brow, the sun already hot enough that I was baking underneath my coat. Anam stopped at a jewelry stall to admire some earrings.

A shout sounded from nearby, and I smiled to myself.

This was it.

The stall beside Anam burst into flame.

The crowd panicked. Screams filled the bazaar and people clamored to get away from the fire. Anam was pushed to the other end of the market by grubby little hands. I hurried down the street, keeping my eyes on her as she was swallowed by the wave of bodies. Durab and Tishk pushed and shouted trying to get to her, but it was too late. There was no sign of Anam as I made my way through the pandemonium of the market, weaving between shrieking women and irate shopkeepers desperately trying to protect their wares from the blaze.

I even bumped into the bulky body of Durab as he shouted Anam's name.

My hood covered my face, and I quickly slipped into the crowd, but he didn't pay me any attention. I stepped into a dark alley, casting a look over my shoulder to make sure no one had followed me before melting into the shadows.

———

"Help! Tishk!" Anam's voice pierced through the alley.

"Can you shut her up?"

"Oomph." A cry of pain sounded and a wheezed response I couldn't make out. "It's taking everything I have to hold her."

"At least we have the rope around her now—argh, she bit me!"

"Get off me! I'll give you my purse. If my brother finds out you've taken me, you'll be executed!"

I raised a brow at her words, and the feeling behind them. It wasn't superiority, but rather genuine fear for the ones who had taken her.

Fear of what her brother would do to these street urchins.

Would Mazin actually execute children? The boy had mentioned that he would burn down the entire city if Anam was taken, but I hadn't thought he was serious.

What had Mazin become? Or was this his true self, a power-hungry tyrant who controlled the city by fear?

I folded my arms across my chest, simmering with a strange feeling of anticipation. Let him come. I would be here, burning Basral before he even thought about striking a match.

The street thieves held Anam at the end of the darkened alley, in a small building that was abandoned years ago. She sat in a chair, bound, with only a shaft of light from a broken roof tile above to illuminate what was happening. I clung to the darkness while I examined her from afar. Her hands and feet were tied, and still she had left two of the thieves nursing their wounds on the floor.

Impressive. Mazin taught her well.

With my lessons.

"We aren't letting you go until we receive our ransom!" The older boy nodded to Yashem.

"Maz will pay your ransom and then tear each limb from your body. Then the emperor will display your heads on a pike at the front of the city," she responded, her words pleading, not vicious.

Truthful.

I stepped out of the shadows, finally making my move. "I think the wise thing to do would be to let the girl go, don't you?"

The boys turned toward me. Yashem was about to say something, but I shook my head. The older one shot him a look.

"Who are you?" he said, following it with a giant wink that thankfully Anam couldn't see. I rolled my eyes and stepped closer.

"Who is that?" she called out, confusion and fear clear in her voice, and she lifted her head as if to see me, despite wearing a blindfold.

"Don't worry Miss Sial, I'm here to rescue you." I turned to the thieves. "I will make it very worth your while to let the girl go." I gave a stern look to Yashem when he smiled broadly. The other boy slapped a hand over his mouth.

I really should have hired better actors.

"Maybe we'll ransom you too!" The older boy lunged, just as we practiced, and I feinted left, landing a soft blow to his middle and spinning around him. He let out an exaggerated howl that sounded as if a cat had been killed. I huffed out my exasperation and fluttered my hand at Yashem as he stood gawking. He nodded and together they ran with the other thieves, leaving Anam and me alone.

To her, it would have seemed like a fight had broken out, and her captors were fleeing from the conflict. To me, I had Anam exactly where I wanted her.

"Hello?" Her words echoed through the now empty building.

"Anam?" My voice dripped with false concern. I threw off my dark cloak and strode over to her, pulling off her blindfold and pasting a fake look of alarm on my fake face.

"Sanaya?" She was disoriented, blinking repeatedly despite the lack of light, and staring up at me with her large dark eyes.

The same eyes her brother had.

I jerked back, my heart hammering in my chest.

Damn him. I would not think of him now, especially when I felt pity for his sister. She was just a pawn. Someone to manipulate, just as he manipulated me.

I steeled my heart, wrapping it in molten metal, impenetrable to any guilt or sadness. The fact that she had his eyes should remind me even more that he was the primary target.

I leaned forward again. "Are you all right? I saw you get dragged into the alley, but there was so much chaos with the fire. I knew I had to do something. Especially when they talked about holding you for ransom!"

At least I could play up the little wretches' dramatic embellishments.

Relief filled Anam's face. "Sanaya—thank you so much. Please get me out of here. Mazin will be so *so* angry I was taken in his city."

His city.

It wouldn't be for much longer.

"As long as you are safe now, that is what matters." I untied the rest of her bindings and helped her up from the chair. "Come, let us get you back to the bazaar. Your guards will be looking for you."

We left the abandoned building and made it back to the busy streets. The air stank of smoke and burned cloth, but the fire was out and the vendors were busy salvaging their stands. A shout sounded from down the street and both Anam's guards rushed to us.

"Anam! Where have you been? We had to tell your brother you disappeared!" Durab's sword was drawn, as if he were about to run through half the people in the market. Shoppers threw him uneasy looks and gave us a wide berth.

Perfect. Nothing like panicking bodyguards to fall right into your trap.

"It was street thugs, Durab. They dragged me into the alley to ransom me."

I stifled a smile. *Thugs* was rather a strong word considering their ages and build, but Anam likely couldn't see much given how fast they'd blindfolded her, which was a very good thing.

"But Sanaya stopped them." Anam's soft gaze landed on me.

Durab and Tishk both looked at me, as if realizing for the first time I was standing there. Again, I felt that uncomfortable itching sensation, worried they would see past the disguise.

I thought about the time I had beat Durab in a bout, and he lay flat on his back with a mouth full of dirt, his sword yards from his grasp.

If he knew who I was, he wouldn't hesitate to use the deadly scimitar in his hands to strike me through. I glanced at Tishk, who was standing beside Anam checking her for injuries. He was the one I was wary of, the one who could figure things out quickly in the training ring and use an opponent's weaknesses against them.

He returned my gaze, sizing me up and down as if I had been the street thug dragging off Anam. Tishk had a permanent distrust of everything.

In response to his suspicious scowl, I presented him with a sunny smile.

"I did what anyone would do, really, I saw two ruffians drag Anam off and I had to help her." I nodded at Anam. "We only met briefly, but I remembered you right away. I'm so glad I could be of assistance."

Anam smiled and reached for my hands. She clasped them in mine, then pulled me into an embrace. It took me a second too long to react, and she held me tight as my arms hung limply by my side. It had been a long time since I'd been embraced by anyone except when I'd hugged my grandmother, and even that had felt wooden and forced. Unbidden tears pricked at my eyes and I swallowed thickly. What was wrong with me?

Kindness was seductive. As Sanaya I could pretend I was kind, that I did things out of the goodness of my heart, and not because I wanted to destroy her brother.

But revenge was much more satisfying.

Mazin certainly wasn't kind when he had me locked up in the worst prison in the empire. And kindness wouldn't help me now.

I leaned back from the embrace, a friendly smile on my face. "I felt a kinship with you when we first met."

A spark of warmth entered her eyes. I knew her, knew the loneliness she felt living in the palace without anyone else, and I preyed on it.

"I couldn't just let you get kidnapped. I had to do something."

"But you risked yourself for me, and that is commendable." She looked up at her guard. "Is it not, Tishk?"

He opened his mouth to respond, some of the unease about me lessening in the set of his shoulders, but the voice that answered was not his.

"It is indeed commendable."

My eyes fluttered closed.

That low rumble always had the power to send me to my knees. But this time I had prepared for him, had counted on him being here.

I turned to face him, brushing out the beads on my kameez and raising my eyes up to meet his.

Maz was immaculate. All in black as usual, the gold on his sherwani coat gleaming in the afternoon light. His sun-kissed hair was swept back, the thick waves of it perfectly neat. I remembered running my fingers through it as he lay in my bed, talking about all the dreams we'd had. I remembered besting him in the training ring, the only time I ever really saw a strand out of place. I stretched my lips wide at his dark glance. A muscle ticked in his jaw, and he seemed to be barely holding himself in check, like a jackal surveying the valley before it pinpointed its next meal. Except there was no prey here.

Then why did I still feel hunted?

"It seems we owe you thanks, Sanaya," said Mazin, circling. His voice was tight.

Oh, you owe me a lot more than that.

He was different than he had been at Casildo's. This time instead of a hint of sadness in his eyes, it was pure murder. Rage darkened his countenance now. The last time I had seen him like this, he'd been in my room, talking about the emperor.

Now someone had stolen his sister, and he was here to make them pay.

"Durab, Tishk. Round up the city guards. I want the bazaar turned inside out. The perpetrators cannot be far. Someone in Basral will know something."

"Yes, sir," Durab said, his fist curling around the pommel of his scimitar.

"And remember," Maz said smoothly, staring at the two guards. "My sister was taken during your watch." His mouth twisted into a sneer. "Don't disappoint me again. Find who took her." That same muscle ticked in his jaw, his eyes blazing.

Durab and Tishk raised their chins, shame painted on their features. They nodded once and left us, their footsteps burning holes in the red earth.

Leaving Anam, Mazin, and me standing together in the bazaar.

"Thank you for saving Anam," Mazin said quietly. "My own guards failed where you succeeded. We owe you a great debt."

"It was nothing," I said, unsure of who he was now. He was so *serious*. So stoic. Like a shadow had passed over him and never quite left.

"It was something to me." He inclined his head, his eyes never leaving mine. I felt a sense of unease steal over me, his expression still too murderous while he watched me.

"My brother is right. You were amazing. You should have seen her, Maz. Well, not that I could." She made a face. "But I heard her. She fought off the thieves and rescued me."

"Did you manage to get a look at them?" His gaze was probing and I stood a little straighter under his attention.

"I'm afraid not," I said, shaking my head with false disappointment. "It was dark, and I was more focused on helping Anam."

"Their age? Any identifying scars or features? Were they short or tall? How were they dressed?"

"Brother! Stop pestering her when she's just saved me. We should be giving her a proper thank-you, not interrogating her. Come, Sanaya." She linked her arm in mine, walking to the tanga that waited for her with the other carriages at the edge of the bazaar.

"Forgive me," Mazin said, his voice low, stepping alongside me and matching my pace. I closed my eyes and savored the rumble of that voice and the way it vibrated through me.

"There's nothing to forgive." My voice was bright, tinny, false. But then everything about him had been false too.

"Have lunch at the palace with us."

I whirled my head to face him, my breath stolen at his commanding words. They had seemed almost rushed, a last-minute invitation, but his face was serious, his mouth set.

"Anam's right," he continued, tilting his head. "We should be giving you a proper thank-you. Let us honor you for what you've done today."

Anam let go of my arm and clapped her hands together. "That's perfect. Let's meet tomorrow at the palace."

"I would love that."

"Then it's settled," he said, placing a hand on the small of my back.

Despite the layers and beading I felt the heat from his palm as if it were on bare skin. I shivered.

If he noticed the movement, he didn't react. He still watched me with that same inscrutable stare.

What happened to you? I wanted to ask. Where had the boy I'd known gone?

He never existed. He was never real.

He withdrew his hand and helped Anam into the carriage.

"Can we give you a ride anywhere?"

I blinked at him, realizing he held his hand out and was offering to assist me into the tanga. I shrunk back. As much as I needed to spend more time with him, to sow the seeds of my own revenge, I needed to gather myself. If I were shivering from his touch I didn't know what I'd do sitting beside him in a carriage ride.

And with Basral soldiers scouring the city for my pickpockets, I had other things to take care of.

"I have my own driver waiting for me. I just wanted to make sure Anam was all right."

He nodded, then rubbed a hand across his chin. "Until tomorrow, then."

"Until tomorrow," I repeated.

I waited until they were out of sight, until the tanga wasn't even a speck on the cobblestone road, before flopping down on the bench next to the banyan tree and cradling my head in my hands.

Everything was perfect. They'd invited me to the palace, I'd ingratiated myself to Anam. It was all unfolding exactly how we'd planned.

Then why did I feel like I was still sitting in that prison, counting the days until my freedom?

Twenty-two

Before

His sword met mine with a sharp echo across the training field.

"You're getting better," I gritted out as I pushed him and rolled away in the dirt.

Maz leapt to his feet at the same time as I and thrust his sword forward, meeting my parry.

"Admit it, I'm as good as you now."

Our blades clashed again as we danced around each other, the steel slamming together with the ferocity of our pride.

Neither one of us was willing to back down.

This was the way it always was when we fought. Fevered intensity, the rush of elation when I landed a hit, and the overwhelming exhaustion when a bout was completed. I couldn't afford to let him know how much better he had become.

"You only wish you were as good as me."

"Your lies are so easy to spot, Dani."

"Don't call me that."

He smirked, knowing he'd gotten under my skin. I felt a flush of heat rise in my chest at his smile. I pivoted my sword, lifting it from his and then sliding the blade down my hand until the hilt rose up and smacked him in the head.

He stumbled back, the smile wiped from his face with the butt of my sword.

"That was uncalled for."

"Use the name Dani again and I'll smack you with the edge of my blade instead of the hilt."

"Touchy."

He raised his sword again to attack, the light catching the steel. I lifted a hand to block the sun and his rushing feet pounded across the ground toward me.

I laughed. "You can't pull that trick if you are so heavy-footed I can hear you a mile away."

My sword rose to meet his, only the impact never came. I lifted my hands from my eyes to find him still, a frown across his face, looking in the distance at something behind me.

"What—"

A scream sounded, cutting me off, echoing through the village. Then more screams, shouts, and cries. A lead weight dropped in my stomach. I twisted to face the village, the houses dotted through the mountainside.

Then the unmistakable rumble of hooves and horsemen.

Maz moved beside me.

If I didn't know him so well, if I hadn't trained beside him, watching for every nuance, I would have said his dark eyes were emotionless, his face a mask of calm as we listened.

But I did know him.

I caught the small tick pulling the edge of his mouth. The fine beads of sweat dotted across his brow. The darkening of his deep brown eyes.

Maz was afraid.

"What is it?" I whispered. My tongue was so thick I could barely get the words out.

His voice was low, and he kept his gaze trained on the mountainside. "Raiders."

I clutched the hilt of my talwar tighter. My father was in the city bringing new swords to the emperor. I was here alone.

I glanced at Maz at my side. *Not quite alone.*

"This close to the emperor? They must have some gall." I licked my lips, cracked from the heat. Terror seeped through me, my pulse hammering against my skin. I had trained daily, under the tutelage of a master swordsmith. There shouldn't be anything I wasn't prepared for.

And yet, I'd never been in open battle. Never without the safety of the training field.

Blood rushed to the surface of my hands and made them come alive. I raised my talwar up. Another scream rose in the air, tearing my heart in two.

This was my village, and these were my people.

It didn't matter that Maz and I were alone. It didn't matter if I was afraid. We could save the village. We could try.

"We have to stop them."

Maz turned to face me, his lips white. Dread wound tightly in my stomach, like a cobra coiling up.

His expression said we were about to die, but not if I had anything to say about it.

"I was getting bored of beating you anyway."

The corner of his lips quirked up and dispelled some of the vacant look I'd seen there.

He gave me a terse nod and I exhaled a large breath of relief. My heart drummed in my ears, the erratic beat as loud as a tabla.

We ran to the village, keeping low until we came to an outcropping of houses and small huts. Smoke billowed from one of them, the thick wafts pillowing into the sky.

A child's cry erupted, and I lurched forward, only to be yanked back by Maz.

"Wait."

"There's a child!" I snapped back at him, but I stayed my feet when I saw two large men exit the hut. One held a burlap sack over his shoulder filled with presumably stolen goods, the other something that made my stomach lurch even more—a bloodied sword.

"They've killed people."

He nodded. "Likely. There will be more men than this, though."

"How many?"

He tilted his head, his eyes not on the raiders standing in my village, but somewhere else, on a memory he'd rather stay forgotten. "Usually no more than a dozen. Raiders don't like working in big groups, it's difficult to stay hidden."

"How do you know this?"

"Because raiders came to my village. They killed many."

I couldn't do anything besides clutch my sword and stare helplessly at him.

"I didn't know."

He shook his head, as if shaking the memory off him. "It happened years ago."

The child's cry echoed again from the burning hut.

"But we can stop them now," I urged.

"Listen to me, Dania, raiders are savage." Maz clutched my shoulders, his long fingers digging into the meat of my arm. "They don't care who they kill or hurt. They only care about themselves. If they get the best of you, you won't be standing anymore."

"Then I won't let them get the best of me, will I?" I stood, swirling my sword in my hand. I knew what the consequences would be if I didn't try, and I wasn't prepared to live with that.

I jumped to my feet and headed to the hut, the child's screams growing louder. The two men stood outside laughing, one picking at his teeth.

I didn't hesitate. If I did, they might call for help. And I didn't need to have battle experience to know I wanted to take on as few of them as possible.

I lifted my sword and swung it, slicing the calf of the first raider who held the sack.

He screamed and dropped the bag, clutching his leg. His friend whirled on me.

He was young, that was my first thought.

Barely older than Maz and me. Much too young to be raiding villages and killing children. He wore a square cap that was graying and frayed, and clothes that hung from him like limp sacks. His sword was rusty, as though he didn't take care of it, though the blood smeared across it looked far more ominous than my gleaming, too clean talwar.

He smiled, as if his fellow raider wasn't howling on the ground, grasping the slashed tendons of his bloodied leg.

"Have you come to fight us, little girl? What fun this will be."

He lunged for me, but I was ready. I pivoted and arched my blade behind me, slashing his outstretched arm.

He released a startled cry. "Bitch."

"Thought you would come up with better names to call me after I made you bleed." I nodded to the blood running down his arm.

"Village girl, there won't be anything left of you by the time we are done."

The other raider was standing now, his own bloodied sword poised toward me. "You can't take both of us on alone."

"She doesn't have to."

Maz's voice was deep behind me, and I hated admitting that it felt like a gust of wind in the desert, lifting me up. We'd never been on the same side before, not really. We'd trained and battled and bloodied each other over and over again. But now, I felt it. I knew he wouldn't let me fight alone.

"How touching. Two village children we can slaughter today."

As if we'd done it before, as if we'd practiced a thousand times, Maz and I both walked around the raiders, winding around them like a dance.

I crashed against the younger raider, meeting his blade with deft strokes. Adrenaline was trapped in my throat, and with each successful parry, I felt bolder, more sure. This was no different from the training field, where I dominated. The raider had been in battle before, but I was better trained, and it showed. I managed to land another hit on him, sliding my sword across his shoulder, and then again catching him in the side. He howled and became more erratic, and my confidence grew. I had him, and I was going to make sure he never raided another village again.

But as the smoke from the burning house thickened around us, the child's cry rent the air.

The boy was still in the house.

My footsteps faltered and I missed the next strike. The raider's sword caught the edge of my hand, and I yelped as the blade bit against my skin, the blood welling up.

"Dani!" Maz shouted as he fought with the injured raider.

But my momentum was lost. The young raider advanced again, his confidence buoyed. The screaming surrounded me. If I didn't get the child, he would be dead.

But if I didn't meet the blade of the raider in front of me, I would be.

I gulped down my frustration, a knot forming in my chest at the impossible decision. On the training field there was only myself and the sword.

But this was what Baba meant when he said that battle was different.

He was right—it wasn't about skill, it was about what happened when instinct took over, about what direction your feet took.

It's about heart.

I rushed at the raider, hoping to catch him by surprise. Our swords crossed and I pushed against him, throwing him off balance into the dirt. He raised his sword again but I brought my own down with such force it was knocked out of his hands. He gaped up at me.

"You're just a girl," he said, his eyes as old as mine. "You don't have it in you to kill."

I looked at his bloodied knife in the dirt, then to the house he'd set aflame.

"Being a girl never stopped me from stabbing someone who deserved it. You picked the wrong village to raid today."

He tried to roll away but I was already plunging my sword down, piercing his gut, driving my blade into his skin and feeling my own stomach churn when I felt his innards give way beneath my blade. He collapsed into the dirt, the life draining out of him.

The urge to vomit was so strong, I nearly emptied my insides over his twitching corpse.

But I didn't have time to dwell on what I had done.

"Maz!" I shouted, gesturing to the house.

"Go," he called back. "I'll find the other raiders."

His raider was on the ground, bleeding out from his wounds. Maz looked toward the rest of the village, as I ran inside the burning house.

The roof was on fire, causing it to collapse on itself, the flames catching the furniture and walls. I coughed at the overwhelming pillows of smoke gushing toward me, following the sounds of crying to the back of the small house.

A child was on the ground, clutching his mother, her body the source of the bloodied sword I'd seen.

"Amma!" He looked up at me, desperate to wake his mother.

"Your mother is dead." I moved to grab him. But he clutched her body harder.

"You don't have time for this," I muttered, and pulled him harder.

"Not without my amma."

This time I didn't reason with the boy, I yanked him away from her body and dragged him screaming from the house.

"Other people need help. You'll die if you stay with her. She's already gone."

I knew I was cold. The child needed more comfort than I was able to give him. But it was me carrying him from this house, and not someone else, not someone warmer or kinder. And yet, because of me, he would live. If he hated me for tearing him away from her, at least he would live.

The child reared back and kicked me in the shin, then ran from the burning house and into the mountainside. I watched him, his cries filling the afternoon air.

But a shout of pain wrenched through me and I turned back to the village with panic in my heart.

I knew that cry.

I ran, hefting my bloodied sword beside me. I stopped short when I made it to the village square. Maz was on his knees and two men circled him. His scimitar was nowhere to be seen. Blood ran down his arms and face, and a raider's unmoving body lay in the dirt beside him. At least he'd managed to take another one out before they got him.

They got him.

But not for long.

Confiscated weapons were piled beside the water well, and next to that a group of village women stood together, holding each other. They were women I'd known my whole life, aunties who had fed me, doted on me, pinched my cheeks and exclaimed to my father how much I looked like my mother. Just the sight of their distress made my fingers tighten on my hilt, the anger rising in my chest like a black cloud, like the smoke of burning mud-packed walls.

I crouched behind the well, forcing myself to stay hidden. I didn't have much time, not with Maz unarmed and two raiders advancing on him. But if I wanted us both to live, I needed a plan.

Maz looked small next to the raiders standing above him and I was reminded of his youth next to the two men.

One of the raiders raised his sword up, ready to bring it down against his neck.

It was too late. I'd run out of time.

I picked up a large stone from the dirt and chucked it at the raider about to kill Mazin.

I could hear Maz's voice in my head as I did it: *That's your big plan? A rock?*

It struck the raider's cheek and he whirled, his eyes narrowing. He put his sword down and began walking to the well where I hid. He stopped before rounding the corner, his attention focused wholly on the women. I was close enough that I was sure he could hear the hammering of my heart.

"Which one of you did it?" The raider's voice was soft, and the women cowered. He swung his bloodied sword in their direction, then pointed at Afra, an aunty who was an elder in our village, who always made the lightest parathas, who folded me into her arms with warm embraces whenever I came back to our village from the city. I bared my teeth, even though no one could see me.

"I'm going to kill every one of you until you tell me who threw that rock. And I will start with her."

Afra raised her chin, her deep voice echoing through the square.

"You'll kill us all anyway. Good job one of us managed to hurt you back."

The raider roared and swung his sword. Afra wrapped her arms around her head preparing for the blow.

But my dagger dug into the flesh of his thigh before he could strike. When he collapsed to his knees, I stood above him, grabbing a fistful of his hair, yanking his head back to expose his throat. Then I slid the sharp edge of my blade across it and threw him down as he choked before turning to face the other raider.

This time there were six standing there, and all had witnessed me kill their fellow marauder. The tallest among them had his beefy hands wrapped around Maz's throat.

"You won't be able to take us all on. Didn't think this through, did you?" The tall raider grinned, showing a mouth full of blackened teeth.

"I did think about it. But I assumed you were all equally inept with a blade."

"We're not the inept ones, girl."

"No? What would you call leaving all your captives next to a pile of swords and clubs?" I gestured to the women behind me. At my words, they all looked over at the weapons.

"We can all fight them," I said to the women of my village, the ones who'd watched me train with my father since I was a child. "They can't stop us all."

Without hesitation the women rushed to the weapons and armed themselves. I smiled as even the youngest girl picked up a katar and snapped it into place over her knuckles.

We were women from a village where one of the greatest sword-smiths lived. We knew weapons.

The raiders looked uneasy, but still advanced on us.

My hands shook, my palms so slick I nearly dropped the hilt of my sword. But the women were braver than I—they rushed at the raiders, beating them with clubs and swords, and giving me the opportunity I needed.

I raced around them, stabbing the arm of the raider who still held Maz and then slashing his neck. He gurgled, pressing his hands to the wound, and released Maz. Maz rolled to his feet, and I threw him a sword.

"We have to help the women."

He grinned, blood leaking from his lip, his dark eyes focused wholly on me.

"You know I'd follow you anywhere, Dani."

Something twisted in my heart, and I was suddenly robbed of breath in a way that had nothing to do with the battle.

He'd said it so simply, almost nonchalantly, but it pierced the center of me like a hot knife through ghee. I didn't have time to turn the words over in my mind, not when the fight had truly begun.

I rushed into battle and Maz followed. We fought side by side until our hands bled and our shoulders ached. And only then, in the quiet after the fight, in the grieving for those lost and triumph that we managed to win the day, did I dwell on that coil of feeling that had struck me when Maz had looked at me like I was a goddess and he a zealot.

I'd follow you anywhere.

Twenty-three

Mazin's invitation was what we had been waiting for. It gave us entry into the palace, and access to the emperor. And if I felt any trepidation about my reaction to spending more time with Maz, I buried it deep. Being near him would only get me closer to my goal, would only help to destroy him further. Something gathered inside my chest, something dark and thick.

Noor and I sat at the back of our tanga as it pulled through the city streets, the palace looming closer.

A breeze rippled through the canvas of the carriage, and Noor sighed in relief.

"It's hotter than Thohfsa's asshole out here. Why are we wearing so many layers?"

I leaned back against the seat. "Because rich people always wear too many clothes to show off how much money they have," I murmured, my eyes on the palace.

Soon, I'd be standing inside it, back in the place where I was arrested. Back in the halls I was dragged through, where my screams bounced off the cavernous ceilings and no one listened. Back where I met Mazin's eyes and realized for the first time who he truly was—a boy who would destroy everything just to get what he wanted.

The building loomed ahead of us—gleaming white columns of marble like a snow-topped mountain towering over the city. It was so imposing you could see it on the horizon for miles—a reminder that wherever you were, Vahid's power was always present. And with Mazin as his second-in-command, his was too.

As we crested the hill I felt eerily soothed—as if everything solidified in my mind. I glanced over to find Noor staring at the palace too, a frown creasing her forehead, and worry shadowing her eyes. She caught me looking and gave me a rueful smile.

"Are you worried?" I kept my tone light. Though Noor talked about her feelings more than I did, she was always reticent when it came to what happened with Souma and Vahid. As if when she spoke about it, it took her right back to when Souma had died.

"Not worried, not about our plan. More so about controlling myself if I see him."

"Vahid?"

She nodded. "Knowing that I might come face-to-face with him in a few minutes makes me want to tear my hair out. I don't know how I'm going to stop myself from pouring a vial of poison in his chai."

"Now you know how I feel seeing Maz."

She collapsed against the seat and threw her hands over her face. "I have no idea how you kept from throwing the dagger directly at Mazin's heart the first time you saw him."

"Trust me, I wanted to."

"But you stayed so calm. Even afterward. I can barely stop shaking and I haven't even seen the emperor yet."

"I'm not calm." I turned to look at her. "I'm furious. I can hide it well because I'm wearing a face that isn't mine, because I know that when I look at Mazin he has no idea who I am. Because if I don't control the storm raging inside me, then all of this will be for nothing. My father's death will be for nothing. And I can't let him—let any of them—get away with what they've done. I'm not calm, just focused."

"You certainly play your part well. I'm not sure I could control myself the same."

"You will. Once you see Vahid, you will be reminded of why we are here."

She threw me a skeptical glance. "You don't appear affected by anything. You aren't even sweating! Does your body just not produce moisture? You don't cry or sweat? Do you produce saliva?"

I looked away. "I cry."

"Since when? You didn't even weep when you found out your father died."

I opened my mouth to respond but the words had dried up. Baba's face flashed across my mind—a memory of him laughing at something I said over breakfast, as he scooped up his haleem with thick bread, the minced mutton and lentils his favorite morning meal. I couldn't remember our conversation, only his great belly laugh that shook his whole body. My father had been everything to me—a mother when my own was killed, a provider by selling his swords to the emperor he hated when we'd needed the money, a teacher when I'd shown an aptitude for fighting. But what he'd been most of all was a friend. Someone who sat with me in the quiet moments, who laughed with me at breakfast, who gave me advice but never judgment. Crying over the loss of him felt too small.

A silence fell over the carriage that was tight with emotion. Noor looked stricken.

"Dani, I'm sorr—"

"Don't apologize." I sat up straight. "It's true. I didn't cry. There was too much to think about at the time, too much to do. It would have been a waste of tears." I pressed my hands against my thighs, gripping the beaded fabric of my trousers so hard a few of the beads popped off. "When he's avenged, that's when I'll cry. That's when I'll grieve. I just hope I'll have that moment."

She nodded and returned her gaze to the palace. "We will. Souma used to say 'the bird sees the grain but not the snare.' We'll make them see what they want to see. And they'll be trapped before they even realize it."

"And the plan?"

Noor gave me a familiar grin and rolled her shoulders back. She held up a hand, folding down a finger for every item she checked off. "While you are charming the pants off mister-only-wears-black, I learn what I can about the palace, the head of the guard, and Vahid's routine. And get as much information as I can."

"Exactly." I picked a speck of road dirt from my indigo kameez. The sleeves of my suit were detailed with blooming lotus blossom embroidery, showing off my dark skin like the gold setting of a ruby.

"That one looks nice." Noor nodded to my outfit.

I smiled. "It's Mazin's favorite color."

Noor reared back in mock shock. "You're joking. You mean it's not black?"

I huffed a laugh. "He wears what he wears in service to the emperor. But I know him better than anyone. I know his favorite colors, foods, what he thinks about when he wakes up. I know him."

I exhaled, feeling the words on my tongue, remembering how they used to feel before, when I thought I loved him.

When I was so sure he loved me.

"You used to. You don't know how a person may have changed." Noor's expression turned hard. "He betrayed you. So he must have surprised you."

I sat back in my seat and chewed on the edge of my lip. "He betrayed me, yes. But I grew up with him. I fought with him."

"And still he handed you over to the guards without a second thought."

Noor's voice was matter-of-fact, and even though the words were true, they still felt like rubbing coarse salt in a fresh knife wound.

I hardened my jaw. "You're right. Thank you for helping me to remember the things I cannot see."

"Especially when it comes to Maz." She raised a brow.

My nails bit the flesh of my palms. "It's hard to have perspective where he is concerned," I admitted, though the words were difficult to get out.

"You sounded like a strangled cat saying that."

"It isn't easy admitting my weakness."

"And is he one?"

"A weakness?"

She rolled her eyes. "No, a fat mango. Yes, a weakness."

I stewed over her words. It was foolish of me to try and deny the truth. I had loved Maz for half of my life. The hatred festering inside me was close to obsession. But I couldn't lose sight of the bigger picture, the goals Noor and I both wanted to achieve.

"Yes."

Noor let out a whoosh of breath that whistled between her teeth. "Well, at least you are honest about it. It's more dangerous when everyone is in denial."

"I'm not in danger of falling back in love with him, Noor," I said dryly. "But . . . I know I am a little blinded when it comes to him. He was the betrayal I never saw coming. He was the one constant I always had, no matter what."

I turned my focus back to the palace looming ever closer, where all my enemies were waiting. "And now he's the one I have to destroy."

The carriage lurched to a stop suddenly, and Noor was thrown forward.

"What—"

Something hit the side of the tanga and my hand went to the talwar at my side. "Get down," I warned her. I crouched down too, peeking over the side of the carriage, to the street beyond. A crowd had gathered, chanting and shouting. They weren't looking at us, but at the palace. A line of soldiers blocked their path, their hands on their swords.

I looked down at the side of the carriage, seeing a rotten, bruised tomato on the stones below.

"Sorry, sahiba," said the driver from the front seat. "The street is blocked off. There are protestors marching." He clicked his tongue in command and the horses began walking backward. The carriage turned around, heading back the way we came.

The crowd grew more irate, hefting stones and refuse at the soldiers.

"What is it?" whispered Noor.

"Protestors," I called back to her. "Against the emperor."

She snorted. "It seems he's already hated by the people of this city."

"That's perfect for us, then."

A rock flew in our direction, and the crowd spied our carriage. I could see the moment their bloodlust found a target. We were wealthy—with our gilt carriage and black stallions—and we had been heading toward the palace. If they couldn't have Vahid, they would have us.

"Maybe not so perfect after all."

Noor watched with wide eyes as the crowd approach us. The shouting grew louder and they pelted the carriage with stones.

Our driver shouted obscenities at them, and I gripped the hilt of my sword.

"Noor, can I do anything to stop them? With the zoraat, I mean."

She shook her head. "No, you are using it to transfigure yourself, each dose has a specific purpose." She clutched the small purse at her side helplessly. "I didn't bring any zoraat with me. I didn't want to chance it in case the emperor searched us."

The driver shouted to the horses and the tanga moved faster, away from the crowd. But it wasn't fast enough. They pressed in on us, intent on blood from somewhere, if not from Vahid.

They were so close I could see the grime and desperation on their faces. I could taste their fear, their anger.

It tasted a lot like mine.

They shook the tanga, and the driver raised his saber to slash at them.

"No!" I shouted to him. I wasn't about to cut down innocent

civilians for the crime of being angry at Vahid. Especially not when I felt the same. "Don't hurt them."

But no sooner had my words come out than bright flames enveloped the carriage, surrounding the crowds, sending them running and screaming.

The horses took off, the tanga lurching down the street so fast I flew backward and landed with a hard smack in my seat. Vahid's soldiers circled the protestors, djinn fire shooting from their hands as they burned Basral citizens alive.

The stench of burned flesh and charred cloth filled the air, and I unconsciously pressed the small dagger pendant at my chest. My own screams were trapped in my throat, held hostage by the shrieks of the dying protestors.

"Stop," I whispered, but no one heard anything.

Our carriage sped away, the bonfire of bodies aglow behind us as we made our way to the emperor's ivory palace.

———

We arrived to a legion of palace guards lined up outside the entrance steps. Noor and I sat silently in the carriage, still in shock over what happened. When I closed my eyes, I still saw the people burning. Murdered, all because they protested a ruler leeching their city with his djinn bargain.

But as we pulled up to the palace, a strange pressure filled my chest seeing the line of guards clad in Mazin's familiar black-and-gold sherwani, with gilded scimitars strapped to their waists, etched with an intricate design carved across the leather sheath I knew very well. A zoraat flower, similar to the lotus but with more rounded petals, and a sword crossing the center of it. The mark of the emperor's high guard, and Mazin the head of them.

When my gaze swept the guards along the marble staircase, I realized Mazin wasn't there greeting us.

We were led into the palace, the floor like a still lake reflecting the clicking of our fine heels as we walked through the cavernous halls.

Not much had changed. And yet everything had.

The last time I was here, I had just been arrested. The last time I was here, my entire world fell apart.

And when I looked up from examining the broken pieces of my life, I had found only Mazin's cold dark gaze staring back.

I bit the inside of my lip so hard a metallic taste hit my tongue.

Good. At least the physical pain would be a distraction from the emotions coursing through me as I walked these halls again.

It was still ostentatiously decorated—gaudy, golden statues, pillars lined with jewels, and detailed carvings finer than the lace edging our dupattas. This palace was the former king's design, but when Vahid had taken over with his djinn magic, he had added to the spectacle of it all. Anyone who stepped inside would know his power. The palace was a weapon of its own—the kind that invoked fear and awe. I glanced over at Noor, silent beside me, her eyes sweeping the high ceiling and widening at the large open-air court-yard at the center.

"This place is as big as a city," she whispered as we walked through the tightly curated garden in the bright afternoon sun. She brushed a finger across a cluster of dark pink roses. "I had no idea Vahid lived like this. Souma's house was very fine. But Souma's didn't compare to this."

"Don't let it fool you," I whispered back. "It's all an act. Souma held Vahid's true power—the one you and I now have. Vahid would be nothing without djinn magic. We've just seen proof of that. Without zoraat, he'd still be a farmer eking out a living in the south."

Anam received us in a sitting area I had sat in often before.

It was a simple room to take tea, if simple meant that the ceilings were still lined with gold, and the cool tiles were an elaborate floral motif of orange, indigo, and fuchsia.

"Sanaya, I heard what happened—are you well?" Anam looked

from Noor to me and back again. "The protestors are getting more daring."

"Yes, the emperor's soldiers managed to . . . subdue them with zoraat." I swallowed the words like they were poison, but still stretched my mouth into a smile. "Thankfully."

I could still smell their burned hair on my clothes.

"What a beautiful room," I said with false pleasantness, attempting to change the subject as I breathed through my mouth.

"I'm glad you love it. It isn't mine, obviously, but I love sitting here. It's rare that I get to have visitors." She laughed a little, though the sound was sad, as if she had just realized the truth of her words.

Mazin had yet to join us, and I kept casting a glance to the doorway. I folded my hands on my lap to keep them from moving and focused on Anam.

Don't get too caught up in this, I reminded myself for the hundredth time. If I lost myself, I would lose everything.

"You are a ward of the emperor's." It wasn't a question, but she took it as such.

"Yes, he took us in when we were children. We had nowhere else to go. I owe him everything." She crossed her arms over her lap, her voice still light, despite the heavy subject.

"What happened to your parents?" My voice sounded harsh in the midafternoon heat.

Noor raised a brow from behind Anam. I rolled my eyes and tempered my tone, making my expression gentler. "My apologies if I overstep, it's just such a unique situation—the emperor raising you."

Anam's gaze shadowed.

"They died when I was a baby. I never really knew them. And neither did the emperor. He had been riding through our village during the fighting with the king and spied my brother with a baby. He decided to take us in. We are lucky the emperor found us when he did."

Lucky.

Maz hadn't told his sister how their parents died. Not how they had *really* died. She only knew the version Vahid told her. I smothered my shock and tucked that information away for later.

"The emperor must be a generous man." My smile felt like a hideous grimace. Every moment I had to hide my true feelings about Vahid, about Mazin, about any of them, it became more impossible.

Anam barked out such an abrupt stream of laughter that I jumped back.

"Oh! I'm sorry. I didn't mean to laugh as I did. It's just that you are the first and only person who would ever describe him as generous."

"And how would you describe him?" This was starting to sound like an interrogation but I wanted to know how Anam truly saw the emperor. Was she putting on an act? Did she resent this gilded cage?

"He is like a father to Mazin and me. He hadn't any children. But he raised us in the palace with every luxury we could want. He gave my brother a powerful position at his side. He didn't have to do any of that."

He wanted to buy your loyalty.

I nearly said the words aloud but stopped. There was something that she wasn't saying. Something just beyond the edges of her sentences that felt darker, truer. Anam knew more than she was letting on.

"But others might say he is . . . a merciless ruler."

A snort sounded from Noor's direction, and I willed the smile on my face to stay unmoving, and my eyes to stay trained on Anam's face.

Yes, we just witnessed the extent of his mercilessness.

Anam busied herself with making tea and I shot Noor a murderous expression. She gave a shrug and slid out of the room, the shadows of the doorway swallowing her up. Either she couldn't take much more of Anam talking about the emperor, or she was finally heading to do what she was planning to do since we got here.

I exhaled as soon as she left and turned my attention back to Anam. It was time I got a few more answers from her about who her brother really was—if she even knew.

"Your brother seemed quite upset in the bazaar yesterday."

Anam looked down. "Yes."

"I suppose it's understandable, he must have been so concerned when he heard you'd gone missing."

"That, or he's angry he doesn't have control of the city like he thinks," she said, with a tilt of her head and a mild smile.

I raised a brow. "And does he? Control Basral, I mean? I know he's in charge of the royal guard and the city patrols, but there seem to be so many problems."

"Oh, Maz has been focused on gaining a foothold in every corner of the city. Every corner of the empire, really. He's been working extremely hard—he's very ambitious."

She said it with pride, as if she admired the things he had done to get here. I wondered if she had ever thought about me, and what he had told her had happened.

I had always seen Anam as sweet, unassuming, an ally. But now I was questioning everything. She knew what Maz did to me—she must. And yet she sat here looking proud of what he did—proud that he betrayed his best friend for a little more power.

I curled my fingers around the bronze knife sitting on the table beside the small pot of honey.

Footsteps thudded in the doorway, and I looked up to see a large figure filling the entrance to the terrace. My breath caught and I released the knife in my hands with a thud.

As Maz stepped into the light, the red sun gleamed off the terrace, and his dark hair shone like liquid night. The threads of gold in his eyes glowed as they lit on Anam, before coming to rest on me. He raised his lips in greeting and I felt the smile more than I saw it. I released a slow breath that I'm sure both Anam and Mazin heard.

I wanted to throw myself off the terrace at how thoroughly my body was still in his claws. But I was supposed to act like this, like a lovesick fool who didn't know any better. I just wasn't supposed to be taken in by it myself.

"My apologies." His deep voice filled the terrace, making everything seem warmer. I tugged at the collar on my kameez.

"There was a skirmish in the west of the city. And I had a lead on those thugs who abducted you, Anam."

I sat up in my chair, my heart pounding against my chest. If Mazin looked at me now, he would see the truth written in my expression. But he was watching Anam, and it gave me a chance to mask my panic. If he had any information on the street thieves, I needed to warn them. But as I willed my heart to slow, logic entered my thoughts. They were children, yes, but I remembered how slippery they were. They could evade Mazin, at least for now.

"Yes, Sanaya had her own troubles near the palace. Basral soldiers stepped in."

Mazin's concerned gaze met mine. I bit the edge of my lip, looking distraught. "The protests were awful. We were thankful for the emperor's soldiers. The crowds dispersed quickly after the fire."

"The soldiers used zoraat?" Mazin's voice was sharp.

"Yes, they must have. It was certainly a sight to see. We managed to get away unharmed."

The same could not have been said for the protestors.

I bit my bottom lip in an effort to look concerned and widened my eyes at him. "I hope your own skirmish wasn't too awful, sahib."

"Call me Maz." His smooth voice slid over me.

I was jolted by the way it sank, like hooks, into my skin. His eyes were the same and yet not. They were tempered by something else—a calculating expression, like a snow leopard, waiting to pounce on its prey.

"Maz," I acknowledged. "I hope no one was hurt."

"A mild protest we quashed immediately, nothing of concern." He swallowed, and I watched the line of his throat. "But we didn't use zoraat on them." He said the words as if he knew exactly what that meant, what I had seen.

His eyes met mine, dark and probing.

"Another protest?" I asked, cocking my head. This would be welcome news to Noor. If there was this much civil unrest in Basral, we needed to exploit that to our full advantage.

Mazin cleared his throat. "The emperor recently raised taxes and there have been a few . . . uprisings in response. But we've silenced them quickly enough."

"I hope it wasn't like last time," Anam cut in. "That was awful."

"What happened?" I didn't have to feign interest. The bigger the fire we could fuel against Vahid and Mazin, the better. I just needed to know where to fan the flames.

"A protest that got out of hand," explained Mazin. He looked down at his hands, stretching out the long fingers. "The emperor gave orders to execute all those responsible for the insurrection."

"It was a bloodbath." Anam shivered. "I'm so glad you weren't hurt, Maz."

I tilted my head. "You were there?"

His gaze met mine, unblinking. "I was."

And we both knew the words I didn't speak: *Were you responsible for the bloodbath?*

And we both knew the answer.

His gold-threaded eyes were the same, but they weren't.

And I knew why.

He'd finally become the villain he'd been so eager to destroy. The man who crushed down desperate people, who betrayed the girl who loved him for power, who became a cold monster, incapable of compassion.

"Thank you for joining us, Sanaya." Mazin sat down beside me, his leg nearly brushing mine.

I gritted my teeth under my smile. Now I had to seduce the monster.

"I hope you know how indebted we are to you," he continued as he motioned to one of the servants and drinks were poured. I tried to concentrate on the ruby candescence of the pomegranate-and-rose tea in my glass so I didn't have to look at the new harshness in Mazin's eyes.

"Anyone would have done what I did to help Anam." I leaned forward, letting my hand fall from the stem of my tea glass and brush the edge of his wrist. He glanced down at his hand, then back to me.

"And yet, no one else did. I think you are being too humble, sahiba." He leaned forward, a smile curling his lips, one of the first I'd seen from him. My heart increased a steady rhythm, and I wish I could say it was anger or even fear. But I knew the feeling for what it was, and it was the same elation I got when holding the hilt of a new sword in my hand, when swinging the winning strike against an opponent.

Excitement.

I gave a gentle, delicate laugh that would have made Noor proud. "I have never been accused of being humble, so I will accept your compliment." I moved my hand back to my glass, making sure to brush my fingers against his skin once more. Then I took a long gulp of my chilled tea—probably too long—and set the glass gently on the table. Flirting wasn't my forte, but I didn't think I was doing too badly.

The servants spooned out a fragrant rice dish, along with spicy pickled mango, and lamb simmered in whole green chilis. I concentrated on eating, barely tasting the heat of the spices despite how impressive the food was. This was the kind of meal I had dreamed about when I had lain on the floor of my prison cell.

"There is one thing I wanted to know." Mazin's voice was light, but deceptively so. The benefit of having known him so long was that I could tell there was something bothering him. An ache of familiarity took me back. I remembered knowing his expressions, being able to convey a whole conversation between us with a look.

"Anam mentioned at the bazaar that she heard a scuffle when she was blindfolded," he continued, leaning back in his chair. "That it sounded like someone was fighting the ruffians who took her. Did you fight off the thugs?" A smile played on his lips, and he had a slight slouch in his shoulders as if he were relaxed and calm. But I knew better.

I smiled back.

"Yes, actually," I admitted, watching his eyebrows rise to his hairline. He hadn't expected that. Good. Sanaya was going to be everything he didn't expect. "I managed to land a few hits on them, before they took off." I took a sip of my drink, the tart floral taste washing away the food and sharpening my mind. I didn't mention that the "thugs" in question were children and that one of them had been shaking with laughter as we pretended to engage in combat.

Mazin smiled, broad and sharklike. He leaned forward in his chair, so close I could smell the crisp forest scent of him. He steepled his fingers together. "Forgive me, I don't mean to offend, but I don't imagine you as the type to fight off thugs." His eyes flitted over my body as if willing me to see what he saw. And I did. Clad in jewels and a heavily embroidered shalwar kameez with a color so deep the dye must have cost more than this wing of the palace. I was a frivolous, beautiful confection. Not a warrior. But he didn't know warriors could wear jewels just as well.

"My mother taught me. She wanted to make sure I could defend myself." It was a lie close enough to the truth.

Mazin tilted his head, examining me still, but with a softer expression. I don't know if he bought my lie, but my words had the effect of doing something else—intriguing him. "She sounds like an intelligent woman."

I inclined my head. "Yes. All the women in our tribe are taught to fight." I wet my lips. "I think it's an important skill. A girl needs to know how to handle herself in an attack."

He propped his chin against his palm, his dark eyes like the mountain sky at midnight.

"Like you taught me, Maz," Anam interrupted with light affection, reminding me that she was still in the room. I looked away from Mazin's intense gaze and back at his sister.

"Anam fought well." I smiled, my voice warm and approving. "When I arrived, she had already hurt one of the thugs. If she hadn't been taken by surprise, there's no doubt she would have bested them."

Mazin looked between us. "Unfortunately, surprise is often the strategy used by opponents to gain the upper hand." He turned back to me. "It's the best tactic one can use in an attack." His voice was plain, speaking without any condescension.

I blinked at him. "Yes, which is why they weren't expecting me." I cleared my throat. "*I* was the surprise."

I raised my chin. That same thrill buzzed under my skin, knowing your opponent had a weapon just as sharp.

"The emperor wanted to thank you himself, but he couldn't get away." His voice was cold again, like when I had met him in the bazaar.

I'm certain the emperor doesn't even know I'm here or who I am.

"But he does want to thank you in person." He rubbed his hand over his chin, and I had the inexplicable urge to put my own hand there, to cup his jaw in my palm and cradle his face. I curled my fingers into the meat of my hand to stop myself from doing something so unhinged.

"There will be a feast at court that he would like you to come to," he continued.

"Oh, but you are welcome back here sooner than that," cried Anam. "With everything you've done, I would love it if we could be friends."

I smiled, nearly a genuine expression. The more access to the palace we had, the more chances to plant the seeds of our revenge.

And I knew Anam was one of Mazin's few weaknesses.

"Of course we are friends. And you must come to my home as well." I looked up at Maz. "I would love to attend the emperor's gathering, especially being new to the city. That is so generous."

He nodded, his expression bemused, as if he hadn't been able to figure me out yet.

At the end of the meal Anam embraced me, and we promised to see each other soon. I began to walk back to the palace entrance, only to have Mazin fall into step beside me.

"You don't need to walk me out," I laughed, looking around for

Noor. But Mazin stuck by my side, and I forced my feet to continue forward.

It was strange walking alongside him again, but even though this time I had longer legs, he still towered over me.

"I meant it," he said, so quietly that I had to move closer to him to hear. "I owe you a debt of thanks. And I always repay my debts." He said it like an oath, and when I tried to brush it off again, I found the words sticking in my throat.

Instead, I nodded. He released a long breath, as if he needed my acceptance. As if he needed the debt.

I smiled at him, shaking my head. "You know, you don't have to pay someone back if they help you. Not everything is a transaction."

He stopped short, and I nearly tripped over my own feet at the abruptness of it.

"But it is. Nothing is without a cost."

"Maybe to you, but not me. When I help people, I have no agenda."

If Noor were here, she wouldn't have been able to contain her laughter at my words, but in my heart, I meant them. I wasn't being Sanaya now, I was Dania. My love never came with a price, even if his did.

"I don't think you understand where I came from, Sanaya. The way I grew up, you must assume everyone has an agenda."

"What an awful way to live." I frowned at his words. "How can you ever truly be free if you measure every interaction in terms of what it costs you?"

"Oh, I am not free in any sense of the word."

"Of course you are." We'd come to the open-air courtyard now, the gaudy manicured orchids and jasmine flowers surrounding us with near-suffocating perfume. Instinctually I leaned closer to him, like even in this body I couldn't get enough of him. We stood next to the large pond, tiger lotus sprouting out of the muddy water like a warning. I waved my arms at the magnificence surrounding us, and I didn't have to fake my next words. Not when I'd lived in true captivity for the past year.

"You live in a palace, not a prison. You have the world at your fingertips." I smiled, hoping it wasn't too brittle. "It's your own fault if you choose to feel confined."

His brow rose. "Is it? I'll have to take my lessons in freedom from you, then."

"I came all the way here from the northern territory—there isn't anywhere that can cage me."

"I like that," he said quietly, turning to face me. "I should like to feel . . ." He licked his lips and my eyes followed the progress of his tongue. *"Uncaged."*

"Perhaps I can teach you." I kept my voice just as soft, even though my heart was hammering in my chest.

He looked at me from beneath hooded eyes. "Perhaps you can."

We'd reached the front steps of the palace and walked toward the tanga waiting at the bottom.

Noor was by the carriage looking decidedly unruffled and not like she'd been combing the palace for secrets.

At the unexpected sight of her I stumbled on the stairs, nearly pitching forward. Mazin reached out to steady me, his hand grabbing my forearm and his arm on my waist. His touch was warm, rippling through me like a brand.

He stared down at me, his mouth slightly parted.

"Are you all right?"

"I hope so." I pressed my teeth together, trying to ignore the fact that I didn't hate the way I felt when he got close to me. I didn't hate the way he looked at me when our eyes met. Like he could consume me.

Like he was scheduled for execution and I was his final meal.

But he's not looking at you. He's looking at Sanaya.

That thought jolted me out of my haze, and I moved half a step closer, enough to see the lighter cracks of brown threaded through his dark eyes. His eyebrows lifted at my sudden nearness, but he didn't move back, meaning I hadn't pressed my luck, not yet.

Underneath the anger, underneath the feeling of wanting to stab him to death, I found myself *missing* this. Missing him. Talking to him. Sharing things together.

Don't fall into your own trap.

I looked over at Noor waiting by the tanga, and her bright eyes met mine. I cleared my throat.

"It was a pleasure to spend time with you and your sister today. I hope in time you will see there is nothing I ask from either of you except friendship. I have no agenda, there is no debt to repay."

He tipped his head down to me and it felt as if my heart was trapped in my throat and the only way I could breathe would be if I removed it entirely.

"I don't have many friends, Sanaya. But I will accept your friendship."

He took my hands in his, then pressed them to his lips. They were warm and dry, and it would be a lie to say I was repulsed, that the only thing I was thinking about was revenge.

Instead of fighting it, I leaned into the feeling, the crackle of fire underneath my skin something I hadn't felt since we'd last been together.

I hoped he felt it too. I hoped his body remembered mine, like every inch of my treacherous skin knew his.

I looked up at him, through my altered eyes.

He gripped my hands and his breath hitched tight in his chest. His pupils dilated, lips parting slightly.

I had him.

I walked to the tanga, my fingers slipping from his, though he seemed reluctant to let go. Finally, he did, and I pulled away, watching him flex his hand against his side after he did so.

Then I climbed into the carriage, leaving Mazin behind in the dust.

Twenty-four

Before

My bedroom window creaked, then shut with a thud. I sat up, my heart in my stomach, my fingers immediately feeling under my pillow for the bite of my blade.

A silhouette stood stark against the glowing moonlight. A scream lodged itself in my throat, fear gripping me in its vise until I slid the dagger out.

But something stopped me from throwing it. There was familiarity in the broad shoulders, slightly caved inward, the determined set of the profile, a recognizable curl of hair standing up in an odd direction.

"Maz?" The fear leaked out of me at the surety it was him, and not a raider who had broken into our home. I released a relieved breath.

But anger quickly replaced it.

"What are you doing? I nearly threw my dagger at you! Don't surprise me in the middle of the night like this, I could have killed you."

He stepped forward then, and I saw his features clearly—hair like he'd been through a windstorm, dark shadows lining his eyes, and a hint of stubble across his jaw. His clothing was askew—which never happened—and instead of his usual black-and-gold outfit that signified he belonged to the emperor, he wore a simple tan kurta with loose trousers and his scimitar in a sheath strapped to his belt. Mud was splattered across his lower half, and he looked as if he'd waded through quicksand to get here.

I curled my lip. "You look terrible."

He huffed out a laugh that I could tell surprised him, as if he hadn't expected to laugh tonight. Then he came to the bed, the mattress dipping with his weight. I moved over to give him room.

My pulse sped up for an entirely different reason than fear. Maz had never been in my room in the middle of the night before, and my treacherous mind was thinking all sorts of treacherous thoughts.

What did his skin feel like under my fingers?

Would he still smell like pine and a mountain rainstorm lying beside me?

Would my name sound the same if he whispered it in my ear?

What sighs would he make if my hands threaded through his hair?

I exhaled and curled my fingers in the thick quilt on my bed. Then I forced myself to shake the thoughts from my head.

At this close distance he looked even worse, his eyes bloodshot, a bruise forming on his chin I hadn't noticed before. Normally, he was impeccable, crisp jacket, combed hair, face so clean it was as if the outside elements didn't dare touch him.

But there was something different beyond what he looked like. He carried an air of heaviness that weighed down the whole room. My eyes narrowed on the bruise.

Anger rose tight and abrupt in my chest.

"What happened? Who did this to you?" My voice was like a harsh knife slicing through the weighty silence, but it seemed to shake him loose.

"How do you know something happened?" His dark eyes met mine, and the moon illuminated the bits of gold flecked in the iris.

"You look awful, and you showed up in my room in the middle of the night, which means you rode at dusk and through the valley in the dark." I cocked my head, looking again at the bruise. "You wouldn't do that if something hadn't happened. Something bad."

A breath eased from him, but I could tell it wasn't one of relief. He was steeling himself for something. Then he turned to me, and this time the glint of moonlight caught the whites of his eyes, causing the darkness in them to stand out. For a minute, he didn't look like my Maz, but rather someone darker, wilder. Someone capable of doing unspeakable things.

My Maz.

That thought jarred me. Since when had I begun thinking of him as *my* Maz?

"Dani." He breathed my name and lifted his hand to my face. I held my breath, suspended in the moment as the callused pads of his hands rested on my cheek. Something caught in my chest, a wild bird struggling to get free. A hawk soaring from a great height, taking an exhilarating dive toward its prey.

"Tell me something true." His voice rasped the words out, a deep scratch like he'd been swallowing sand.

"What?" I shook my head, clearing it from the feel of his hand.

"Tell me something true, something real." He looked at me earnestly, almost desperately, his lips pressed firmly together and a muscle ticking in his jaw. "I need something true right now." He lowered his hand from my cheek, but I still felt the heat of him on my skin.

"Maz, what is going on? You aren't acting like yourself."

He touched his forehead to mine, and my heart pounded between us, so loud I was surprised he didn't look down and see it beating against my loose cotton kurta.

"Vahid killed my mother."

I sucked in a breath, the air whistling between my teeth. If my fingers weren't still gripping my quilt for dear life I would have reached up and given him the human contact he looked like he craved.

But we weren't that to each other. I wasn't sure if he even wanted that.

But now he was in my room, on my bed. Looking at me like he did.

Everything was crashing together in my mind, my heart, my lungs. It wasn't that I didn't know what I wanted, but that admitting it might cost more than I was willing to give up.

"Maz, I'm so sorry."

"Don't act surprised," he said with bitter amusement in his voice. "You've always hated the emperor."

I snapped my gaze back to his. "I'm not surprised he had something to do with her death. He burned whole villages during the takeover. When he found you, you never saw your parents die. Vahid never does anything without an agenda. He isn't altruistic and you know it."

"I always thought he was truthful with me. I always thought I knew where I stood with him. He wanted loyalty, yes, but I thought he provided that to *us* in return. It was a transaction I thought was fair. I didn't realize it was tipped against me from the beginning."

I chewed my bottom lip, my eyes going again to the bruise on his chin. "How did you find out?"

What did he do to you?

"He told me." Mazin's mouth flattened. "After I came back from the north and didn't manage to quell the rebellion there. The smug bastard came out and told me. That he'd been lying to me all these years. That he'd killed her as she was trying to run back to us. That I was a failure just like her." He rubbed the side of his jaw where the bruise was, and I noticed blood caked in the edge of his lip too.

"He hit me, then dared me to return the strike." He gave a bitter laugh. "If I had, he would've eviscerated me. I've seen him burn people from the inside out. He always did like holding all the power and using it against those who had none."

I closed my eyes, tamping down my rising rage. I didn't usually have the kind of comforting words others did, and never managed to say the right thing to provide reassurance. I wasn't warm or soft or kind.

So I said the only thing that made sense to me.

"If the emperor were here, I would slit his throat." My voice was low and rough in the darkness of my room.

"Oddly, that makes me feel significantly better." He laughed a little, running his hand through his hair and looking up at the ceiling.

I followed the path of his fingers and bit my lip. "It should, I'm quite handy with a dagger." My voice was lighter than before, matching his tone, giving him some reprieve.

"Don't I know it." There were still shadows lurking in his eyes that I wanted desperately to chase away.

Tell me something true.

I leaned toward him, my heart in my throat, my voice low and quiet. "The first time I saw you, I wanted to wring your neck."

Maz stared at me, then let out a disbelieving laugh. "I know you have trouble being sensitive, but there might be a better time to talk about that." He tilted his head. "And likewise."

I swallowed past my panic and kept speaking. "I think you are nearly as good a swordsman as I am." My voice spilled out of me like hot chai, dispelling the cold that had crept in when Mazin talked about his mother's death.

Dawning understanding flitted across his face as he realized what I was doing. "Dani—"

I carried on, my breath rushed, like I had been running, not letting him stop the words from falling out. If he stopped me, I wouldn't ever say this.

"Sometimes, when we fight, I stare so much at your arms that I get distracted." My face was so hot I was surprised it didn't light up the room. But I had said it.

I had told him something true.

Maybe too true.

Maz choked out an incoherent sound, but I continued. I could do this. I could keep going. This wasn't just for him anymore, it was for me too. What was my life if I wasn't honest with the people I cared the most about?

Tell me something true.

I couldn't stop now.

"The other girls in the village are jealous I spend so much time with you. For the longest time I couldn't understand why." My words grew soft.

I wrung my hands in the folds of my kurta, keeping my eyes locked on his. I felt an unfamiliar fluttering, the feeling of stepping off a cliff. My fear was contained in these haunted dark eyes looking back at me, in the words that sprang from my mouth so quick I could barely contain them.

"But as we spent more time together, I understood," I continued. "Because you have more honor in your toe than the emperor has in his entire body. Because others gravitate to you, they *like* you. You are brave and strong, and *good*. You told me to tell you something true, but the only lie I could ever tell is how much you matter to me. Because it scares me too much to tell you that."

Maz's breath caught. His mouth opened, but no sound came out. He looked as stunned as I felt.

But the words were between us now, and I couldn't take them back. As uncomfortable as I felt at voicing my feelings, it had been more uncomfortable to hide them, like a steel mask slowly weighing me down.

"The emperor lied to you, and I'm sorry for that." I moved closer to him, my voice earnest. "But you built a life for you and your sister, and you can't regret that. You don't have to follow Vahid forever. You don't have to do his bidding for the rest of your life."

Maz reached out and did what I hadn't dared. He cupped my cheek again, the pad of his thumb tracing my lower lip. I inhaled sharply, the surprise of it catching me off guard. His finger drew so lightly across my mouth and yet it felt like he was painting with wildfire against my skin.

He leaned into me, so close his lips were inches from mine. We stayed like that for a beat, a frozen tableau, but the darkness made me bold. I closed the distance between us, pressing my lips to his, catching his gasp in mine.

Something in my chest ignited.

I had surprised him, I could tell, but not for long. A second later he was kissing me back, and we were meeting each other with the same fervor, testing and exploring this new ground. He slid his hands to the back of my head, threading his fingers through my hair and tipping my face back. My mouth opened wider and our tongues met in a hot, messy frenzy.

I was dizzy with it, with him. I sighed against his mouth and his teeth dragged against my lower lip. My hands gripped at the collar of his tunic, pulling him closer to me, like I wanted to consume him.

It was new and yet it wasn't. We'd been drifting toward this place for so long that it felt like a natural progression. Him kissing me, my hands on his chest, his fingers in my hair.

Finally, he eased away from me, letting out a long breath. I watched him, waiting to see who we were now—if he was still Maz and I was still Dani and we existed as we always did.

Finally, he spoke. "You think I'm as good as you with a sword?"

I punched him hard on the shoulder and he fell back against the bed, laughing.

"That's the *only* thing you have to say?" I scowled at him, but I couldn't hide my smile. We had kissed. I still tasted him on my lips. And we still laughed together like nothing had changed.

When everything had.

"I believe I said *almost* as good."

He shook his head. "No, you distinctly said *just* as good." He grinned back at me.

"You told me to tell you something true, and I've told you several somethings." I folded my arms across my chest. "We *did* several somethings."

"Just one thing," he said, his voice soft. That pain was still there, I could see it behind his eyes. But the shadows seemed less deep. And even though I hadn't kissed him to give him that reprieve, I was glad that it did.

"You get distracted by my arms? I should fight you with my shirt off more often, maybe I'd win more."

I rolled my eyes. "Maz, I still have a dagger, and I'm never afraid to use it."

He leaned toward me, his face now serious. I breathed him in, the crispness of a mountain forest in the morning, the comfort of a thick quilt while waiting out a storm. This felt right. Whatever was between us, whatever we had cultivated with our training, our teamwork, our fierce rivalry, and now this kiss, it now felt right.

"I care about you too, Dani." His voice was solemn, with a gentleness to it I'd never heard before. My heart felt as if it were on fire, as though it would light up the entire room.

"And for the record," he added, the humor returning, "I don't think I'm comparable to you with a sword at all."

I gave a small smile, still distracted by what he had confessed to me, about that kiss and what this meant for us now.

He swallowed, the knot at his throat bobbing. "And thank you, for making me feel something other than consuming rage. Because my only two options were either to murder the emperor, or come straight here."

And he had chosen me.

Just by saying those words, he had told me so much.

He had chosen me over vengeance, despite the riot of emotions he must be feeling about the death of his mother. Despite knowing that the man who raised him had done the most despicable thing—he hadn't sought anger, but solace.

"Is that why you rode through the cold desert in darkness?" I asked, looking again at his muddied clothes, the torn sleeve.

He nodded, then moved his hand down to clasp mine. "I knew that if I could just get here, if I could just see you, I could hold off on doing anything rash. That we could talk things through and

I wouldn't do something that would endanger Anam. If I attacked Vahid, it wouldn't be me he would destroy, it would be her. And he knows that. He knows he can control me with my sister. So, I came here." A rueful smile played on his lips. "Because I knew you would tell me to calm down."

I watched him, heat rising in my belly. "Didn't you know I would just tell you to cut out the emperor's heart?"

He laughed, and the sound lifted my heart higher. "Yes, but you also ground me. When you fight you never act rashly. It's always calculated, always precise. As if you know what move I'm going to make before I do it. I want to be like that. When I come for Vahid, I want it to be all planned out." He looked out of my bedroom window, and I followed his gaze.

From this side of the house the torches of the city shone in the far distance. You could almost make out the outline of the city, the towering palace sitting atop the hill. The place where the emperor asserted all his control.

I nodded my head in understanding. "You want justice for your mother."

"I want retribution." He tore his gaze from the window. "I want to know my mother didn't die for nothing, and that her son cared about what happened to her." He gripped the edge of the bed so hard his fingers were shaking, and I knew that if the emperor were here right now, he might not be able to hold himself back.

And I would help him.

A cat's cry startled both of us as Jalebi jumped on my bed and began rubbing her dark body against Maz. Maz laughed as he scratched behind her ears and her purring practically shook the whole bed. I was glad for the interruption, it gave me the chance to gather my thoughts, to center myself from the storm that this night had turned out to be.

"Traitor." I nodded to Jalebi. "She probably wants to sleep next to you." I felt my face heat at my words, not realizing their implications until they flew out and were sitting between us. *Did I want to sleep next to him too?*

But Maz didn't react to them, instead he scratched her belly, then swatted away her paws when she tried to attack him. He smiled, then closed his eyes as if blocking everything else out. I noticed for the first time how tired he looked, the circles under his eyes like craters in his face.

"I probably should get some sleep. I rode all the way here in a rage and didn't think of how exhausted I'd be." He moved to get up. "I'll go to the main room and lie on the divan."

"Just sleep here," I blurted out, thankful he couldn't see how red my face was turning in the dark. But I'd just kissed his face off, told him I admired his muscles and cared about him, I couldn't possibly be embarrassed about anything else now.

He hesitated, his eyes darting around the room as if looking for a safe place to land. "Are you sure?"

"Of course. You'll get more rest here than in the main room. My father wakes at sunup to start at the smith." I chewed at my bottom lip, not entirely sure what I was suggesting, but just knowing that I didn't want him to leave.

We'd shared something monumental between us, and I couldn't go back to sleep on my own knowing he was in the other room, looking up at the ceiling just like me.

Maz looked from the bed to the door.

"It's fine," I repeated. "Stop making it strange," I said with laughter in my voice even though my own pulse was jumping out of my skin. He was watching me with that same wild look he had before, and I felt it in the pit of my stomach. I turned away from him, not daring to meet the intensity of his gaze anymore. Instead, I shuffled to the other side of the bed, moving against the wall to give him room to lie down.

The bed dipped with his weight, and I held my breath so long my lungs were burning in my chest. He adjusted his body under the quilt and lay his head back against the pillow beside me.

My body was completely frozen.

I was too nervous to even breathe, so instead I released my breath in shallow puffs. A huffed laugh touched my hair after Maz settled against my back.

I bristled and turned my head to look at him. "What?"

"It's like sleeping next to a wooden board."

Anger spiked my blood and I scowled. "Excuse me," I retorted, crossing my arms over my chest. "But I've never slept next to a boy before." I moved as close as I possibly could to the edge of the bed to give him more room away from me. "I'll stay over here."

"No, don't do that." He cleared his throat, and I felt the heat of him behind me, moving closer to me on the bed. Every nerve ending in my body became alive with the knowledge that he was pressed against my back, lying alongside me, the back of my legs pushed against the front of his, his solid chest like a wall behind me, my bottom tucked into the apex of his thighs. When I thought I couldn't stand the awkward silence any longer, his arm snaked around my waist and his body pressed even closer. I exhaled heavily.

"Is this okay?" His voice was tentative and gruff, and if possible that endeared him to me even more.

I smiled to myself, my heart lighter as I placed my hand over his. "Yes."

"You can relax now," he mumbled into my hair, sounding drowsy. "It's me who should be worried if you sleep with a dagger under your pillow every night."

The muscles in my body eased as I let go of the uncertainty, even though my heart still pounded in my ears. But now he was next to me, it felt natural. As if we had been doing this all our lives.

"At least I'm prepared when someone breaks into my room in the middle of the night looking like a desert marauder," I retorted.

His chuckle rumbled against me, and I closed my eyes, feeling the vibrations ripple through me.

"Desert marauder? That sounds quite dashing."

A laugh escaped me, which abruptly ended when the pad of his thumb began tracing the underside of my arm. My stomach flipped. But it was a slow, contented touch, one that felt soothing and not like he was trying to instigate something. I relaxed back against him, and silence stretched out long and easy between us. His breathing was steady as his hand dropped away and fell softly to my waist. My eyes were growing heavy, but I wanted to stay awake a little longer to savor this feeling, to experience his arms wrapped around me for the first time.

I was certain he was asleep until he spoke.

"Thank you, Dani."

Twenty-five

"Tell me everything." I leapt on Noor as soon as the carriage took off, trying to get the thought of Mazin pressing my hand to his lips out of my mind.

"Well, while you were making moon eyes at Mazin, I was gathering some useful information. The security in the palace is atrocious. I managed to get to the kitchens and gossip with the kitchen maids."

I leaned back as we hit a bump in the dirt road, the cloud of dust in our wake causing Noor to cough and rub her eyes.

"What did you hear?" I didn't wait for her to recover. I was eager to get back to the plan. Back to reality. Back to hating Mazin. I could feel myself slipping into familiar ways, and cursed myself for the hold he seemed to have over me.

"There is a group of rebels in the city," Noor said, still rubbing the dirt from her eyes, "fighting against emperor Vahid and calling him a usurper. They've caused significant problems throughout Basral, but apparently Vahid has tried to crush them with a crackdown on all protests."

"Hence his awful display today. Anam mentioned something similar—that there was a protest recently that turned into a bloodbath. And Mazin had been there."

Noor nodded. "Yes, Mazin was there. The rebels wanted to bring down Vahid and the control he has over zoraat in the empire. They say he doesn't belong on the throne, that he was only given it by a djinn."

"Not a terribly original argument," I said, looking out of the tanga at the red-gold city streets around us. The breeze from the speed of the tanga whipped through my hair as I watched people turn to us curiously. Most people kept their heads down in fear, scuttling through the streets as the noise of the carriage reached them. Of course they would; if they dared to protest against anything, the emperor would burn them alive.

Vahid had promised freedom, choice, a way out of poverty. Instead, the djinn power had corrupted him.

"Vahid himself tells the tale of being gifted zoraat from a djinn. He just acts like he was chosen to rule because of it, instead of being polluted so much by the magic of the unseen that he wanted to control it all."

I flexed my fingers, thinking of the last dose of zoraat I had taken just this morning. I thought of that black tendril of power curling around my finger like a snake under my skin. I still wasn't even sure if that was real, but if I wasn't careful, Vahid's greed might happen to me. I needed to remember that in all this, I couldn't allow myself to be taken by the djinn power too.

"You and I agree with the rebels' cause at least," Noor reasoned, and turned to look out to the city as well. The wind brushed the ends of her short curls, and she looked much younger in the afternoon sun. Something had changed about her, something I couldn't put my finger on. She seemed a little more focused after leaving the palace, and I wondered if being in Vahid's house had made her think of Souma.

"I think there is opportunity here," she continued.

"You mean work together with them? The rebels?" I leaned back against the plush seat and folded my arms over my chest.

It was a good idea. The seeds of antagonism were already there, we just had to add to it.

"Or at least help their cause. They want the same thing we do, to see this empire of lies fall." She hesitated and looked at me.

I noticed her nervousness. "What is it?"

"We can also use the zoraat in . . . other ways. Ways that Vahid won't see coming."

I looked back at the passing streets. A mother was on her knees clutching at her child who appeared ill. She wailed in distress, crying out for help. People walked past her doing nothing, leaving her to fend for herself. I signaled to our tanga driver to stop and handed him a bag of coins to give to the woman.

The emperor had the resources and power to help people, but he had chosen not to. In the end it would be his own actions that would bring him down, not ours.

I had been hesitant to use zoraat; the feeling of power flooding through my fingertips was far more seductive than I had thought. I didn't need its full power to achieve my revenge.

But perhaps it was about more than just my revenge. Maybe it was about giving Basral—about giving the empire—something different to hope for. And maybe it was time to step things up.

"Tell me how," I said to Noor, watching the sobbing woman clutch at the bag of coins with hysterical relief as she ran off with her child to visit a healer.

"When I was working under Souma, there were blends that we created to help the crops, to bring the rains, to flood the clay earth with growth. The emperor uses it all to help his own crops, to control the amount of food production and the prices of resources. But I can also do the opposite."

I chewed on my lip. "Target the crops, you mean?"

"Yes. The crops, the livestock. Creating a blight they wouldn't see coming."

"They'll think him cursed," I murmured, working it all out in my mind. "And more will rise up against him." I toyed with a tassel dangling from the edge of my sleeve. "But people will starve. They'll die."

"Not if we have our own food stores. We can purchase land bordering the city."

"It's a good plan."

She grinned. "Don't say I'm not useful just because I can't fight."

"I never said you weren't useful because you can't wield a sword, just that you weren't *as* useful," I corrected. "And besides, the beauty of a plan like this is we can take Vahid down while not looking suspicious, until his empire is crumbling around him."

"We can undermine his rule without even getting near him," agreed Noor.

I licked my lips, tasting the remnants of the rose petals from the chilled tea at the palace. I wondered briefly if Mazin's mouth would have the same lingering taste. I shook myself, not letting my thoughts fall further into the trap of him.

I didn't want to use zoraat more than I already had, but if I could undermine the emperor's rule using the magic, then it was worth the use.

My body reacted with dark elation at the thought of using the djinn power again.

It was like an itch at the back of my skull, a constant need that had begun to trickle out of a crack that was forming. But if I took more, it wasn't because I wanted to, it was only to put our plans into place. Once this was all done with, I would stop taking it.

An unsettling voice whispered at the end of my thoughts, that same voice that had spoken to me when I'd first touched the zoraat.

Revenge.

The word danced on the breeze.

More.

I leaned into it with a soft sigh.

That voice had known what I wanted, and it had tasted the anticipation on my tongue. It felt wild and troubling to listen to it, but it also felt as if I were about to dive off a cliff in the darkness.

The rush of using zoraat scared me, and whatever that voice was, whatever the zoraat was doing to me every time I consumed it, I didn't want to think about. But behind that fear was something darker, something more dangerous.

Want.

It was tugging at me like a consuming need, thrumming through my veins every time I breathed.

"Prepare the blend of zoraat to take Vahid down," I said to Noor, and turned to face her. She had the same look I felt in my heart. Not exactly happiness, but something a little closer to satisfaction.

"Give me something that will tear this city apart."

———

"What exactly am I looking at?"

"Just wait."

"Her?"

I pointed to the beautiful woman in front of the schoolhouse, the whitewashed building standing out in the wealthy neighborhood in the north end of the city. We were far from the dirt and stink of the shanties that brewed with discontent at the rising food prices and Vahid's control of healer magic.

Here the air smelled sweet, and the children and stray dogs were well-fed.

The woman I gestured to waited outside the school, her hair wrapped with an emerald dupatta, and she wore a simple white kurta. A loud bell rang and children began filing out of the schoolhouse, running to the nearby play park and scattering in all directions.

"Her," breathed Noor.

I followed her gaze to a young girl, no older than six, in a neat uniform, holding her book bag in front of her like a shield.

The woman in the green dupatta took her hand and together they walked away from the school and down a wealthy street near the palace.

"That girl is who Casildo values most." Noor crossed her arms over her chest and nodded.

"Casildo has a daughter." I exhaled at the information. "One who doesn't live with him."

"A daughter with his mistress. He keeps her hidden. What I've learned from tailing him the past few days is that he has more enemies than just you. He's cheated others in Basral. He's turned people in for bending rules that he himself bends."

"In other words, he keeps his daughter secret in case they come for him."

"But we are already here."

I stared at the girl's retreating form, her chubby legs not yet grown into her body. "Yes, we are."

———

Noor began preparing the blends we needed to damage the emperor's crops on the dressing table beside my bed, grinding up the different-colored seeds with a deftness that spoke to her doing this for a long time. She had to blend the zoraat in my room because it was off-limits to the servants. We couldn't risk anyone seeing the emperor's highly valuable djinn magic when it was so restricted in use. I eyed the ochre piles, knowing soon I would be consuming them, and a new power of zoraat would be at my fingertips once more. I tried to dampen the exhilaration my body felt at the thought.

Every time I ingested it, I felt the same burning pain, but also an acute wave of relief. By the end of the day the need for more was aching in the back of my teeth.

I knew what this feeling was. Baba had explained it when we came to Basral and I had seen men drowning themselves in bottles of dark liquor, or children dragging their mother to a healer after she'd drugged herself to oblivion.

If I wasn't careful, zoraat would consume me too. But as long as I had my revenge, I knew that need would always win out.

"You're not going to hurt her, are you?"

Noor's cautious voice broke through my thoughts. She didn't look up at me; instead she continued to crush the vibrant seeds and separate the powder into tiny piles.

I spun my dagger on the table, watching the glistening light against the blade. I didn't have to ask who she was talking about; my mind hadn't stopped spinning since I'd seen Casildo's daughter—two wide dimples, still trusting in everything and everyone.

"We are going to do to him what he did to me." I lifted the dagger and threw it at the well-worn spot on the wall by the door. "But don't worry. I'll give Casildo a choice."

"That didn't quite answer my question."

"He keeps her hidden for a reason, which means he's afraid." I chewed on my nails, the only thing on my body that felt familiar. "Probably afraid that someone will do to him what he did to my father. What he did to me."

I looked up at Noor. "The most frightened people are the ones that do the frightening. And no, I don't have plans to hurt the child."

"Well, right now we can't take him down when he has more guards than the palace."

"Do you know how many times I tried to escape prison?" I asked her, my mind going back to those days, and every route I had tried to take before Noor dug through my floor.

Noor shook her head.

"At least ten. But in each one I learned that nothing is impenetrable. You just need the right opportunity."

"And what is that?"

I picked up a new dagger, taking aim at the door again. "We are going to make one."

———

I visited an old friend of my father's in the south of Basral, another swordsmith who he would visit when supplying the emperor with weapons. I knew the man had a store of swords he didn't show anyone, ones that my father would marvel at. He didn't sell to anyone—

and hardly any even knew of them. But as soon as I invoked my father's name, he unlocked his storeroom and pulled out the most beautiful scimitar I'd ever seen.

"It is said that this is the scimitar Naveed used to kill the azi," he whispered to me, encouraging me to examine the blade. I choked back a whimper as I held it in my hands and stared at it.

"Thank you," I said in a hushed whisper.

"It is you who I should be thanking. The swordsmith you spoke of gave this to me for my keeping. I've been waiting for someone to claim it since." He hesitated. "I didn't believe what they said about him. He cared only for his daughter. He wasn't going to commit treason."

I exhaled, my chest tight.

He gave me the scimitar with his blessing.

We spread a story that Sanaya Khara had found Naveed's own mythical sword.

I knew Casildo wouldn't be able to resist that, not with the fountain in the middle of his courtyard depicting Naveed's famed battle. Its worth and value surpassed any in Casildo's collection. It wasn't long until Noor spied one of Casildo's soldiers sniffing around the house.

He wouldn't buy it from me, I knew that. He knew I wouldn't sell it to him anyway, not if I was a collector. But most of all he had acquired my father's knives through theft. Why would this be any different?

"Tell our guards to have the night off for the festival," I said to Noor, the same night she told me we were being watched by Casildo's men. It happened at the perfect time, right before Ijal day, a festival celebrating the harvest in Basral. "And make sure Casildo knows about it. Sahiba Khara is so generous that she gave all her servants the night off."

By that evening, the sword was gone.

Noor stroked the empty case where the scimitar once lay. "It would be obvious that he took it."

202 ◆ Emily Varga

"Casildo believes he is above reproach, that he has the emperor in his pocket."

"Luckily, there's someone who we can use to our advantage."

The second person on my list, and another way to gain the trust of one of my betrayers while destroying the other.

"Darbaran," breathed Noor. "He's now head of the city guard."

"Street thieves know all the city gossip. Yashem told me that Darbaran lost quite a bit of money to Casildo."

"Bad blood." Noor crossed her arms over her chest. "He'll want to clear that debt."

I nodded, my mouth pursed. "Contact the city guards tonight. I want an accusation of theft made against Casildo immediately. Then we will see where his loyalty lies—with his family? Or with himself?"

Twenty-six

The night was dark, the moon clouded over by the pregnant clouds lurking in the sky, ready to erupt with monsoon rains.

Guards lined the streets, and a crowd had begun to form outside Casildo's home, as curious onlookers stood around to see what the fuss was about.

I waited outside for Noor and my other betrayer, Darbaran.

The last time I had seen him, he'd arrested me for treason and dragged me by the hair into the palace dungeon.

My hand tightened on the hilt of my knife when I spied his pock-marked face and smug grin.

He wore that same expression when he'd locked me up.

But he was next.

So, while I remembered the part he played in my arrest, it would only be a matter of time before his downfall as well.

At last Noor walked out of the house escorting an affronted Casildo.

"You dare?" he sputtered, marching outside. "I'll have your head when the emperor hears of this!"

He glared at Darbaran. Then his eyes alighted on me.

I pulled my hood up, making sure my face was covered. Casildo would know it was me—he'd have to know. But I wanted city gossip about Sanaya's involvement to be limited.

Darbaran lifted a bag and threw it on the street at my feet. My scimitar spilled out.

I didn't bother to draw back my hood, to study the blade on the ground. I knew it was the one he had stolen.

"This sword was found in sahib Casildo's home. In accordance with Basral law, stealing is prohibited."

Casildo looked like his eyes were about to bulge from his head. "This is preposterous! I don't even know where that came from."

"What is the punishment for thievery in Basral?" I asked, my voice ringing out. Casildo was red-faced, even in the darkness of the square. Whispers sounded around us.

"The work camps," spat Darbaran with glee. Maybe it was because Darbaran loved using his power to cause suffering, or because his debt with Casildo was now expunged, but it was clear he was getting joy out of this.

Casildo blanched white at the mention of the grueling work camps Vahid had implemented in the north.

"You stole from me," I said clearly, stepping forward, still shielding my face. "And no one contravenes the law in Basral."

I licked my lips, preparing for the performance. "But there is one exception to that law."

The guards moved to arrest him.

"Wait!" he shouted, desperation lacing his voice. "What exception?"

A feral grin spread across my face. "You are allowed"—I said the words slowly, relishing them—"to have a family member take your place if you so choose."

Casildo gaped at me. "But I don't have any family."

"Now that isn't true, is it?" My voice was deceptively soft.

I stepped closer. A frown creased Casildo's forehead as he squinted up at me.

"You have a daughter. She can take your place. The law will accept her blood instead of yours." My words were just above a whisper.

Casildo staggered back and clutched at his chest. I wanted to laugh at the irony—in this city children were sent to the work camps every day—orphans, those that worked as pickpockets and swindlers. But a child of a wealthy merchant—that was unheard of. That was shocking. When I had gone to prison, no one had said a word.

Except my father.

Let Casildo do to his own daughter what he did to me.

"It is the law," I repeated. "You are allowed to have someone else serve your reparation. It's your choice, either you or your child."

I could see his mind working as he narrowed his eyes. That he didn't immediately denounce the idea had triumph flooding through me.

As if to hammer home my point, Noor appeared with his daughter, taken from her bed in the north of the city—the sweet-faced, dark-haired little girl who clutched a small doll to her chest. She couldn't have made a better martyr. The woman who had picked her up from school was also there, being held back by Darbaran's soldiers as she wept and lunged for the girl. Casildo looked as if he might vomit. He dragged his gaze between the little girl and me.

"Fine," he spat, not looking at his daughter. "Take her instead."

I released a low breath. Murmurs sounded all around me.

He had done it.

He had actually chosen himself. In the end, he wouldn't even save his own daughter.

The woman with the emerald dupatta let out a low wail.

"Baba?" His daughter's voice was pleading and soft. Noor shot me a look but I didn't return her glance. I clenched my fists tight and willed the steel in my heart to remain for this next part.

If I looked too closely at this little girl, if I remembered my own trauma at being arrested, at feeling so alone I could break in two, then I wouldn't be able to do what needed to be done.

This girl had just seen someone she loved betray her and give her up for his own greed. It was better she learned this lesson now.

"A coward is always a coward," I murmured, mostly to myself, but Casildo heard me. His gaze shot up, and his eyes narrowed. I smiled at him, letting my teeth show.

"What did you just say?"

"You would let your own daughter go to the work camps for your crime? Sentence a child to be imprisoned?" This time my voice carried over the crowd. People had started gathering in the square around us.

"Is it better that the child have no father?" he sputtered. "I can get her out once I speak to the emperor."

"Have you no honor?" someone shouted.

Casildo looked around us, his eyes widening. He finally seemed to notice the crowd that had amassed around him. The angry, protest-driven crowd that was now pressing in on us.

Jeering and shouting filled the square.

The crowd had turned on Casildo.

"Wait," he cried weakly at the furious mob. "Wait, I didn't mean . . ."

"I thought you were a pillar of this city, sahib? Hm? Now you steal and suggest a child take your punishment?" I shouted the words across the square, inciting the throng of people, bringing the frenzy to a peak.

"You said . . . you said . . ." he sputtered, his hand going to his heart, looking less like a powerful man and more like a scared little boy.

I bent down, getting on my knees in front of him, ignoring the screams of the mob. Noor and the guards were keeping them at bay now, and only Casildo could hear my words.

"This is what you like to do to people, isn't it?"

He looked up at me, his eyes wild, but my question cut through the fear.

"What?"

"You heard me. I've just done what you do. I took everything from you—your reputation, your family. That's what you did to my father, isn't it? You used his trust, his love for his child, and you destroyed him."

Casildo looked me full in the face. "Your father? Sanaya, I've never met your father."

"You're too smart to be this foolish, Casildo. My father trusted you. And instead of helping him, you warned the emperor and got him killed."

Understanding lit in his eyes.

"Dania?" he whispered, his voice barely audible. His face had blanched white as his eyes roved over me. He shook his head. "You can't be her. You look nothing like Dania."

I smiled at him but said nothing. A look of horror washed over his face.

"I took everything from you, just as you did from me."

I stood and surveyed the incensed crowd, then turned back to him. "By the way, there is no exception to the law. You must serve in the work camp yourself. But now at least everyone knows what kind of person you are."

"Casildo will be arrested, not this girl," I called out to the crowd.

The mob cheered and Casildo collapsed on the ground, weeping into his hands. Noor gestured for the guards to take him away. I grabbed Darbaran's arm lightly, and he gave me an oily smile. My skin crawled just being near him.

"Put him on the transport tonight. The faster you do, the richer you'll be."

Darbaran nodded, his eyes lighting up.

I watched as my father's betrayer was taken into the night begging for mercy. His daughter was at the edge of the crowd in her mother's arms, head buried in her chest. At her father's cry, she lifted her head. For a second, our eyes met, hers a pale, blazing green and mine dark with revenge.

I wondered if she would come for me too, when she was older.

Noor stepped in place beside me. "What do you want me to do?"

I tore my eyes away from the little girl.

"Make sure she gets everything." I jerked my head toward her and her mother. "Every ounce of Casildo's fortune. She should want for nothing."

Noor nodded and began walking away, but I stilled her with a hand. "Except the swords." My voice was low. "I want them back."

Twenty-seven

The mix of zoraat that Noor blended burned down my throat like the aftermath of vomiting—sharp, acidic, and it coated my tongue with a bitter film.

I gagged. Noor stood beside me with a grim expression.

"I didn't think I would need another dose this soon."

"Remember that in order to keep the shape of another human being, the zoraat needs to be consistent. For anything else you generally just need to take what you need for the job at hand, just like a djinn healer might if they need to heal a specific ailment. But transfiguration is a very strong power. And it requires strong magic."

I collapsed on my bed, the embroidered coverlet bunching up under my prone body.

"And for the crops?" I murmured.

"I'm working on it. The blend should be ready soon, I just have to tweak a few things. But that one won't be as bad—this one is about changing the very essence of your body, your skin, hair, eyes, voice. Everything that makes you, *you*. In order to use that specific djinn power, it takes pain and exposure to zoraat."

I pressed my hands against the wall, shaking with the force of the poison coursing through my veins. I looked up at them, shocked to see the black veins covering my skin once more, this time spreading from my fingertips to my wrists.

Startled, I sat up and spread my hands wide in front of me—but the skin on my hands was now brown and unblemished. I blinked. My hands were the same, and entirely still mine.

I knew zoraat wasn't poison—that wasn't how anyone in this empire referred to it.

Magic.

That's what they called it. To wield the power of the djinn was a privilege. But it didn't feel like that. Every time I swallowed another mouthful of zoraat my body simultaneously recoiled and begged for more. It was like eating fire that burned you from the inside out, when you were so cold you'd do anything to get warm. I was made of clay and the djinn of fire, and consuming their power was to transform the human body into something other. Something unseen.

I gasped and doubled over, this dose taking my breath away.

"It wasn't this bad before." The words came out like they were being pulled from my mouth with a sharp hook.

"You already had some in your system, so it should be a little easier." Noor's voice was practical. "But I've never transfigured someone for this long before." Surprisingly, her frank honesty calmed me more than her sympathy.

"It feels like my blood has ignited." I coughed and my mouth held a slight metallic taste.

"That means it's working."

I raised my eyebrows. "Or killing me."

She inclined her head. "That too."

I huffed a laugh that caused my body to shiver with pain. "Don't make me laugh." I groaned and clutched at my stomach.

Something cool pressed against my head and Noor made a soft murmur.

I collapsed onto the floor as my vision blackened.

"You were sleeping for a while." Noor's voice cut through the haze in my brain. I coughed and sat up.

I was facedown on my bed, blood crusted to my nose, and my skull feeling like it had been split in half. I lifted my fingers up to feel my face—checking the bridge of my nose, the angle of my cheekbones. I exhaled in relief, though it was still disconcerting to be in another body.

I looked down at my hands, still mine, still scarred and still the thing that grounded me in all this. I examined them for any trace of the black spidery lines that had crawled up my hands earlier. Nothing.

Noor was sitting in a chair beside the bed, tinkering with the zoraat.

"How long was I out for?"

"Most of the afternoon."

"How often do I need to do that?" I couldn't handle something like that every day.

But that dark, wild part of me that rejoiced in the magic flooding through my system, at the power in my hands, came alive.

That scared me most.

She scrunched up her face. "This one was a stronger dose. It should last longer." She studied my face. "We can draw them out a little more. I just didn't want you in a situation where you started changing back into your real face without warning. I wouldn't want that to happen while you were in the palace."

I bit my lip, wincing at the pain of the small movement. "No." I grimaced. "We wouldn't want that."

I imagined what Mazin's expression would be if I suddenly turned into Dania before his eyes.

He would run me through where I stood. My hands curled as if gripping an imaginary dagger. I would welcome him to try.

Noor let out a low laugh. "I don't even want to know what you are thinking about right now with that look on your face."

"I'm thinking that I'm going to have to speed up my revenge plan so I don't have to consume much more of that."

And so black spidery veins don't appear on my arms, and so I no longer hear voices whispering about revenge.

That would be nice too.

I sat up in bed as Noor brought me a fresh cup of chai and put it on the nightstand.

"I told the servants you had taken ill," Noor murmured.

"That's not wrong."

Noor chewed on her bottom lip. "The amount of zoraat you have to consume for transfiguration is difficult, and I've never dealt with the repercussions of it before. I can see how hard you are taking it, and we don't have to do this. We can do something different to get our vengeance—or we can stop this plan entirely. We can just sell the seeds, or . . ."

"Or?"

"Or destroy them." She stood up and proceeded to pace around the room. "I thought about doing that while working for Souma. Just setting fire to the whole crop and letting the powers return to the djinn where they belong."

Something in my stomach recoiled at the thought of all that power being set aflame.

That was the last thing I wanted to do. Zoraat was giving me the chance to make those who had wronged me pay.

I wasn't about to give up this opportunity. And Noor shouldn't be about to either.

"Is that what you really want? To let Vahid get away with what he did?"

Noor ran a hand through her short curls. "No. That's not what I want. But this is destroying you. More than I thought it would. What good is revenge if we die while doing it? Then who is it for? Your father wouldn't have wanted you to die to avenge him. And Souma wouldn't have wanted me down this path."

I took a sip of the chai, the warm, milky tea soothing my ravaged throat. "Souma isn't here," I said quietly, my voice low. "And neither is my father. And we both know the reason why." This time I stood, my legs steadier than I predicted. "If we do nothing, their death means nothing."

Noor sat back heavily against the divan. "I could kill them," she said quietly. "Then you don't have to do this."

I snorted. "Noor, you didn't even want me to kill Thohfsa. You can't kill anyone." I sat beside her. "Why don't you want me to do this?"

She looked up at me. "You're the first friend I've had since Souma. I don't have anyone else. And yet I'm helping you destroy yourself. What kind of friend does that make me?"

"A friend who understands exactly what it feels like to lose everything." My voice rose a little too loud, but I couldn't control it. Or I didn't want to. I could feel my eyes burning. Rage was cold and dark in the back of my mouth. "To be imprisoned for a crime you didn't commit. To lose the person who cared about you the most. You know *exactly* what that's like."

Noor wiped a tear from her cheek. "And what will you do when it's over and you no longer have revenge?" she asked fiercely, the words ripping from her. "What will either of us do?"

I looked away from her.

"Then we'll be free." The words sounded hollow, like I was trying to be convincing instead of truthful.

The truth was, nothing else mattered if I didn't get revenge.

The truth was, I would destroy myself a thousand times if it meant getting retribution for my father.

"Free?" She laughed to herself, a bitter sound, before looking at the open window that framed Vahid's palace like a target. "We'll be free? Or broken?"

I shook my head, that black, dark anger rising in me once more, as if it were starting to take charge of me. Words spilled out of me, words I couldn't control, words that seemed dictated by something else.

"If you don't want to be here, you can leave." I pointed toward the door.

Noor stood up, her hands planted on her hips. "I'm trying to save you here. I'm trying to save us both."

"I don't need saving," I said, the voice not my own. It wasn't even Sanaya's. It was dark and deep and rageful. "I only need one thing. And it's clear you didn't care that much about Souma if you are willing to give up now."

Noor inhaled sharply, looking as if I'd stabbed her.

I blinked, and the rage melted away, replaced by shame at Noor's stricken face.

"How dare you?" she uttered, her voice low and vehement.

I stood up and held out my hands, guilt lacing my tone. "Noor, I'm sorry—I know you cared for Souma. I didn't mean that. I . . . I don't know what came over me."

I knew I couldn't explain it. Couldn't rationalize what I was hearing, seeing, feeling. I scrubbed my nails through my hair. I needed to take responsibility for this, but it felt a little like I was losing my mind.

Noor's eyes narrowed with seething anger I'd never seen before. "You know nothing about my relationship with Souma. You lost your father, yes. But I never really had one, not until I finally found Souma. He taught me how to fend for myself, how to do something no one else could do. You talk about revenge as if you are the underdog, but you were loved your whole life. I was nothing. Abandoned. Forgotten. He was the only one who ever gave me a chance." She pressed her arms to her sides. I looked down at her hands, which were shaking. She followed my gaze and clasped them together to still their movement, scowling at me. "And you still have your grandmother. You still have someone who loves you. I have nothing and no one. Vahid took the only person who ever gave a damn about me, and you say I don't care? I don't want revenge?"

She looked away, back to the open window, back to the palace. "I care what happens to you, Dani, because I know what it's like to lose everything. If you spend everything you have chasing this, you might not like what's left over."

"What's your solution, then? Just give up?" I threw my hands in the air. "I can't do that."

My words were edged with desperation, panic in my chest at the thought of no longer pursuing this.

At the thought of no longer consuming zoraat.

"I can't let them walk free, not after what they did." I rubbed the back of my head, still aching from the latest dose, now also ringing with Noor's words. "And you have me. We are in this together—you and me. Just don't give up now, not when we're so close."

Noor's shoulders sagged. For the first time in a long while I really looked at her. Shadows lined her eyes, and she was so pale. She wasn't consuming zoraat, but this was taking its toll on her too.

Noor sat on the edge of the bed, looking deflated. "I don't want to give up either." Her voice was more measured. "I don't want Vahid to get away with any of it. But I don't want to lose myself in the process." She took a steadying breath. "And I don't want to lose you. I'm here to help you, for whatever you need. I owe you that at least after you came back for me at the prison."

"You don't owe me anything." I shook my head. "We helped each other escape that place. We are both here because we have the same goal. And more than that, we want each other to succeed." My eyes met hers, hoping to erase my previous words. "I want to help you get revenge for what he did to Souma, just as much as I want revenge for my father."

"I want to do this, Dani. But I'm allowed to try to stop you if I think it's killing you."

I nodded. "I'm not going to take more zoraat than I need. We are going to finish this. For my father, and for yours. And after it's all over, we are getting as far away from here as possible. We'll leave the whole empire."

Noor exhaled, the fight draining out of her. "Well, we don't have to go *that* far."

I laughed, relieved that the tension had been dispelled, relieved that my awful words didn't drive Noor away for good. But the feeling I'd had when I'd said them stuck with me. It was as if the person who had said those awful things to Noor wasn't me at all.

"So." Noor's voice pulled me out of my thoughts, and I was thankful for the distraction. "Who's next?"

Twenty-eight

Darbaran sat alone at the café, drinking coffee from a golden dallah pot that must have cost the equivalent of his entire year's salary when he was a guard. Now that he was wealthy, and ran the security of Basral, he bled the city coffers dry with his corruption.

"We already know his weaknesses quite well." Noor sat across from me pretending to read a book while I sipped my tea.

"It's certainly not coffee."

She smiled, her eyes on her book.

Greed.

The easiest thing to prey on. But it was more than that. Darbaran preyed on the weak, taking advantage of women and girls and abusing his position to feel powerful. I wanted to make him feel helpless instead.

"We greased his palms well enough when he got Casildo out of the city before the emperor got wind of it. They say he'll do anything unsavory for money. Basral's city guard is so corrupt all you need is gold. And I thought it was Mazin who controlled this city. Turns out it's actually Darbaran."

Noor inclined her head. "From what I can glean, Mazin attempts to crack down on the corruption. But Darbaran has done quite well since your arrest."

"He solidified his loyalty by framing me for murder." I thought back to his weaselly face when he was dragging me away, and that smug smile as he pocketed the glass poison vial beside the body of the dead chief I had supposedly killed. "I'm the one who made him his fortune."

"Fitting, then, that you will be the one to take it away." Noor smiled in his direction and took a bite of a rose water pastry ball sprinkled with pistachios.

I lifted my cup to my lips, savoring the last drops of chai at the bottom of the glass. This one had crushed almonds, and it tasted sweet and earthy.

"His own greed will be his downfall."

I placed the glass on the table and flexed my hand. "Let's put on a show for our dear captain."

The feast was the most extravagant one I'd ever been to, and I couldn't believe I was the one hosting it. Tonight, I'd be adding another brick in the tomb of Darbaran.

"Sanaya, your home is amazing."

I held my arms out to Anam as she entered through the double front doors. Her heels clicked across the front marble, her kameez shimmering moonlight. My throat constricted when I saw who was coming in behind her, stepping through the front doors, his dark coat immaculate, the gold embroidery gleaming.

"A pleasure to see you here, Mazin."

"I couldn't very well let my sister attend these festivities alone." His gaze swept the entrance, and then landed on me. I knew what he saw—my glossy mahogany hair coiffed to perfection, a maroon shalwar kameez setting off my complexion, black kajal lining my eyes, and bejeweled bangles adorning my wrists. I spared absolutely no adornment and no expense. I looked like a bride, which was exactly what I wanted Mazin to think of when he saw me.

His bride. A girl he could marry, fall in love with.

A girl who would devour his heart.

He inclined his head. "Thank you for inviting us this evening." His eyes roved over me, touching on my shoulders, my wrists, my hips. "You look magnificent." His voice was low but confident, not self-deprecating as he would have been when I knew him. As if he said this sort of thing to girls all the time. Once again, I was struck by how much he had changed, how commanding he had become.

I gave him a small smile and lowered my lashes. I was happy to play the part of the simpering fool if that's what he needed to prop up his ego.

"Are there black swans in your pond, Sanaya?" Anam interrupted us with a squeal and pointed to the courtyard where a glimmer of the large fountain outside could be seen.

"Yes, we acquired them last week. Go take a look for yourself. I adore them, but they will snap your fingers off if you get too close."

"I'll take you, sahiba." Noor gave Anam a small bow and led her outside. Which gave me the chance to be with Mazin alone.

"I'm sure you will be busy welcoming your other guests," he said smoothly, though he didn't take his eyes off me.

"Not at all," I responded, making my voice flustered, as if I couldn't catch my breath around him. It wasn't difficult given that my heart was slamming against my rib cage. "There are plenty of diversions throughout the house that will entertain them. I couldn't wait to meet more of the emperor's court, and I thought what better way to do so than have my own party?" I gave a small laugh.

"You've certainly made an impression on the city already," he commented, walking alongside me as we moved through the house. We paused every now and then to watch the fire-breathers or street performers that Noor had recruited for the evening.

"Basral has been good to me," I said simply, gesturing to the throngs of people surrounding us.

"I'm sure if we were to venture to your home in the mountains, we would receive the same welcome?"

I paused, because the words were not a statement but a question. And I was again faced with the sense that I was being interrogated.

So, he didn't quite trust me yet.

I laughed, a rich, throaty sound. He stared at me, something flashing through his expression that replaced the calm, confident mask he usually wore. But figuring out what he was thinking was like trying to hold water with my fingertips.

Then he smiled in return, a rare dimple popping in his cheek, the one I used to try to make appear when I joked with him during training.

"I've never heard you laugh like that," he said, his voice deep and smooth. "Was what I said funny?" He inclined his head.

"Yes, actually. If you were to come to my home in the mountains, you'd probably be in for a fight. But after you proved yourself with a blade, you can be sure you would receive a fine welcome."

"You have an interest in swords, and you bested my sister's attackers. You spoke to me at the palace about how your mother taught you to fight. It seems as if you'd be a skilled opponent yourself, though you don't give that impression."

I felt the sting of anger, which I tried to tamp down. But even though Sanaya might be, Dania wasn't the kind of girl who guarded her anger.

"A girl can't know how to fight and dress well?" I asked, arching my brow, telling myself I was supposed to be agreeable and compliant, the very opposite of myself.

His mouth popped open and he appeared momentarily speechless. "Not at all," he rushed to say, for the first time abandoning his self-assured tone. "Just that it surprises me."

"Why?" I said harshly, and a few guests looked over at us. I gave them a tight smile and kept walking with Mazin.

"Why?" he asked blankly.

"Why should it be a surprise? You taught your sister to fight. I'm assuming you've seen other. . . . girls fight? We are no different from you. Putting on a pretty outfit doesn't mean we can't slit your throat."

I winced, my words cutting a little too close to what Dania would say. But everything else about me was so different—from my eye color to the curve of my chin. There was no way he would suspect me based on a turn of phrase.

He smiled then, and the smooth Mazin was back. I felt a pang of disappointment. I wanted him unsettled, I wanted his real self when he spoke to me, not this unshakable man with shadows in his eyes and false smiles.

"I've seen other women fight, yes. I've fought alongside one of the greatest swordswomen for many years. But I didn't mean to offend you. Only that I find your interest in it refreshing."

I was brought up short by his mention of the greatest swordswoman.

Was he referring to me? He must be. I looked at him from the corner of my eye, but he still watched me with that same smooth mask.

"I've had some training with a blade," I said with a laugh. "But I'm no expert. I prefer to admire them, collect them, yes, but I'm not the best wielding them."

"I'm not sure I believe that—we'll have to have a bout sometime."

I swallowed thickly, my fingers burning to grab the hilt of my dagger, which was strapped to my thigh, and engage in a fight with him right there. But if we ever fought, he'd know exactly who I was.

And if he entered a bout with me with a blade, he wouldn't get out of it alive. I wanted him alive for what I was going to do to him.

I leaned forward on the banister overlooking the entranceway. We'd made it upstairs, and could oversee everyone who entered the house from this angle. I looked down, keeping tabs on which guests arrived and waiting for one person in particular to show his face.

"I'm afraid I wouldn't make it very long with a heavy sword. I'm just happy to collect them, really."

"It's a pity what happened to Casildo's sword collection—stolen immediately after he was arrested. I went to the house and it was completely gone." Mazin's voice was rough. "There were some knives in that collection I tried to buy from him. I would have liked to have them."

My eyes narrowed, wondering if he was talking about my father's swords. I had to bite my tongue to stop from telling him he would never have them.

Not as long as I was alive. He didn't deserve to own anything created by my father.

"I was heartbroken," I said, allowing my voice to crack slightly. "Such beautiful swords, lost."

I didn't mention that the entire collection was currently safe in the cellar of this house.

"I cannot believe what I heard about Casildo after he was arrested. Thievery, extortion, bribing city officials. Thankfully he's in the work camps where he belongs. It seems I'm not a very good judge of who is trustworthy or not." I rubbed the back of my neck, looking chagrined.

"Don't be too hard on yourself. Casildo fooled many." He looked away from me.

"He seemed to be held in high esteem. It was where you and I first met, after all. I certainly didn't expect a man respected by the emperor to be such a rogue."

"Sometimes it is those we trust the most who will betray us," he said softly, still not looking at me.

I paused at the words, a near-exact echo of the ones Noor said to me when we were in prison together. I pressed my hands against the banister to still their shaking. Or to stop myself from reaching out and strangling him.

"What do you know of betrayal?" I tried to soften my voice, but it still came out clipped and forceful, an accusation instead of a query. As if I were saying he couldn't possibly understand what it was to be deceived.

Mazin looked at me then, a question in his eyes. He opened his mouth to say something, but instead a commotion near the door had us both turning our heads to look at the entranceway.

A loud laugh cut through the din of the party, and the cruel edge to it coupled with the raucous shouting told me exactly who it was.

Darbaran.

The guest I had been waiting for.

"What is he doing here?" Mazin stiffened, his stare drilling into Darbaran, who stood near the door with friends he'd brought along with him.

"The captain?" I said, trying to hide my humor behind faux innocence. Mazin had always hated Darbaran, and for good reason. The roach had preyed on the women in the palace. But Sanaya didn't know that. Let Mazin be my rescuer if I needed it.

"He helped me recently and I am so thankful for the additional security he provided after my home was robbed." I smiled at Maz as he continued to stare at Darbaran with venom in his eyes. "You don't like him?"

Mazin snapped his gaze to mine, his face smoothing over again. "Darbaran used to be at the palace. He was captain of the royal guard. He . . . isn't my favorite person." He studied me, as if deciding how much he could trust me.

Not at all, I almost told him. Instead, I gave him my most wide-eyed stare, hoping that I conveyed naïveté.

He licked his lips and my eyes went straight to his mouth.

"May I be discreet?"

"Pardon?" I looked up at him. "Oh, of course." I cleared my throat. "Do you know something about Darbaran I do not? After Casildo I'm terrified about who to trust."

"You can't depend on Darbaran," he said bluntly, his mouth thinning. "I can't say much more, but please don't entrust him with your safety." He looked so concerned I nearly laughed. Darbaran wouldn't be able to harm me if he were surrounded by a thousand city guards.

I leaned toward Mazin. "And who should I entrust it with, then? You?" I said the word softly, and it sat between us like an anchor.

For a moment we stared at each other. I couldn't tell if I had pushed the issue too far. But then Mazin moved closer, until we were only a few inches apart.

"If you like."

I released a breath, my heart beating as if I'd been in battle.

He'd wanted a swordfight, and this was no different, but instead of talwars, the weapons we used were words. Our bodies. This was a battle of intimacy, of landing the right strike, testing your opponent. If you rushed ahead, if you put the wrong foot forward, you could lose everything. But I was nothing if not good at waging war.

I wet my lips. "And what do *you* like?"

He let out a low chuckle that went straight to the pit of my stomach.

"I'd like you to be safe," he answered softly. "You did save my sister, after all."

"And that's the only reason?" I arched a brow. "Because I saved your sister?"

His eyes grew dark, and I could feel the heat from his body like it was drawing me to him, I a moth and he the hot flame. He flexed his hands and I stared down at the long fingers, hands I knew as well as my own.

"I am concerned for your safety, Sanaya."

"And nothing more?" I breathed, pushing as far as I dared. I had never flirted before and I was starting to think I might be quite good at it. Except for the fact that I currently needed to fan myself in my elaborate frock, so heavily beaded I wanted to peel it off my skin.

"Would you like there to be more?" he countered, a smile playing about his lips, but a dark heat in his eyes.

Oh yes. That's exactly what I want.

I tried to ignore how thick my tongue felt, or the loud hammering of my heart. I let out a steadying breath. I could not allow him to get the upper hand here, not again. I was in control of this.

I walked to a nearby alcove and Maz followed, walking behind me as if I were leading him on a string.

"I find myself intrigued by you, Mazin." My voice was soft and he leaned forward to hear. I gave a slow curl of my lips and moved farther into the shrouded alcove. "You protect your sister fiercely, you are loyal to your emperor, and you are worried for my safety." I raised a brow. "And yet you are aloof—holding yourself at a distance. I can't read you as I would wish." I pressed my hands to my side to quell the jitteriness of my nerves, ready to give the whole thing away. A part of me wished I was more sophisticated with men, that I had more experience manipulating and seducing.

But Mazin was the only person I'd ever been with, and it was difficult to keep my emotions at bay. I had to feign intimacy when my body was used to the real thing with him.

"And how would you wish to read me?" He was closer, his chest nearly touching mine. We were partially obscured by a curtain and I felt the rise and fall of his breath.

"I would read you like a novel. From cover to cover, learning everything about you."

He tilted his head. "Leisurely, only taking me out when you felt like it?"

I snorted. "Is that how you read your novels, Mazin? How uninspiring. No, I mean in a fierce frenzy, by candlelight, devouring you until I finished every page and committed it to memory, and then I'd flip right back to the front and start again from the beginning."

His eyes flared, glowing bright, those flecks of gold in the rich brown coming to life like embers. He pressed in on me further, so that my back hit the wall. I wore a coy smile on my face, daring him to push this more. I wanted everything, I wanted him here in this moment, thinking he had me.

"Ah." He bit the edge of his bottom lip, his eyes roaming over my face. "Perhaps I'm just reading the wrong things. Shall I tell you how I would read you?"

I shivered, hugging my chest as if my arms could guard my heart. I'd forgotten exactly what it was like for him to turn those dark eyes on me.

He seemed to take my silence as assent, and he continued. "I'd read you like scripture, a prayer. And all the worship I felt, I'd heap at your feet." His words were low, like he was actually praying, or reciting an incantation of the djinn, words for whispering magic and power.

I sucked in air through my teeth, the tension between us tight. It made me remember all-too-familiar things, his arms wrapped around me, his lips buried in the crook of my neck, his hands on my thighs.

I looked up into his blazing eyes, taking control of the moment. "Just my feet?"

He moved so quickly I couldn't catch the movement—faster than any swordplay we'd had. His mouth slanted across mine hot and urgent, his body sheltering me like a banyan tree in a monsoon.

And I nearly sobbed.

It was everything I remembered. Everything that was real between us. It made me want to cry for the girl I had been, hopelessly in love, reckless and far too trusting.

I kissed him back.

Kissed him even though it set my skin on fire, even though it caused a swirling storm inside me clashing between my head and my heart, my body sighing in relief at being touched by him again but my head recognizing him for what he was—the boy who had given me everything and then burned it all to the ground.

My hands clutched at his dark sherwani, my head spinning. I wasn't sure if it was to pull him closer or stab him with my dagger.

But I wouldn't do that. Not yet. Not until I burned him up inside like he burned me. Until there was nothing left of him but this wanting. Until he begged for me like a dying man in the desert, and I the mirage that could have saved him.

And in the end decided to let him starve.

Twenty-nine

"I didn't want to interrupt you and Mazin eating each other's faces in the alcove, but we have a problem."

I scowled at Noor and crossed my arms over my chest.

Mazin and I had jumped apart as soon as Noor's cough had cut between us. I mumbled an excuse and allowed her to drag me away to my bedroom. I couldn't even look at Maz, not after I'd nearly lost myself in that kiss with him. I touched my fingers to my lips as if I could taste him all over again.

But as Noor spoke, a single clarifying thought entered my head and refused to let go.

He thinks you are someone else.

The way he kissed me, held me, breathed me in, he wasn't doing that with me. He was doing it with Sanaya.

If there was anything that should douse my old feelings for him, it was this.

He obviously never had the same feelings for me, otherwise, he wouldn't have been able to kiss someone else like that. I certainly wouldn't.

You want to kill him, I reminded myself.

My heart felt like it was splintering in half, which made no sense because I thought he'd already torn it out.

I buried my head in my hands and groaned. It was time to move forward with our other plans, to shift the focus to someone else. Noor's earlier words filtered through my mind.

"What do you mean, problem?" I said through my hands.

"Darbaran is not taking the bait."

I lifted my head. Darbaran was the very last person I wanted to discuss at this moment.

"Then sweeten the pot for him," I said with exasperation.

"How? I've made subtle offers about gold, jewels. More money than he can dream of. I've offered him everything."

I looked around my room, my eyes landing on the floor, remembering what was hidden beneath it. "Not everything." I sat back in the tapestry-upholstered chair. "If greed motivates him, then we need to prey on that weakness."

Noor straightened, then gestured to the door. "Be my guest."

I set my shoulders, determination steeling my spine. One thing was going to go right tonight. And if I couldn't get the upper hand with Mazin, I sure as hell would against a weasel like Darbaran.

<hr />

Dabaran took a long drink from the bottle in his hand, then broke off with a laugh, spitting the dark spirits into the nearby pond. His friends were jumping around the fountain, making screeching noises at the swans.

I wanted to leave them to the mercy of the swans and sit back as they pecked their eyes out. Instead, I plastered an amused smile on my face and walked toward them. Darbaran was going to feel like this was his plan, after all.

"Thank you for attending my party."

There were three others with him, two clad in maroon kurtas signifying that they were city guards, and the third in the same dark kurta as Darbaran. All of them gave me a look that made my skin crawl.

"And for bringing your . . . charming friends."

He leered at me, but then, that was Darbaran's usual expression at the girls who walked by him. I had slammed the edge of my heel into his foot more than once when I'd visited the palace with my father.

"The pleasure is all mine, sahiba." His gaze snaked my body, but I forced my face to remain impassive, as if I didn't want to rip his throat out.

He was only a few years older than me, with a face like a mongoose—small, snub nose, beady eyes, and a permanent air of being unwashed. Despite his newfound wealth, he didn't look more polished than he had prior to my arrest—he still gave the impression of a street criminal, except in finer clothes.

"Tell me," he said, sidling up to me. "How did a woman from the northern tribes come into such wealth?" He eyed the bangles on my wrist and his eyes gleamed.

I bristled at his words, obvious with his tone that he thought the people of the northern tribes were below him. I thought of my beautiful mother, and her tales of growing up in the north as she braided my hair beside the hearth.

"Well," I kept my voice light, though I could hear the tight anger behind my words. "There *are* plenty of resources in the north, and plenty of wealth." I gritted my teeth. "But that is not how my family is wealthy . . ." I made a show of looking over my shoulder at his friends and moving closer to him, dropping my voice to a whisper. He lowered his head to catch my words.

"Oh, saab, I shouldn't say." I looked to either side and waited until his friends had moved closer to the swans on the other side of the pond. "I wouldn't want anyone to get the wrong idea. You know. It isn't exactly . . . *legal.*"

His eyes widened in interest.

"But, sahiba, you can trust me. I would never tell a soul." His voice was slimy and coaxing, and I could sense the excitement he was attempting to hide.

I gave him a relieved smile and clutched at the gold filigree necklace resting on my chest. His eyes followed my hands there, and he gave a calculated look, tabulating how much it cost.

"That is good to know. You've been so helpful, especially in dealing with Casildo."

"I do what I can with the ruffians in this city." He spat on the ground and ran his tongue along his teeth.

"And I am *so* grateful." I stepped over his glob of saliva on the ground. "But I actually need more help. I'd like to move a . . . certain *product* without detection. An *illegal* product."

His eyes sharpened on me, fierce with anticipation. "I can help with that, sahiba."

I pulled back and shook my head. "No, no. I shouldn't involve you." I bit my lip. "It would be incredibly lucrative, but I can't ask you to do something that might risk your position."

"I don't mind a little risk now and then," he said greedily, then seemed to catch himself. "Not when helping a newcomer to our city, I mean."

I smiled, letting my teeth show.

He dipped his head close, as if we were confidants. Raw onion and stale sweat filled my nostrils, and I put a hand over my nose to block the smell.

"What can I help with, sahiba?"

"It's not something I should be sharing here." My eyes darted around. The garden was fairly empty now, with people leaving the heat of the outdoors and retreating into the cool house.

Darbaran's friends were now being chased around the garden by the swans who had finally had enough of their teasing. Servants were scattered about the grass attempting to corral the birds to no avail.

"I've come into possession of a significant amount of a controlled *resource . . .*" I deliberately let my voice trail. "One that only the *emperor* usually has access to. And I need a way to sell it, quickly. I had a previous buyer, but that avenue has since dried up." I clasped my hands together in an attempt to look earnest.

Darbaran stared at me, his mouth slightly ajar, and I could see the wheels in his tiny brain turning. "You mean . . ." He couldn't even form the words.

"Yes," I breathed, pressing a hand to my chest. "That's exactly what I mean."

A strange light entered his eyes. "How much do you have?" He whispered the question, as if he wasn't sure if he could still speak.

I bit my bottom lip, dragging out the suspense. "A considerable amount." I paused. "Certainly more than I can move by myself."

"You realize what this means?" His voice rose with excitement. "The emperor has completely eliminated any leaks in his production. It would be worth more than we can even imagine." His gaze was pinned to the middle distance, greed lacing his voice like rose syrup, already counting the money he'd get from selling zoraat.

I looked up at him with a hopeful expression. "You can help me, then?"

His gaze turned sly, a dark smile edging the corner of his mouth. "Sahiba, it would be my honor." He placed a palm across his chest. "However, this would be a great personal risk to myself. It will be expensive, especially to be so discreet."

"Of course. Whatever it costs, I will pay it."

Those words had him practically vibrating. "I will also have to take a percentage of the profits. I'm sure you understand," he said smoothly.

I made my eyes go wide. "Of course, Captain. I would absolutely insist."

"Then we are agreed." Darbaran held out his hand. For a second, I thought about ignoring it, so I didn't have to touch him.

I thought back to when I was being arrested, and he had put his hands all over me, dragging me through the halls of the palace after Maz turned his back. I thought of the look on Darbaran's face as he grabbed me, more roughly than he needed to, and how he had thrown me into the holding cell in the palace dungeon before I was transported to the prison.

Bile rose in my throat as I took his fingers in mine and gave his damp, sticky hand a quick shake.

"I'll have my servant, Noor, contact you about next steps." I pulled away from him, resisting the urge to wipe my hand off against the side of my frock. "I should have a shipment ready for you shortly, if you can line up a buyer?"

"Oh, I will have plenty of interest in this, sahiba," he said, his voice bubbling with glee.

I headed back to the house, but a movement near the banyan tree caught my eye.

Someone faded into the shadows the moment I turned, but not before I saw the barest hint of a black-and-gold sherwani.

Thirty

Before

"I told you to leave me alone. I have nothing to say to you." Anam's voice cut through the stillness of the palace, and I paused at the vehemence of her words. I had no idea who she was speaking to, but I knew it wasn't anyone I was going to like.

"What are you going to do?" the voice replied with a sneer. "Tell your brother?"

I frowned from my plush seat on the verandah, hidden behind the door. I tried to place the man's voice. It was nasal, like a whine, and out of pitch, if someone's speaking voice could be out of pitch.

"Of course not," Anam shot back. "I know how to take care of you myself."

I smiled, pride filling my chest as she stood her ground. But I wasn't about to let her deal with this man on her own.

I came around the door to find a pinched-faced young man with his hand gripping Anam's wrist. He was wearing the same dark sherwani as the palace guards, but he had a golden sash slung over one shoulder. I tried to remember what that sash meant, but my thoughts were clouded by a flash of anger at him grabbing her.

"Did you lose the dagger I gave you, Anam?" I said loudly, my fingers hovering over the talwar sheathed at my hip.

They both jumped and the young man whirled on me.

Anam used his distraction and wrenched her arm from his grasp. A red imprint from his fingers stood stark against her skin. I narrowed my eyes and took a step forward.

"Well?" I inclined my head.

Anam stared at me, seeming to remember I had asked a question. "I . . . No. I didn't lose it." She took a hurried step toward me.

"Then why does this man still have his eyes?" I turned my gaze to him and smiled.

Anam blurted out a laugh, but the mongoose-faced man stared at me.

"Who are you?" He curled his lip and looked me over, his gaze stopping on my plain kameez, then at my hand resting on the knife at my hip. "This conversation does not concern you. And how were you allowed to bring a sword into the palace?"

"I am the daughter of the emperor's weapons master." I crossed my arms. "*Who* are *you*?"

"This is Darbaran, he's the new captain of the palace guards." Anam moved closer to me. I didn't miss the hurt way she wrapped her arms around herself, the delicate patterned embroidery on her kameez pulling tightly.

I looked him up and down, taking in the sneering boy who was trying to make Anam do something she didn't want to. "*This* weasel?"

"Dani!" Anam reached up, covering her laugh with a hand.

The weasel turned bright red. "If you keep talking to me like that, I'll have you arrested," he sputtered, reaching for his sword.

"You won't even get a chance to unsheathe your scimitar before I've sliced your hand off."

I turned away from him.

Never expose your back to an attacker. I could hear Baba's voice, but I ignored it.

The sound of metal pulling from its sheath sent a rush of excitement up my spine. If Darbaran attacked, he'd regret it quickly.

"Darbaran, I don't think you should do that," Anam pleaded.

"It's okay, Anam, maybe we should let him try."

"Who do you think you are?" he spat.

I glanced at him over my shoulder.

"I already told you who I am. If you don't know, that's your down-fall." I pulled the talwar from its home. "It won't take much effort to cut you down."

"You do, and the emperor will have your head."

I shrugged. "I'd gladly give my head for a good cause. And it seems like ridding you from the world would be a fantastic benefit to everyone."

"Darbaran, just go," Anam said, her voice low. Then she put her hand on my arm. "Leave him. He's not worth it."

Darbaran's beady eyes slid to her and then back to me, and for a moment we just stared at each other with steel in our hands.

"I'll leave," he said finally, sliding his scimitar back. "But not because you've avoided punishment. It's because I have other duties to attend to. Don't think I've forgotten this."

I rolled my eyes.

"I, on the other hand, have already forgotten you before you've even left." I smiled sweetly, enjoying the way his face turned a mottled red before he marched through the doorway of the garden terrace and disappeared.

"You shouldn't have mocked him like that," Anam said quietly, coming to stand beside me. A shaft of sunlight lit her hair from behind, making a faint hint of red come out. Mazin had that same tint to his hair, and sometimes I found myself staring at the multitude of shades in the sunset. "He does have influence at the palace."

"Why?" I frowned, thinking he couldn't be much older than Maz. "He seems too young to be captain of the guard. What happened to Hassan?"

"Hassan was fired—Darbaran took his place. He's the son of a friend of the emperor—a prison warden. I think the emperor enjoys having people be in his pocket so he doesn't have to question their loyalty." Anam's voice was a whisper, and she bit the edge of her lip as if she couldn't believe she'd said those words herself.

I certainly couldn't believe she said them.

"Why, Anam, that's as close to treason as I've ever heard from you." I threw her a smile, knowing she knew my opinion of the emperor. Since Maz had confessed to me what Vahid did, my ire for Vahid had only increased.

I had never spoken to Anam about it and had no idea if she knew Emperor Vahid had killed her mother. I assumed Maz would tell her in time.

I walked back to my chair on the terrace and sat down. Anam settled beside me, and I stared at the mark on her arm that would be a bruise tomorrow. One that she might have to explain to her brother. She poured us some hibiscus tea and then took a long sip.

"But in all seriousness, where is that dagger I gave you? You shouldn't have to put up with boys like him."

She smiled and relief shot through me after seeing her fear when Darbaran had his hands on her.

"I didn't wear it today." She looked down at her silver suit, the blouse light and floaty with small mirrors embroidered in a floral pattern. Her straight trousers were threaded with dark blue beads in a similar pattern. "It didn't go with my outfit."

I stared at her. "A knife goes with *every* outfit."

"You only say that because you clearly pick your outfits based on your knives. Most people do it the other way around."

"I do not," I huffed, looking down at the rust-colored kameez my father insisted I wear for the palace. If I could get away with wearing my simple training kurta to the palace, I would. Especially because Maz and I usually ended up sparring in the training field with his friends anyway. The talwar I brought was one of Baba's most beautiful ones, with gleaming emeralds set in the handle. It offset the dark red of my outfit perfectly.

I frowned. "Hm. I guess I do match."

"You always do!" Anam collapsed against the divan.

"What was that about?" I made my voice serious. I didn't want to spook Anam if she wasn't ready to talk about whatever was happening between her and Darbaran. "Does Darbaran always talk to you like that?"

"Oh, that was nothing. Darbaran wanted me to join him in the gallery. But I told him I was meeting you for luncheon."

I watched her. "That wasn't the first time he tried to force you to do something you didn't want to do." I inclined my head. There was a familiarity in the way they dealt with each other.

"Yes, and next time I will have my dagger with me." She nodded, a little smile on her lips. "Don't worry so much about it."

"Should I be mentioning this to your brother?"

She sat up. "Absolutely not. He will just get even more impossible and protective than he already is. I won't be allowed to leave my room at this rate."

"Learn to defend yourself and you can prove you don't need any protection," I said reasonably. "Maz isn't the type to cage you in."

"He isn't, but he believes the same as you. I should learn to fight. But I'm not like the two of you, I have no interest in fighting."

"Yes, but do you have an interest in staying alive?" I took a sip of the tea and Anam grabbed one of the biscuits sprinkled with candied pistachio and took a large bite.

"Why should I, when you are nearby?" she said, speaking between mouthfuls.

"If he does anything else, tell me," I said firmly. "I don't like him."

"I promise, I'll tell you." She looked toward the garden, avoiding my eyes. "Just don't tell my brother what happened today."

"Tell me what?"

Maz walked onto the terrace wearing the same black sherwani as Darbaran, but it looked crisper, more refined. As if wrinkles and dust didn't dare land on him.

"About her taking up her training again," I said smoothly, meeting Anam's pleading gaze. I didn't make eye contact with Maz—he'd have been able to tell I was lying. "She's grown lax."

Mazin sighed. "She won't listen to me anymore." He looked at Anam with a stern expression. "We might not always have the protection of the palace, you know."

She gave a loud sigh. "You worry too much. No one can touch us behind these walls."

"I bet the king thought that too," I said, taking a sip of my tea.

"Yes, but he didn't have the power of the djinn."

I raised my glass to her. "True."

Anam crossed her arms and glared up at her brother. "What are you so worried about, anyway?"

"We can't always assume we will have this forever, Anam." He spread his hands out, gesturing at the palace. I knew they had come from a small village, and he told me about the poverty he had grown up with. Anam had been a baby when the emperor had taken them in and didn't remember.

"You can't depend on always having protection." His eyes looked haunted. I flexed my hand, nearly reaching for the hilt of my knife again. It made me want to stab someone, imagining what he went through when his parents died, knowing he was the only one who could look after his sister, realizing he had no choice but to depend on Vahid.

Maz lived as if any moment, his safety could be taken from him.

"I agree with your brother that you should go back to your training, but I disagree with him on one thing." I sidled up to Anam.

Maz cocked his head in my direction. "And what is that?" His voice was irritated, but I was glad it had replaced the bitterness.

I raised my glass and winked at Anam. "You can assume you will have me protecting your back forever."

Thirty-one

"Did he buy into it?" Noor's voice cut through the panic that had descended over me since I left the garden. Someone else had been there with Darbaran and me, and I didn't want to voice who I suspected it was.

Was it Mazin watching us? And how much had he heard?

We said goodbye to our final guest and I turned back to Noor. "I gave him exactly what he wanted. A chance to be richer than he ever thought possible. What do you think he did?"

Noor rubbed the back of her neck. "You told him the truth, then? That's a risky move."

"This entire business is risky. But we went into it knowing that."

I flopped down onto a divan filled with jewel-toned pillows and massaged my temples. It was all going to plan, but if Maz had overheard anything I'd said to Darbaran, we had him to deal with.

"You want to talk about it?"

Noor sat beside me and gave me a pointed stare.

"Talk about what?" I brushed an invisible piece of dust from the end of my blouse, determined to avoid the subject of Mazin for as long as I could.

Noor snorted. "Nice try, but you are definitely giving me the details right now."

I put my hands over my eyes and groaned. A pillow hit me in the head.

"Ow!" I sat up.

"Stop being dramatic, that didn't hurt. You kissed him." It was an accusation. One she had every right to make.

I had kissed him, it was part of the plan to kiss him.

But Noor and I both knew it wasn't part of the plan to kiss him like *that*. Not with his hands tangled in my hair, my arms around his neck, pressed against each other like we were about to combust.

He thinks you are someone else.

And that was the worst part. I couldn't wish away my feelings about him, they had been part of me for years. It was natural that they would come to the forefront when we were together. But I was hoping I could channel that, control it. But when he kissed me, he wasn't kissing Dania. He was kissing Sanaya and feeling those things for her.

I had forgotten that.

"Don't say it out loud, it makes it real." I grimaced into the pillow.

"I wasn't expecting to have to peel you two apart, that's for sure. But . . ." She paused as if considering. "This *is* what you wanted," reasoned Noor. "Isn't it?"

I exhaled heavily. "I thought so. But it's harder going through with it than I thought."

My hands instinctively curled into fists at my sides. It was much easier to hold a dagger, for my weapons to be blood and blades, not my lips, my thighs, my skin.

It was simpler to stab someone in the chest than lose my heart.

"You mean you can't coldly seduce your previous lover who betrayed you without any old feelings rearing their ugly head?" She crossed her arms.

"For once can you be serious?" I chewed on my lip. "I struggle with the idea that he wants someone else."

"Because when he's kissing you he thinks he's with someone else?"

"Yes."

Noor cleared her throat and leaned back against the wall. "You want me to be serious?"

I nodded.

"Then here I am, being serious. You still love him." She jabbed her finger in my direction and I stared at her outstretched hand.

The words sank into my gut. I had avoided admitting it but I could feel the truth, deep in my bones.

And still, denial choked my words. "You said it yourself—he betrayed me, had me arrested, left me to be tortured and to rot in prison." I broke off bitterly, scraping my hands over my face. "How could I still love someone like that? How foolish would I have to be?"

"It isn't so easy to turn feelings on and off, Dania."

"It was easy for him!" I lurched to my feet. My heart thundered in my ears and I wanted it to drown out Noor and her reasonableness.

"But you aren't Mazin. You aren't like him." Noor walked over to me. She placed her hands on my shoulders and stopped my pacing. We stood there for a minute, rooted to the floor. "You aren't a cold-hearted beast."

"Aren't I?" I laughed, a bitter sound, the rough scrape of a sword against stone. "I will become one." My words were low. A soft whisper followed them, like an echo, but an entirely different voice to mine.

Yes.

"Did you hear that?" I looked over my shoulder toward the empty hallway.

"Hear what?" Her forehead creased, looking in the same direction before turning back to me. She shook her head. "I like Mazin's sister. Are you still going to destroy her too?"

I tore my gaze away from the dark corridor and back to Noor. That voice sank into my skin with dread, the same one I'd heard in Souma's cave. But Noor never heard a thing.

Maybe I was losing my mind after all. Noor stared at me expectantly, and I realized she was waiting for my answer to her question.

"Maz didn't care about my family when he took them from me."

"The girl is innocent."

"So was I," I hissed. My face was hot with emotion. "I shouldn't have to justify myself to you. You of all people should understand."

Noor swallowed, and I could see her jaw working.

I narrowed my eyes. "Just say it, I know you want to."

"You can't just extinguish your feelings, Dania. You aren't like that. You'll end up hurting yourself more than you know."

I laughed. "You think I care what happens to me after this?" I could feel something black and dark entering my chest, as if I were being taken over by my hatred, and it wasn't me talking, but my revenge.

"I am a tool of vengeance now," I uttered. "I exist to destroy those who came for me and my family." I could feel my fingers tingling, a similar feeling to the one I got before lifting my sword for the first time in battle. That's what this feeling must be—battle lust.

Why else would my blood feel like it was on fire? Why else did I want to scream until I was hoarse?

If Noor thought I couldn't turn my feelings off, fine. But I could turn them into something else. Something I was good at.

Noor stepped back from me, shock painted on her face. "Dania, your eyes . . ."

"What?" I reached up to my face, confused.

"I . . . nothing, it must have been the light. I thought I saw . . . never mind. But you don't mean what you are saying—you can start a new life, after this is done."

I whirled away from her, the anger beating in my chest now directed at Noor.

"A new life would mean nothing if they were still living. If I knew they had gone unpunished."

"Dani, have you seen Mazin? He does not look as if he's gone unpunished."

That brought me up short. "What do you mean?"

"Does he look well to you?" She rubbed her chin. "I have no reference for what he looked like before, but *now*? Now he looks *haunted*."

I had noticed the change in him, but hadn't dwelled on it. If it was guilt that ate him up inside, then at least he had some sort of conscience. But it didn't excuse what he did.

"His eyes are shadowed," she continued, throwing her arms up in the air, and started pacing too. "He doesn't go anywhere or do anything. His entire world is running Basral, commanding the emperor's soldiers, helping rule the empire with an iron fist. He doesn't dream. He exacts. He's obsessive and focused and has clearly dived off a fucking cliff after you left. He regrets what he did to you."

"I hope he regrets it. He's going to regret so much more before this is done. I'm going to take away the last bit of happiness he has."

Noor examined me. "So, you're determined to go through with this?"

"Have I given you cause to think otherwise?"

She wet her lips, considering. "I don't know. Something . . . something in the way you were with Mazin tonight." She looked away, out the window, toward the palace. "It made me think you might be changing your mind."

My mouth popped open involuntarily. "Have you changed your mind?" The words fell in the room like a stone.

She looked back at me, her reddish-brown eyes glistening. "I haven't. But I'm worried about you."

I tried to rein in the anger pounding against my chest. Because it wasn't Noor I was mad at, I was absolutely furious with myself.

Noor wasn't wrong.

Not that I was about to change my mind, but I could feel myself softening toward Mazin. When he touched me, I couldn't keep my feelings separate from my hate. It was as if I were forgiving him for what he did.

I clenched my fists so hard my nails bit into my palms.

He would never be forgiven.

I crossed my arms. "I'm not changing my mind. And there's nothing to be worried about."

Noor nodded, though her eyes were still shadowed.

"Mazin's own actions caused this," I continued. "Not mine. His sister's fate will be on *his* hands. They are already bloody."

Noor nodded. "And Darbaran?"

I snorted. I hadn't even thought about Darbaran during this conversation. "He'll be so far into this he won't know what hit him until he's in prison."

"A fitting place for him," she answered.

"Perhaps they'll even put him in my old cell."

Noor smirked. "We can only hope." She walked to the window and set her hands against the sill. "I'll set the plans with Darbaran in motion. In the meantime, we have other things to worry about. More than Mazin. More than Darbaran." She looked over her shoulder at me. "There is someone who is a little too comfortable in all this."

I tilted my head. "Vahid."

I hadn't forgotten that Noor was here for revenge too.

"He won't be." I shook my head. "We're going to set his empire on fire."

Noor nodded tightly. "I've prepared the zoraat blend. The emperor won't even be able to use his own zoraat supplies to combat this blight. We can be ready as soon as we like."

It was an abrupt change of subject, but we both needed it. It was late, the early light of dawn creeping over the house and filtering slowly through the windows. "And the land we purchased?"

"It's ready too."

"I don't want the people in this city to suffer if they don't have to. I want them to see that the blight is only related to Vahid. All our crops will be more than enough to feed the city. But we'll hold off for now."

"What will you do in the meantime?"

I inhaled, lining all the pieces of my plan up in my head. "I have an appointment with some thieves."

Thirty-two

"How many can you get?" I cracked my knuckles, finding familiar comfort in pressing my hands together. Because now I was standing in tepid wastewater, rats scurrying past my feet, with a face that wasn't mine asking a child if he could wrangle other pickpockets to do my bidding.

"As many as you need, sahiba." Yashem picked at his teeth as if he was barely paying attention to what I was saying, but I knew he was taking in every single word. His green eyes were pale in the darkness, and his face surprisingly clean considering the last few times I'd seen him he'd had dirt-streaked cheeks and artfully placed bruises to look more pathetic. Now he looked like a tidy young boy, not the usual bedraggled street urchin.

I scanned the alley, checking to make sure he was alone. If Mazin heard what I'd said to Darbaran in the garden he might be monitoring my movements even now—but this was a message that needed to come from me.

"I have thieves in all four quadrants and eyes and ears from every single tribal state. There isn't much we can't provide, information, persuasion, *anything*."

He said that last part with a gleam in his eye, as if he knew I had come to him with something outside of the norm. But he didn't know how far I was prepared to go.

"And the hawk?" I said, letting Mazin's nickname roll off my tongue. "Do you still fear him?"

He inclined his head, considering. "I'd be a fool not to, sahiba. He pays just as well as he punishes, so there are always those willing to work for him. But you have something he does not."

"More money?"

The boy's grin was a flash in the dark. "If it were about money, sahiba, you would have been caught long ago. The hawk is willing to pay significantly for information about who snatched his sister."

I snorted. "If you turned me in, you'd have to turn yourself in." But something in his words caught my curiosity. "What else do I have?"

"You aren't working with the emperor. Vahid has starved this city with his greed, and there are many who want to see his rule fall."

"Well, I can help with that," I drawled, my voice steady, despite the blackness opening up in my gut. With Casildo it had been a little too easy—like a trial run for the rest of them. But now, I was starting down the path of destroying an empire. And if it didn't work, I could take all these people down with me—Noor, the pickpockets, the citizens of a city willing to revolt against an emperor for freedom, not knowing they'd be doing it to service my revenge.

"I need the whole city." My words fell in the stillness of the alley, taking up the rest of the space between us.

Yashem's eyes widened. I felt oddly satisfied at his surprise, to see someone as jaded as the young thief taken aback.

"I've got your attention." I leaned against the wall behind me, taking in the hint of fear in his eyes.

"Can you do it?" My tone indicated I didn't believe he could, but it was his arrogance that made him take the job in the first place. I needed him on board for the next steps too.

Yashem opened his mouth to speak, and then clamped it shut, his eyes narrowing. "What is this about?"

I swallowed, the lump in my throat becoming impossible to ignore. "Does it matter? I just need to know if you can do it. If you can control the city."

"You want to know if *you* can control the city, isn't that it? If *you* can command the people, manipulate them with a whisper in their ear and a coin in their pocket instead of those who possess the might of the djinn."

"Yes." I gritted my teeth.

He toyed with the cuff of his kurta. I waited, watching him.

"It's gonna cost."

"I can pay it," I said immediately, then chastised myself for responding too quickly.

His eyebrows rose. "You can pay enough for the whole city?" he scoffed. "Enough to pay off every pickpocket from here to the palace? Enough to incite a riot?"

I crossed my arms over my chest, unbothered by the fact that Souma's gold might be gone at the end of this, but what use did I have with money except to avenge my father?

"That's exactly what I can do."

He chewed on his lip for a moment, then shook his head. "It will take more than just suggestion. You'll need a reason to drive the mob. Something to incense them in the first place."

"We'll have that. I just need you to help spread the unease, to talk to the gossiping aunties in Basral about the cursed rule of Vahid and infiltrate the minds of the common people."

"We can do anything, sahiba, if the money is right."

I nodded, a sense of calm washing over me. "Then wait for my signal."

———

Noor stood at the edge of a lush field in the dawn light, her cropped curly hair in stark contrast to the fields of yellow behind her. "How long do we have?"

"There aren't many guards around the city crops, they mainly guard the cultivation of zoraat. Here, they just watch to make sure no one is stealing from the emperor's farmers. We have a little time before the next rotation comes through."

"Then we'd best get to work."

Noor pulled out a vial from her pocket, this time the blend a deep green instead of the mixture of the burnished red I'd been consuming to change my body. My stomach flipped with the anticipation of another dose, the insane urge to snatch it out of her hands nearly overcoming me. Instead, I tried to breathe through my nose to control myself.

"If you are worried about the pain, this won't be as potent as the one you've been taking," Noor said, misinterpreting my expression. It wasn't pain I was worried about, but the inability to not be a slave to the zoraat filling my body.

"It doesn't matter, it must be done." I bit my bottom lip so hard I tasted blood. "There isn't as much of it this time."

"It's a more basic mixture than what you've been taking. We only need it for one job after all, and not to transfigure a human body, so the magic is less complex. You shouldn't feel a thing."

I opened the vial and downed the blend in one, that familiar burn pricking my throat. But Noor was right, it didn't have the same piercing pain accompanying it. This time, it was just a frisson of energy to signify the djinn power had taken hold. There was a burst of power in my blood and I stared at the field before me.

Noor began explaining, gesturing to the fields in the distance. "Usually when we dealt with crop magic, we had the wielder—"

"I know what I need to do." The answer was thrumming through me, whispering in my ear, telling me what the next steps were without any prior knowledge.

The dawn rays glowed brighter as the sun rose, and Noor fell silent, waiting.

When I had transfigured my face, I concentrated on pushing the djinn power there, reforming my bones and skin and cartilage like clay under my fingers. That's what Noor taught me, that's what it took to transform a body into someone else.

But with the earth it was different. The soft dirt beneath my hands was like a deeper, pulsing life force. Something older and stronger than myself.

I extended the djinn's power into the dirt, like I was lighting a fire from below, and unleashing its molten core to the surface. My hands were hot, and there was a tugging sensation from under my skin as I poured the djinn magic into the ground. There was a rumbling sound, as if the earth had quaked. I felt the vibrant root system of the plants, healthy and pliant under the nurturing of djinn magic. They spoke to me as if they recognized me, my power descending past the surface and taking hold of them.

Too late they realized that I wasn't there to provide nourishment.

The roots screamed against the energy I was pumping into the soil and I felt the tips of them begin to shrivel and burn against my onslaught.

"I can already see the difference." Noor's quiet voice cut through my connection. I looked up, seeing the plants had already blanched, their life burned away.

A pit formed in my stomach, the certainty that soon the entire field would be turned to ash.

The guilt continued as tendrils of discoloration began to spread to the other nearby fields, the green leaching of color like someone bleeding out after they've been stabbed. Noor's gasp echoed across the now pale field.

I followed her gaze and watched as the blight traveled farther, to the fields beyond. As if I had poisoned the entire earth.

A bead of sweat formed at my temple, and I pressed my hands to my sides to still their shaking.

I had done this. I had taken away a food source for an entire city and done it all to foster a revolt against an emperor.

My mouth tasted like ash.

"They'll blame Vahid for this blight. They'll have to. No one has entire crops die on them overnight."

Noor sucked in a breath. "They'll say he's no longer favored by the djinn, but cursed."

I looked out over the fields, now a wasteland of shriveled plants.

"I'm counting on it." My voice was low, a promise.

"What are you doing?" A gruff voice cut between us, and we both whirled at the sound.

A large guard was heading our way, his uniform worn but tidy, his forehead creased in concern.

Noor leapt forward, her head bent in deference. "Saab, we were just out for a walk and got a little lost."

I bowed as well, skirting to the side of him, my hand on the hilt of my sword at my side.

The guard frowned, his eyes flicking between our dark cloaks and placid faces. I knew what he was seeing—we were in clothing too fine to be thieves and had manners too polite to be vandals.

He scratched the back of his head, his eyes narrowing on us. "I'm going to have to report this—"

The butt of my sword smacked the side of his head so hard he fell to the earth like a stone.

"I'm impressed, you didn't try to kill him." Noor put her hands on her hips as she surveyed the guard lying prone on the ground.

"Why get my hands bloody when we can make him look like a drunk instead?" I rifled through the pack that hung from his belt and pulled out a flask of beer. I doused him in it, throwing it on the ground beside him.

I crossed my arms over my chest and looked over the guard. "I'll spread the news that the emperor's fields have gone fallow. Then the panic will come."

Noor watched me with a grim face.

She didn't look like a woman who was getting revenge, more like one who had lost everything and was trying desperately to hold on. But then, maybe I did too.

I wasn't sure what either of us would be once this was all over.

Happy? Satisfied?

I couldn't fathom ever feeling either of those things right now, not with this dark hole in my chest where my heart once was.

But the only thing that kept me going was this drive, this physical need in my gut that couldn't leave them alone, that couldn't let them get away with what they'd done.

"Noor, let's burn his city down."

Thirty-three

Darbaran was cloaked in darkness, waiting by the edge of the wide river that wound itself through Basral. He was alone, without any city guards with him.

I shouldn't have been surprised, but a part of me was. He sank into my plan perfectly, like a fat stone thrown into a lake. He could have tried to turn me in—Noor and I had a contingency for that—but he was here to satisfy his greed, the one thing he couldn't resist.

"I see you are a man of your word, Captain." I let my voice bleed into the night, a soft hush, luring him in further.

"Of course. Do you have the goods?" His tongue ran across his teeth, and he flashed an unsettling grin.

Noor threw the canvas bag of zoraat at his feet. The top of it opened to reveal the small djinn seeds, glistening like multicolored stones in the torchlight. He bent down and picked up the bag, his fingers shaking.

Darbaran huffed out a laugh that was whisper soft. "Yes, yes," he said, mostly to himself. He licked his lips, then looked up at us. "I can get a pretty penny for these, sahiba. Just wait and see." His eyes gleamed as bright as the seeds in his hands.

254 ◆ Emily Varga

"I don't know what I would have done without you, Captain." I made my voice breathless. "If I obtain more, can you sell those too?"

He tried to smother his surprise but was unsuccessful. A dark giddy feeling built in my chest.

"Of course," he responded, a little too fast. "But how will you get more?" He pressed the bag of zoraat to his chest.

I gave a little laugh. "I can't give away all my secrets, can I, Captain?"

He looked faintly annoyed.

He would find out very quickly where I got these from.

"Who will you sell it to?" Noor asked, probing gently.

"I know some nobles who will pay handsomely for access to this kind of power." He patted the bag. "But don't concern yourself with that." He returned his gaze to me. "It will get sold faster than you can blink." His cruel laugh cut through the night air. "I already have buyers lined up."

I smiled, and it felt feral. *I'm sure you do.*

"Then you are my savior, Captain." I looked down, making myself smaller. Let him think he was in control here. It would be him rotting in prison before long.

I waited until he had put the zoraat in his saddlebag and rode away. Relief filled me as he disappeared down the dark cobbled street with the illegal djinn magic strapped to his horse.

Now. Now he would know the meaning of what he had done to me. *Revenge.*

I took a surprised step forward, squinting at the darkened street. I'd heard it again, that whispered voice, the same one from Souma's tomb, and again at the town house. The voice that was in the still parts of my brain when all was quiet, that seemed to thrum under my fingertips when I drank my morning tea or took my daily dose of zoraat. My hands curled into fists involuntarily, that familiar darkness seeping into my skin once more.

"Did you hear that?" I narrowed my eyes at the alley, then whirled on Noor. "That voice?"

Noor squinted in the direction I had been looking and came to stand beside me. "No, I didn't hear any voice. Shall I go check it out?"

I shook my head. "No, no. I think I'm just hearing things."

Noor examined my face closely. "Your eyes seem . . . different. Maybe I should tweak your dose." She grabbed my chin and tilted my head toward the torchlight.

I pulled away.

"I'm fine. I just want to focus on our plans."

Noor looked as if she was about to say something, but thought better of it.

"You know what to do?" I tried to change the subject, but I couldn't stop looking at the street where the voice came from.

"It's already in motion," she replied. "Though I must say, he was easier to deal with than Casildo."

"I told you, he just needed the right incentive. Greed is his motivator. He wants to be rich. But more than that, he wants power over those weaker than him."

I breathed, pushing that unsettling voice from my mind and thinking of how satisfying it would be when Darbaran was finally thrown into the same prison as I was.

"Too bad where he's going, he won't have any power at all."

———

I stirred my chai, sitting on the divan and waiting for Noor to come back. When the door creaked open, I turned.

"Is it done?" I held my breath.

"Yes." She nodded. "They picked Darbaran up this morning. Along with the stolen zoraat lifted from one of the emperor's healers a few days ago."

I closed my eyes and exhaled slowly. I mentally crossed off another name on the list.

Just two more.

Two more and I could be done with this. An ache settled on my shoulders, like one more burden had been lifted from them, leaving only the pain of the impression behind.

Two more names and I could open the floodgates locked around my heart and allow myself to grieve for Baba. For the life I was meant to have.

I looked up at her. "Do you know what they intend to do with him?"

Noor shrugged. "Ship him off to the same prison we— Did you hear that?" Noor turned her head sharply toward the open courtyard door leading to the garden beyond.

I sat up, reaching for my dagger.

A thud sounded outside, followed by a shout that was abruptly silenced. I slid my katar from its sheath before I stood, my pounding heart echoing in the otherwise silent house.

"How many guards do we have out there?" I hissed at Noor.

She moved closer to me, her eyes wide, her hand gripping her kameez at her chest. "At least four."

"Not enough," I muttered. The zoraat was safe, at least, not any intruder could just break in and find it. But if someone wanted to rob us, they needed to make an effort to overcome the security in this place. But then they would be left to me.

I moved to the open door, creeping into the courtyard as quietly as I could, my bare steps a whisper across the stone floor.

But I wasn't fast enough.

A blade kissed my neck, surprisingly steady considering the hand that held it.

I turned my head as Darbaran's stale breath puffed out and he moved out of the darkness. His twisted face was illuminated by the torches lighting the room.

Noor let out a strangled scream, but I held up a hand. I still held my dagger in the other, and I wasn't sure how deft Darbaran was with a sword. If he had taken me by surprise now, then he could move as quick as I and I didn't want to risk using my dagger when his sword was pressed against my leaping pulse.

"Bitch." His fowl stench wafted, the pungent odor of sewer water and sweat, with a slightly metallic, familiar tinge underneath.

I pushed past my panic and focused on that metallic smell. My eyes scanned his body in the dark, trying to find its source.

There.

A dark red stain spreading across his abdomen like spilled paint. He was injured. It was deep.

I smiled.

"Darbaran," I drawled, my voice like rose petal honey. "I wasn't expecting you back so soon. Did you sell the product already?"

"The product you *stole,* you mean," he growled, his whole body reverberating with anger. "Then framed me for the theft and tipped off the emperor's soldiers." He coughed, a wet, squelching sound. "Good thing I knew a few people to bribe."

I cocked my head. "You didn't know the right people, if you came out of it with a wound like that." I looked pointedly in the direction of his stomach. "It's deep." My voice lost its false charm, instead becoming what I felt inside—cold, fierce.

He laughed, his teeth smeared black with blood. Then his face grew serious.

"Why?" he snarled, stepping forward into the light, pressing his scimitar harder into the soft curve of my neck. Noor moved in my periphery, creeping closer in our direction, but I shook my head almost imperceptibly. Darbaran could slit my throat in a moment, and then she'd have to fend against him on her own. And Noor was no good with a weapon.

We needed to do this my way.

"Why what?" I arched a brow.

He pushed closer and my flesh gave way beneath the sharp sting of his blade. I let out a hiss of pain as a thin trickle of warmth beaded toward my chest.

"You know exactly what I'm talking about." His voice grew louder, and I could hear the desperation in his words. He was cornered now, a mongoose in a trap, and I the jackal.

"Why did you set me up?" he bit off. "It was too organized. Too specific. You weren't trying to make money off this, you were out to get me specifically. Why?" His beady eyes were bloodshot and wild, and they were hyperfocused on me. He leaned closer.

"What did I do to you? Tell me before I spill your blood all over your pretty floor."

His blade was already stained red, and my neck burned with the proof of it. My eyes flicked to the courtyard where the prone body of a slain guard lay. So, that had been the noise we heard earlier. I brought my eyes back to Darbaran.

I'd compensate the guard's family, but a life was still taken.

A life that wouldn't be gone if it weren't for me.

I was sick of people like Darbaran who thought they could do whatever they wanted, kill and use and imprison whoever they wanted while they got rich in the process. That darkness rose up inside me again, the rage building until the edges of my vision blackened and a beast in my chest took hold.

Not a hawk, not a jackal, but a halmasti, the giant wolf hunting on the edge of the mountains. Rage made me confident, and I suddenly wanted Darbaran to *know* it was me, not this lacquered, pretty mask. But the real me, the girl he had condemned to a life of prison, torture, even death, all for coins.

I felt for the thread of djinn magic that had transformed me. I felt for it, and I pulled it *back*.

My nose, my eyes, the bones in my cheeks—I took everything away that was Sanaya until it was *my* face.

Until I fit in my own skin again.

Dania, daughter of the slain weapons master.

Dania, forsaken by her best friend.

Dania, looking at one of her betrayers.

"You want to know *why*?" I spat the question coming from my own voice this time, deep and certain.

Darbaran shrank away from me, his eyes wide, lips parted. He stumbled back, lifting his sword from my neck and clutching the blade in shock.

"*You.*"

"Me."

I kept walking forward, and he fumbled, falling over his feet until he was on his backside looking up at me.

"I'll tell you why." My voice was soft, the hiss of a blade cutting through the night air. "Because you had a choice. You chose to betray me, to sell a girl for money, to frame her for gain. And so, I chose this." I lifted the glistening dagger in the torchlight of the garden, where the guards I had hired lay dead. Anger burst inside of me. But there was something else there too, savage, elemental.

The power of knowing this was righteous anger.

A history of women and girls being wronged by men who never had any consequences.

Now I would be the consequences.

"I choose vengeance. I choose death. And in the end, that's what you chose too."

Darbaran lurched up, swinging his sword in the air, but I dodged the strokes of his blade easily. He stumbled, the blood dripping steadily down his leg and across the parquet floor. He swirled around, running at me again.

"I knew they should have executed you when they had the chance, but that idiot boy wanted you alive."

I inhaled sharply but didn't have time to process his comment.

Darbaran charged at me, recklessness making him unpredictable. His sword missed me by inches. I struck his blade down with the edge of my dagger but couldn't get close enough with my knife to land a real hit given how wildly he was swinging.

I needed my sword.

I maneuvered myself toward the room behind me, spying my tal-war hanging on the wall over the divan. I dove for the doorway, but Darbaran cut me off with his sword raised above his head.

He wavered on his feet, looking as if a strong wind could blow him over.

He let out a howl, lurching forward. But before he could strike, he pitched facedown onto the stone walkway in front of me. I gaped at him as he lay on the ground, groaning.

Noor stood behind him, holding a large dahl pot in her hand.

Darbaran struggled to his feet with a grunt and whirled on her, his sword pointed in Noor's direction now. A roar sounded in my ears, drowning out everything, until I could only hear the faint sound of screaming.

And I realized that sound was coming from me.

I was too late. I would get there too late.

Noor would die.

"No!"

Darbaran rushed at Noor with his scimitar, and panic filled her face as she lost her footing.

I ran full speed at them, shoving Noor out of the way at the same time Darbaran's sword plunged toward her. Burning pain lit my body as his scimitar pierced my abdomen instead.

I looked down at the golden filigree hilt of the scimitar lodged in my stomach and realized this, too, was a blade made by my father. I raised my head, coming face-to-face with Darbaran and every inch of his triumphant smile.

Pain clenched in my heart—not just the pain of the curved blade impaling my body, but the denial of justice, the unfulfilled vengeance piling up inside my chest so that the pressure was too great to bear.

No. I clenched my teeth and stared at his smug, disgusting face.

No, it would be harder than this to best me.

My fingers clenched tightly over my father's katar dagger, the bite of the snake pattern on the hilt forming an impression on my scarred hand. Darbaran's face was so close to mine, close enough that I could make out the yellow threads in the whites of his eyes, the speckled pores in his nose. Close enough that I could watch the victory in his face twist into stunned agony when I sliced him across the throat with my knife.

His mouth dropped open and he tried to move it.

Once. Twice. Forming words with no sound.

But I had enough for the both of us.

"You were destined for this end," I whispered to him, his lifeless body dropping to the ground. I sank to my knees beside him, then fell to my side, my hands holding the hilt of my father's sword, the blade that had killed me.

Perhaps I was destined for this too.

Thirty-four

"You don't get to die yet." Noor's desperate voice filtered through the darkness. "You can't leave me in the middle of all this shit and expect me to dig my way out. Not today," she muttered, but I could feel fear behind the words. Fear that I shouldn't be able to recognize. Not when I was dead.

"You aren't dead. Not yet."

I must have said the words out loud, but when I tried to respond, a rough groan burst out instead.

Noor's voice echoed around me once more, but my insides were twisting together, burning, a river of lava running through me instead of my blood.

I howled, arching my back, the pain worse than the sword lodged in my body and piercing my intestines.

"I've made the best healing blend of zoraat I know. If this doesn't work, you're officially too stubborn to listen to anyone else."

"That's rich coming from you." I coughed the words out, my voice wet, my tongue tasting metallic.

Suddenly Noor's face snapped into focus, her features sharpening, her concerned gaze flooding my view. I blinked a few times and scowled at her.

She released a startled gasp and clasped her hands to her face. "It worked!"

I coughed and sat up. Noor helped me, pressing her hand to my stomach as if she were trying to feel for something. Belatedly, I realized there was nothing there.

Darbaran's scimitar was gone.

Why isn't it there?

Warmth trickled through my stomach, the feeling of djinn magic being used *on* me, instead of me using it myself.

I snapped my gaze to hers.

"You consumed zoraat? But what about your vow?"

Noor pursed her lips, her hands shaking against my stomach. "I couldn't just leave you to die in the courtyard, could I?" I didn't miss the catch in her voice.

I stared at her, an unfamiliar lightness filling my chest. "Yeah," I scratched out. "You could have."

She shook her head. "Well, I didn't. And you should be grateful."

I touched my stomach, prodding at the area that had just been a gaping hole. Now the skin was unbroken, not even a scar to speak of.

"It's completely gone," I said, my voice filled with wonder. I had seen djinn magic change the bones of my face, the skin on my body, but this seemed somehow bigger than that.

"I don't even feel pain anymore." I poked at my abdomen.

"Well, I can't promise you won't still get cramps on a monthly basis, but at least you aren't dying of a stomach wound anymore."

"All the djinn power in the world and it can't even get rid of cramps?" I propped myself up on my elbows feeling as if I'd aged a hundred years.

She smiled, but it faded just as quickly.

"I thought you were dead," she said finally, sitting back on her heels.

"*I* thought I was dead. And I thought you were about to die. You shouldn't have gotten involved. I was handling him."

She rolled her eyes. "Sure you were. Darbaran was about two seconds away from stabbing you *and* me. At least he only got one of us."

"You're welcome." I glanced over to his lifeless body on the courtyard, surrounded by a dark pool of blood. "How long was I out?"

"Not long, a couple minutes. I checked the guards too. He killed two of them, the other two were just knocked out."

I exhaled, a familiar pain lancing through my heart at the additional lives on my conscience. "Darbaran should have never gotten in."

"We'll double security." Noor thought for a minute. "And I'll dump his body in the fields outside of the city."

I snorted. "It's what he deserves." I stood up, my legs so shaky that Noor had to support me.

"You showed him your face." Her words were quiet. I lifted my hands to my face, touching features and skin and hair I hadn't felt in weeks. It felt good to be in my own body again.

"I wanted him to see who was responsible for his downfall."

Noor bit her lip.

I narrowed my eyes. "What is it?"

"Did you hear what he said about wanting you to be executed? But 'that boy' prevented it from happening? Do you think he was talking about Mazin?"

"Probably," I said, resigned. "I don't really know what he meant." I shrugged. "Mazin likely wanted me to suffer as much as possible."

I leaned back and looked up at the sky, bright with stars. I remembered other stars, on other nights, and the person I'd been looking up at them with had been him. Perhaps Mazin couldn't bring himself to have me killed after everything we had shared. Perhaps he wanted me imprisoned but not dead.

I shook myself. Nothing good would come of thinking that way. My father was still dead. And Mazin hadn't said a word to defend me when I was arrested.

It was the same as if he had killed me.

Noor looked as if she wanted to say something else.

"What is it?"

"Or . . ." She held up her hands at my expression. "Hear me out. Or he was saving your life."

I turned to look out the north window, the palace lit up in gold. I felt like I was being pulled in two—that raging, dark vengeance ready to light Basral on fire, and that other part of me that felt alive and free when Maz kissed me again.

But which half of me would win?

And which did I want to?

Thirty-five

If I thought the party at our town house was opulent, the emperor's put it to shame. There were street performers folding themselves into small boxes, tigers on golden leashes, and zoraat entertainers that pushed beyond the bounds of imagination.

I suppose when you held the key to a djinn power, you could imagine anything.

"I just watched a woman transform herself into a cobra and then eat a man she had just turned into a white-bellied rat. Who even *wants* to see that? I nearly threw up." Noor shuddered.

"The emperor and his cronies, apparently." I looked around distastefully.

Noor surveyed the room with a scowl, as if she could conjure the emperor with her eyes.

"Vahid likely won't reveal himself until later," I said with a low voice. "The emperor always did have a flair for the dramatic." The few times I'd seen him he was with my father, looking at his swords. I didn't understand why he even wanted to own swords in the first place if he held djinn power. He had told my father he liked the way it felt, to hold something not forged from magic but by human hands.

"I've never seen the effects of so much zoraat in one place." Noor swept her gaze over the crowd.

"The emperor controls the use of it, but he likes to show off. He likes everyone to know the power that only *he* has access to."

Noor raked her hands through her short hair. "Which is why he killed my father."

I pressed my hand to her upper arm. "Just remain calm. He doesn't know who you are, and he can't hurt you."

We both paused in horror as a man who had just consumed a vibrant yellow dose of zoraat split himself in half and then fused his body back together again.

"Oh, I think he can hurt me." Noor's was voice low and bitter as she watched it too. Sweat formed on the edge of Noor's brow and she shifted on her feet nervously. She looked terrified.

I grabbed her wrist and dragged her away from the performers. "Don't focus on that." I scanned my eyes over the crowd, checking Mazin wasn't nearby either.

"You telling me not to focus on all this is like saying to ignore the sun on a hot day. It's all around us." She waved her hands at the grotesque performances.

I huffed a breath. She was right. But I needed her headspace clear right now for what we needed to do next. "Vahid uses this to show his power. To assert his control. But we have one thing he doesn't."

"And what is that?"

I touched my hand to the dagger held in an opulent sheath at my waist, as if the weapon was used more for decoration than murder, beautiful, not dangerous. Exactly how I wanted to appear.

"Me."

Noor rolled her eyes and huffed out a laugh.

"Walk around. See if you hear anything about the rebellions or the crops we destroyed. We need to be able to plan our next steps."

Noor nodded and then faded into the crowd, purpose replacing the fear that had been on her face.

I watched her disappear before glancing down at my hands and jerking with a start. Curling tendrils of black spread up from my palms to the inner part of my wrist. And this time I wasn't imagining them. They were there, imprinted on my skin like dark ink stains. I pressed my fingers to my cheeks, feeling to make sure Sanaya's face was still there, that the djinn magic hadn't somehow worn off.

What was happening to me?

I searched for Noor in the crowd, but she was already gone.

She might no longer be afraid, but fear was now locked away in my heart, threatening to burst free and ruin us all.

———

I wove through the crowd, moving upstairs away from the zoraat performers and to where it was quieter. I needed to get my head on straight before the emperor came. A pair of black dress gloves were left on a banister, forgotten by a zoraat performer, and I shoved them on my hands to cover the dark veins. I walked over to an alcove hidden by a brocade curtain where I could figure out what was happening to me.

But a hand grabbed my arm and pulled me back.

I spun on my heels, my knife out of my sheath faster than I could breathe. A stark inhalation paused my blade.

"I thought you just liked to collect knives. Seems like you *do* know how to use them as well."

My stomach flipped as I met Mazin's dark, unreadable eyes. We watched each other for a moment, the tension between us thick, my dagger still pressed against his skin. Until his mouth quirked up in one corner. My shoulders relaxed, and I dropped my arm, resheathing my dagger.

"I know a few ways to protect myself," I said, forcing a smile in my voice.

"You think you need protection at the emperor's feast?" His mouth was still tilted in amusement and his eyes flitted away from me. He gestured at the guards standing against the nearby pillars, surrounding every inch of the palace. Luckily, they hadn't seen me pull a knife on the emperor's second, but Mazin didn't seem particularly bothered by that.

"It doesn't matter how much zoraat is here, the emperor still would not risk a single seed leaving the premises."

"Just because he protects his magic doesn't mean he'll protect the people inside," I said archly, realizing too late how I sounded—close to treasonous.

But Mazin didn't look aghast. Instead, he seemed to be assessing me—his eyes sweeping my form and coming to rest once again on my face. "That's very true."

I lifted my chin in surprise, but if Mazin noticed he didn't let on. Instead, he leaned against the rail, surveying the crowd below, his forearms braced against the wood.

I bit the edge of my lip. "I didn't expect you to agree."

He turned his head. "How can I not?" He smiled faintly, but it didn't reach his eyes. "I see how much value the emperor places on his magic. How obsessed he is with the cultivation of it." He gave a twist of his lips. "And it's grown worse this past year."

Goose bumps rose on my arms at how honest he was being with me.

"Worse?" I breathed the word out, not wanting to stop him from this thread of conversation.

"He's become a slave to his need for magic," Mazin said bitterly. He looked as if he were going to say more but thought better of it. Then his eyes softened. "But I do not wish to discuss him with you tonight."

I do.

I needed the conversation to stay on Vahid. If I could get Mazin to talk more, then perhaps he would reveal more of the emperor's secrets. "We are here at his behest, are we not? It seems fitting to discuss him."

"Even if we are insulting a man in his own home?"

I arched a brow. "Is it his?"

Mazin drew air sharply through his teeth and I felt a rush of exhilaration in my chest.

Even I knew that was too far. I had all but proclaimed Vahid a usurper.

"It's his home if you want to keep your head."

"I've always rather undervalued my head."

"But it's such a pretty one."

I gave him a sidelong glance, my heart flipping. But again, I had to remind myself, he wasn't talking about me, but another girl.

"Are you flirting with me about getting beheaded?"

His eyes lit up. "I can't think of anyone else who might even consider it flirting."

"And yet, after our kiss, I can't think of anything but."

We hadn't seen each other since we'd kissed, and I took a risk mentioning it. I flexed my fingers, stopping myself from reaching up and touching my lips, stopping myself from remembering his being pressed to mine.

Not mine. Sanaya's.

He straightened, an uneasy look flickering over his face.

Had I pushed too much?

"I think about it too," he admitted, as though he didn't want to.

I smiled inwardly. If he was thinking about Sanaya, then it was a step closer to having his heart. And I wanted it, badly. I wanted to feel it beating in my hand, to feel his love, his emotions, his trust, before I crushed them beneath my boot.

"And yet here we are, two people standing around, discussing execution, when we could be really doing what it is we both want."

His mouth dropped open and a surprised laugh came out, a throaty, deep sound that rumbled through his chest.

I closed my eyes, and for a second I was back where we used to be, in the training field, his laugh echoing through the mountains, warming the pit of my stomach like fire.

"You never cease to surprise me, Sanaya."

"At least I'm never boring."

"No. Never that." He huffed out another laugh and then looked at me again. "I have something to show you. Will you come with me?"

He held his hand out, and I stared down at it, the calluses as familiar as my own, the long fingers perfect for holding the hilt of a sword, or for interlacing between mine.

I placed my gloved hand in his and he clasped it tightly, like we were already lovers, like he was taking me to a clandestine meeting spot, like I wasn't going to deceive him as he did me.

Thirty-six

Before

"Dani, can I show you something?"

I looked up at Maz's earnest face, and then down at his outstretched hand, and scowled. "Is this a ploy to get me back after I trounced you in the training field?"

He laughed, and the sound was deeper than I remembered.

"I promise I take my losses fairly."

"Good, because you have so many of them." A rueful smile curled my lips.

"How long will your father be with the emperor?"

"Hours. The emperor likes to go over every aspect of the sword. I don't know why, it isn't as if Vahid uses them anymore."

"Maybe he wants to be sure he will be able to fight even if he doesn't have access to any djinn power?"

"Well, then he needs lessons in swordplay as well as having fancy blades," I retorted. Then I looked up at him. "What did you want to show me?"

He rubbed the back of his neck, suddenly looking sheepish.

"It's in my room."

I blinked at him. "Is this just an excuse to get me into your room?"

"What? No." He turned the deep shade of a plum, the flush

creeping up his neck. I was laughing, but at his reaction, my humor dimmed. Suddenly my friendly teasing made my own skin hot. I brushed the neckline of my kurta, as if I could dust off the uncomfortable feeling that I had hit close to a truth I hadn't wanted to admit.

We'd kissed.

We'd fallen asleep with his arms wrapped around me, his breath on my neck. Sometimes I thought I'd imagined it all. But then he'd look at me with dark eyes, or our fingers would brush and it would become real again.

"What, then?" I heard myself say.

"It's easier to show you."

In all the times I'd visited the palace and practiced with him in the training yard, he'd never taken me to his room. The dining hall, the private salon where we would sit with his sister, but never his bedchamber.

Not that going to his room would have been strange before, but now I couldn't help but feel the heat of his body as he walked in front of me leading the way, couldn't ignore the rush of excitement in my chest as we made our way up the stone steps.

He opened the door to a large area, larger than I had supposed, with a front room connected to a bedchamber and a verandah overlooking the city.

I whistled long as I surveyed the lavish surroundings. It certainly bested my little room.

"The emperor wanted to ensure his adopted children were well taken care of," he said a little ruefully. "Anam's room is down the hall."

I walked over to the verandah and surveyed the city below. It stretched out like a bloated dust storm, thick and heady in some places, and sparse and grimy at the edges.

"At least you have a good view," I said flatly.

Mazin cracked out a laugh as he sat on the edge of his bed, rifling through the drawers next to it, looking for something. "You hate the city."

"True." I bit my bottom lip, weighing my next words. "So do you," I said softly.

His head shot up, his expression wary. "I never told you that."

I shrugged. "You didn't have to. You always seem so confined here, like your jacket is buttoned too tightly and you can't take in air. You were like that when I first met you. But in our village, you are more relaxed. Like you take the stick out of your arse when you arrive and put it back in when you are with the emperor."

He angled his head. "I can't tell if you are complimenting me or not."

I snorted. "Neither can I."

I walked over to the divan and collapsed on the plush cushions.

"It's different in the village." His voice was quiet and low, and something made me look up, made me think twice about wrapping myself in the prickly humor that I always did when emotions were too close to the surface.

"There's not the sense that everyone is watching you, waiting to see what mistake you will make. And no one seems to care about bloodlines, or how my true parentage will come out in the end." He sighed and walked to the balcony. I watched him, tracing the line of his shoulders with my eyes as they fell with the relief of shedding whatever he had been carrying. "When I'm in your village, when we train, when I'm with you—I feel like the only thing I'm being measured on is my skill with a sword."

"You are," I said simply. "That's the only thing that matters."

He looked over at me. His dark hair was silhouetted against the deep orange of the sky, and his eyes seemed sad.

"Maz?" I sat up. "What's wrong?"

"It's like I said. You don't care about who my family was, I don't have to overcome something about myself that I can never change. With you, I feel like I can be myself."

Something in my heart cracked at the sound of his voice. "Why do you sound so miserable about it?"

He gave a tight laugh. "Because I've just realized that your village is where I feel the most free. The rest of the time I am here, and mostly trapped in this cage." He gestured his arms at the over-the-top bedchamber.

"It's certainly a gilded one, though."

"It is, at that."

I picked up a handful of pistachios from a bowl nearby and popped them into my mouth, unsure how to respond. What was our friendship now that we'd kissed, confessed our feelings, held each other in the darkness? If he was free with me, what did I feel when I was with him?

Did I feel the same as when I sparred with anyone else in the training field?

No.

I knew that for certain. With him, when we danced on the open sand, our swords flashing in the sun, it was like lightning across an empty desert. When our blades met, it was a sigh of relief.

He felt like my match.

I choked on a pistachio at the realization, hacking a cough into the pillow of the sofa. Maz came around in alarm and began pounding me on the back. "Dani? Are you all right?"

"I'm fine," I choked out, waving him away. I sat up when he offered me some cold hibiscus tea and drank it greedily.

You've never been a coward, Dania.

But now, I felt like I was. He'd given me something real, and I'd just eaten some nuts in response.

I lifted my head, my breath catching at how close he suddenly seemed. He leaned over me, his eyes shadowed. Heat crept up my neck, but I didn't tear my gaze away from his.

You've never been a coward.

"I feel the same, by the way," I blurted out, my words a croak in my throat.

"What? You feel like you are in a gilded cage too?" He laughed lightly, not meeting my eyes, and I recognized what he was doing.

Giving me an out.

We hadn't talked about our feelings since that night a few weeks ago that almost felt like a dream now. But he'd been by my side for years, and when he went away, I yearned for him. When I heard the sound of his stallion's hoofbeats against our village path my heart rejoiced.

I wasn't going to let his be the only confession today.

"With you I feel like I can be myself too," I said quietly. "I feel free."

His soft intake of breath echoed in the silence between us.

And then, because I wanted to prove that voice in my head wrong, because I wanted to overcome that niggling piece of fear that told me to doubt, told me to stop, told me to do anything but what I was about to do, I leaned forward and pressed my lips to his for the second time.

There was a beat of time in between my lips meeting his and his meeting mine back, and in that space, all the fear I held in my heart consumed me. What if he regretted what we did? What if, in the cold light of day, he wasn't interested anymore?

But then he kissed me back.

A hawk took flight in my chest, the power of its wings beating out of my skin and willing my whole body to soar.

He cupped my chin with his hands, the roughened calluses against my face making me lean in closer, devour him more ravenously, until we consumed each other.

I lay back on the sofa and he tumbled down with me, propping himself up on his elbows.

I unhooked the gold buttons lining his sherwani and peeled the coat from his broad shoulders. He then shrugged his tunic off.

I'd seen him shirtless before, especially after training when he washed himself off at the water basin beside the field. I'd always looked away, not wanting to be caught staring, not wanting anyone to notice the emotion flushing up my cheeks. But now, I had no cause not to stare.

"You're making me nervous. This is how you look right before you are about to stab me." He gave a small laugh.

"You know I never like to do anything halfway."

"Yes. It's disconcerting to have you put that focus on *me*."

I inhaled sharply. "Unwelcome?" I asked hesitantly.

"Never." One word, said with a vehemence that took my breath.

"I . . ." I didn't know how to have this conversation, but there was something I had to tell him, so I wet my lips and began again. "Sometimes I get bad cramps," I blurted out. "When it's my monthly time."

He stared at me. "Do you have them now?" he asked, confusion lacing his voice at my abrupt change of topic.

"No, I'm not . . ." I shook my head and took a deep breath. "I'm not explaining myself well. Afra Aunty gave me pakaal tea to ease them. I drink it regularly." I swallowed past the lump in my throat. "It's . . . normally used to prevent pregnancy."

"Ah." A flush crept up his neck as understanding dawned.

"Yes. Now excuse me while I go throw myself off your balcony."

He laughed, pressing me down to the divan when I attempted to get up. "No, don't do that. At least not before I've had my way with you."

I swatted at him, but my hand stayed on his chest. We both looked down at my fingers laid hesitantly against his skin. I ran them down, feeling the small scars littering his body, many of them from our fights.

"I've marked you," I said, wonder in my voice as I swept my fingers down to his navel. He sucked in a breath and I stopped my hand, my fingers curling into my palm.

Then his smile was slow and deliberate and I felt like I was about to combust. "Shall I tell you my favorite ones?"

He grabbed my hand, not waiting for me to respond, as if I could find my voice anyway. It felt like being at the edge of a storm, knowing the way forward was dangerous, but wanting to feel the cool rain on my face. He placed my palm against the side of his taut stomach, and I felt the raised skin there, like a hook.

"This one." His words were low. "Do you remember it?"

I tried to smile, but it was getting increasingly difficult to maintain light humor with the dark intensity of his eyes.

I don't even know how to forget.

"Of course. I'd just begun to train with scimitars."

"I thought I'd best you then, given I'd used mine so much more, but you swung your sword at the last moment, catching me in the side."

"I was beside myself," I blurted out. "I could hear your cry of pain in my nightmares for weeks. How can this be your favorite? The dirt turned red with your blood, I thought I had finally succeeded in killing you."

I felt the lift of his lips like they were against my own skin. "It was because of what happened afterward. You stitched me up, berating yourself the whole time, administering the salve with a touch so gentle I didn't know you were capable of it."

I swatted him on the arm and he leaned forward so his lips were inches from mine. "It was the most we'd ever touched outside of training, and I knew then I'd never be able to get you out of my skin. You marked me, but in more ways than one. I couldn't stop thinking about you, the way your hands felt. The apologetic smile when you applied the salve, the way your eyes grew dark when you concentrated on the stitching."

"What you are saying is that you liked it when I stabbed you." My laugh was a little breathless, my attempt at humor stuck in my chest. "Only I could find a boy who was as bloodthirsty as me."

He lifted my hand to his cheek, and I felt a long, ridged scar there, underneath the stubble along his jaw. "This one?" he asked, his voice as breathless as mine.

I swallowed. "The first time you beat me in an open fight. I'm sure this is your favorite."

He barked a laugh and it rumbled through him, making me

deeply aware that he was shirtless on top of me. "Not because I won that bout, but because of afterward. Do you remember?"

I thought back to last year when it happened. It had been at the palace this time; my father had been commissioned to outfit the royal guard with new weapons and he'd been summoned more often than usual. I met Maz at the training yard, the ground flush with green grass instead of worn dirt, the knives so polished I had ached to bloody them up. We fought, and Maz had used my own move against me—sliding his sword along the edge of mine and then flicking backward so I lost momentum. But not before I had slashed him with the broad sword, marring his victory just a little bit with a wound of my own. I thought back to what we had done after the fight and remembered the sugary taste of kulfi on my tongue, the ice cream dusted with almonds—a rare treat we never had in the village. But mostly, I remembered the feeling of laughter rumbling in my belly and throwing my finished kulfi stick at Mazin's face after he brought up winning against me for the millionth time.

"Afterward," I said, thinking as I processed the memory. "We ate kulfi in the grass, and you told me about your mother." I smiled, remembering Anam running around, grateful we were finally paying her attention. "Then we played lattoo with your sister until her spinning top broke."

He nodded. "Your father joined us and we had dinner at the palace."

I nodded, thinking about the small room we'd gone to, not a large palace dining room, but a warm, cozy space usually used by the servants. Maz had told me that he and Anam normally ate alone at the palace.

"The best stewed lamb I'd ever tasted."

"It was the perfect day."

I nodded in agreement. He lifted my hand to the center of his palm.

"This one?" he murmured against my wrist.

I inhaled, my heart pounding so hard it was all I could hear. A spidery scar sat on the inside of his hand like an engraving. "Our first fight." I breathed out slow to calm my jumping pulse.

"Sometimes I rub the center of my palm when I'm missing you."

I closed my eyes briefly.

Then I took his hand in mine, placing his fingers on the outside of my knuckles on my right hand. "This scar is from the talwar my father gave you. Before you went north with the emperor."

He gave a slow smile. "You were so angry I'd managed to lay a hand on you."

I arched a brow. "I vowed you never would again."

He placed his hands on either side of my face. "And now?"

"I'd gladly retract that."

His breathing changed, hitching in his chest, and I felt the deep sound reverberate through me. His lips captured mine again, and then he helped me out of my light kurta, both of us taking off the remainder of our clothes until it was just our skin and the marks of our past between us. We'd helped each other heal them, but it was more than the outside scars. We'd been two lonely people who had been given solace in each other. I knew what Maz meant when he went through all the memories we'd had together. We had become intertwined, we were part of each other, and with him, I felt at home.

I brushed his back as he moved against me, feeling the other scars laced across it, many of them from the ugly parts of his life, the ones I knew he didn't want to remember.

"Shall I mark you again?" I asked, my thighs around his hips, my lips against his. "Shall I make you mine?" I whispered, tasting the salt of his skin.

He laughed against my mouth. "You already have."

I arched against him, the feel of us pressed together like stardust across the clear night sky, and together we mapped our voyage home.

"So, it really was just an excuse, huh?" I asked, my words on the edge of laughter.

Mazin rose up on his forearms, his hair delightfully mussed, a quizzical expression on his brow.

I grinned at him. "You asked me to come to your room so you could show me something?"

Clarity smoothed his face, and he hopped out of bed, not bothering to hide his nakedness as he went to a large wooden closet at the end of the room.

"You could at least throw something on," I groaned, a flush of heat rushing to my cheeks at the brief flash of nudity. I sat up and wrapped my hastily flung kurta around me.

"But that would have slowed me down," he called out, rummaging around the cupboard.

He returned with a triumphant look on his face, and I tried to look anywhere but at him.

"Put some clothes on!" I shouted, shielding my eyes.

He barked out a laugh. "How are you this sensitive? You've seen my body thousands of times."

"Not like this," I grumbled. "And not immediately after we . . . not like this."

"Fine. I'll get dressed. But take this first."

I snatched the box from his hand without glancing at him. He gave a rich laugh and threw on the long ivory tunic he'd discarded on the floor earlier.

"There, stop your blushes and open it. Proof that I didn't drag you to my bedroom to take advantage of you."

I arched a brow. "I think you'll find that *I* took advantage of *you*," I said, crossing my arms over my chest.

He leaned over and kissed me. "So you did. Now open it."

I unfolded the pressed paper wrapping the outside of the small box. Curling wildflowers dotted the outside. I lifted the wooden lid from the top. Underneath was a small golden dagger, a pendant with a real blade, no bigger than my pinkie. The dagger had a halmasti head, and a curved edge, just like one my father had made.

"How did you . . . ?"

"There is a jeweler up north who crafts custom pendants like I'd never seen before. He creates work for the emperor so I wouldn't be surprised if he supplied him with zoraat. He bends gold and steel into masterpieces. I asked him if he could create this, and he did it."

"It's perfect," I said, my throat thick with emotion.

"I finally found jewelry you'll wear." He gave me a lopsided grin. "And of course it's a dagger." Then he grew serious. "You'll wear it, won't you?"

I thumbed the scar on the edge of my knuckles and looked into his dark eyes. "I'll never take it off."

Thirty-seven

Mazin led me to his bedroom. I should have felt elated at this turn of events. This would be one more moment I would use against him, one more way I could take my revenge.

But all I felt was the sick churning of my stomach, and growing dread with every step. I wanted him to suffer, but I wasn't sure if I was ready for this.

Not yet.

We ended up at the room I knew well, though he had no idea I'd been there before. The lamps were already lit, and they cast a soft glow around the dark room. I couldn't help but remember the last time I was here, and how different things were. Back when we could tell each other any secret, confess any regret without fear of judgment.

Back to when I loved him.

And now, I was different.

But he was different too, even though I was the one with the new face. I cast a surreptitious glance his way and spied the dark stains under his eyes, as if he hadn't slept in a year. His face was gaunt, which frustratingly made him appear more handsome. It was as if some of his boyish youth had deserted him, and in its place he was cold, calculating. A killer.

I understood that, because I was too.

We were what he made us.

"You have something to show me?" I asked, as if we both weren't here for another reason entirely. My breath was trapped in my chest and the pressure was unbearable. I pressed my hands to my thighs to still their shaking.

I needed distance. I needed time to get myself under control before I went down this dark road.

"Yes," he said, his voice straightforward. He went to his desk, a dark mahogany that replaced the cabinet once sitting there. I swept my gaze around the room to find that other things were different too—the room appeared darker, as if the hollowness from his eyes had seeped into the fabric and walls and created a room of shadows. Gone was any color, any life. He once had a painting of a jasmine flower on the wall his sister painted, and that too was removed, with a faint outline from where it had been. Mazin walked toward me, but a movement from the other side of the room drew my gaze.

A small black shadow moved closer from the darkness. I jumped back, my eyes adjusting, trying to make out what I was seeing. Had Mazin been consuming zoraat too? Had he summoned the shadows to life? I slammed into Maz behind me with a gasp, and he pressed a steadying hand to my shoulder.

"What . . ."

The creature jumped out of the darkness, leaping for me, and behind my shock and dread something registered in the back of my mind.

A cat leapt into my arms, a cat that had once been mine.

And if I felt like I couldn't breathe before, now I was drowning. I clutched the dark ball of fur to my chest, my eyes burning.

I couldn't cry. Not now. I bit my lip so hard I drew blood to dispel the tears.

I scrambled for a response. "I wasn't expecting a cat in your room . . ." I broke off awkwardly.

"Jalebi usually avoids strangers. I'm sorry to have scared you." He said the last words with a faint huff of amusement, as if it was impossible to be afraid of the cat clinging to me.

He moved to take the cat from my arms, but I shifted away from him, holding Jalebi close.

"No, it's fine. I was just surprised." I stroked her head softly. "She's lovely." I buried my head in her fluffy neck and closed my eyes at her answering purr. I had forgotten how much I missed her, and how much of my old life I didn't realize I longed for.

He inclined his head. "Don't let my sister hear you say so. Jalebi tends to attack anyone else who comes her way. The cat is a bit feral."

I bristled at his derisive tone. "Why do you have her, then?"

He paused, a slight smile on his face. "She belonged to someone I once knew and I wanted to make sure she had a home."

I couldn't stop the scowl from crossing my face.

She would have her true home if you hadn't arrested me, you selfish bastard.

"That's so thoughtful of you," I said through gritted teeth. I probably looked as feral as Jalebi.

He rubbed the back of his neck, as if suddenly self-conscious. "Anyway, this is what I wanted to show you."

He handed a box to me and I put Jalebi down on the bed. She gave a mewl of protest, but I turned my attention to the intricate wooden chest. It was much like the one he had given me in his bedroom before, except this box was larger and unwrapped.

"A gift?" I asked, my voice wary. I remembered his last one, something I thought I would treasure forever. Instead, it was a reminder of his betrayal, and its cold bite still rested against my chest.

"Of sorts. I found it when I was in the south dealing with the rebellion there last week." He gave me a rueful smile. "It reminded me of you." His voice was soft, almost as if he daren't speak the words.

Inexplicably, heat rose in my belly, and my chest felt as if it would burst.

I wanted to cut out my treacherous heart and throw it on the carpet.

It wasn't me he was speaking to, but Sanaya. It wasn't me he thought about, but the creature I had created. And still, my face flushed with his attention, my pulse beat wildly. It was as if my heart couldn't reconcile with my head and it was the thing controlling all my emotions. I tried to cut it off, as if I could stop the flow of blood to the organ lodged in my chest that was the reason for all my weakness. But still, my fingers shook as I opened the box.

Inside a dagger blazed, smooth camel bone fashioned into a cobra head, an elegant curved blade with a silver filigree sheath.

A knife. He'd given the girl who wore jewels a blade just like he'd given the swordfighter a necklace. At least he was consistent in his contrariness.

"I don't know what to say." My voice was trapped. "It's beautiful."

Beautiful was too inadequate a word. The camel bone was polished to gleaming, the cobra so detailed I could nearly feel its scales beneath my fingers.

"I knew you'd like it." He watched me with dark eyes, his expression closed. I shut the box with a thud that echoed between us. I swallowed past the thickness in my throat, past this uncomfortable sensation I couldn't quite put my finger on. It couldn't be guilt, not when he had done so much to me. Not when he deserved what I was about to do to him.

"I love it," I bit off, knowing I had to say something in response.

It was a lie, and I could hear it in my words. Because right then, I hated that knife with every inch of my skin. I hated that it made me think of him as human, as someone who buys something thoughtful for someone he's thinking about. And mostly, I didn't know whether I wanted to kiss him for giving it to me or wrap my fingers around the hilt and plunge it into his chest.

Mazin moved closer, his dark presence like a shadow, the relief of shade on a hot day. I put the box down and pressed my gloved palms into my thighs, my thoughts a riot of confusion. For one moment I closed my eyes to make everything stop, and I savored the sudden silence.

And in it, I heard that voice again.

Revenge.

My hands burned from where the dark curling stains were. This time, the voice was a soft whisper. It sounded suspiciously familiar, though I couldn't place it exactly. And since no one else ever heard it but me, I'd come to realize the voice was coming from inside my head.

But it was so hard to remember I was here for revenge when Mazin surrounded me with all the memories that had made me love him.

My eyelids fluttered open and Mazin came back into view.

I needed to trust my gut. That was the one thing that had gotten me through every battle, every fight.

I leaned into him, savoring the familiar between us. In his room, surrounded by him, surrounded by *me*.

Then his hands, those calluses on my shoulders, cupping my jaw.

He kissed me, his lips meeting mine in a question, one that I answered readily. I pushed down any of the trepidation I felt and just thought purely of *him*. Of the way he made me feel, of the sounds in the back of his throat when he pressed me against him. I kissed him back with everything I had, and suddenly it wasn't enough, and we were flying together, spiraling down a mountain of anger and passion and such fierce longing I could barely breathe.

And then the sick churning in the pit of my stomach, that gnawing growing deeper, darker, like an abyss ready to swallow me whole. And all the while the same thought kept replaying in the forefront of my mind.

He thinks you are someone else.

He thinks you are someone else.

My insides roiled. My mouth tasted of ash. I pushed away from him with everything I had, practically throwing him against the wall.

Our heavy breaths filled the silence of the room. His dark eyes were wild as they took me in, lips red from our kiss.

"I can't," I said desperately, not caring about his response. I couldn't go down this road, no matter what my vengeance was. Every part of my body rebelled against what I was doing, against who I was becoming.

If I led him here, Mazin wouldn't be truly saying yes. He wouldn't have agreed to be with *me* but with Sanaya.

"I can't," I repeated, touching my hands to my swollen lips, letting my words hang in the air. Then I raced out of the room, not bothering to wait for a response, not taking the dagger he'd just given me, desperate to escape this fate I'd built for myself.

Thirty-eight

I ran through the halls of the palace, holding myself together as much as I could until I found a vacant room to hide in, away from the performers and crowds. I stood in the darkness, back braced against the door, my heavy breath the only sound besides the muffled revelry beyond.

Then I broke apart.

I finally allowed the tears to fall.

For my father.

For all the love I'd had in my heart for Mazin.

But most of all, for me, because even though I'd escaped prison, it felt remarkably like I was still there.

Sobs choked my body as I folded over, my face pressed to the floor, and cried for everything I'd never have again. I wrapped my arms around myself, feeling the cool marble against my skin, wishing not for the first time that I could go back in time to when choices seemed easy and every step wasn't a betrayal against myself or my family.

Eventually my ugly sobbing stopped and I pressed the heel of my hands to my eyes, wiping away the tears.

I sat up slowly. This was what I would allow myself.

This small bit of emotion, before I donned my armor once more and went out to the battlefield. I threaded my fingers through my hair and massaged my scalp to ease the ache there, wishing I had some of the heated mustard oil from Afra Aunty to calm me.

The emperor hadn't even arrived at the festivities yet, and I couldn't stay hiding in this room. I wouldn't break. Not now. Will was the only thing keeping me going and seeing this through.

I got up and paced around the dark room, drying my face and letting the emotion drain out of me to be replaced by a steel blade. Somehow I managed to open the door again, walking back into the throngs of people laughing and exclaiming over the djinn power on display. But its true power—more than just street performer tricks— was on display too, they just didn't realize it.

It could transform you into a living weapon. It could reconstruct the skin you wore, reform your bones.

You could conquer empires with it.

My eyes searched the room for Noor, but I didn't see her dark cropped hair. After a few moments, the throng of people began quieting and the performers stopped ingesting zoraat. The noise hushed to a whisper, and the people stood, waiting.

The emperor was coming.

I only had a few memories of the emperor, from when my father had taken me to the palace. That Vahid chose to use me as his political pawn showed that he had taken more notice of me than I ever supposed. Or perhaps it was that Mazin had been the one to suggest me.

From the upper level of the palace the crowds parted. The emperor walked through them as if he was born to it.

But he wasn't. Vahid had started as a humble farmer before making a bargain with a djinn that had helped him take an empire.

None could doubt the grandeur of his outfit—the golden sherwani, the buttons made of diamonds, curled emerald shoes embroidered with silver and pearls, and a gold circlet emblazoned with rubies and topped with a jewel made with the most precious commodity of all—djinn magic.

If you looked past his outfit, Vahid was a plain, average sort of man. Still, beneath his graying hair, his sallow skin with a yellow cast and unassuming short stature, were the glittering black eyes of a usurper.

It was always his eyes I was most wary of.

Those were the eyes of someone who had been eaten up by their desire for power.

He moved through the people and spoke a few words to members of his court, those sycophants who had kissed his feet when he'd come to the capital. He walked closer to me, and I gripped my dagger tight, tucked into the pocket of my kameez.

I could just end it now. My knife could pierce his heart, stab through his brocade coat, and bleed out all the zoraat from his veins.

It would be over.

He walked closer, the throng parting around me, and I had assumed Vahid would pass right by me. However, he paused, his sweeping gaze holding my own. Then his eyes slid over my head, landing on someone else behind me.

Mazin.

I didn't want to face him. Not after how I'd just reacted, what I'd just nearly done. I steeled myself to meet his eyes, taking a long breath and straightening my shoulders. Then I turned my head.

And came face-to-face with Thohfsa.

Thirty-nine

"I wasn't expecting you here yet, warden."

The emperor's voice rumbled behind me, but I barely acknowledged his words, nor her response. In front of me was Thohfsa, the woman I'd stabbed clean through the stomach with a rusty sword. The one who had tortured and terrorized both me and Noor.

Noor.

A jolt of panic shot through me at the realization that I had a disguise, a new face carved from djinn power, but Noor did not.

And Thohfsa knew exactly who she was.

I tried not to react, not to change my expression in the slightest at seeing Thohfsa standing close enough to touch. But it wouldn't have mattered anyway because she barely acknowledged me. Instead, she was staring at the emperor with an unhinged gleam in her eyes, as if she were a hyena and the emperor a butcher with a bucket of fresh cuts. I knew a devotee when I saw one.

Vahid had given Thohfsa power, something she'd never had before, and she had gotten drunk off it.

My eyes swept her body, trying to find some evidence as to how she could be standing before me. Her black hair was oiled back, and the permanent sneer she usually wore was replaced with a beatific smile.

She looked like she was in excellent health, which shouldn't be humanly possible.

Because it isn't humanly possible.

My mind searched back to the day Noor and I escaped. Thohfsa had brought a djinn healer to the prison that day to heal Noor. Thohfsa could have healed herself that way too—if my blow to the stomach hadn't killed her, then she would have had time to summon the healer before the blood loss became fatal.

I curled my fists against my palms, watching her greasy smile as she spoke to the emperor, remembering the last time she beat me, and the welts I'd had from the leather of her belt.

I would just have to kill her all over again.

"Is there a reason you're staring at me, sahiba?" Thohfsa's nasal voice pierced through my thoughts. She had turned her unbalanced gaze on me.

"I thought we had met before," I said calmly, my face a still mask as I reminded myself that she had no idea who I was. "But I can see I was mistaken."

She tilted her head, a sly look entering her eyes. "Are you so sure?"

I inhaled sharp panic. It wasn't possible she knew. The emperor stood behind me and cleared his throat.

"I have an update for you on the situation we discussed," Thohfsa said to the emperor, her eyes not leaving mine.

He narrowed his eyes. "Not here."

She nodded tightly. Then the emperor turned his gaze back to me, his bright eyes narrowing. I felt something crawl over my skin at his attention. This man had orchestrated my family's downfall, didn't care who he killed or destroyed as long as it furthered his goal of more power.

"Who are you?"

294 ◆ Emily Varga

I opened my mouth to speak, but Thohfsa beat me to it. "This is Sanaya from the northern tribes."

I startled, my heart jumping to my throat. But a smile curled on her face and she continued.

"She's come to curry your favor for her father. I also heard she rescued your adopted daughter from a bunch of street thugs." Thohfsa laughed, a high-pitched sound that sliced through my skin like a whip. How did she know all that? Had she been asking about me in the palace? I curled my fists at my sides to still their shaking.

"Ah yes," the emperor responded, his voice mild. "Mazin mentioned something about you." He nodded in my direction, his eyes sliding over me without really taking me in. "My thanks for helping someone in my household."

Someone in his household. Not his child. Not his daughter. If Anam died I wondered if he would even notice. Something dark gathered inside me. This man didn't care about anyone but himself.

Not me. Not my father. Not even those he had raised as his children.

Revenge.

That voice slithered inside me, around me, echoing in my ears. I could do it. Right now, I could grab my dagger and with a flick of my wrist slash the fleshy part of his neck before he could use any of his djinn power.

"It was my pleasure, your excellency," I heard myself say through gritted teeth as I bowed low. Now was not the time. I didn't care about what happened to me after it was done, but I still had to deal with Mazin and I had no idea where Noor was.

And seeing Thohfsa and the emperor together had shaken my confidence. I had wanted to speak to the emperor, to get closer to him, but not like this. This felt like Thohfsa calling the shots, controlling the situation, for a reason I wasn't entirely sure why yet. But the emperor was oblivious to my turmoil and walked away, speaking to other courtiers and warlords who had come to pay their respects.

I cast my gaze around looking for Noor in the crowd.

"Looking for your little sidekick?"

My heart froze at that nasal voice.

Your little sidekick.

Thohfsa knew.

She knew who I was, who I *really was*. My body snapped to rigid attention, muscle memory recognizing danger and battle.

Even though we stared at each other with hatred in a crowded room filled with revelry, we weren't pretending anymore. We were in combat.

I pressed my hand to the knife under my kameez, not letting her have the upper hand anymore. She had terrorized us in prison and used her power to try to break me. But now we were on equal footing.

"If we weren't in the middle of a packed room, I would gut you again." My voice was low, and so quiet. But I knew Thohfsa heard it by the thinning of her lips and flaring of her nostrils.

"Not even bothering to deny it, I see," she breathed, her lip curling.

"What is the point? Looks like you know everything already," I said, dangerously soft.

"We'll see what secrets you spill when the emperor is interrogating you." But her words weren't vehement, held no conviction.

A bluff.

"You would have told him already. You've had ample opportunity." My eyes roved over her mulish face as something dawned on me. "No, you want something from me."

In that moment I also knew why I hadn't seen Noor yet.

Rage filled my veins, hot and consuming. I advanced on Thohfsa, so close that she couldn't mistake how much I meant every single word I was about to say.

"Where is Noor?" I growled, unsheathing my dagger, not caring who noticed the flash of my knife in the crowd. "If you don't release her, I will make you wish you had died the first time I killed you."

Thohfsa was a brutal dictator in the prison she ruled, but toe-to-toe with me, she couldn't win and she knew it. Her eyes widened, but she stood her ground.

"She should have hid her face too, you know. Imagine my surprise when I saw the little maggot walking around as calm as you please in the middle of the emperor's palace. I knew then you two had found it—Souma's treasure." Her voice cracked, but she kept going, her confidence growing with every word as my own diminished. "And you are going to give it to me. All of it." She smiled like a shark after tasting first blood. "If you don't, your friend won't be alive much longer. And I will reveal everything to the emperor and he'll take his price from you."

I exhaled, trying to calm my bubbling panic, wishing that Thohfsa didn't have power over me yet again.

"You could do that anyway," I said with faux nonchalance, cooling my previous tone.

She wouldn't know how much power she truly had. Nor how much I owed Noor. "But you don't want to share Souma's treasure with Vahid, do you?" I cocked my head, examining her. After everything, Thohfsa's actions were still dictated by greed, by the need for power.

"The emperor won't share. He would take it all and leave me with a pittance." She spat on the floor. "But make no mistake: I will give you and Noor to him in a heartbeat if you do not give me the zoraat."

I growled, low in my throat. My well-formulated plans were slipping through my grasp.

"I'll give you the zoraat," I said finally, watching her expression turn gleeful. "Just tell me where Noor is."

"I'm not a fool. I'll give her to you after the treasure is in my hands."

I shook my head, the dagger still in my curled fingers. But I couldn't kill her now because I might never know what she did to Noor. "I won't give you anything until I know she's safe and alive."

"Fine. Meet me at the edge of the bazaar by the banyan tree tomorrow at sunset. I'll have your friend, and you'll have my power."

I nodded tightly and waited until she spun on her heel and left, trying not to imagine all the ways I'd let Noor down and hoping she wasn't already dead before I could figure out a plan to get us both out of this.

Forty

I went back to our house in Basral and pulled out all my father's choicest weapons. I had every kind of sword, a multitude of daggers, and a crossbow. I had zoraat and gold that could hire as many mercenaries as I wanted to bring down Thohfsa. But it would all be for naught if Noor was already dead and Thohfsa had told the emperor anything.

Thohfsa was greedy, just like Casildo, just like Darbaran. I could use that weakness against her. But I couldn't risk keeping the djinn magic if that meant Noor's death. And I couldn't leave her to die.

I exhaled through clenched teeth, trying to think through a plan that would have Noor and me walking out of this alive and still bring down Thohfsa, Vahid, and Mazin. The need for revenge was still scorching through my veins.

But if Noor was alive, no matter what vengeance brewed in my blood, I could make sure she stayed alive.

We had done this together. We'd escaped and planned and mourned our fathers together. And now I had to figure out a way to get her back.

I lay down on my bedroom floor, the cool stones sharp against my cheek.

If I gave up everything I had in exchange for Noor, then who was I?

The girl who didn't fight for her father's memory, who let the people who had killed him and betrayed me go free? If I gave up the zoraat in exchange for Noor's safety, then I was forsaking retribution for my father. If I ignored Thohfsa and pursued my revenge, then my only friend in the world would die.

The pit in my stomach seemed endless, like a gaping wound that would never heal.

If I left her, how was I any different from Mazin? Casildo? Darbaran?

Cold rage drowned me, my vision darkening like a flickering torch. I could even feel it at the back of my teeth.

I pulled off the gloves encasing my hands and examined the black stains on them. They'd spread, sprouting from the center of my palm and the end of my fingertips and curling up my wrists. It was like a strange tattoo—as if I dipped my skin in dark paint and let the droplets curl up my arms. What did it mean? Was I taking too much zoraat? Was it infecting me like a poison?

I didn't even have Noor to ask anymore.

But with each passing moment it was harder and harder to contain the fury and bloodlust.

I closed my eyes and felt a familiar power coursing through me—this time it had nothing to do with djinn magic or zoraat, but my own power, the one that had got me here, that had gone back for Noor in the infirmary and that had propelled us out of that prison.

I changed out of my heavy shalwar kameez, put on a plain black tunic and leggings, and tied my hair back. I had a chance to get Noor back, and I was going to use it.

I could do this, and I could still win.

Even without any magic at all.

But I was going to rescue Noor *and* keep the power we'd taken.

With new purpose, I packed up the weapons I needed and prepared to leave. But as I walked past the large mirror in my room I paused.

Something stopped me, something not quite right with my reflection. I reached my hands up to my face, my cheeks, my nose.

I looked like *me*.

I realized with a jolt that tonight was when I had needed to take an additional dose of the zoraat, and that the power must have been already wearing off, at a more rapid rate than before.

I scrambled for the bag containing the djinn seeds, hidden under two stones in the floor. I hauled it out and opened it.

The multicolored seeds glittered back at me in the moonlight, different amounts, different textures, and wholly unknown to me.

Noor hadn't taught me how to blend the mixture, and I didn't trust my own knowledge. It could either work just fine or burn me from the inside out.

I sat back on my heels and curled my fists into the ground.

Then I screamed my voice hoarse into the night.

This couldn't be how it ended. I would have to face Thohfsa and her guards with my sword alone.

My sword, and my true face.

But what if I failed?

Finally, I lifted one vial up, a single dose of the right amount and color of what I'd seen Noor use most often. It was dark red, the powder fine, like sand. If I swallowed all of it, surely that would give me enough power to transform my appearance and free Noor.

Or it would kill me.

My hands shook, the glass vial poised on the edge of my lips. Did I need this power?

But before I could swallow the rest of the zoraat, a heavy thud sounded from the courtyard, the noise like a body falling, followed by shattering glass.

I shot to my feet. Noor had tripled the number of guards since Darbaran's attack, it should have been impossible to break through our security.

Was it Thohfsa, reneging on her deal and coming to take me by surprise at home?

Maybe she had told the emperor who I truly was, and Vahid had surrounded the house with his soldiers.

I picked up my talwar from the bed and walked down the hall, heading to the garden. The house was eerily quiet. I paused at the edge of the hallway, spying a maidservant standing by the divan, staring outside, a broken glass at her feet.

"Vira?"

She didn't move. Thoughts whirred inside my brain, screaming at me, trying to make sense of what I was staring at. I moved closer to her, my sword held high, and looked at her face.

It was frozen.

Her face was a mask of shock, eyes wide, fixated on the garden outside, the effect an unsettling macabre statue standing in the main room.

I waved my hand in front of her, but she didn't even blink.

My fingers tightened around the hilt of my blade. My breathing was hoarse and loud in the silence of the house. The air was cool as I walked outside. A guard stood in the corner of the garden, also unmoving, his eyes on me, as if he couldn't look away.

Dread crawled up my spine, and I felt the heavy sensation of the presence of someone else before I saw them.

Soft breath landed on my neck.

I whirled, my sword raised. But it froze in my hands. I tried to swing the blade, but my arms were fixed in midair.

A figure stood in a long cloak that reached the cobblestones. Dark eyes glowed from underneath the hood, watching me with hunger.

"Who are you?" I breathed, terrified my words were as frozen as the talwar in my hand.

"You know who I am."

I closed my eyes, not wanting to voice what I suspected.

302 ◆ **Emily Varga**

Because saying it out loud meant this had turned into something far beyond my control. That not only did I have to deal with my own world, but another one too.

An unseen one.

There was a beat of silence so long it felt as if a lifetime stretched between us. And then I said a single word, the one I had been afraid to utter.

"Djinn."

Forty-one

The djinn who stood before me smiled, his teeth straight and white, like small chips of diamonds in an ageless face.

He looked human like me, just older. Or younger. I couldn't quite tell. And he stared as if he knew me, which I found much more troubling.

I didn't want to be known by a djinn.

"You are different from the last human I bargained with. She had a black vengeance in her soul that could not be contained. But Vahid had the same hunger as you."

His ageless voice shot through me, cold and impersonal. Then his hold on me lessened, and my frozen limbs thawed until my sword dropped. Words stuck in my mouth like cold ghee, but I pushed past my fear. Noor was still captured, and I didn't have much time to help her.

"You are the djinn that gave Vahid his power?"

The djinn smiled again, as if he took delight in my question—no, as if he took pride in it.

"Vahid was a simple farmer then, raging about the injustices of the kingdoms." The djinn chuckled, though his face barely moved. "He rambled about how the children in his village died from starvation, and that he would make the king pay for creating the famine. He had such *hatred* manifesting inside him." The djinn sounded gleeful. "I warned him that if he wanted my power he would have to accept the cost as well. I warned him, but you see, he didn't listen." The djinn's eyes were ravenous.

I inhaled sharply, a word he used burning my insides like acid.

"The *cost*?" My voice was a whisper, and I wasn't sure if I was more scared of my question or his answer.

The djinn leaned forward, his eyes gleaming. "Surely you feel it? Hmm? The leaching of yourself. The darkness that is eating away at you the more you consume. Some take years to feel it. But humans that use as much as you do, that *feel* as much as you do, they experience it almost immediately."

My mind whirled. That voice I kept hearing. Those instances of deep anger that made me feel like I was going out of my mind. The moments where it felt like the rage had blackened my vision. It had nearly taken over when I'd been with Mazin, egging me on to get revenge, but my own small voice had fought back. I clutched the hilt of my sword tight, my fingers unsteady, despite knowing my blade would do little good against the creature before me.

"Why are you here now?" I desperately wished my voice didn't shake, and that I could stand firm on my feet, instead of edging away from him like my skin wanted to leave more than I did.

He smiled again, that haunting, intense stare. "To offer you the same bargain I offered Vahid—a piece of my power. A piece of djinn magic that will give you your vengeance."

I inhaled, my breath catching in my throat, my chest feeling like it would explode.

But there was something bitter at the back of my throat, and I turned one word over in my mouth.

Bargain.

This was not a gift. It would always have a cost.

"I already have access to your power, djinn. I don't need to bargain for it."

"You have access to a grain of sand compared to what I can give you. If you want to save your friend, I can give you everything you need to do it."

I exhaled, knowing he spoke the truth. I had no chance of saving Noor with the power I had now. If he gave me something I could destroy Thohfsa with, I could take Vahid down . . .

But what if this magic was more than I could afford?

"And in return?" I backed up another step. "What is the price I would pay for such power?"

The djinn's eyes lit up like the fire inside him was stoked. "The price would be the use of your body."

I reared back, stumbling on a step before I could stop myself. I opened my mouth to say something but the words didn't come out. Fear bubbled in my stomach, turning my skin to ice, cooling the sweat on my brow and making my skin clammy.

And yet . . . *and yet.*

"I would possess you, inhabit your skin, and fully live in your realm," he continued.

"You're in my realm now," I pointed out, gesturing to the courtyard around us, to the night sky lit up with stars. "And you have power here. My servants aren't moving. My guards are frozen stiff. You stopped my sword without touching it. What more could you want?"

"These are tricks," he hissed, taking a step closer. "I am limited by what I can do here. But in a human body, I would not be. I could channel my power through you, much like your precious zoraat that you consume."

"And why would I give you use of my body, when I already have a portion of your power?"

"Because I can give you everything you've wanted. Everything you dream about in the darkest parts of yourself."

"What is it that you think I want? I'm not like Vahid. I don't do this for power."

"Don't you? Haven't you always wanted the power to destroy your enemies? You practiced with a sword until your hands were bloody. You built a wall around yourself so you would be untouchable. But yes, you want more than power, I will grant you that. You want something far more interesting. Retribution. Revenge. That I understand very well. I can give you the power to destroy an empire. To eviscerate a man and take from him all that he loves. That is what you crave, is it not?"

I pursed my lips together. I wanted my revenge, but I didn't want to become Vahid for it. But Noor was still being held by Thohfsa. If I didn't do something, she'd be dead. Maybe I could accept death if it was just me, but Noor deserved to live, to be free.

A sound from the garden turned my head, soft footsteps echoing through the courtyard. One of the guards walked toward me, as if he hadn't just been a statue for the past few minutes. He came closer, and I blinked, seeing the man clearly for the first time.

Out of the darkness came a man that wasn't a guard at all. My heart lodged in my throat, my breath stuttering.

It was someone altogether impossible.

"I never thought I would see you again." His soft voice called to me, deep and steady, the one who always calmed me when I needed guidance.

"Baba?" His name was pulled from me, drawn out as if I didn't know my own language.

I whipped my head back to the djinn beside me, who watched with firelit eyes. "What have you done?"

"Tricks again." He shrugged, the gesture as unnatural as his presence. "But effective. Humans are so controlled by their past. It dictates everything you do."

I forced breath through my nostrils, my hands clenching my sword hilt so hard I thought it would crack in half.

As the illusion drew closer, I even smelled my father—soft smoke and flame, earthy hot iron mixed with the slightly acrid scent of molten steel. Memories flooded me—sitting in a chair at the end of the smith as my father stoked the fire, the sound of his knife scraping against camel bone as he carved in the evening, the pride I felt in my stomach when he laughed at a joke I told him over a plate of hot dal kachoris.

And now that same man was standing before me, the gray in his beard shining in the torchlight, the deep wrinkles on his brown face I had mapped like the constellations of stars above us.

Except my father was dead.

My stomach fell like an iron weight, and I closed my eyes to block out the sight of him.

"Take him away." I forced the words through my set teeth. "I don't want to see him anymore."

"But you do," said the djinn in my ear, with a low, self-satisfied whisper, suddenly so close I could touch him. "You want to see him so badly you would cut out your own tongue. I can feel it, the longing. The agony. The anger. I'm almost drunk from it." His cold breath brushed my neck. "It's why I'm here." The djinn waved his hand over me. "Because of you. Because of the *rawness* of your need for vengeance. Because of who you've lost, and what you plan to do about it."

"He was taken from me. This is not my father."

"Your father was murdered, you were betrayed, and since then you've only had one purpose. Tell me, what would you do if you had unlimited power? If you could do anything you wanted to the people who stole your life? Would you make them pay the cost?"

I stared into my father's dark eyes, crinkled at the corners from laughter. His mouth lifted and he gave me the same grin I'd always known. The one he gave before tousling my hair affectionately and correcting me on the right way to hold a dagger.

My father cocked his head. "What are you looking for, beti?"

I exhaled, searching for something that made him unnatural,

unfamiliar. But he felt as real as the sword in my hand. "The answer, Baba."

My father leaned forward, his hand reaching out to touch me. My lungs contracted in my chest.

"Don't," I whispered, my voice cracking. His hands paused in midair, a question in his gaze. When my mother had died, my father picked up the pieces of our life. My nanu had been broken, inconsolable, and I was left with the loss of both of them. But my father was the one constant in my life, the one who loved me no matter what happened.

Finding out about his death caused my heart to crack open, the blackness spilling inside, hardening my insides with more rage than I thought imaginable. I hadn't had him to comfort me then, when I'd most needed it.

If I felt his hand on my shoulder now, I would fall apart.

And I couldn't fall.

Not now, not when it wasn't just my revenge in the balance but Noor's life as well. What if my only living friend died because of me?

The cost of my body was something I'd pay a thousand times if I knew I could get my father back. But that wasn't what the djinn offered.

No one could bring back the dead, not even the djinn.

But if I could save someone else. If I could save Noor. What would I give for that? What would I do?

I looked up at the djinn, wrenching my gaze away from my father, as much as it pained me to do so.

I had the answer, I'd always had it, I just didn't know if I had the strength to see it through.

"I accept the cost," I said, my voice causing an odd vibration across the garden, like a ripple in a pond. I kept speaking before I lost the nerve, before my legs gave out and I crumpled to a heap on the ground. "But I want more than what I have." I tightened my hands on the hilt of my sword, remembering the other lives Vahid had taken, destroyed, starved. The protestors burned in the street. Mazin's parents, slaughtered in their village. He had systematically destroyed the king-doms with his own greed. Now I would take them back.

"I want the power to free Noor and burn this empire to the ground. I want the emperor dead. And . . ." I paused, remembering a set of dark eyes I'd sworn to forget, the touch of someone I thought loved me until I knew better. "I want Mazin to watch it. All of it. I want him to know that I was the one who took it all away, before I kill him. That is my bargain, djinn."

I dropped my sword on the ground and held out my hands, study-ing the lines, the scars, the bumps and ridges that made them me. On top of those scars the black spidery veins crawled up my arms from the center of my palms, like slick oil bleeding into my skin.

But my hands were still mine. Every cut and mark was *mine*.

And I was about to give them to a djinn.

My stomach was a dark pit eating away at me. Everything in my body rebelled against this decision. This would give me what I wanted but take away everything I had left.

I looked back at my father, but it wasn't his warm smile I saw anymore. It was the djinn's, those icy teeth glittering, now razor blades in the moonlight.

"Done."

Forty-two

I watched Thohfsa from behind the closed bazaar stall, the moonlight outlining her form like a glowing beacon in the night.

She came alone, with no sign of Noor at all. If she had at least brought Noor, I could have fought her with my sword. But I couldn't take the chance Noor was out there waiting to be killed if Thohfsa didn't come back for her.

"Where is she?" I let my voice slice through the night, as my sword would have. "Where is Noor?"

Thohfsa's head jerked up, her mouth twisting into that familiar sneer. "She's safe for now." Her gaze swept over my face, void of the magic that had disguised me previously. "I'd forgotten how ugly you were."

I rolled my eyes. "I want to know Noor's still alive."

Thohfsa chuckled. "The little worm is still alive, she's of no value to me dead." Then she raised her lit torch in the air and whistled low.

A light went on in a building at the edge of the bazaar. Noor was illuminated in the window, a knife pressed to her throat and a look of misery painted on her face.

Relief flooded through me that she was alive and here.

I could work with that.

"Let her go," I growled, advancing on Thohfsa.

Thohfsa held up a hand. "If you harm me in any way, her throat will be slit. You won't have time to save her, not with all the djinn magic in the world."

You don't know how much I have.

I nodded tightly and opened the satchel at my side, unfolding the bag of zoraat and glancing down at the seeds one last time. This was what had given me the power to exact vengeance on Darbaran, Casildo, Vahid, and Mazin.

But I didn't need it anymore.

I glanced up at Noor in the window, the one friend I had left. If I couldn't save her, all of this would have been for nothing. I picked up the bag, ignoring Noor's cry of protest, and chucked it at Thohfsa's feet.

"There."

She bent down, picking it up with a greedy smile. "Is that all of it?"

"Every last seed."

"How do I know you're not lying?"

I gestured to my naked face. "Would I walk around like this if I were lying?"

Thohfsa nodded, then gave a low whistle again. This time the methodical, insistent sound of boots marching on cobblestones filled the courtyard.

Hundreds of them.

I watched Thohfsa, utterly still, memorizing her smug expression.

"Did you really think I wouldn't give you up?" She tucked the zoraat in her pack. "Did you really think I would let you go free?"

Noor cried out in the window and I jerked my gaze to her. They hadn't killed her, not yet.

Soldiers surrounded me, but I barely spared them a glance, not even when they drew their swords.

"Thohfsa, did you really think I would ever trust you?"

She narrowed her eyes, but before she could make a move, I reached for the power simmering beneath my veins.

The power I'd given my life for, just to have access to.

There was a slight tugging, then a snap as it flooded through me, a thousand burning needles stabbing my skin and filling me with djinn fire.

Then, every soldier surrounding me turned their blades the other way. Toward Thohfsa.

I could feel their lives. Their blood.

Tricks, the djinn had called it, but it was as if I were moving clay models of the soldiers and forcing them to do my bidding. Their faces were placid masks, their bodies mine to command.

"What . . . ?" Thohfsa fumbled with the bag at her hip, scrambling for the zoraat, as if it would help her now. But Thohfsa never really knew what to do with power when she had it.

"You traded Noor for djinn magic, which was a poor exchange for you."

I waved a hand and the soldiers advanced on her. She pulled out a handful of seeds, stuffing them into her mouth.

The soldiers kept advancing.

"The thing about having zoraat is you need to know how to use it."

In a few moments, Thohfsa began to gag, and her legs buckled from underneath her. She clawed at her throat, her eyes bulging, sweat pouring from her face.

A line of guards parted as I walked through them. I crouched down to Thohfsa. "This time, you *will* die."

"Dania."

Noor stood at the edge of the square, her dark eyes wide at the crowd of soldiers surrounding me. I stood, facing her.

"What have you done?"

Forty-three

"The emperor will know we are here. Thohfsa wouldn't have brought the soldiers without telling him."

Noor crouched down to Thohfsa, who had stopped thrashing and moaning and was now motionless.

Dead.

Noor looked up at me, her mouth grim.

"What did you do?" Noor repeated, her voice so low I had to strain to hear her. Her eyes flickered to the soldiers, then slid back to my face. From her pained expression, she assumed something terrible.

And yet, it was so much worse than her imaginings.

I bristled at the censure in her voice. "I did what I had to in order to save you," I shot back.

"Bullshit," she snapped at me with ferocity.

I blinked.

"You did it for yourself." Her eyes flashed with hurt, as if I had destroyed her instead of saving her.

"Why do you even care?" I threw up my arms. "You can go wherever you please now. You're free."

I felt a darkness eating at me, anger bubbling to the surface, the manifestation of frustration that Noor wasn't even grateful for all I had done. There was a rage I couldn't calm, a flood of dark emotion threatening to take me under.

"Why do I even care?" Noor looked incredulous. "Are you a fool? You think I've been helping you for weeks because I had nothing better to do?"

"I think you feel like you owe me for coming back for you at the prison. Well, now you don't. I release you of any obligation you once felt."

"Oh, you don't think it was because I had nothing better to do, you think it was out of *obligation*?" Her eyes were fire, her body vibrating with fury.

"Why are you shouting at me? I just saved your life."

Her eyes narrowed. "And I am grateful. But I am not here with you because of obligation."

I swallowed, my throat thick. "Then why?"

She gaped at me. "Because I'm your *friend*, Dani."

Warmth filled my chest, contradicting the darkness inside me. But I looked away from Noor's pleading face and thought instead of Baba's smile, of his soot-smudged hands. Of the djinn-created ghost of him that had stood in front of me.

"Did you forget about your own revenge against Vahid?" My voice cracked, and I was desperate to hold on to something, even if it was vengeance.

"No revenge is worth this!"

"Worth what? My life? That was the plan all along. I knew what I was getting into."

Noor huffed a bitter laugh. "It isn't worth whatever you've done to yourself. The control you have on those soldiers is not due to zoraat. I know that better than anyone. Whatever you did to control human bodies, it isn't worth it."

I was silent for a moment. "How do you know it wasn't zoraat that gave me this power?"

She bit her lip, looking back at the soldiers in the square awaiting my command. "Because I know what zoraat can do, I've worked with it for years. What you did, it wasn't in the realm of possibility. Which means you must have had help." She folded her arms. "You were visited by a djinn, weren't you?"

I exhaled. "Yes. The very same who bestowed his power on Vahid."

Noor made a sound of distress before pursing her lips together. "And what did he want from you in return for all this power?"

"Nothing I wasn't willing to give," I said bitterly. Then I let out a slow breath. Noor wasn't the one who deserved my anger.

"Noor," I reasoned, holding out my hands and tempering my voice. "When Thohfsa took you, I had nothing left. I gave everything I had to end this, once and for all. I will do what I promised to do."

"At the cost of what? You are being consumed by this vengeance—it isn't going to get you what you want, your father is never going to come back. And he wouldn't have wanted you down this path either."

I laughed, a harsh sound. "You know nothing about what he would have wanted. I owe this to him." I clenched my fists, any attempt at civility gone. "Do not make the mistake of thinking I won't go through you to get to them."

Noor raised her eyebrows, whistling low. "Are you threatening me now? Look at what this power has done to you. I know that anyone who loves you wouldn't want you to destroy yourself in a quest for retribution."

"But they don't get to make that choice, I do."

"And I'll ask again, what will it cost you?"

I pressed my lips together and stared at Noor.

She sighed and ran her hands through her hair. "There's no use arguing with you, and we don't have much time. I'll go to your grandmother, make sure she's safe. If you won't tell me what bargain you made, at least remember this." She took a step forward, grabbing a hold of my wrists tightly. I was so startled I nearly lashed out at her, feeling my new power rise to the top of my skin much too fast.

"The djinn can't own your body or soul, no matter what they say.

Souma talked to me about the djinn often, I think he might have known one once. You don't have to sacrifice everything for vengeance."

Her eyes were pleading, as if imparting this would somehow save me. But she didn't realize I was already gone.

"I'm going to finish what I have to do, no matter the consequences." I crossed my arms to hide my trembling.

Noor released a sound of frustration before swinging onto the saddled horse I'd brought. She looked back at me.

"I'm not in the mood to be lectured at again," I warned.

"I wasn't going to. This is a warning and a small piece of advice. The emperor's soldiers will come once they realize Thohfsa isn't coming back. Go to Vahid first and catch him at his own game. And, Dani"—she gave one rueful shake of her head—"don't change your appearance anymore. Let them see who you really are. Let Mazin hear it from your lips."

She rode a few strides before I called out to her.

Our eyes met, mine dark, hers bright. I remembered the first time she'd burst through the floor of my cell, the day she'd given me hope that I could be more than what they'd made me.

"Thank you."

She nodded, her mouth pressed into a thin line. Then she rode out of sight.

Now I was alone.

Perhaps truly for the first time since I'd come back.

I walked toward the palace and the future I would take with my bloodied hands.

Forty-four

My boots echoed across the cobblestone streets as I walked to the glittering sandstone palace in the center of the city. Blockades had been set up to quell the recent protests, with piles of burned bodies yet to have been cleared. The palace was surrounded by a circle of death. This was what Vahid had done when his subjects rose against him.

This was what I had done too.

I'd stoked the flames that burned the bodies. I'd incited the people to destroy Vahid, and now I was also responsible for these deaths.

Basral had begun to wake up, and people glanced my way nervously. I knew what they saw: a girl with murder in her eyes, clad in black boots, a sword strapped to my back and dark hair unbound. I met their gaze until they looked away, until they could no longer face whatever they saw in me.

The palace grew closer and burning power flooded through me. By the time I reached the foot of the palace steps, an army of soldiers stood in front.

But Vahid had assumed he would be dealing with protestors, city folk who could be subdued and burned alive by zoraat fire.

He wasn't counting on someone more powerful than he.

The soldiers had consumed zoraat—I could tell that by their

smiles when I approached, the way their swords twitched in their hands. My own fingers flexed as if to reach for the talwar strapped to my back. But I didn't need that weapon, not when I had the power of a djinn in my blood.

I sank my hands into the dirt—the same thing I had done when I'd destroyed the emperor's crops. But this time, instead of pulling for the thread of life, the roots of crops and trees, I felt for the earth itself.

And I shook it.

A crack sounded. Soldiers shouted as a pillar from the palace fell to the ground. Then, the earth began to shake, rolling through the city, shattering glass and cracking stone. A line of soldiers charged at me, their swords turned to blades of fire, transformed with djinn magic.

I swept through them, djinn fire pouring from my hands as they dropped to the ground, piles of ash, just like the bodies of the civilians they'd burned on the outskirts of the palace.

Elation filled my blood.

This, *this* was worth the cost of everything.

To be able to destroy Vahid like this.

Dark clouds gathered above, a storm building, as if to contribute to my violence with its own force.

I drew my sword from my back and walked up the front steps of the palace that still shook with my power. People ran screaming, and any soldier I encountered I cut down with a blade of white-hot light. My steps clicked across the marble as I strode to the throne room with purpose.

I stepped into the center courtyard, open to the dark skies above, and filled with Vahid's manicured garden.

A row of zoraat plants lined the room, the emperor always reminding guests of where his power had come from. I lit them on fire, the flames fueled by my blood, the smoke rising to the blackened sky.

Footsteps sounded behind me. I prepared myself to cut down more soldiers, even Vahid himself.

But I wasn't yet prepared for *him*.

Forty-five

Before

I blinked, trying to reconcile the mangled body lying at my feet with the robust warlord who had been very much alive this morning. Alive and angry, when I had threatened him. His hands were curled and black, the same ones that had drawn his sword and pointed it at me just earlier. His mouth was wide and frozen, a silent, agonizing scream passing his lips stained black with djinn poison.

Djinn poison.

But who would have poisoned him?

A broken vial lay beside his body, but it held no clues as to who had done this.

I had wanted to kill the warlord this morning, it was true. He was rumored to have been the man responsible for my mother's death in the uprising, and my hot temper had gotten the better of me when I had threatened him. But the death I had wanted for him came at the tip of my blade, not from poison.

A noise from outside the doors echoed through the palace.

I cast my eyes around, but it was just me and the dead warlord. Maz had asked to meet me here, but he was nowhere to be found.

Another sound like thunder rumbled in the distance.

I needed to tell someone the dead warlord was here. I needed to find Maz.

As if I had summoned him, the door burst open and Maz strode through it, his face as somber as his midnight sherwani. I exhaled, something releasing in my chest. Maz would know what to do.

But he was followed by about twenty guards.

"Maz," I breathed, the relief coursing through me.

The emperor would be furious about this. A warlord killed in his palace? He was already having problems quelling the rebellions in the north, he'd have another if they suspected he'd just murdered one of his greatest opponents under the guise of hospitality.

"I was just about to come find you," I said, gesturing to the body at my feet.

There was certainly no love lost between me and the warlord. "I found him here. He's dead."

"Dani." Maz's face was a cool mask. "What are you doing here?"

"She's at the scene of the crime!" Darbaran leapt forward, his scimitar drawn.

Out of reflex I grabbed the hilt of my sword and stepped back.

"See? She moves to attack me! The captain of the palace guards!" His little mongoose face was pinched in fury and I wanted to kick him in it.

"Oh, shut up," I said as I rolled my eyes. "It's painfully obvious I had nothing to do with this."

I turned to Maz with faint amusement, but stopped short when he didn't return the look. Instead, on his face was the same impassive expression.

Something tugged at the back of my mind, and I felt drawn out of myself, as if I were watching what was happening from far away.

"Maz?" I winced at the sound of my voice—almost pleading.

"You cannot be serious," sneered Darbaran. "She's standing over his dead body. The emperor must be told. She's murdered a warlord under his own roof!"

"Oh, and that's very convenient for him, considering this warlord leads one of the biggest factions against him," I snapped.

But the moment I said it, I knew it was wrong.

I'd never had a problem with saying the exact thing that was on my mind and not caring about the results. But now, I recognized that I should have bitten my tongue.

All twenty guards unsheathed their swords and pointed them at me.

Sweat beaded at my forehead. My hands grew damp. I tightened them around the hilt of my sword, because if I didn't, my entire body might be shaking. But I wasn't about to let them skewer me without putting up a fight.

I slowly sank into a fighting stance and lifted my own blade.

Mazin was still standing there, frozen.

"Maz," I forced myself to say calmly, without screaming, even though every fiber of my being was ready to scream this whole palace down. "*Do* something."

He could command these soldiers. He could stop them from advancing on me.

That seemed to shake him out of whatever trance he was in, and he too reached for his blade.

I shook my head in confusion; why was he arming himself?

Why didn't he just tell them to stand down?

His face was stone; the only proof I had that he was still listening to me was the slight tick in his jaw.

Rising horror washed over me.

He couldn't.

Maz couldn't tell them to let me go. Not with a key warlord from the northern tribes dead at my feet.

He walked toward me with his sword drawn and I realized what he was doing.

He'd have to fight his way out with me.

We'd have to make a run for it, then figure out who killed the warlord. I couldn't take on all these soldiers. But with Maz by my side, we could give ourselves a fighting chance. The benefit of this warlord's death to the emperor wasn't lost on me. But I wasn't about to go down as his scapegoat.

And at least I would have Maz with me.

I cast him a grateful smile, but he didn't return it. Instead, he stared at me with inscrutable eyes and remained standing alongside the guards.

"Dani . . ." His voice was soft and low.

"What are you waiting for?" snarled Darbaran, leaping forward. "If you don't arrest her, I will." He looked me up and down, eyes narrowing. "And if she resists, I'll use force."

"Touch me and I will cut your disgusting hands off."

"You won't have hands yourself after this, girl!" he shouted back.

"Mazin!" I screamed at him, trying to get a reaction out of his stone face.

I wanted him to snap out of it, to leap forward and take me by the hand so we could both escape together.

We'd get his sister, then go back to my village and tell my father and Nanu to pack our things.

Then we'd run.

I met Mazin's intense gaze. That wild, dark look had entered them, the same one from the night he'd come to my room and told me Vahid had killed his mother.

But if we run, we'll be on the run for the rest of our lives.

And suddenly I understood.

He was never coming with me.

He wasn't going to fight this together.

I was on my own.

The bottom dropped out of my stomach. My mouth turned dry. I moved it, but no sound came out. I lifted a hand to my lips as if by touching them I'd remember to speak. But the only thing I remembered was Mazin kissing me just that morning. The warm press of his mouth as he had smiled against my skin.

But now, his eyes were cold, oddly vacant, taking on some sort of dark determination I'd never seen from him. I clutched my talwar like a novice, desperately looking around the room. The windows were too far to jump from, and the guards were blocking the only other exit.

I couldn't make it. Not against twenty guards and Mazin. Not without him.

"Dani." His voice was soft, as if he were coaxing a wild desert stallion, calming it right before he slung the rope around its neck.

That wasn't going to be me.

"How dare you?" I growled at him, pointing my sword in his direction. If he wasn't going to join me, then I would do this myself.

Mazin's face grew shuttered, his eyes narrowing on my blade. Then he turned to the guards at his side.

"Arrest her."

My lungs collapsed, my heart freezing in my chest.

He'd finally chosen, and he had chosen Vahid.

He'd chosen the man who had raised him, who had killed his mother. And suddenly, the dead warlord at my feet made much more sense. It wasn't an accident, them finding me here. It was all part of a plan.

"You did this," I hissed at Mazin. If I didn't know him so well, I wouldn't have noticed the flinch that crossed his features almost imperceptibly. Dark shock shot through me at that flinch, at those confirmed suspicions. But his face gave nothing more away.

"Dani, don't make this difficult. Don't fight and you won't get hurt."

"Don't fight?" I laughed, the sound manic, panic spilling from my mouth.

My laugh echoed off the palace ceilings like the sickening crack of bones. "You don't know me at all if you can say that." I turned to the guards. "Go ahead, try to arrest me. See what happens."

"Dani." Mazin's voice was sharper now, urgent and low. "Don't do this."

"Don't tell me what to do ever again." I lifted my sword over my head, preparing myself. "You mean nothing to me now. And it will be a pleasure to cut you down."

"Dani, stop. You'll die." His voice was low, but I knew his game now.

"I'll die anyway once the emperor gets a hold of me." I took a step forward. "I might as well go out fighting."

I moved forward at the guards flanking me, hoping to cut through them first and carve a path for myself. But Mazin's inaction ended as soon as I moved. He spun around me, unsheathing his own blade.

My breath caught in my chest, and I narrowed my eyes. "Are you actually going to go up against me, Maz? You'll lose."

But before he could respond, Darbaran rushed at me and I whirled to face him. Out of the corner of my eye Mazin stepped behind me.

I couldn't fight them both.

I inhaled, centering myself before battle. Is this how I would die? Being stabbed in the back by my ex-lover?

The glint of Mazin's sword reflected off the window behind me and I turned.

I would be damned if he didn't look me in the eye when he cut me down.

But he was holding his sword backward, the hilt facing me. I frowned, taking a step back, confusion warring with the rage of his betrayal. Until I realized what he was about to do.

No.

I opened my mouth to scream, the sound catching in my throat. I raised my own sword up, but it was too late.

He brought the hilt down against the back of my head.

I plunged into darkness, my legs giving way as I dropped like a stone to the floor.

Forty-six

"Get out of my way."

"Dani—"

My face was my own again, and he knew who I was. But my name on his lips brought back memories I wanted buried. The way his voice dipped low at the end, remembering the feeling of his fingers brushing across my shoulder when he whispered it in my ear.

"You don't get to call me that, not anymore."

"What should I call you, then? Sanaya?"

My head shot up. He knew.

He took a step toward me, as if he couldn't imagine me hurting him, as if I didn't hold my dead father's sword in my hand ready to slice his throat.

I lifted my sword high. He continued walking, his steps methodical and slow, his own sword still sheathed. He made no attempt to draw it.

"Thohfsa told you who I was?"

"You think I didn't know it was you?" His words were low and quiet, but I heard them clear across the courtyard. He tilted his head, examining me, roving over my now undisguised face, and I felt strangely vulnerable again. Anger rose in my chest, anger at myself that he still had the power to make me feel.

I moved back a half step, that anger burning into my tone. "You can't have."

"You didn't change your hands," he said, his voice a little rough. He held up his own right fist and pointed to his knuckles.

"I remember every scar on your body. Especially the ones I gave you. I felt that scar across your knuckles when you first came to the palace."

My heart lurched. I remembered the way he'd held my hand that day. The slow way he'd bent over and kissed my knuckles. His lips had brushed right over my scar.

"You knew and didn't say anything?" My skin felt cold. "You knew it was me. The entire time when we—"

I thought of our kiss, about when I had come to his room and what we had almost done. About every time I had flirted with him, when I had thought I was manipulating the situation. But the entire time he'd been doing the manipulating.

Fresh rage bled through me, as well as the hot flush of shame that he had outsmarted me again, even when I had been most on guard.

"I wanted to see what your plan was. And . . . I felt guilty. About what I'd done." He looked away, his lips thinning. "And I wanted to know how far you were going to take this. I would have stopped it before we . . . But in the end it was you who stopped it." He took a step closer. "I didn't know you'd escaped. The warden never told anyone. You escaped one of the most savage prisons in the empire. Then you came right back here. Why?"

"You know why," I growled as we circled each other. "You betrayed me. You betrayed my father. And now he's dead." I advanced, my voice nearly cracking with the weight of my anger. "You stole my whole life from me."

His expression was anguished but hard. "I was trying to get you out of there."

I pursed my lips together. "I don't believe you."

"Did you not wonder why you hadn't been executed? Your father would have been spared had he not been killed before I could intervene. I managed to smuggle you out to the prison and save your life."

"You sentenced me to suffer!" I shouted, that black rage seeping through me. Those whispered words, that voice that I recognized now, the djinn's voice, saying the same word over and over and over.

Revenge. Revenge. Revenge.

Maz's face was stricken.

I kept walking toward him, my sword raised. "You sentenced me to be tortured and tormented." My words were guttural, and with every step, his eyes grew bleaker. "To wonder why the person I *loved* had betrayed me. So why would you try to save my life when you had already destroyed it?" The last words were a whisper, ravaged and soft.

Mazin's fists were curled at his sides, his knuckles white. "Because it was the only thing I could think to do to save you. And they would have killed you."

"No, you just wanted me to live in agony."

"I didn't want that either." He shook his head, his eyes pleading.

"Then why?" I hated the way my voice cracked, I hated that I cared about his answer. I hated that I couldn't just run him through with my blade without thought. But I needed to know. I needed whatever answer he could give. "Why?"

A muscle ticked in his jaw, and he looked away, as if he could no longer meet my eyes.

"Vahid killed my mother. He laughed about it. I was never going to let him get away with it. But everything went wrong. Instead of rallying the northern tribes to overthrow the emperor, the warlord's death was blamed on you."

"So, you admit you staged it?"

He shook his head, his mouth grim. "No. It was my plan to work with the warlord, to take the throne from the emperor and overwhelm his forces. But the man was dead before I even had the chance."

328 • **Emily Varga**

"Liar!" I spat. "It was you who killed him. You who left his burned-out body for me to find."

"Why would I do that?"

"Because after everything, you still chose the emperor. Getting rid of the warlord was convenient. His death might have started a civil war if it wasn't blamed on me. I was the next best thing."

"Dani, I was going to get you out of that prison, I promise. But first—"

"First you had to watch my father die and pursue your own vengeance? Is that it? Even if your story is true, even if you didn't plan this entire thing to frame me, you still let me take the blame. All so you could get your own revenge on the emperor. You owed me more than that."

"You're right," he said quietly.

I reared back. "What?"

"I owed you more than that. But I couldn't have fought my way out of the palace with you. I had Anam to think about as well. What would he have done with my sister if I had left? I had her to protect."

Anam.

I tasted the acid in my mouth as he said it. I wanted to make him say the words. I wanted him to admit that he'd thought of everyone else but me.

Thunder echoed through the halls of the palace, and I looked up into the open sky of the courtyard, the heavy clouds darkening our figures, blending our shadows into one.

Rain splattered, thick droplets pounding the floor. A monsoon began to pour, the sheet of rain like a scream.

"Dani, the choice I made . . ." He shook his head. "It was the wrong one. I chose revenge over you. I chose it over everything."

His words grated on my skin, an echo of my own. But I brushed them away like the rain pounding my shoulders.

"Let me prove it to you now. Tell me what you want, Dani."

"What I want?" I lifted my sword in front of my face, the rain beating against the blade. "I want my fucking cat back."

I lunged at him, my sword pointed at his heart. My hands were slick, my vision blurry, but when it came to Mazin I saw clearly. I saw everything. He wouldn't be the one to take it all away from me again.

He finally drew his own blade, but raised his scimitar in defense instead of attack, flicking my blade away. But I knew him. I knew his body, the muscles in his arms, how long until he would tire, his ticks and habits.

I knew how to beat him.

I kept coming. Again, and again, and again. I arced my sword up overhead, meeting his blade in the flashing rain.

"I don't want to fight you."

"You don't have a choice."

He defended every attack I wagered against him, but never advanced himself. His face was a mask of anguish, but I recognized that determined clench of his jaw, the small crease in his forehead.

He was holding himself in check, and I wanted him to unleash. I wanted him to burn with hatred as much as I did, to fight like he meant it, to fight like I had meant something—anything—to him.

"Had you already plotted against me when we were together in your room?"

His eyes flashed dark as I chipped away at his stillness.

"And when we talked about your mother? Did you know then that you would abandon me to Vahid, just as she was?"

He slashed at my sword, but his blade faltered. My own slid down his and sliced his arm. He winced but sidestepped my next attack, spinning and lifting his scimitar to slam against my sword.

"When I opened my heart to you? You knew then that you were going to crush it, didn't you?"

I ducked low, my sword swiping to the side and the blade catching him across the middle before he fell back. He grunted, slamming backward, the rain pounding against him.

He got up on his forearms and flipped back up onto his feet before I could rush at him.

This time he moved against me.

I felt the rush of satisfaction as his sword hit mine, at the anger I saw bleeding into the darkness of his eyes.

"No!" He shouted the word, the rain amplifying the sound. "None of this was planned. None of this was what I wanted." His voice was hoarse, the stone facade of him finally cracking. "I wanted Vahid to suffer, not you. But you got caught up in it."

"And my father?" I twisted, slamming the hilt of my sword into his jaw. His head snapped back and he stumbled. I pressed forward my blade aimed at his chest.

But he pivoted at the last moment, and I caught him with the tip alone, a slice across his chest where his heart would be.

If he had one.

"What did you think would happen when I was arrested? You knew my father would come for me."

Pain laced across his features, making something break in my chest. "I thought I had more time."

I laughed, the bitter sound swallowed up by the rain. "You had it all planned out, you just failed to let anyone in on those plans."

"My revenge was supposed to be quick, easy."

"It wasn't."

"For neither of us," he agreed.

"Excuse me? You want me to pity you? You who live in your golden palace, who does the bidding of a man who murdered his mother to protect a sister who would likely be better off away from here? What do you know of betrayal? What do you know of anything that I went through?"

Mazin pushed my sword away with his, the sheer brute strength of his arms overcoming mine. I would never beat him that way, but I was faster, smarter—my tactics were always to weigh a man's weaknesses and use them to my advantage. He slashed the air in front of my face, more in an effort to ward me away from him. But I danced backward, arcing my blade.

"You think I don't understand?" His voice was guttural, his face close to mine as our swords pressed together in silent struggle. "You think I didn't mourn the death of your father too? I loved him like he was my own."

"And yet your loyalty suggests otherwise."

"I thought I could destroy Vahid!" shouted Mazin, and he pushed my sword away.

I lowered it.

"I thought I could undermine the emperor's influence in the north with the death of their beloved warlord and then finally take the throne from him."

His eyes were feverish, his mouth a bruise.

I gave him a grim smile. "And so, we come to the truth of it. You wanted the throne, not to protect your sister. Not revenge. This was never about anyone but you."

"I wanted revenge," he growled, the words reverberating through my body like I'd said them myself.

Because I *had* said them.

"Revenge for my mother. And look what it cost me. Tell me, what is your revenge costing you?" He threw his sword onto the white marble, then unbuckled the golden clasps of his sherwani. He peeled the plastered fabric off his body, the pale kurta beneath already soaked through with rain. The fabric had molded to his body like a second skin, and I could already see the scars beneath, could practically feel the ridges of them with my fingertips.

"What is your revenge costing you?"

He fell to his knees on the floor, looking up at me as if waiting for his execution.

"I am a shell of who I was for what I did to you. For what I did to your father. And still Vahid sits on that golden throne. Still he rules over the empire after all he has done."

He placed a wet hand over his chest. The rain had lessened, and now it was a dull drizzle. "You think it didn't feel like my heart had been eaten out of me when they took you away? Knowing that they had you, knowing you were imprisoned and I couldn't do anything?"

My sword was still. I tried to will my hands to move, to lunge forward and pierce him through the chest as he had done to me when he had me sent to that prison. But something stopped me. He knelt before me baring everything, as if there was nothing between us but this truth, this fight, this shared misery.

He said he hadn't betrayed me, but even if that were true, he'd abandoned me to get revenge. Was that any better?

I raised my sword with a scream that tore through me, the rage and hurt and anguish ripping through my body like a mad river.

Still, he didn't move. Those dark eyes watched me, as if he was perfectly fine with whatever I was about to do—even if I were to stab him through the heart.

My arms were aching and frozen, unable to move.

"What is your revenge costing you?"

Noor had said something similar, but I hadn't listened. I felt the storm of djinn magic still igniting my blood, and I knew I didn't have to fight Mazin with a sword to kill him. I could choke his body of life with a snap of my fingers. That dark rage engulfed me, dictating my sword like I was standing at the top of a mountain and ready to dive off into oblivion. I was at the point of no return now, the fury of the djinn magic so intense it was difficult to see straight, the bloodlust drowning me.

"Dani, I love you."

I closed my eyes, wishing he'd never said those words. They called me back to myself, to who I truly was before all this, before my father's death, before everything I knew and trusted was torn away.

And what about what I had done? Who I had become in order to best him?

My blade wavered.

"Dani." He said the words softly, so soft I could barely hear him over the rain. "I'm sorry."

I dropped my arms.

My sword hit the stone floor with a clatter. My knees followed, until I was on the ground, the rain falling around me.

"Dania."

His voice pierced my chest, because no matter how much I tried to outrun it, to dismiss it, to avenge it, half of my heart was still his. Even though he'd cleaved it out, it was still his, and I couldn't stop giving it to him.

He came toward me, his hands open.

And I took them.

Forty-seven

His hands were warm, despite the rain, and even though I had a swarm of emotions running through me, it still felt good to touch him. His fingers threaded through mine, and I closed my eyes at the sensation.

"Why can't I kill you?" My words sounded desperate, wild, with none of the viciousness I had felt. Even though I still had the djinn's power in my veins, it felt muted somehow.

"For the same reason I haven't been able to sleep properly for the past year. Because when I dream, it's always of you. When I fight, it's your voice in the back of my skull. We are part of each other. Dani, I can't ask for forgiveness for what I've done. I should have fought for you. I should have put you above my need for vengeance." He swallowed and closed his eyes. "I thought I could do more to help you. And yes, I wanted to take power from Vahid. I wanted him to know what it was to be powerless. But I should never have sacrificed you for that chance."

He was so close I could almost taste the raindrops on his lips, but I still felt torn in two.

Who was I without my revenge?

I must have said the words out loud, because a fire lit in Mazin's eyes and he looked at me, like truly seeing my face for the first time in over a year. "You're Dania."

"But I'm not. I don't know what I am anymore. Perhaps not even human." I curled my fingers, channeling that pulse of power under my skin.

I thought about what I had done to all the soldiers that had stood in my way at the command of the emperor. Of the prison guards I had cut down. And suddenly I felt . . . tired.

Noor's face, pleading with me, filled my head. And then Anam, who still had no idea who I truly was, but who had trusted me even when I had donned another face. And I thought of my nanu, still waiting in our village. If I stopped now, maybe I wouldn't have to destroy everything.

A burning sensation took hold of my veins, as if the magic inside me knew the decision I wrestled with. If I gave up this power, would the djinn still claim me?

Even if I condemned myself by making this bargain in the first place, I knew I would be lost if I let it burn through me. It felt like the zoraat mixture I had eaten but amplified by a thousand. And that same dark wrath was still present, lurking underneath the surface, threatening to spill over.

When had I ever let anything else take control of who I was?

I turned to Maz. "Where is Anam?"

"She's safe, I sent her away because of the increased protests in Basral. And I didn't know what you had planned to do."

"I would never harm Anam," I uttered, knowing it was true when I still had control of who I was, but with the djinn power, how could I know for sure? Was I still me?

"I was afraid you'd tear down every stone to get to me." He ended his words with a huff of laughter, and an uneasy smile as if he couldn't quite trust this truce between us.

Neither could I.

"I almost did." I exhaled.

I didn't know if I forgave Maz, but I no longer wanted to murder him, and that was something.

"Vahid expects me to come for him," I said slowly, testing the words on my tongue. "And I . . ." I choked on my next words and met Mazin's eyes. I must have betrayed a sense of my panic, because his own widened.

"I made a bargain with a djinn," I finally bit off.

I felt Maz's deep intake of breath, the shock reverberating off his skin. I couldn't stop myself now, or I would never get the words out.

"I bargained with him to use his power to destroy you and Vahid. And he expects me to fulfill that bargain." I couldn't bring myself to say what would become of me once I did. I exhaled slowly. Then I picked up my talwar from the ground and stood, offering my other hand to Maz. His eyebrows rose to his hairline. I tucked my chin to hide my smile, but nearly lost my footing when he took my hand with his own callused one. I helped him to his feet, and for a moment we just stared at each other.

"So what will you do?" he asked softly, his eyes dipping to my lips.

I swallowed, then gave him a rueful smile, settling into this familiar and yet new feeling between us.

"Well, I've never been one to do what men expect."

Forty-eight

We left the palace behind, the city disappearing in a cloud of dust. Every djinn-soaked drop of blood in my body rebelled against it—I was leaving the emperor and my revenge behind.

Despite that, my heart felt free.

We rode through the valley and to my village on Mazin's stallion, and I tried not to think about how good it felt to have his arms around me again.

I hadn't quite shaken the need for revenge, the guilt that my father died and I wouldn't be avenging that death. But Noor was right. Baba wouldn't want me to destroy myself for it.

Even though I might have destroyed myself already.

The insides of my hands were filled with black curling vines that ran up my forearms. The djinn had marked me, and I couldn't outrun my own skin.

I had made a bargain, but I wouldn't be fulfilling my end of it.

And when the djinn came for me, I would need to be ready.

The sky swirled with a dark storm that seemed anything but natural. Lightning cracked overhead, and the darkness opened up to pour down its wrath.

"I don't think we can go very much further!" Maz shouted in my ear over the pounding hooves and screaming rain. "Rakhna can't take much more of this, not with the lightning!"

He turned off the well-worn dirt road and raced toward a large apricot orchard surrounded by an outcropping of houses and a white-walled caravanserai.

We arrived at the caravanserai soaked to the bone.

Sheets of rain pounded the little village, despite its sheltered position in the valley. The apricot trees swayed under the power of the wind, unripened fruit flying from their branches. A herd of goats was being corralled into a nearby shelter, and villagers were running for cover all around us. No one was traveling in this storm, not even the emperor.

An old woman met us at the door of the caravanserai holding two cups of hot chai. I downed the liquid immediately, relishing the scalding tea pouring down my throat.

Maz had left to put Rakhna in the stable, and I waited for him in the entranceway.

"The djinn are angry."

I whirled around. "What?"

The woman gestured to the blackened sky overhead. "The djinn. Only they could produce a storm like this. But I wonder why they are so furious."

Thunder crackled above us, as if proving her point. The woman was wrapped in a red dupatta with frayed edges and curling jasmine flower embroidery, and her eyes were a warm, rich brown in her weathered face. I had stopped at this village a few times with my father on our way to Basral, but we'd never come to this caravanserai before.

"Maybe someone has offended them," I said, hiding my stained hands in the folds of my wet kurta.

Maybe someone has gone back on a bargain.

But this storm didn't seem like the djinn who had bargained with me. When I met him, he seemed emotionless, confident. This was the storm of bitter anger.

It raged down on the tiny valley village until rivulets of water ran through the streets and along the edges of the caravanserai. They had protection against flooding—heavy rains would devastate valley towns such as these. But if the rain continued as it was there would be problems.

"Do you need a room?"

"Pardon?" My head shot up, meeting her kind eyes.

"You and your companion. There's only one room left. And with the way things are going you might want to take it because we are going to be inundated with travelers heading to Basral."

I stared at her. We thought we would wait out the storm here, but a chance to get dry and change my clothes from the sopping mess I was in would be welcome.

"Yes. We'll take it," I said, not letting myself dwell on what that meant.

"Of course. I'll have Attaf bring up some of the mutton nihari we have on the fire. It's good and will warm you."

"Do you have another kurta?" I asked, clinging to my sodden clothes. "Or anything to get dry in?"

"He'll bring some things up for you and your friend." The woman leaned in close to me. "I'll also send some pakaal tea as well," she said, her voice low. "In case you need it." I felt my face turn red hot at the mention of the herbal tea used to prevent pregnancy, but she swept away before I could respond.

The woman looked up as Maz stepped through the door, rainwater dripping from his shoulders. He wore his sherwani again when we ran from the palace, and the woman's mahogany eyes went wide as she took him in.

"Sahib." She bowed her head. "Forgive me, I didn't realize the emperor's man was here, I would have had a servant take your horse."

"It isn't an issue," Mazin said smoothly.

I was struck by how much older he seemed since I came back. I was only gone a year, and yet his shoulders filled the entranceway with a presence he didn't possess before I was arrested. Or maybe I just never noticed it before.

"I got us a room," I said hastily.

Mazin blinked.

"To warm up," I said, my cheeks heating. "And to get out of these clothes." I gestured to my wet kurta.

Mazin looked down at me, then his eyes shot up just as fast.

"I mean, to change into dry ones."

My face was so hot I wanted to throw myself into the raging storm and never come out again.

"Of course," he responded, clearing his throat.

The woman behind us smothered a laugh. If possible, I grew even more embarrassed because I'd forgotten she was still there. I didn't even want to bring up the contraceptive tea she'd offered.

"Your room is upstairs, to the left, sahib." She handed Mazin the key. "Your food and extra clothes will be along shortly." She nodded to us, then shuffled to the kitchen.

We proceeded up the stairs in silence, walking past the travelers in the dining room watching the storm through the windows with awe on their faces.

Dark clouds were raging above Basral, swirling in a frenzy of violence. We were safe inside for now, but how long until the emperor came after us? How long until the djinn dogged my steps?

I continued up the stairs, stepping into the vacant room slowly, my stomach dropping with a lurch when Mazin closed the door behind us. The fire was lit, and I moved closer to it, rubbing at my freezing skin to bring feeling back into it. I turned around and stopped at the sight of the bed sitting in the middle of the room.

The silence stretched out between us, thick with anticipation.

A knock sounded at the door, which startled us both. A small man, presumably Attaf, bore a very large tray of food in one hand, and dry clothes and towels in the other.

"Simple clothes, sahib, but they are dry and warm." Attaf hustled in, placing the tray on the small table by the fire and the clothes on the end of the bed. "And Badeea makes the best nihari outside of Basral. You won't be cold after this."

"Thank you," Mazin said, closing the door behind him.

Then Maz turned to me. "I can go, give you the room. I'm happy downstairs anyway, I can monitor the storm and be ready when it's time to leave."

"Maz, we've shared a room before," I scoffed. "In fact, we've shared much more than that." I raised a brow, there was no point in skirting around the obvious now. "And you are soaked. At least get changed and eat something. No one is traveling and it looks like the storm is going to go all night. And you certainly can't sit out there *all night*."

He let out a heavy breath and still seemed uncertain.

"What's wrong, you think I'm going to kill you in your sleep?"

Maz looked up, a wry smile in the corner of his mouth. "The thought had crossed my mind."

"By all means, go sit in the dining hall if you're scared."

That dimple came out again, and I caught my breath.

"I never said I was scared of you, Dani. Maybe I *want* you to try to kill me."

"I can't tell if you're flirting by asking me to kill you or not."

The smile faded from his lips. He walked toward the fire, his back to me, his sherwani already beginning to dry in the warmth of the room. I wasn't cold anymore, not nearly as much as I had been, but my cotton kurta was still soaking wet against my skin.

"When you were arrested," he said suddenly, "when I persuaded Vahid to throw you in prison, I thought it was the safest place for you while I tried to figure something out. I knew you wanted me to fight—but I couldn't leave her. I told my mother I'd protect Anam. I swore to her I would." His voice broke, and he raked a hand through his hair.

"I understand," I said, coming up behind him. "More than you know." I thought of Noor, whom I'd only known a short time, but whom I had forged such a strong bond with that it was unimaginable to abandon her. And Anam and Maz only had each other. I understood, but it hurt more than I wanted it to.

"I still hoped you would fight with me. That you would fight *for* me. And I was devastated when you didn't. Why didn't you tell me about your plans to overthrow Vahid?"

He turned to me, his eyes stark. "Dani, I've seen Vahid torture people with zoraat to obtain information from them. I didn't want to put you in that position. I thought that if I could mobilize against Vahid with the north, then we'd have a chance at real change. But then the warlord died, they arrested you and killed your father—all my plans crumbled. And the only thing I could think about was surviving, keeping Anam safe and breaking you out. But the prison warden made freeing you nearly impossible. I tried everything, every method of bribery, every possible way I could. I even laid the groundwork for your escape until . . ."

I was scared to ask anything, scared to speak, because as much as I wanted to hear this story, it felt like pouring salt on a fresh knife wound. I wanted to know, and yet I didn't. I wanted to bury my vengeance and anger and yet it was still part of me, tattooed on my hands for all to see.

But I *needed* to hear what he had to say.

For me, for us. I needed to see if I could close this hole in my heart, to see if it was done between us.

Or if he was still mine and I was still his.

"Dani, I love you."

"Until?" I prompted.

"Until you showed up, looking like someone else, asking after your father's knives. But the way you spoke, your gestures, even the way you bit your bottom lip—it was *you*. It seemed impossible. For all I knew you were still in prison, still locked away while I was going out of my mind. When I spoke to Sanaya and felt . . ." He trailed away, looking at the flames. They danced off the planes of his face, his cheekbones high and proud, eyes fathomless depths. A scar curled over one eyebrow that I didn't recognize, and it made me remember that he'd lived a life while I'd been in prison. He'd been given scars I didn't know about either.

He raked his hands through his hair again. "I thought I was going mad," he whispered. "Every time we spoke, it felt like I'd finally snapped. I was imagining you in someone else . . . I thought it was my mind trying to cope with what I'd done. We even got word of a sighting of you in your village, and I sent soldiers to investigate. I wrote to the prison, demanding to see you, but the warden wouldn't agree. She said nothing of your escape. I know now she likely didn't want the emperor to know that two very important prisoners had broken out of her supposedly impenetrable jail." He lifted his head, moving closer to me, and my heart hammered in my chest.

"But then I touched your hands. And I *knew*. I felt the scars I'd given you, felt the memories we'd lived together." He took another step, until he was inches away and the heat from his body was like the fire itself. My fingers flexed, wanting to reach for him, but I kept them pressed to my side. After everything, could I fall into this again?

Or maybe I'd already fallen, I just didn't want to climb back out.

"Maz . . ."

"Did you think I wouldn't know you? I'd know you with any face. Any skin. Any hair. A thousand djinn could disguise you from me and I'd still be able to find you just by the sound of your breath."

I exhaled, the space between us so small he could likely feel it on his cheek.

"Tell me you can never forgive me, and I'll go. Tell me you hate me and I won't bother you again."

My body swayed toward his, my skin knowing my answer before I could say it out loud.

"Because unless you tell me that, my foolish heart hopes and dreams and imagines. I can't make right what I did, I can't change it. But I can beg. I can promise that in all things, in all ways, I belong to you. And I will never let you feel as though I didn't fight for you again."

His voice was the crackling flames, the beat of my heart, the breath in my lungs. It drowned out the dark magic in my blood, the whispers of the djinn, and the doubting thoughts in my head.

"No," I said, my words clear and sure. "I can't tell you those things. I can't because they wouldn't be true. And we promised we'd be true to each other, didn't we?"

He closed his eyes, his hands uncurling at his sides. I reached up and cupped his cheek, and whatever barrier there was between us shattered at my touch. And then he was holding me, pressing me to him, mouth on my lips, at my throat, fingers in my hair. I kissed him back—it was impossible for me not to, I felt like I would die if I didn't.

I peeled back the coat from his shoulders, and my own wet kurta joined his on the ground. We tumbled onto the bed, his lips on my skin, hands at my waist, my thighs. We were in a frenzy together, the storm outside matching the one between us, except instead of rage and wrath it was every memory we'd shared, every slight touch and heated glance. It was a lifetime of passion and rivalry and pain and hope.

And it was us—every messy, apprehensive, fervent part of us, together as we'd always been. It was my scarred hands in his, his tongue against my pulse, my legs around his waist. It was who we were, and who we became, and I knew that he was right.

He would always know me, would always see me.

Just as I would always see him.

———

"The storm is lessening."

I watched the window as Maz traced lazy circles around my hip with his fingers.

"We should go soon, then." His voice was soft, and I knew he wanted to stay as much as I did. But we both had people counting on us, and we couldn't let them down. "Vahid will be coming."

The mention of his name doused the cozy warmth of our caravanserai room and brought me back to reality.

Unfortunately, it also prickled the magic underneath my skin, like the djinn power in my veins knew exactly what Vahid's name meant.

We dressed hurriedly in the warm clothes given to us by Attaf, and Maz ran to get his horse saddled.

I joined him at the front of the caravanserai and he put his hands around my waist to lift me onto his stallion.

But he paused.

I looked down at him, his stillness making me wary.

"What is it?"

"Nothing." He shook his head. "Whatever happens next, whatever the emperor rains down on us, I wanted to remember this moment, just as you are right now."

He swung up behind me on the saddle, his arms strong and sure as he led us back through the valley to my small mountain village. Hope was a bird rising in my chest and it felt as if we could overcome anything, as long as we were together.

I just wished I knew what was coming.

———

Once we reached the edge of my village, Maz urged the horse faster, until we came to the little house my nanu was staying in. Noor should have been here by now, but I saw no sign of her, nor her horse.

Dread washed over me. The village was too still, too quiet. It had felt the same when we'd found out about my father.

I dismounted and ran into Nanu's house.

It was empty, the ashes in the hearth cold, a cup of chai untouched on the mango wood table.

"Where are they?" I whispered, my voice cracking.

Maz stood behind me, his steady presence a balm to my rising panic. Did I ever think that Mazin standing beside me would be a relief again? But now it felt as though I could breathe again. I leaned back against him and felt his surprise at my unexpected touch before his hands came up and he clasped my arms.

"We'll find them," he murmured against my hair.

"Noor and Nanu are the only other people I have left."

"We'll find them," he repeated, sweeping his eyes around the small cottage. "But they aren't here."

We left the house, the early rays of dawn filtering through the empty streets. A sound echoed across the square, the smashing of glass, and a muffled groan.

Mazin and I both reached for our swords at the same time.

I knew the direction it came from.

"The smith." I looked at Mazin.

My father's house.

The last time I'd been there I had learned of his death. I'd cursed the man now beside me and promised I would find retribution.

But all I wanted now was to find the people I cared about and get them out of this alive.

We jogged to my old home, falling in step beside each other, like an old dance we both knew the steps to.

I knew Maz, knew his moves, his breath. I felt the burden on my shoulders ease now that we were on the same side again. We stopped on the edge of the village, watching the smith and the little house connected to it from a distance.

I cast a glance at Maz as he crouched beside a stone wall, his scimitar in hand, dark eyes focused on the smith. He flicked his gaze in my direction and stilled, the shadows playing off the angles of his face.

That feeling of anticipation rushed to my stomach when he turned those intense eyes on me, something that didn't feel like relief or calm or comfort, but altogether like dropping into a dark sea. Something I never thought he'd make me feel again.

"What is it?" His voice was lower, rougher than before, and I wondered if working together again had made him realize those same feelings.

"It feels good," I said, my abrupt way of blurting out uncomfortable truths catching us both off guard again. "Having you beside me again."

His eyes darkened, and he drew closer, close enough so that I could hear his low words.

"I'm sorry I ever made you think I wasn't."

I exhaled, the quiet ferocity in his voice shaking me.

We crept closer to the small stone building surrounding the smith, but no other sounds came from it. I finally pushed through the door, my sword in hand ready to take on whatever I would find there.

But every room was empty, the same as it was before.

All my father's possessions gone, the house still looted.

Until I got to the final bedroom—my parents' room.

There a figure sat on the bed, alone, closed in on itself, almost resigned.

"Nanu?"

She started and looked up at me, her light eyes a little brighter than usual, her crinkled, dark skin the color of burned embers. But something seemed . . . off.

"Dania." Her voice was plaintive, not a question exactly, but an acknowledgment. As if she had been waiting for me.

I rushed forward, wrapping her small body in my arms. She was cold and didn't return my embrace.

"Nanu, are you all right? We thought something had happened to you—the house you were staying in—"

"I'm fine. Really," she said in a disconnected sort of way. As if she were talking to me from a long distance.

I frowned, my eyes sweeping over her. "What are you doing here alone, Nanu? Where is Noor? She was meant to find you."

Had Noor even made it to the village?

At the mention of Noor's name, my grandmother's pale fire eyes flashed. "Dania, your friend could not be trusted." Her words were a hiss, an unfamiliar savage tone, and I stepped back from her, unease filling my stomach.

"What do you mean?" My eyes swept the room, as if Noor was hiding somewhere.

"Noor came here, yes. But she betrayed you, my granddaughter."

Something wasn't right, and I shook my head in confusion.

I had been betrayed before, but the certainty that sat in my heart was unlike anything else—Noor wouldn't do that.

"Nanu, what are you talking about?"

A muffled cry sounded from somewhere nearby, and I realized Maz hadn't joined us in the room. I took a step toward the door, but Nanu's hand shot out, gripping my wrist so tightly I let out a gasp of surprise. Her strength took me off guard, and I jerked my hand away, but she didn't release it.

"Don't go," she said, her voice raspy.

My eyes scanned the room, trying to pin down the uneasiness flooding through me. "Nanu, let go."

"Your friend has abandoned you," she repeated in that detached voice. "Left you for Vahid."

Something glinted from the corner of the room, something dark and smooth. My eyes focused on it, and I saw them then, like small oval pearls I couldn't ever seem to escape.

Djinn seeds.

A small bag of zoraat rested on the nightstand. The same bag I had given to Noor before she left. My breath caught in my throat, and I whirled on my grandmother.

"Nanu, where did you get those from?"

Her gaze flicked behind her, and I wrenched my arm free. Everything in me said to draw my sword.

But could I? Could I pull a weapon against my own grandmother? Something splintered in my chest as I laid my free hand on my dagger.

But I couldn't shake this feeling, this churning in my gut that something wasn't right.

My gaze returned to the seeds. Why was the zoraat here?

And if it was here, it was entirely possible that the woman standing before me was not my grandmother.

"You aren't my nanu, are you?"

She gave me a curious stare, as if she were confused by my question. I swept her body for anything else that could identify her—that one piece of physical evidence that a person needed to keep before they could transfigure themselves.

But nothing. She was exactly the same, her eyes, her weathered hands, each silvery wisp of her hair. Even her smell was the same—a woody, mountain scent with hints of crocus flower. Her skin was papery, her eyes bright—she was still my grandmother.

"Why would I have to pretend to be someone else? That didn't get you your vengeance, did it, girl?" Her voice wasn't cruel, but factual, as if she were merely curious.

I opened my mouth but the words dried on my tongue. Confusion warred with fear and the depths of something else thrumming through me.

Revenge. Revenge. Revenge, it whispered.

But the words were not for me this time.

"I saw your Mazin riding into town with you," Nanu continued. "Wasn't he the one who sent you to prison in the first place?"

I wrinkled my forehead, frustrated at the abrupt change of subject. "What happened to Noor?" I repeated.

And where is Mazin? I cast a glance to the hallway hoping to see him. I still had the djinn's power leaping at my fingertips, but the less I could use it the better. And I certainly didn't want to use it against Nanu. I eyed the seeds on the bedside table again.

If my grandmother had consumed any, there was no telling what she could do.

But what would she need djinn power for?

"Noor is weak," she snapped. "I'm surprised at you for surrounding yourself with people like her. Like Mazin. People who stand next to you just to absorb your strength. You are a warrior, like your mother. You don't need to surround yourself with weaklings as your mother did with your father."

My breath collapsed at her words, at their meaning. My skin felt white hot as something rose up inside me. Something bigger than djinn power, something that changed my entire worldview.

I knew that my grandmother and my father hadn't really gotten along, but I didn't realize the extent of her dislike. I stepped back, bumping into the door behind me. Nanu had never spoken this way about my mother and father, ever.

A fleeting memory tickled at the back of my mind, from before my mother was killed. A memory of my nanu as an entirely different woman. Not this silent, tightly coiled person. And then, the night my mother was killed, I remembered that. The way she howled and tore at her hair. The way she screamed and pushed me away.

How my father tried to calm her, even though he too had just lost his wife. But she didn't want to speak to anyone, instead moving out of the house and living alone in the village. Since my mother's death, Nanu became distant like some part of her died as well.

But the way her eyes glittered, it was as if something in her was now alive.

Like there was a viper under her skin.

Cold tendrils of fear ran down my spine as she advanced on me, her pale eyes huge and round.

"Baba wasn't weak," I said slowly, trying to understand what was happening. "He was the strongest person I know."

"You didn't know your mother well enough, then. She could have ruled over the northern tribes. Instead, she chose your father and came here." She spat on the floor. "And got herself killed."

"Mama was killed by a northern tribesman, Nanu. It wasn't Baba's fault."

"He let her go there, unprotected. He angered the warlord that killed her, refusing to fashion him a sword. Her death was on his hands as much as the man that slit her throat."

My mind whirled, the realization hitting me that Nanu had felt this way my whole life. And I'd never seen it until today. And now I saw everything.

It was as if the sky were caving in and I had no room to breathe anymore. My chest was tight, about to combust from the pressure, my eyes burning, though no tears came.

"The warlord," I said, the words barely leaving my mouth. "The northern warlord I was charged with killing. That was you, wasn't it?"

The confirmation was written all over her face. Her mouth flattened, nose flared. She looked guilty, but also . . . proud?

The northern chief had been murdered, and all this time I had thought it was Vahid trying to quell a rebellion.

But it was my grandmother, getting her revenge, and condemning me to this forsaken path.

I stumbled back, my mouth like dust, my djinn-tattooed hands shaking. My own grandmother had been the reason I was imprisoned.

"He was the chief who killed your mother," she confirmed, her hands reaching out for me. "I knew he was coming to Basral, the first time in years since he killed my girl. I'd never felt such need for retribution. He stole my life from me. And when I thought I would explode with the injustice of it all, a djinn came to me. I bargained for a small amount of power—just enough to do what needed to be done—and I destroyed the man who killed my daughter." Her eyes shone brightly, sweat coating her upper lip as if she were ill, her skin gray and waxy.

I couldn't move, couldn't speak. I stared at my grandmother, realizing I never really knew her. She had made a bargain with a djinn, she had traded for the power to seek vengeance.

We were more alike than I thought.

"I watched him writhe as his insides burned up," she whispered, her voice as soft as a caress. "As his skin bubbled and his blood boiled inside him. It wasn't enough. It wasn't enough pain for what he stole. But still, I knew satisfaction. I knew strength. More than I had in years."

She looked at me, those pale green eyes—my mother's eyes—boring into me, eating at me with her revenge.

The warlord deserved to die. I did not blame her for her vengeance. I would have done the same, I thought bitterly.

I *had* done the same.

"I knew you were headed to that room," she continued, and my lungs froze. "I had heard your plans." She closed her eyes. "There was one more person who deserved punishment for your mother. And I knew if you were arrested, he would try to help you."

A sharp pain splintered inside me, but she kept speaking, oblivious to the agony she was causing.

"I encouraged your father to try to save you. It wasn't difficult. He charged to the palace, scimitar in the air, and did for you what he never did for my daughter." Her voice was low and rough, the hatred pouring out like bitter tea.

"He loved you more than he ever loved her. That's why he didn't go with her to the north. That's why she's dead. She deserved better than him. She deserved better than both of you." Our eyes met, and I was taken aback by the darkness in hers.

"Nanu. *You* killed Baba." I rolled the words on my tongue like poison, my mouth numb. I still didn't want to believe it. "You had me arrested. I was beaten, tortured. Imprisoned for a *year*."

"But you survived." Nanu clasped her hands together, her eyes taking on a bolder gleam. She approached me steadily and I wondered if she had consumed the zoraat.

"I thought you would be executed. I counted on it. Then I would have fulfilled my bargain—I needed to give something up. You, for the warlord. You, for your father. But you lived." She watched me with a terrifying intensity.

"Because you are *strong*," she continued. "You are like me and your mother. You were forged in the fires of hatred too, made new by your revenge. I watched you when you came back, you were someone who could light this world on fire, who could make it yours. I was going to kill you then, but in the end, I couldn't. Not when you reminded me so much of her. You could destroy Vahid, crush anyone who stood in your way. You had vengeance filling your soul, *just like me.*"

She reached a weathered hand out to me, as if I were going to take it and clasp it to my breast, as if I didn't want to swing my knife and chop off every one of her fingers for killing my father, for wishing me dead, for giving up on us all when my mother was killed.

"I knew then that you were worthy of her. A daughter that could burn the earth to the ground with the power of the djinn."

She reached for me again, and something in me snapped. "You killed Baba. You condemned me to death. You destroyed your family for a daughter who would have hated your actions. Mama *loved* Baba. And she loved me. And you destroyed the things she loved in her memory."

I exhaled, the back of my eyes burning. I lowered my sword. "I am *not* like you. I will not throw my entire life away anymore on a path that leads to nothing but death and ash. That is not what Amma would have wanted for either of us."

My grandmother dropped her hands, and her face took on a grim cast. "Then it appears I will get a chance to fulfill my bargain after all."

The door behind me moved, the glint of a scimitar flashing through it.

"Dani." Mazin's eyes flicked between my grandmother and me. "I found Noor. She's okay. She was immobilized and tied up, but I couldn't free her. I think it was djinn magic."

I whirled my eyes back to my grandmother. "So, you did consume the seeds."

She scoffed. "You think I would waste that power? You had it all at your fingertips. I thought you were smarter than this." She looked at Mazin. "But you chose someone weak to be beside you as well."

"He's not weak," I uttered, my voice low. "Weakness is destroying your only family for vengeance, killing those who love you for your own gain." I lowered my sword and took a step forward. "But you don't have to do this, Nanu. You can still come with us." I slid the sword into its sheath. "We'll destroy the seeds, make it so no one can ever use them again." I swallowed a lump in my throat, thinking of everything she had done to my father, me, Maz. So many lives destroyed for revenge.

But the cycle ended here.

"I forgive you, Nanu. I forgive what you've done."

My grandmother watched me for a long moment, her eyes bright. "Forgive me? There is nothing to forgive. I gave you the chance to be strong, to forge your own destiny, and now you've thrown it away." She reached into the pocket of her dark shalwar, pulling out a handful of seeds. "But I won't throw it away. I am going to steal it for myself."

She stuffed a palmful in her mouth, the dark seeds glistening like tiny bugs, blackening her gums, her mouth, her tongue.

I lunged forward, grabbing at her wrist. "Nanu, stop! You have no idea what this amount will do to you."

I had seen Noor be so careful, grinding up the seeds quietly, measuring out each portion diligently. I'd seen Thohfsa collapse and die from eating too much.

When the djinn magic was in your blood, you felt invincible.

I felt the pull of it now with the power in my veins, and I fought to control it. I tried to still her limbs but I was too late. She'd eaten them, and her eyes were alight with zoraat. She roared in pain, clutching at her throat, her eyes bulging. Then she turned her wild, feral gaze on Mazin and me.

I looked at Maz, our eyes meeting, everything I wanted to say to him contained in that one glance. Fear. Longing.

Love.

And then I opened my mouth and uttered one final word to him. "Run."

Forty-nine

Maz didn't question me or hesitate. He took off through the door and shouted for Noor.

"Nanu, you don't want to do this."

"You don't leave me with any choice. Don't stand in my way."

"I'm not going to hurt you." I felt the djinn power running through my veins prick at my senses. A hot flame of magic was ready to burst out of me, to consume everything, the house, my grandmother, myself.

But I didn't want that path anymore.

I didn't want to kill Nanu, despite what she had done. It wouldn't end this circle of hatred, of vengeance.

"You couldn't hurt me if you tried."

"I have more power than you," I said carefully, raising my palm up and letting her see the blackness inking my palm and the hot flame within it. "I don't want to use it."

Her eyes burned bright. "So, you've made a bargain too." She smiled, too stretched, like skin pulled over a skeleton. She had become something other than human, as if the djinn had inhabited her and pulled out her humanity, leaving her with a husk of a body fed on rage.

She advanced on me, but this time, I stood my ground.

Was this who I would have become?

Was this the future that awaited me?

A woman wretched and shriveled with her need for vengeance?

No. Not anymore. You had to choose to become this, to forsake all joy in favor of destruction.

That would not be me.

She took another step forward and I lifted my palms again. Unease flashed through her eyes. And then a different kind of look altogether.

Her face creased in agony, and she unleashed a low howl.

"Nanu?" I moved toward her hesitantly.

"Don't call me that," she snapped, jerking away from my outstretched hand. She curled into herself. "You are no granddaughter of mine," she croaked out.

Then she lifted her hands, those pale green eyes bleeding into black. My breath caught in my throat as tendrils of darkness spilled from her fingertips, glossy, as if she'd spilled a bottle of ink into the air and it took flight. They curled around me, a viper tightening around its prey ready to choke the life away.

I could have raised my own hands in defense, could have used the djinn power pounding against my pulse and light the dark on fire.

But I didn't. I wanted to see how far she would go.

"You could have loved me," I whispered. "All these years, you held yourself back and I never knew it was because of your grief over my mother. But you could have opened yourself to loving me."

"Like you opened yourself after your father died? You came back for the same thing. Revenge."

The spiraling black veins grew closer, an echo of the ones crawling down my hands. They closed in, the air around me turning cold, then unbearable.

I called on the borrowed djinn magic that burned under my skin, waiting to erupt. It wrapped itself around the blackness, swarming it like a hive of bees. A column of fire burst from me and enveloped the sack of zoraat beside the bed, alighting like a puff of desert scrub.

Then I walked through the flames, toward my grandmother.

Her eyes widened, her face blanching.

"How did you do that? How much did you have to consume?"

"I didn't consume any. I was given this by the djinn himself."

"Djinns do not *give*. You traded something considerable for a taste of that power." She tilted her head, her black eyes knowing. "Your life, perhaps?" She watched my face carefully, and I realized she'd been doing this to me for years, assessing, evaluating. "You think I'm the dangerous one when you bargain for much more?" She watched me. "You *are* like me."

"I'm nothing like you," I bit off. "I am capable of changing. And even if I did something I regret, I can atone. I can make it right."

I wanted to believe that.

I *had* to believe that.

Because there was no way I could fulfill that bargain I made. Not when I saw where it would lead me.

"It's not too late, Nanu." I held my hand out to her again. "You don't have to do this."

She shook her head, her eyes still wild but sad. "Keep your forgiveness. I don't want to be forgiven. I gave my daughter justice. I gave—"

She broke off, a choked sound cutting off her words. Her hands went to her neck, gripping the skin hard.

"Nanu? What is it?"

She doubled over and screamed, more black tendrils spreading from her hands, filling the room around us.

"I . . . can't . . . I can't," she gasped, and I knelt next to her writhing form. She screamed again, and I saw that her tongue had shriveled inside her mouth, her teeth blackened.

"The seeds." She had taken too many, and not in the right quantities. She must have taken different quantities to Thohfsa, giving her power temporarily before poisoning her.

I swallowed, my throat thick, my eyes burning with unshed tears.

Nanu had killed my father. Betrayed me and got me arrested. Did she deserve my kindness? My empathy?

I exhaled, placing my hands on her. I wouldn't destroy my soul for revenge, no matter what she deserved. "I'll try to help you."

I closed my eyes and pulled at the power that bound me to the djinn. So far it had bent to my will when I had called upon it. Something whispered inside me, dark and deep. I could save her, I knew I could.

I pressed my hand over her mouth as she convulsed with the stain of the poison inside her. I concentrated on flushing her body of the toxin. She screamed, but I held fast, stopping her wriggling with an arm wrapped around her middle.

"I'm trying to help you, Nanu."

But the more I flooded her with power, the more I realized I needed . . . more.

The zoraat wasn't responding in the way I thought it would, it was resisting me.

I would need more power, more strength, perhaps everything I had.

Nanu stopped struggling at the same moment my arms went slack. I released her and she got on her hands and knees on the floor.

"Help me," she begged, fear lacing her voice. "Get it out of me."

I wet my lips with my tongue, trying to tell her with the right words. That I wanted to try, but it would take all of me.

"I can't."

"What?"

"It's too much. I can't save you without destroying myself."

She coughed, black liquid spilling from her throat onto the date palm mat. "You won't even try for the last of your family?" She gripped her stomach. "Help me!" she screamed.

I hesitated. "I don't owe you this," I said finally. "I don't owe you all of me. Not after what you did. Perhaps not ever. And if you loved me, you would never ask it."

She gave a gut-wrenching cough. "I thought you weren't devoted to vengeance anymore? You are punishing me for your father's death."

I knelt down beside her, bringing my voice low, almost indiscernible. "This isn't revenge. This is cause and effect."

"Dania." Her voice was pleading, a high whine that sliced through my heart. But there was someone else in my heart too, and Baba would be here with me now if it wasn't for her. Noor and Mazin were still here. I was still here. In the end, my loyalty was with them and myself.

"I can't help you, Nanu. Not at the cost of myself."

She doubled over, crying out again as her nails began to turn black. Pain and guilt and misery lanced through me, but I turned away from her.

I walked away from the room, my grandmother's screams the last thing I heard before I finally shut the door to my baba's house.

Fifty

"Are you okay?" Maz's steady voice called out as I tried not to think of my grandmother dead of the zoraat she had consumed. I tried not to think of me walking away from her, of the choices we'd both made to get here.

Death by her own revenge.

Will that be me?

Noor and Maz waited at the edge of the village, with Mazin's horse saddled and a pack mule waiting behind it. Noor sat on the dirt, her hands and ankles magically bound together, a tie that was once around her mouth now loosened and drooping around her neck. I exhaled with relief at seeing her unharmed; her round eyes met mine and she nodded. Souma's treasure was slung over the back of the pack mule and a single bag of zoraat remained.

"No," I answered Mazin, "I'm not okay."

My eyes narrowed on the zoraat.

I walked past him and snatched up the bag of seeds from the side of the mule.

"And I won't be until these things are destroyed. All of them."

I threw the bag on the ground, my chest heaving, a thousand screaming voices echoing in my brain.

These seeds were death.

My grandmother's. Baba's. All the protestors in the city fighting to survive. The power inside my veins rebelled at what I was about to do, but I ignored it. Instead, I concentrated the energy inside me into a single spear of pure flame and aimed it at the bag. In a flash it lit up, a flame so hot it turned bright blue before blazing red. It was over quick, the bag of zoraat burning to ash.

The ground was scorched black where the sack had been.

"Seems a bit of an overreaction," Noor called out. She lifted her hands in the air. "Care to remove of these djinn-made bindings if you are going around burning things?"

I did the same to the rope tying her hands, concentrating my power there until they sputtered into a small flame and disintegrated.

After Noor was free, she stood, looking from me to Mazin. "The last time I saw you, you were trying to murder him. Now what are you? Friends?" She crossed her arms. "Or something more?"

"I changed my mind about the murder," I said, putting my hands on my hips, deliberately ignoring her other question.

"Have you?" Maz raised a brow. "That's a relief. I thought you might take up the sword against me again." He smiled, and I returned the gesture.

That feeling fluttered in my chest, familiar and yet new. I didn't know this Mazin, and yet he still set my body aflame like no magic that existed.

"I think I liked it better when you two wanted to kill each other," groaned Noor.

I shot her a look. "Noted."

"Your grandmother?" Mazin asked, and I didn't meet his gaze. I felt the sorrow of her death, even though she had been responsible for everything. It was an odd clash of emotions—grief warring with anger. I understood why she had done it, which was perhaps what scared me most of all. That she had loved my mother so much it had trumped all other relationships and prevented her from seeing what she still had left.

Noor's eyes were pinched with concern.

"She took too much zoraat," I explained. "She couldn't handle it. I tried to . . . purge it from her, but it would have taken all of me. That wasn't something I was willing to give."

Noor looked down at the ground, as if another memory preyed on her. I glanced to Maz whose dark eyes were bleak. We were all haunted by death here, and it was time to finally banish those demons.

But I allowed myself one moment, one small instant of grief.

I wrapped my arms around myself and closed my eyes, thinking of my mother, father, and grandmother. All the people who were now gone.

Mazin's sure footsteps came closer, until he dropped an arm across my shoulders and pulled me in against his chest. I pressed my face into his sherwani and inhaled—lemons, woods, and morning. All the things that made me think of him and I'd wanted to expel from my memories I now helplessly leaned into. He pressed his hands into my unbound hair and pressed his lips to the top of my head as I sobbed against his shirtfront.

My grandmother may have made her choices, but the sounds of agony she made as I walked away would stay with me a long while.

I waited a few moments before pulling away from him and wiping my tear-streaked face with the back of my hand.

"Thank you," I said low, realizing how hard it was to get the words out.

"Always," he said, watching me with those inscrutable eyes.

Noor's voice cut through my thoughts and pulled me back to the present. "The plan is, we pick up Mazin's sister and get out of this damned empire before Vahid finally comes for us. We have enough wealth to make a life somewhere else and get away from all these djinn-obsessed people." She leaned back against a low date tree behind her.

I toyed with the sleeve of my kurta, turning my words over before they all spilled out of me. We couldn't leave it like this.

"I have a different plan."

Noor's mouth dropped open. "Dania, we've been following your plans since you and I met. All it has gotten us is an army of people trying to kill us. Please, tell me you have a suggestion that isn't walking back into the mouth of the demon. We all know you are fond of that."

I puffed out a breath. "We need to go back to the city."

"I knew it." Noor covered her eyes with her hands.

I held my own hands up. "Noor, you know as well as anyone what those seeds can do. We need to get rid of them. *All* of them."

Desperation leaked into my voice. If there was one thing I could do to atone for all this mess, it was this. I wouldn't let more lives be destroyed.

Noor sat up. "You want to go after the emperor's djinn fields."

Maz walked over to me, his dark gaze determined. "I agree with Dania."

Noor made a sound that was half laugh, half cry. "Of course you do! You're as senseless as she is! And don't think I haven't forgotten you both also want revenge on Vahid."

She looked up at the sky. "He took just as much from me and I want retribution too. But heading back there is madness. Revenge didn't give any of us what we truly wanted, so why don't we leave it behind us?"

I shook my head. "Noor, this isn't about revenge. It's about making sure this power doesn't stay in the hands of anyone who is going to use it to destroy. It's about stopping the cycle."

Noor looked up at Maz, her brow raised.

"It's a little about revenge," he admitted.

Noor folded over, burying her head in her hands. "I hate both of you."

I hoisted myself up onto Mazin's horse and he leapt up behind me. Noor looked up, her face wretched but with a determined set of her chin. I knew that look, I'd seen it before after we'd broken out of prison and she agreed to come with me.

"You know it's the right thing to do," I called out to her.

"I know," she said miserably. "And strangely enough, I think Souma would have agreed with you." She rubbed her shoulder.

"Noor, you don't have to come with us. You have Souma's wealth. You said it yourself, you can go anywhere, be anyone."

"And miss out on everything? I'll come with you. But I'm not happy you are making me ride the mule."

She stood up, and her face turned serious. She glanced at the treasure, the last remaining piece of Souma strapped to the mule she was about to get on, and I knew she was thinking about her father. "I want to destroy all the zoraat there is and take Vahid down with it."

"Now who's out for vengeance?"

She got on the back of the mule and brushed her hair from her face. "I take my lessons from you."

Fifty-one

We headed back to the city under the cover of night. Patrols of guards roamed the road, stopping everyone to and from Basral, but Mazin and I knew this valley. We zigzagged through the cold desert, ducking behind snow-capped sand dunes and sneaking through the mango orchards in the lush part of the valley, avoiding the well-used road along the lake.

Noor led us to the zoraat fields, the place where she'd lived with Souma. Guards and soldiers were scattered all over the city, quelling the rebellions from every corner. The soldiers watching the emperor's zoraat fields weren't prepared to guard against the djinn magic coursing through me and I sliced through their protections easily.

Finally, we stood at the edge of the fields, zoraat plants stretching out for miles. We were on the north side of Basral, and by the time I'd incapacitated all the guards we knew Vahid and his army were coming for us. There was no way he would let us take away his power without a fight.

But he was already too late.

I put my talwar on the ground and sank my hands into the earth, feeling for the zoraat roots. Once I had them, djinn fire shot from my fingers underground, devouring them from the inside out, lighting a powerful blaze across the sky as djinn fire engulfed the crops for miles.

The heat from the flames pushed us back to the edge of the fields, and we stayed to watch the zoraat plants burn. His most valuable possession, responsible for so many dead. Smoke rose high in the air, a beacon. The night sky swallowed the billowing black pyre. Noor took some of my djinn fire, lighting flaming torches to take care of the remaining plants. She walked from field to field, torching the plants with my inhuman djinn fire.

Horse hooves pounded closer, Vahid's army approaching.

"What have you done?" An anguished scream echoed across the fields.

I whirled around to see the only figure I hadn't been able to confront with my vengeance yet.

And the only man who united all three of us in that common goal.

The flash of flames lit up Emperor Vahid's face, painted as it was with a ghoulish mask of outrage.

Behind him, his army stood, waiting for his command, their eyes glazed from their consumption of zoraat.

"My fields . . ." He balled his fists up, and I startled at the threads of black also spiraling down his arms.

His blazing eyes scanned the fields, landing on the three of us.

"You." He pointed my way, his eyes black with hatred. "I should have had you executed."

"Vahid." Maz stood beside me, his quiet presence making me feel stronger than I thought possible. He nodded at me, reaffirming that he was standing beside me, even in the face of the emperor's fury.

But it was my wrath the emperor had to contend with now.

"We've burned your fields," I said, crossing my arms. "And we've destroyed Souma's store of zoraat. You won't have djinn power to control this empire anymore, to kill anyone who stands against you. Without it, you are nothing."

He took a step forward, but he looked strange compared to when I'd last seen him at the feast. He was shrunken, shriveled, unsteady.

His skin looked much older, and sallow, as if an illness had taken hold of him. His lips were gray black, and his cheeks held a hollow space I'd only seen on the dying.

He looked like my grandmother had.

"The djinn power is killing you. Look at you."

"Look at yourself," Emperor Vahid sneered. "Look at your hands. I smell it on you. You'll know soon enough what it will do to you."

"We've taken everything from you," cut in Maz angrily. "You won't control the city now, not with the riots and rebellions. Nor will you have control over the kingdoms. The north has started mobilizing against you again. You've lost, Vahid."

Vahid's face turned a mottled purple. "I took you in. Saved you and your sister from your pathetic existence. Gave you power. In return you should have worshipped me, not betrayed me."

"I'm sorry that I have no respect for the man who murdered my mother," snapped Mazin.

"I made you what you are, boy."

"No," said Maz, tipping his chin at me. "She did."

Heat flooded my body, and it had nothing to do with the djinn power. Maz's faith in me made me feel stronger than if I had the power of a hundred djinn.

I glanced at Noor, and the emperor followed my gaze and gave a harsh cry at seeing what she was about to do. Noor moved toward the final field with her djinn fire. The emperor lurched away from us and raised his hands, intent on stopping Noor from burning the last one.

I raised my own and felt the power he had smelled on me rise to the surface. It was intoxicating, and I understood why Vahid had fallen under its spell. You could push aside the repercussions of such a power if it made you feel like you could own the earth.

But I had seen what revenge had done to Nanu, to Maz, to myself.

And I wouldn't let more lives be destroyed by it all.

"Stop." I felt the djinn fire rise in my blood. It called out to Vahid's own, and I felt an answering tug.

I latched on to that thread of power in Vahid. And then I pulled.

Emperor Vahid staggered and dropped his arms. He turned from Noor and gaped at me.

"What are you . . . ?"

"I was given a gift too, by someone you might find horribly familiar."

Vahid's face blanched white against the black sky.

"No," he whispered, his voice so faint I thought the sound might have been the wind. "What did you promise him in return?"

I tilted my head, wondering what *Vahid* had promised him to have such a look of fear cross his face. "Something I am prepared to give, if it comes to it."

If.

Was there an *if* in this bargain that I made? Perhaps not. But that didn't mean I wasn't going to try. I closed my fists again. There was only one thing I could think to do.

Feeling the edge of the emperor's power again, I webbed my own magic to his. This time, instead of a gentle prod, I felt for the sum of it all.

And then I tore it from his body.

Vahid screamed and collapsed into the field on his hands and knees.

Maz pressed his hand to my arm. "Dani, what are you—"

"I know what I'm doing," I said quietly. "Trust me."

Maz breathed, then stepped closer, his presence centering me. "Always."

I then extended my power to Vahid's armies along the edge of the field, ripping the zoraat from their bodies too, pulling it from their blood. It was what I had tried to do with my grandmother, but she had consumed too much, and it was already too late.

But now, I knew the feel of the black tendrils coiled inside the veins of another person. I knew what I needed to do to eliminate them. I unraveled the djinn magic, like pulling apart an intricate stitch threaded through their veins, until his armies had nothing left.

Until he had nothing left.

From the corner of my eye, I saw Noor light the last field ablaze and run to us. Mazin unsheathed his sword as Vahid staggered to his feet and lurched toward me.

But as he did, the air grew thick and slow.

Maz's sword paused in midair.

Noor froze in the middle of the field.

Vahid stopped and rose to his full height, looking beyond me, his face flooded with fear.

I turned, knowing without looking who was behind me. The waxy skin, the row of small, shining teeth. Eyes filled with a smokeless fire.

The djinn had come to claim his price.

Fifty-two

He was so close, I could see every fine line on his skin, as if he were wearing a mask of a person over his face. His eyes glowed with a violent rage, and it took everything in me not to take a step back.

But this creature would not see me afraid, even if I desperately was.

"The time has come to pay the cost."

The djinn curled his fingers, and the dark fabric of his robes rippled at his movement. He licked his lips, and I could sense that he was waiting for something he had wanted for a long time.

"My revenge is not complete." I gestured to Vahid, who wasn't moving despite not being frozen by the djinn.

"Kill him, then." The djinn's lip curled. "He's outlived his use anyway."

"We had a bargain, djinn," cried Vahid in desperation.

The djinn's eyes glowed brighter. "And I have fulfilled my part. You have given me what I need, but this girl offers me something more."

"I'll give what she has, then." Vahid gestured to me. "Give me the power you gave her. It isn't fair." His voice was the needy whine of a small boy.

"You think I want your body now? You are old and ill. You have exceeded your use." The djinn turned his eyes to me. "Finish your vengeance, I have come to claim what's mine."

But underneath the djinn's anticipation, I felt an urgency that seemed at odds with what I knew of him. I got the sense that he wanted me to kill Vahid *now* for a reason. He wanted me to fulfill my bargain because there was a chance I wouldn't.

Couldn't.

"Why did you come now?" I watched him, saw the way his eyes flicked back to the emperor. Something had happened that had made him appear, that had alerted him somehow.

"Because I want what is mine," he growled, moving closer to me.

"What did you say about your power earlier? Tricks?" I waved at Maz and Noor, still unmoving. "Stop trying to intimidate me. I know you can't do anything."

"No?" The djinn's voice became dangerously soft. "It's my power that runs through your veins, girl."

"And I am the only person who can give you what you want. You want possession of my body so you can have your full powers in our world? You must wait for our bargain to be complete."

"It's my power that runs through your veins."

He was right.

But what if there wasn't any power?

"You preyed on my vengeance. On his." I gestured to Vahid. "But you don't receive anything if my bargain remains unfulfilled. If I don't achieve my revenge."

"Kill him!" shouted the djinn, pointing at Vahid. "He is the reason your father is dead! The reason you were tortured and rotting in a prison. If you take his life now, you get everything you've ever wanted."

"No," I uttered. "If I take his life, *you* get everything you've wanted. But I still have your power, which I'm guessing can only be used through me."

The djinn pursed his dark lips, his eyes nearly bulging out of his head. And then I guessed what had brought him here so quickly, and why he had seemed so enraged.

If Vahid and I had no power, then the djinn didn't. And I had been in the process of removing Vahid's power and burning all his zoraat to the ground.

I turned back to Vahid and raised my hands. I snatched the remaining thread of power in him, that last bit of fire that warmed his blood. Vahid screamed and crumpled to the ground at the same time the djinn lunged for me.

I moved backward, scrambling away from him.

I gave up what I had most wanted for the past year, the reckoning I had finally sought to claim. The power that ran through my blood would have helped me get there.

But I still had plenty of my own power left.

This time, when I felt for the djinn magic in my system, I pulled it inward, condensing it into a bright, concentrated piece of flame.

Then I expelled it.

I purged the djinn flame from my body, and it had nowhere to go but in the burning field of djinn crops themselves, lighting up the dark sky like a bonfire.

The horizon exploded in a white-hot fire, the heat cascading over us.

The djinn behind me screamed and wrapped his hands around my throat. We toppled to the ground as the fields burned around us, the flames growing higher, Noor and Maz trapped within them, unable to move.

His grip held me like an iron vise as I tried to push him off. He was choking me, his long fingers wrapped around my neck, his teeth so close I thought he was going to rip my throat out.

I looked desperately at Mazin and Noor, still frozen from the djinn's power, in the path of the flames eating away at the fields surrounding them.

I had done this.

My need for revenge had meant the two people who had come to mean the most to me would die.

I had made this bargain with the djinn, and I had decided these consequences.

This was cause and effect. Just like my grandmother. Just like the plans I had set in motion to put us all here.

And I couldn't just lie down and allow that to happen.

My hands searched for anything, running along the ground for any rock or weapon. Blindly I gripped the only thing I could: Mazin's dagger pendant around my neck.

I ripped it from my neck and stabbed the djinn in the eye.

He reared back with a scream, black ichor streaming from his wound. It only gave me a brief reprieve, but it was enough for me to take in air, to ward off the darkness creeping over the edge of my vision, threatening to pull me under.

"You are mine," the djinn howled.

I had nothing left. No djinn power, no sword, no hope.

"Winning the battle isn't about skill, Dania. It's about heart."

Baba's words pierced the fog and focused my thoughts. This wasn't about fighting, not anymore. This was about my friends, about love, about forgiveness.

I pushed the djinn off me and scrambled away, looking at Maz and Noor who were about to be consumed.

"Release them!" I screamed at the djinn. "They'll die!"

He laughed at me in response, my dagger pendant still sticking out of one of his eyes.

"You think I care about that? Give me what I want, and I will release them. Give me your body so I can reign over this realm and flood this world with fire."

"Well, as wonderful as *that* sounds, I'm not going to give you anything."

A movement flickered from the periphery of my vision, but I trained my gaze on the djinn. He advanced on me again.

I made no effort to move. I could sprint to Maz, but Noor would still be lost. The only hope of saving them both was to stop the djinn's hold on them.

But before the djinn could reach me, he stopped. A twisted look of shock passed over his features and then his gaze dipped down to his chest.

We both looked down to see the tip of my talwar piercing his chest, black blood slowly pooling from the wound and beginning to drip down his body.

At once the grip the djinn had on the world seemed to lift, the air clearing.

Noor's scream sounded across the field as I watched Emperor Vahid dig my sword out of the djinn's back.

Fifty-three

"Dani." Maz's voice pierced through the haze, and he gripped my shoulders, shaking me hard. "Dani, we need to get out of here."

Vahid pushed the djinn's body off my sword, and black blood spilled across the dirt. The djinn was lifeless, and whatever form he had taken in this realm was gone.

My necklace fell to the ground, the small blade covered in dark djinn blood. I scooped it up, clutching the pendant tight in my hand.

Vahid's eyes were black and deep, and gone was that spark of fire in them from earlier. Instead, he seemed hollow, empty.

Maz looked up at him and inhaled a sharp breath.

The emperor watched us both. "Go on then, do what you both want to." He held his arms out wide, the flames raging around him. Heat pressed in on us from all sides, the sole path to freedom being steadily eaten by the wild djinn fire.

"I have nothing now. Take your vengeance."

Mazin gripped the hilt on his scimitar so tight his knuckles turned white. My eyes flicked to my bloodied knife on the ground.

The person before us was no more human than the djinn had been. He was a broken creature, knees on the ground, gaunt cheeks, a look that no vengeance of mine could ever replicate.

He was already destroyed.

The djinn power in my veins was gone too. Whether it was from the djinn's death in the human realm or my own actions trying to expel the power out, I didn't know. But I did know that I didn't have the same rage dictating my actions.

"Let's go," I said to Maz, stepping away from the emperor.

"Wait," said Mazin, staring at Vahid.

I glanced at Noor. She had escaped the fire and was shouting at us from the other side of the field. She looked over at Vahid too, her eyes burning as hot as the flames in the field, and I knew what it cost her to turn away from him. We all were pursuing our own vengeance, and it was time to let it go.

"Maz, if we don't leave now, it will be too late."

"Come with us," Mazin said, his eyes still fixed on the emperor.

Mazin held out a hand. I expelled a shocked breath. After everything Vahid had done, I hadn't expected Maz to reach out to him.

The emperor went still, looking as stunned as I felt.

"Didn't you hear what I said?" Vahid asked, his lip curling. His body shook, and he resembled a frail bird, barely strong enough to hold his head up. "I said take your revenge! Kill me!"

Mazin shuddered but couldn't seem to tear himself away.

"Maz." I tugged on his arm. The flames were pressing closer now.

He finally looked my way, those dark eyes meeting mine. I knew what it cost him to do this, but I wanted Mazin alive.

We deserved that.

I searched for my words quickly, aware that we had a very narrow space of time left for escape. If I didn't convince him to leave with me now, I'd have to bash him over the head and drag him out of the flame-soaked field.

Which I wasn't opposed to doing.

"You may not want revenge anymore, but don't give him any more of yourself. If he wants death, let him have it. Don't let his actions . . ." I cleared my throat, saying these words to myself as well as Maz, thinking of how I felt about my grandmother, and the lives she had ruined. "Don't let his actions destroy your life. You may have given him forgiveness, but that doesn't mean you owe him kindness."

Mazin's shoulders sagged as if I'd given him permission to let go. Then he took my hand, walked through the flames and into the clear path beyond.

———

Noor stood and watched the fire reduce the rest of the fields to ash.

She had been like this since I told her Vahid had stayed and that Mazin and I had left him behind.

"What are you looking for?" I asked, stepping close to her.

"Proof that he's dead." She didn't take her eyes off the blackened fields.

"I don't think you'll find it." I shook my head. "Not with that blaze."

"No. But at least I would see Souma's life's work destroyed. Zoraat is what killed him, just like Vahid. Both of them enslaved to someone else's power."

Her gaze stayed trained on the smoldering crops, and I'd never seen her so broken and alone. I licked my cracked lips, hoping I hadn't lost her after all this. "Did you get what you came for?"

Noor finally pulled her gaze away from the scorched earth. "Did you?"

A wry smile crossed my lips. "I asked you first."

"I came for revenge, but I'm leaving with something much more worthwhile. Friendship." She huffed out a laugh and gave me a tentative smile. "How do you feel?"

I knew what she meant. I flexed my hands, the black stains on my skin gone. I reached for the dark power that once filled my veins and to my relief nothing answered me. The only voice answering was my own.

"I feel . . . normal. As if I had never consumed zoraat. I can still lift a sword, which is all that matters to me."

"And here?" Noor pressed her palm flat against her chest. "How do you feel here?"

I chewed on my bottom lip, lifting my eyes to Mazin who stood a little distance away. He was staring at the fields too, but at my glance he looked in my direction.

"I feel raw, hurt, but still alive. And that's got to count for something."

"Yes," Noor said, following my gaze to Mazin. "It does. You don't have to live the narrative your grandmother did."

"I can choose," I said, for the first time believing it was true. Believing that I had my own power, my own freedom, the ability to make my own destiny, and not be held back by the past.

"And what do you choose?"

I looked at Maz again, and he met my eyes, a smile touching his lips that was more than a little quizzical.

I clutched the pendant in my hand, the blade that represented who I was. And I looked at Mazin, the person I could make a future with, despite all the loss and pain and heartbreak.

"I choose him," I said to Noor. "And I choose myself."

Epilogue

The light was good for training today.

Sunlight peeked through the gray mottled clouds, and a cool breeze blew across the field, giving my students a much-needed reprieve from the heat.

"One more drill," I called across the sea of trainees, which caused a chorus of groans.

A cup nudged my elbow and the scent of steeped mint and cardamom wafted toward me.

"Another? They'll be cursing your name by the end of the day."

I took the tea from Mazin gratefully and inhaled. "At least they'll know how to block properly. Which is more than I can say for Imran right now."

Mazin put his arm around my chest and pressed his lips to my hair. I closed my eyes and leaned against him, inhaling him as well. Woods. Lemon. Morning.

Hope.

Then I opened one eye and barked out an order. "Yalina! Keep your arms up! You nearly stabbed yourself with your own scimitar!"

"I love it when you screech commands in my ear while I'm kissing you," he murmured into my hair.

I snorted. "Don't you have council meetings in Basral to be in?"

"Anam's there. She always said she wasn't a fighter, but she's been waging more war in those council meetings than we have on the battlefield."

"I always knew she was a warrior." A smile curved my lips as I imagined her facing off with the leaders of the other kingdoms, creating an empire all on her own.

We stood there for a moment, watching the students run through another training drill, each holding a sword made by my father, each putting it to the use he intended. Our village smith was alive again, with a new purpose, just like me.

"You've got a visitor."

I looked over to where Maz gestured and saw Noor leaning against the fence, a saddled stallion beside her, a travel pack over her shoulder. My chest constricted at seeing her, and I straightened, pulling away from Maz slowly, despite his sound of protest.

"Finish the drills for me?"

Mazin gave a nod, concern crossing his features as he watched me. He stepped into the yard and shouted out instructions.

I walked over to Noor, meeting her at the gate and hopping over the fence.

"Your school has come a long way," she commented, nodding at the training yard. "It's impressive."

I followed the direction of her gaze, watching my students with pride.

"I always knew you'd do something amazing." She said the words so softly, they were almost carried away by the wind.

"I'm not sure about amazing. I'm not building an empire or anything. But I love it."

"You *are* building an empire. Just because it isn't made of kingdoms and djinn doesn't mean it isn't powerful. And it doesn't mean that you aren't an empress ruling over it all."

"I rather like the sound of being an empress."

My grin faded as I eyed her travel pack and stallion. "And you?" I dared to ask. "What will you do?"

She released a heavy breath and tilted her head back in the sun, her wild, short curls blowing in the wind. "That's the question I've been asking myself. After helping Anam and Mazin destroy the last remnants of zoraat, there isn't really a big need for an herbalist in Basral."

"You are always needed here," I said quietly.

She shot me a grateful smile. "And I would happily stay here and cultivate mountain plants for the rest of my life, curing all the ailments of your would-be assassins."

"Sword masters. Not assassins," I corrected.

She quirked a brow. "Whatever you say. I refuse to believe this isn't a secret assassin school." Then she blew a curl of hair out of her face and gave me a serious look. "I would be happy here, Dania."

I sighed. "But it's not enough."

She shook her head. "I want to track down my mother's people. I have unanswered questions, and before I settle down and become an old village aunty, I want to find where I come from. I want to know my family."

"Well, you always have family here. Whenever you choose to come back."

"I know. And I will be back." We stood in companionable silence until Noor leaned back against the fence and gave me a once-over before letting out a chuckle.

"What?" I punched her in the arm.

"I'm just thinking of how different you look from when I first saw you—dirty, bloodied, and scrambling on the floor of your cell, accusing me of being a ghoul."

"Trust me, a bath did *wonders* for your appearance too." I gave her a small smile, remembering the moment we met, and all the rage and fear inside me.

But there was yearning too. A dream that there was something beyond the walls of our cell, more than what we were condemned to. Noor helped me see that.

"Digging the wrong way and ending up in your cell was the best thing that ever happened to me, you know?"

"Me too."

My eyes burned with the things we didn't say to each other, but our parting embrace spoke all the words we needed.

———

Maz walked over to me, long after Noor rode away, and leaned against the fence.

"Noor left?"

I exhaled, looking up at him, the shadows haunting his eyes not quite gone, but less. I knew mine were the same. Anger and grief had taken so much from me, but they had given as well. Mazin standing beside me, wearing a blue tunic in the afternoon sun, was one gift I never thought I'd have. Noor's friendship was another, and though my heart didn't want to see her go, I knew she needed to find her purpose, like I'd found mine.

"Yes, to find her mother's people."

"She'll be back." His voice was so sure I ached to believe it.

"I hope so."

"Dani, I don't think anyone can keep away from you for long."

I arched a brow. "You're just talking about yourself now."

"That's probably true. I can't last in Basral for more than a day before I'm urging Rakhna back here."

"Or maybe you just like Afra Aunty's cooking."

He laughed, long and rich, and my heart leapt at the sound, as it did whenever I heard it. We were broken and mending and lost but slowly we were finding our way back to who we once were with each other, with every laugh, every whispered word and soft kiss.

He leaned in, his eyes darkening under my gaze. "Why are you looking at me like that?"

"How am I looking at you?"

A slow curve of his lips had my heart racing faster. "Either like you want to kiss me or stab me. I can't always tell with you, but for some reason they are both equally as exciting."

I laughed, unsheathing my talwar at the same time as he drew his scimitar. "Shall we put on a show?" I nodded to my students. "Then you can decide if it was the stabbing or the kissing I wanted."

He grinned but kept his eyes on me. "Or both? If I'm going to have the stabbing, there better be kissing after."

"Follow me, then." I advanced on him, but stopped when his eyes grew serious.

"Dani, you know I'll follow you anywhere."

I clutched the hilt of my sword tight, terrified to lose this moment, but never more sure of how I felt about him. "I know."

Our blades flashed in the afternoon sun, meeting in the air like old friends.

And when it was done and the students had gone home, it was just him and me, healing the scars we couldn't see, being for each other what we most needed in the dark.

Acknowledgments

I never thought I'd get to this moment, the act of writing acknowledgments in my own published novel, but it is only with these people that this is possible.

First, I must acknowledge Mara Delgado Sánchez, and all the thanks I owe to you for everything you did to help bring this book into existence. Your belief in my writing and this story kept me going and is the reason I can live my dream of being a published author today.

To everyone at Wednesday Books who helped make this book into a reality, I thank you from the bottom of my heart. Thank you especially to Sara Goodman, Cassie Gutman, Meghan Harrington, Alexis Neuville, and Brant Janeway.

To my UK team at PanMacmillan, thank you for your enthusiasm and support and for being so absolutely excited for my words.

The biggest possible thanks to my agents, Laura Rennert and Paige Terlip. Laura, you are so enthusiastic and possibly the kindest human I've ever met, and I'm thankful to have you in my corner. Paige, I cannot believe I was lucky enough to land an agent like you—someone who fits me perfectly, always gets what I'm trying to do, and is a hustler through and through. Thank you for everything you've done for me. I can't wait to have a champagne toast with you in a castle somewhere in Scotland one day.

There are so many people I need to thank who helped make this book a possibility and supported my career—without you I wouldn't be here at all.

To Cheryl Binnie, who jumped headfirst into this book and gave me the most insightful, fantastic feedback I've ever gotten. You shaped this story and made it what it is. I will trust you to the end of time with my words, and I am so grateful I met you on a little retreat in Scotland.

To Adrienne Young—your generosity with your time and advice knows no bounds, and everything you do for the writing community astounds me. You help writers like me believe they can do this thing and make it a reality. Thank you for everything you and your Writing With the Soul community has done.

To my Writing With the Soul community, thank you for your words and comments on my early drafts of this book and for the support you've given my novel. Special thanks to those on the Story-tellers Retreat in Scotland and Saltwater Farms, and especially Erynne, Jamye, Morgan, Gretchen, and Rachelle.

Kristin Dwyer, though I still don't believe we are real friends, I am so excited to maybe be your pretend friend and send you ranting text messages / voice notes occasionally while you make fun of me. That actually might be true friendship, now that I think about it.

To Naomi Louise Jenkins, never did I think meeting another writer on an *88 Cups of Tea* podcast discussion group would lead to one of the most important friendships of my life, but I am so thankful for you and your belief in me as a writer.

To my law friends: Melanie Pituch, Samantha Boyce Bal, Delna Contractor, Jesse Bonner, Kay Turner, Maria-Rose Spronk Johnson, and Elise Doherty. Your support means the world to me, and even though I'm pretty sure you don't know what I'm talking about half the time when it comes to books and publishing, you still listen and support me through everything. I love you guys.

Thank you to Diane Meronyk, Maureen MacKenzie, Nikita Oliver-Lew, Ilana Davine, and Paul Johnson, whose friendship and support over the years have been a lifeline.

To my business partner and work wife, Holly McCord Lonseth, I'm so grateful to have your support and start a business with you that promotes each other's dreams and goals. To my assistant, Caleigh Hunt: girl, you know I couldn't have done any of this without you.

To Jena Colpitts—there's no one else I'd rather exchange hilarious law memes with. You make my life infinitely better.

To Siobhan Keller, for being one of my biggest supporters and cheerleaders, much more than a mom friend and maybe more like a sister—thank you for absolutely everything.

Thank you to the Canada Council for the Arts, who generously provided a grant for the creation of this book.

Thank you to the authors who generously blurbed and supported and read various versions of my book, taking time out of your busy schedules to do so. Thanks especially to Judy I. Lin (especially for our dinners, which are the best), Adalyn Grace, Stephanie Garber, Rachel Griffin, Ashley Woodfolk (who gives THE BEST advice), and Akshaya Raman.

Thank you to Susan Dennard, whose wise words and advice have helped me navigate this journey of being a debut author.

Thank you especially to my sensitivity readers, Sidrah Rana and Aamna Qureshi: without you the book wouldn't be what it is, and I am so thankful for your knowledge and expertise.

To my 2019 Pitch Wars Crew: The Writing Folk. I feel like I've known you all my life, and I cannot believe that pure luck brought us all together. I wouldn't know what I'd do without you, and the support, love, and friendship you've given me. Chatting to you all every day has made me the writer I am and I am the luckiest writer in the world to have you. Sami Ellis, Vaishnavi Patel, Elora Ditton, Kaitlyn Hill, Amanda Helander, Anita Kelly, Anna Sortino, Avione Lee, Briana Johnson, Briana Milano, Brighton Rose, Gigi Griffis, Hugh Blackthorne, Kat Hillis, A. Y. Chao, Lani Frank, Mara Shatat, Piper Vossy, Siana LaForest, Cate Baumer, LC Milburn, Chandra Fisher, Sarah Mughal Rana, Tanvi Berwah, Molly Steen, Maiga Doocy, Ridley Adams, Kate Dylan, Victor Manibo, Angel Di Zhang, Katie Bohn, and Sophia Mortensen—you are my writing family. Many of you read the early pages of this book, and many versions, and I love you to pieces for the help you gave. Thanks especially to LC Milburn and Chandra Fisher, for the amount of times you read literally every draft and gave so much of your time and knowledge. Angel Di Zhang, I'll never forget your comments on my early draft where you highlighted a joke and said, "This is very funny." Truly, I will take that compliment to my grave. Thanks to Vaishnavi Patel, who always knows when to text me and give me a pep talk and whose author blurb I want carved into my gravestone, if I'm honest.

To Sami Ellis, I don't think this book would have existed without you. You helped me take it from a kernel of an idea to a full-fledged plot, and I feel like every writer is missing out by not having you as a brainstorming partner. Thanks especially to Lani Frank, who is responsible for the title of this book, and honestly I get chills whenever I say it.

To Sarah Mughal Rana, words simply cannot express what you've done both for my writing and my life. You helped shape this book but also supported and encouraged my connection to a heritage and culture I thought I could never have. I learn so much from you every day, and I have no idea what I would have done without you—certainly this book wouldn't be here. Thank you, thank you, thank you.

Thanks to my brothers, Karlo and Richard, for all your love and support.

To my husband, Andrew Buchan: I wrote the first draft of this book on maternity leave with a newborn baby and a toddler at the same time, and there is no way I could pursue any of my writing goals if I didn't have your support. For every day you took the kids out so I could write, for the times you booked a hotel room for me when I was on deadline, and for the way you believe in me and my dreams, I am forever grateful and thankful. I wouldn't have been able to write books if I didn't have you in my corner, and I am grateful for you every single day.

For my mom, who showed up when I was on maternity leave with my first baby and kicked me out of the house and forced me to take a break and write—you taught me that my own dreams were worth going after, and you gave me the support to get there. We are so, so lucky to have you and you remind me always that producing art is powerful, important, and worthy.

For my kids, Thomas and Zora. It's because of you that I write at all, and I hope to capture even a thimbleful of the imagination you both have. You are my reason for everything, and I love you more than anything.